The One I Love Most

For Sebastian,

with the best tomatos ☺

Kathrin Jakob

THE ONE I LOVE MOST

Kathrin Jakob

Copyright © 2021, by Kathrin Jakob

Self-publishing

info@kathrinjakob.com

The One I Love Most

By
KATHRIN JAKOB

Content Warning

These content notes are made available, so my readers can inform themselves if they want to. Some readers might consider these as spoilers.

The content of this book includes, but might not be limited to:

- Curse words: occasional curse words
- Eating disorders: short mentioning and brief description of Anorexia, Bulimia
- Sexual language: occasional naming of private body parts and sexual actions.
- Narcissistic abuse: description of characters and conversations
- Emotional Abuse

*To all the women who have
ever doubted themselves.*

Preface

Maybe.... I can manifest the life I want by writing a book about my life. I will tell it as it happened, with the ending of my dreams. So many people talk about scripting. I'm going to take it to the next level.' — My 'thinking-out-loud' thoughts from over a year ago.

I've been feeling the urge to write a book. I love reading novels, and whenever I love something, I feel like I have to try it myself. And I'm a horrible oversharer anyway. I love telling stories, my stories, the ones that move me. And if nothing else, it's something to read when I'm old and wrinkly. This is not a 'coming back from the dead' or 'defying all odds' story. It's simply a part of my journey. Somewhat ordinary, and somewhat unique.

I know how much it helps me, to find myself in someone else's art. And it's such a gift when people can resonate with my songs, something I wrote, or something I shared in a conversation or on social media. There's nothing better than having that connection, and feeling understood. And maybe, just maybe, somebody will feel that way reading this.

Disclaimer: Most names in this book are changed, but almost everything happened exactly like it is written.

Now

I know everything will be OK, despite my existential fears linked to my visa status in the United States. Going home to Germany and traveling back gives me so much anxiety sometimes that I almost don't want to go home at all, even if that means not seeing my family.

Just now, my sister sent a picture with a ring on her finger to our family WhatsApp group. A couple of months ago, she and her now-fiancé Michael announced that they are having a baby. To all of our surprise, they had planned it. We just didn't know about those plans. And of course, we are happy. When Natalie FaceTimed me back then and surprised me with the news that I'd be an aunt, I couldn't hold back my tears. They just came out.

But since then, I'm also having this growing sense of *Biological-Clock-itis* (yes, I made that word up), which I've heard and read about so many times in movies, magazines, and novels. It just didn't seem like something I'd ever experience. Why would I not have a boyfriend and potential father of my children at 29? Yet here I am, single, struggling with my legal status in the country I chose to live in, far away from fame, riches, or the comforting prospect of my own family, which I always thought I'd have much earlier in my twenties.

I am not in a rush to have children. Even though my younger sister, by one and a half years, seems to be far ahead of me now, basically married and a mother. I do, however, feel the rush to meet the man who will make all of this possible for me. The one who makes me so happy I can't think of anything else. The one who is honest and has genuine intentions towards me. And on top of that, is a semi bodybuilder without posing on Instagram, has a great smile, shares my passion for saving and not eating animals, has a job, is healthy, and can be romantic. Those are just a few things on my list, and quite honestly, I'm having a hard time believing that such a man does exist for me at this point.

It's Christmas Eve. We're eating sausages and sauerkraut at my grandma's place, just like every year, except that this time it's just my mom, my dad, grandma, and me. And Bennie, the Yorkie, who at his age doesn't hear or see much of what's going on anymore. Natalie used to be here with us, but she has her own family now. And for the first time, I start to feel really old. What am I doing with my life? Will I be the crazy aunt in America? The one with no husband but a bunch of cats? The one with all the crazy ideas but no actual career? The one who is too weird to fit in anymore, in a small place like this?

"Please eat more sausages. We have so many left," my dad says. And then addressing me: "I also have some of yours left, I didn't make them all, but I can put more in the pan." By "my sausages," he means the vegan ones. We might still follow our Christmas Eve tradition, but I insist on only eating vegan, and my family is more than OK with that, even if they haven't decided to switch to an exclusively plant-based diet themselves. I do pride myself in having made a positive impact in their lives as well, though.

"Thank you, Dad," I say. "I am completely full. By the way," I casually remark, "I don't think I want to go to church tonight."

Christmas Eve service, basically in the middle of the night, always used to be something I looked forward to. Even after I moved so far away from home, it was always nice seeing familiar faces from the old days and talking to my old friends, even if it was just for a couple of minutes. But today, I don't even feel like I belong here enough to go there. And I'm tired.

"Are you sure?" my mom answers. "I mean, it's OK if you don't want to come. You can still think about it. But don't you usually like seeing all your old friends after the service is over?"

"Yeah," I agree, "It's nice, but everybody fizzles out within five minutes, and it's not really worth it."

So many of my "old friends" also attend the Christmas Service at our church. I used to be in a youth group for a big chunk of my teenage years. I think some of them resent me and assume that I think I'm better because I moved to LA. The other ones who still greet me with the same enthusiasm year after year basically don't know me anymore, and catching up in five minutes at midnight is simply not possible. So, it's never more than a "How are things going in LA? Do you have a green card already?"–"It's good, and no, not yet, still working on that. How are you?"–"Oh, you know, the same old."

"I'll stay up, but I'm gonna watch TV instead tonight. You guys said it's not the same anyway since Pastor D left, and Natalie said they aren't going either."

I had gathered enough reasons to skip Christmas Eve Service and not feel bad about it.

Back at home, as I'm sitting on our couch, cuddled in a blanket, watching *Three Wishes for Cinderella,* the Czech version of Cinderella, a Christmas classic in Germany, my phone in my hand, I start to feel very lonely. I know it was my choice not to go to church with my family. But I would have felt lonely there, too. I feel lonely because I don't have a man in my life. I feel behind. And even though I wouldn't want my sister's life, and my parents aren't one of those happy, stuck to each other couples, I can't help but feel like a third wheel. It's not how *they* make me feel. It's just what *I* feel like. I am alone; I don't have a boyfriend; I pity myself.

I can't even use my dating app here because it only shows you people who are within a certain radius. And as far as I know, all the men in any reasonable proximity are either married, in a relationship, complete dorks, or way too young for me. And apart from that, why would I even want to meet someone here if I'm going back to Los Angeles in a few days?

I google *dating apps that let you search anywhere in the world.* 'Coffee meets Bagel' comes up. I've heard about this before but haven't used it. I push the download button. I mean, what else am I going to do anyway? I can just browse while I'm stuck in the German holiday stillness. And while I'm at it, I am also downloading *OkCupid*, 'which I have used before. I have a faint memory of it allowing me to set my location anywhere I want.

I feel pretty desperate, having downloaded two dating apps at once, while I should just be enjoying the holidays with my family, not longing for some imaginary boyfriend. But right now, I am alone, with Bennie and Bounty, the gigantic cat. And who is going to judge me? I set up my profiles on both apps and set my location to Pasadena, where I live when I'm in LA. After about half an hour, I have uploaded enough pictures and info about myself to where I feel confident to start swiping.

Coffee meets Bagel only allows me to swipe through six people per day, which I went through in no time. "What a waste," I'm thinking. I go on *OkCupid* and swipe through about 100 guys in LA before getting frustrated and putting my phone away. I try to pet Bounty, who in return runs away from me after he leaves a nice big scratch on my left arm. I sigh and further cuddle myself into the blanket. I don't know where I belong anymore. I have two homes, and yet I always long for the one where I'm currently not.

Fife minutes later, I hear the front door opening and my parents come in. I'm happy they're home. "How was it?" I ask.

"You didn't miss anything. Except, your friends did ask about you," mom says. "They all asked, 'Did Kathrin not

7

come home this Christmas? 'and I had to catch them up on everything you've done recently."

I don't even know what she would've caught them up on. I don't think I've done many exciting or interesting things in my life recently, or accomplished anything significant enough to be worth telling. But my mom sees all of that a bit differently. She's my mom, after all.

"What are you watching, daughter?" My dad comes into the living room, looking at the TV screen and then at me. He never actually waits for an answer. "Anyone care for some mulled wine before we go to bed?"

"Bring it on," mom says, and I agree. I don't drink much alcohol anymore, but tonight I think I can do with a cup.

Then

I'm sitting on one of the two couches in the foyer of the music school where I just started working. It's been a few months since I graduated from music college, and I'm glad I found a job in a school that's close by and owned by another German immigrant, Fred. I feel good here, apart from my usual everyday insecurities, like the fact that I'm at my heaviest weight so far. That still doesn't make me fat, or even close to obese, but it does make me wear leggings with a skirt on top, all stretchy materials because I can't get myself to buy bigger-sized jeans, when I'm sure I'll have to lose the weight again. And buying something now would essentially be a waste of money.

My hair is long, and for the most part, bleached blonde. It doesn't stay nice and straight anymore, even if I make the effort to straighten it out with an iron. It's thin, and unless I take an hour to curl it, it makes me feel kind of sloppy, the way it hangs down my head and shoulders. So on most days, I just put it up in a bun or some sort of ponytail, which also makes me feel unattractive, but at least I feel like I look a bit more cleaned up.

As I'm sitting on the couch, waiting, gazing down at my converse sneakers, while casually chatting with our shy receptionist Sally, Eddie comes in through the door, immediately engaging everyone in the room in fun conversation, playing with the little kids and throwing them up and over his shoulder. Eddie teaches drums here, but I haven't seen him for the last month or so. He must have been gone for a while. But even so, I have noticed how popular he is with the kids and how much energy he brings into this place. It makes me smile.

"Hey Karin," he says, noticing me looking at him. "What's up with those shoes of yours?"

I correct him, "It's Kathrin. And what do you mean?"

"I'm sorry. My bad. Kathrin. I was just thinking, a woman like you should be wearing something more classy."

"Oh yeah?" I say, acting sassy and confident in this conversation, when in reality I am everything but, and I question every word that comes out of my mouth. "Like what?"

"Like a pair of Js." He wiggles his feet and does a quick funny dance in his Jordans. "I'm sure they would look cute on you." And then he disappears into the drum room.

"Whatever," I'm thinking. I just can't place him or put him in a box. He's different. And somehow, that's weirdly intriguing. On the other hand, I have a strange feeling of discomfort. Most people aren't that forward. I look at Sally, and we both shake our heads and chuckle. I lean back on the couch and wait for the next ten minutes to go by until my next piano student comes in.

I didn't plan on becoming a teacher of any sort. I was so brave to make the big move overseas and study music here, leaving everything I knew behind. My family has always supported me, and my friends have always been cheering for me, despite not wanting me to leave Germany. And now I'm giving piano and singing lessons because I don't believe I could actually make real money with my music. I'm too shy, not thin enough, not fit enough, and haven't practiced enough. 'Too 'too many things. It's not that I'm not grateful for this job and the fact that it allows me to still live in this expensive city. To be here while I build a career and make the connections that are going to get me where I want to be. Only, I am not building anything but more insecurities and more excuses to not do what I really came here to do.

~

That night, I get home, and Baloo greets me with a loud and persistent "Meoooowww" as if he's trying to say, "Where have you been all day, Mom?" Baloo is basically my family here, especially since Alana moved out a few months ago to work at Disneyland. We were in the same program in music college and lived together in a two-bedroom apartment, with several roommates in our living room, over the span of three semesters. There was the girl who was supposed to move in with us but then ditched us. Then there was Xavier, a guy who found our ad on Craigslist, who was high at least half the time and made the grossest sounds in the shower. After that, my new short-term best friend Dora moved in. But she moved back to Norway after just a few months. I still miss her dearly. She was and still is a soulmate. So then, another school friend moved in who then started dating our neighbor. After that, we brought in one of the new girls from school who, at one point, had half of her family living in our living room for a month when they visited from overseas.

Alana and I adopted Baloo about four weeks into living here, and it felt like we were a little family. She now feels like a sister to me. I just don't see her much anymore. She now lives in Anaheim, which, with light traffic, is about an hour away from Pasadena. I already went through two other roommates since then. It's only been four months since Alana moved out, and finding a cool girl to live with was quite tricky and exhausting. Luckily, I seem to have found a good one at last: Liu. She not only loves Baloo, but also shares my plant-based eating habits. She usually works all day and then spends her evenings at the library, from where she easily brings back ten books at a time.

I pick up my furry, four-legged friend and hold him tightly against my chest. "What would I do without you? Do you even know how much I love you?" He starts purring and pushes his head sternly against the palm of my hand, using both of his cat hands to grab my arm and pull my hand in tighter. He is the cuddliest cat I've ever met. And as a Siamese, also one of the loudest cats I've ever met. He's the cat I always dreamed of having. The one that sleeps in your bed with you, spooning, and comes to you and likes to be picked up. The one you have a special bond with. That, I am sure, we have.

When Alana and I went to the shelter to look at cats, Baloo picked us. He stretched out his little arm towards me from the cage he was in. He said, "Please take me home."

At least that's what I thought he was trying to say. And even though we weren't even planning on getting a cat that day, he stole our hearts, and we ended up bringing him home that same afternoon. If only my relationships with men were as simple and straightforward. Maybe I am too picky, but perhaps I just don't want to settle for something less than what I want. Maybe my standards are higher than what I can offer in return, and so I will always run after someone who's 'too good for me.'

Now

Three days after my pitiful Christmas Eve, I arrived at the LAX airport late in the afternoon. Even though the seat next to me was empty, I barely got any sleep. As I'm standing in line to go through customs, I feel the heavy weight of my backpack and my additional hand luggage bag weighing me down. I always overpack. And I always end up putting way too much weight into my carry-ons. I could've just left all those books that I didn't read anyway, here in LA in the first place.

I feel sweaty and gross. I've been traveling for almost 24 hours now, including the drive to the airport and a layover in Amsterdam. It's three o'clock in the morning in Germany now. I got up at four am the previous day. I like to pity myself. My phone doesn't have reception here, and my tired brain is just trying to occupy itself while I'm standing in this forever line, my shoulders burning from the weight of bad judgment. The closer I get to the officers sitting at the little booths, the more nervous I get. My hands are starting to get sweaty, and my heart is beating just a little faster. I've been through this so many times now, and still, it's scary every time, especially since what happened two years ago. I know I'll have to go to what they call *Secondary Inspection.* It's nothing new. I know I'll be stuck in this airport for at least another hour. And until then, I won't be able to relax.

~

Two hours later and I still sit in Secondary Inspection. This is where they bring people with incomplete papers, people who have overstayed their visas in the past, people who got married and have green cards, but seem in some way suspicious to the officer, people traveling on a travel visa, but have spent so much time here that the authorities think they might be working illegally. Some people simply have a spelling mistake on their papers. And then there's me, sitting, waiting, trying to stay calm, trying to read a book, but finding myself unable to concentrate.

This room is shut off from any sunlight or windows, like all of the customs area. The walls are plastered in "no mobile phones" signs with a big circled and crossed-out phone, printed in black and white. And still, there are people who either haven't noticed the signs or just choose to ignore them. The officer by the door loudly yells, "Put your phones away!"

There are seven windows, each with a chair in front of it, but I'm noticing that there seem to be a lot fewer officers than usual. Only two windows are serviced by officers, either talking to someone or working on the computer. The wall organizer in the back is filled with passports from different countries, which belong to the people sitting in the rows of seats in the middle of the room. I try to make out mine, but fail to do so. At least 20 passports are waiting to be processed. I sigh and decide to, once more, take out one of my books. Maybe this will calm me down.

"I said put your phones away, or I will take them," the officer yells even louder this time.

At the same time, I overhear a conversation between a female officer and a woman, who's from Denmark, it seems.

"I'm asking you again: What are you doing here?"

"I am here to visit my mother," the Danish woman says with an accent.

"But it says here that your mother's residence is in Denmark."

"Yes, but she is also here right now."

"And how come you are visiting for so long? Three months? How do you afford this trip?" the officer asks again.

"I have savings, I will be traveling around a bit, but I will stay with my mother for most of the time."

I know the officer is trying to figure out if this woman is trying to get some illegal work in while she's here, or even worse, just trying to stay in the country indefinitely once they let her in.

"If you end up working here, or if what you are telling me isn't true, you could be banned from coming to the United States for the next 15 years. If you tell me the truth now, it won't be that bad."

"I am not lying," the young woman says. "I am just visiting my mother."

The officer stands up and lets the woman sit at the window for another eternity. At least that's what it feels like. I try to glance at my phone while I keep it hidden in my bag. Anne offered to pick me up, but I can't even tell her when I'll get out, and I know she'll want to go to bed early. I see I did get a text from her.

Sorry, but it's getting too late. Can you take an Uber?

Yes, I figure I can. I just can't wait to go to bed tonight, hug Baloo as tight as I can, and worry about everything else later.

After another 20 minutes, the female officer in the first window calls my name. "Jakob!" It's not a question calling my name, like in other, friendlier places. It's an order. I grab my excessive number of carry-ons and make my way over to her window.

"There you go." She hands me my passport, already stamped on the visa page, and sends me on my way, no questions asked. I'm glad I didn't have to explain again what happened.

When I'm finally in my Uber back to Pasadena, and my airport anxiety has left my body, at last, I notice how tired I really am. I can hardly keep my eyes open while my Uber driver can't stop his casual banter. I know he's just trying to be nice. I'm back! Back home. Even if I just came from home.

~

The next day, I managed to sleep in, even though I was sure my jet lag would wake me up early. I'm just too much of a long sleeper. Baloo is in bed with me, curled up next to my head on my pillow. I missed him. I'm glad I have almost a week before I have to teach again. I just have to sing a gig on New Year's Eve and rehearse with my bandmates in two days. If it weren't for this gig, I probably would have stayed in Germany longer. But I'm going to make a good amount of money from this, and I always think I'm not doing enough live performances anyway.

Truth is, I get a little self-conscious when I'm the center of attention, especially when I'm in heels, and especially when I am supposed to entertain people. I feel the anxiety rising within me as I'm thinking about this event, the songs I'm going to sing, which I haven't sung before, the dress I'll wear, and if I'll be able to move elegantly enough, but also portray fun and energy at the same time. I also remember that I should be studying some songs a bit more. As soon as that thought hits me, procrastination takes over, and before I know it I'm on my phone opening up Instagram, Facebook, emails. Everything but getting myself out of bed and starting my day by unpacking my huge Mickey Mouse suitcase, or practicing said songs.

Once my millennial brain lost interest in all the different social media platforms, I open up *Coffee Meets Bagel*. I mean, it sucked pretty bad at the first view, but I might as well give it another try. If I only get six swipes every day anyway, I'll be through those in less than a minute and can move on with my day, which so far hasn't accounted for much. *I* haven't accounted for much. I look at the first suggested guy on my app, Cesar. Weird name.

Doesn't look bad, but also not amazing. He says he loves steak. That's a no. I quickly push the 'X 'button to indicate I'm not interested. If somebody goes out of their way to mention how much they love meat, I just don't think they're the best fit for a passionate vegan. Next, I see a guy kneeling, posing with a little boy in a baseball outfit. They don't look like they're related, so I keep browsing his profile. I am not entirely against the idea of dating someone who already has kids, but I imagine it to be a bit more complicated. Nick has a cute smile. I swipe to the following picture and see him in a beach setting with his back to the camera. He has a shirt on, but I can see that his arms and back look very strong. And wide. I swipe again and see him in running gear, his face covered in mud, next to two other guys, smiling adorably again. There are no six-pack pictures here, and that's a big plus. His profile is pretty empty, and because I want to know more, I hit the heart button. *Congratulations! It's a match!* A message pops up, motivating me to send Nick a message.

"Maybe later," I think.

I get up and brush my teeth, have my breakfast smoothie and finally grab my iPad to have a look at these songs.

Then

I can't believe Eddie asked me out on a date. He said it's not a date. But what do you call it when you want to take someone out for some fancy French Toast and you barely know them?

I don't know exactly how old he is, but he is definitely a bit *too* old for me. I don't know what to expect. Why did I say yes? Maybe because he kept asking me. He didn't just ask once. He basically made me say yes. About a week ago, he started calling me *Bunny* at work. I laughed it off at first. How weird. He said, "It's because you only eat plants, and you look like a bunny rabbit when you chew your food." Now I think it's kind of cute, even though I'm not sure how to feel about being called a pet name at my workplace. Luckily, he doesn't say it in front of my students.

It's Sunday afternoon, and I'm out eating all-you-can-eat with Alana at *Rahel Ethiopian Vegan Cuisine*, when I get a text from Eddie. We had exchanged numbers at last because he was so insistent about the French Toast Meet Up that we figured it would be necessary to communicate, to make it happen.

> Hi Bunny Princess. 🐰🍓🍪🥛🥖🥗

THE ONE I LOVE MOST

Are we still on, to go get that amazing French Toast tomorrow?"

I put my phone away and sigh. Alana questioningly looks at me.

"This guy from work wants to buy me French Toast. It's not officially a date, but I guess in some way it is? And I don't know how to feel about it. He's not exactly my type. I'm not even sure I have a type, but I think he's quite a bit older than I am, and my coworker told me he has a kid." It all just comes bursting out of me.

Alana looks at me sternly. "Just do what feels right. Follow your gut." And then she adds, "If it doesn't feel right, don't go out with him."

"I don't know, Alana. It's kind of set in stone already."

"Well, if you feel like you can't back out, just go and have fun and see how you feel after. And tell me where you are going, you know, just in case."

"Thank you, Mausi. I will."

She and I have been calling each other *Mausi* almost since we've known each other. It's a cute German nickname, but she's been calling her cats *Mausi* all her life. When I heard her use it over the phone, talking to her mom and her cats in Mexico, the two of us started using it as well.

Alana is still working slowly on her first plate of food as I'm getting up for the third time to get more of this delicious vegan *Injera* flatbread, *Shiro, Fasolia,* and all the other mouthwatering dishes I don't know the names of. My college buddy turned sister has a body shape that one could argue is the opposite of mine. Not only is she only five feet tall, and therefore almost half a foot shorter, but she's tiny all the way around. Therefore, she doesn't eat that much, or maybe it's the other way around. She has the shape I always wanted when I still lived in Germany. Small, petite, not too many voluptuous curves, and cute. Her dark hair is growing back strong from a buzz cut earlier this year, and her face resembles a Latina version of Scarlett Johansson. By saying I am her opposite, I don't mean I'm tall and fat. At five foot five, I consider myself a normal-sized woman. My butt has always been the widest part of my body, and with my waist being the slimmest, that gives me an hourglass shape which I never felt was appreciated by the general public in my home country, or by me.

Women, for as long as I could think, have always wanted to look like young girls, as thin and straight as possible. My curviness always made me feel like too much. Especially now. I've gained weight since I moved here. My dream of becoming a hot stick figure seems even further out of reach, which is why I went from being vegetarian to being vegan, figuring all I'd be able to eat from then on is vegetables, but oh, was I wrong. I basically live in a vegan mecca; there are so many vegan junk food options in Los Angeles. At least I have a cute face, I tell myself. And none of these thoughts can stop me from enjoying this food right now.

~

THE ONE I LOVE MOST

Once I'm back home, I decide to text Eddie back. Even though something in me doesn't want to go, and I have this weird feeling, I also don't want to cancel. I need to get out of the house more anyway. And it's probably just my *inner pig dog* (as we Germans call our comfort zone) that's holding me back. I'm not meeting anyone, not going out, just hiding in my bed when I'm not at work. I will not listen to it this time. I'm just going to do it.

> *"Sure. What time did you think of going there? I have to start work at 2pm."*

Immediately, my phone croaks with an answer from him.

> *"YEEAAHH. Meet me on the corner of W 2nd street and Delarmo Ave in San Pedro, that's where I live. And I can drive from here. I'm so excited. If I were a puppy, my tail would be wagging!! I hope you'll like the French Toast."*

WOAH! That's a little overenthusiastic, isn't it? I wish Alana was still here. Talk about a casual meetup for French Toast.

I type in his address in Google Maps and can't help gawping when I see how far he lives. How does he drive up to Pasadena twice a week just to teach a few lessons? It says it's 40 minutes away without traffic.

Hesitantly, I start typing again. At this point, I really don't want to go anymore, but now I'm even further in, and backing out would be horrible, especially after his wagging puppy tail analogy.

> *Omg. Eddie! That is so far. But ok. I just have to be back by 1pm at the latest.*

> *I will come and get you then. Or we can do it on a day that you don't work?!*

Phew. I got away. At least for tomorrow.

> *Friday I dont. That might work better.*

He then offers again to pick me up, and I decline. Being stuck in a car with someone for that long might not be a good thing.

> *Ok, if you come down here, we can go to the beach or the park afterward if you want. I think you just might like it out here.*

Why is he so uber engaged? He barely knows me. And he claimed this wasn't even a date. I don't know about this. But let's just get it over with.

> *Ok. That sounds nice.*

> *Awesome. I can't wait!!*

I know. I can see that. I almost want to text him that, but instead, I just text back a simple smiley. Let's not make him think I'm interested in him pursuing me in any way.

~

THE ONE I LOVE MOST

On Thursday evening, I'm starting to have second thoughts again. The way he's texting me and approaching me just seems *way* too flirty. I'm not interested in him like that. And before he gets even more excited, buys me brunch, and expects something more from me, I want to be clear about how I feel and how I don't feel. Also, I don't really want to go. My comfort zone is pulling hard right now to try to keep me at home instead of driving through all of LA to a guy I'm not interested in like *that*. So, I draft a text and send it.

> Hey Eddie, Good morning. I'm still able to come down there. I just wanted to let you know that right now, I'm not really looking to date. I just want to make sure we're on the same page, and I have a feeling you have different intentions. In that case, I don't want to waste your time or money.

That should do it. Now it's clear. I won't have to go. I basically already rejected him.

Fifteen minutes later, my phone croaks with an answer from him.

> Don't worry Bunny! I'm not looking for anything! No need to worry! I don't want you to feel like there's anything more than simple friendship and fun and laughter and just getting to know one another. No need to worry about a thing. Promise.

Still hesitant, I type.

> *Ok. Sounds good. What time should I be*
> *there then? 10ish?*

~

Luckily, there's not too much traffic anymore. It takes me forty-five minutes to go to the address Eddie gave me.

> *I think I'm here.*
> *I'm parked on the street. I'm in a blue Scion.*

> *Give me a few minutes. I just ran to the*
> *grocery store.*

What? He knew I was coming. I'm even a few minutes late. It's not like I showed up early or anything. But OK, I guess I'll wait. Luckily, there are smartphones you can waste all your time on, and that's exactly what I'm doing.

After ten minutes, a golden Honda pulls up next to my car, with shiny rims and the tinted passenger window rolling down. It's Eddie. 'What in the world have I gotten myself into, and when can I go home? 'I think to myself.

"Hi Bunny," he says with a big smile on his face.

"Hi," I manage to get out. "I think I have to use the bathroom before we go anywhere. Would that be OK?" I'm nervous, and I could've done without going to his place, but a girl's gotta go when she's gotta go. "Also, is my car OK here for now?" I'm always worried about street parking in LA, but apart from that, the neighborhood doesn't quite live up to Pasadena's cleanliness. There's trash lying around on the street, and next to me is a small park with nothing

26

in it other than some guys on BMX bikes, gathered in a group.

"Your car is fine here, Bunny. Do you want to just hop in the car with me, and I'll bring you to my bathroom?"

How weird. I thought he lived here. But OK. There's no going back from here. Alana knows where I am, and Eddie works with me, after all. They have his address. He holds the car door open for me from the driver's seat. I sit down on the old, shiny beige leather. He turns the car around and immediately turns right into a parking garage. "We just have to take the elevator up."

As he opens the door to his studio, a big kitchen island greets us first thing. It looks nice and somewhat fancy, definitely much nicer than our apartment. But I notice there's no furniture. He must have just moved in here.

"I'm so sorry for the mess. If I had known you'd come in, I would've cleaned up." He busies himself by grabbing two fluffy-looking rugs from the floor and bringing them into what I'm assuming is the bathroom. "There," he says, "All ready for you to go in now. I just have a no-shoes policy."

"Of course," I answer. "I don't like to wear shoes inside either."

I take off my shoes and make my way into the bathroom, a small jungle with fluffy white bath rugs, several plants, two sinks, huge mirrors, and a candle he must have lit just a minute ago. Why? I don't know. But this bathroom looks nice. Elegant but cozy. Impressed, while relieving myself, I think, 'maybe this isn't all super bad. 'I feel a little more comfortable now. Let's just see what else the day brings.

"So what's your favorite fruit, Bunny?" he asks when we're finally on our way.

"My favorite fruit?"

"Yeah, every time I ask what you like to eat, you say fruit."

"Fair enough. Hmm, let's see," I answer slowly. "I really like white sapote and durian. Have you heard of that?"

"White Sattate and Dorian? Last I checked, Dorian was a name, not a fruit," He laughs.

"No. DUrian. It's what they call the stinkiest fruit on earth. It smells like gasoline when you open it, but it's quite creamy and good when you actually dare to bite into it. They only sell them at Asian markets, though, and mostly frozen. And they're expensive."

I'm rambling. Not too long ago, I started experimenting with a raw vegan diet after juicing on and off for several months. Once I switched to mainly fruits, I started having all this energy. I haven't felt better in my life, as long as I can remember. I started going to 'Fruitlucks' by the beach, where everybody brought fruit to share, and there were always a few generous people who brought durian. I became so passionate about healthy eating, and I loved how I felt. My mind cleared up, and all of a sudden, I really wanted to go running instead of having to convince myself for hours before I finally put my Asics on and got going.

But going out with friends wasn't the same anymore. With this newfound diet of mine, I started to alienate myself in so many ways. Giving up alcohol wasn't the worst thing. Going out to eat and smelling the food, not being able to order anything off the menu was tougher. And then there were the conversations with basically everyone I knew. "Eating that many bananas isn't healthy. You can overdose on potassium." Or, "You know this isn't sustainable, right?" Or the good old, "Animals were put on this planet for us to eat them." I knew how I felt, and I knew that most of these comments were just general belief statements without actual research, but it started to become really exhausting, justifying my way of life. So, I slowly but surely transitioned back into a "normal" vegan diet while still trying to keep the first half of my days filled with fruit.

"Stinky fruit? Eddie says skeptically. "OK, and what about Sattapo?"

"Sapote?" I chuckle. "Sapote comes in different varieties, even one that tastes like chocolate pudding. But I don't wanna bore you with exotic fruit talk. I also like normal fruits like strawberries, mangoes, and figs."

"Figs, huh?"

"Yeah, they're in season right now, and they're so good. And so healthy."

"OK, Bunny, I'm not sure that's true, but maybe we'll have to try them sometime."

"OK," I offer hesitantly.

Fifteen minutes into our car ride, I decide to ask Eddie where that oh so special place is that supposedly has *the* best French Toast in all of LA, that I was supposed to eat despite my vegan-ness. He wouldn't tell me earlier; he just kept saying it was a surprise. Until now. He says, "We're going to Costa Mesa."

"Costa Mesa?" I blurt out! "That's super far. I mean, to get French Toast."

"It's not that far, Bunny Rabbit," he counters. "Nothing is too far to have you try the best French Toast I know of."

That damn French Toast, I'm thinking. Why did I agree to this? I don't even eat dairy or eggs anymore. How in the world did I let him convince me to do this? Probably because in the beginning, it sounded like a small deal. Getting breakfast somewhere really quick. And this is probably why he didn't tell me how far we'd be going, because he knew I wouldn't have come.

Another twenty minutes later, we pull into what looks like a plain old regular strip mall in Costa Mesa. The parking lot is packed. I don't see any fancy restaurants, just regular shops. 'Is this a setup?' I'm thinking. What is this?

Eddie asks me to stay in the car, so he can open the car door for me. This feels so silly. No man in Germany would ever make the effort to open car doors for me. None that I've known, at least.

"Over there," he points out the direction we're going. In the corner of the strip mall, behind two square pillars, is a small eatery called "Plums Café" with some outside tables on what looks like a sidewalk. Not impressed, I think to myself, 'At least we're here now.'

The waitress seats us at a small round table outside. After almost three years of living here, I finally got used to the fact that you can't just choose any table, like in Europe, where you walk in and sit down at any table of your liking, and one of the servers will find you.

The outside tables are made of metal, and so are the chairs. It's the typical garden furniture lots of people have, and the chairs always seem to be slightly wiggling, including the one I'm sitting on right now. I still feel somewhat uncomfortable, sitting across from a man I don't really know, who seems to have some weird obsession with me. The size of the table in between us isn't really helping. As the waitress brings our menus, Eddie grins at her with big shiny white teeth and says, "We already know what we want. We came here for the best French Toast." And then he adds, looking at me, "But you should maybe have a look at it anyway to see if you want to order something else."

'Something else? 'I'm thinking. 'We came here for that freaking French Toast, and now I can just order something I could order anywhere else in LA?'

"OK, yeah," I say instead.

The waitress smiles and says, "I'll give you guys a few minutes," and then disappears back inside.

I start looking at the menu and see *freshly squeezed orange juice* for $5. "They have fresh orange juice," I say. "I think I'm good with that." I wouldn't be cheating on my fruity diet as much if I just had that and a few bites of Eddie's French Toast.

"Oh yeeeah," Eddie says. "We're definitely gonna get the OJ. But what else do you want, Bunny? You should get something to eat. A sandwich, maybe?"

"Oh. OK," I hesitantly say.

I start looking at the menu again, and they do have a vegan sandwich. So, after three minutes of mentally going back and forth between the sandwich and the fruit cup, I end up choosing the sandwich, being sure that the fruit cup would just be cheap cut-up fruit in a tiny bowl, like at most other places.

Five minutes later, the waitress brings out two rather small glasses of orange juice. "These are tiny," I think. Eddie takes the tiniest of sips, holding it like a fine lady would, his pinky finger standing off, and exclaims, "This is good fresh-squeezed OJ." I give it a try and nod in agreement, adding a "mm-hm" to which Eddie responds: "Let's have a contest," and starts chugging down the orange juice. Immediately I pick up my glass again, which I was gonna sip on carefully throughout the rest of our visit at Plums Café, and start chugging as well. Both our glasses are empty. I can't help but laugh, and Eddie addresses Susan, our waitress, and orders two more glasses.

That's $20 worth of orange juice alone. But OK, I didn't ask for it. As soon as our second round of orange juice comes out, he looks at me challengingly and says, "Let's go." Unbelievably, I take on the challenge a second time and laugh so hard that I have to be careful not to spray all the expensive orange juice back out at him through my nostrils, which is something I do when I laugh very hard while drinking something. I manage to get all the juice down, still laughing hard. This is different, I'm thinking to myself. Not bad. But that was it for the orange juice. And as soon as the thought left my brain, Eddie ordered a third round, which ended up accompanying our food, and we enjoyed them at a slower pace this time.

While the food wasn't bad, I wasn't overly in love with it either. The sandwich was on the fancy, small side, and I tried a couple of bites of Eddie's French Toast, which wouldn't make me want to drive all the way to the next county just to have it, but it also wasn't bad. At this point, I am well aware that it never really was all about the French Toast.

On our way back, he mentions his other plans for the day, also involving me. "If you have some time left, I would love to take you to the beach in Pedro, and there's another beautiful place I'd like to show you. I think you'd really like it."

I am having a good time so far, I'm thinking to myself. Even though the amount of time I've spent in cars today, and the distance I've driven for this breakfast, and the amount of time spent with a man I barely know, do make me feel a bit uncomfortable. But I'm laughing. And I've wanted to laugh more. Even in the car, he still makes me crack up by being silly about pretty much everything we talk about.

KATHRIN JAKOB

"OK, sure," I say. "I really can't stay that much longer, but I haven't been to the beach in a bit, and that actually sounds nice."

"Yaaayy," he gleams at me. "You're going to love it. I'm so excited I get to show you my favorite spots. You can take your shoes off and walk in the sand barefoot. You'll love it."

There's this excitement again. Why is he this excited about showing me all these things? He barely knows me. It doesn't seem fake, but at the same time, it doesn't seem like normal behavior either. But then again, aren't I the one who always says I don't want normal? Maybe this is how Americans date, I'm wondering. I haven't had a real boyfriend here yet, and maybe things here are just *that* different. Perhaps this is a proper date, and I don't have to feel weird about it. At the same time, if this actually *is* a date, I don't know how comfortable I am with the thought of being pursued by him. He's at least ten years older than me, has a child, lives on the other end of town, and is as different from me as one can be. But he did say this was just friendship. I recall our text conversation last night and allow myself to relax.

"And here we are! If you want to take your shoes off, I can carry them for you."

Now

I still can't believe it's 2019. Where did the time go? I will turn 30 this year. And I'm far away from a promising career, marriage, kids, my dream home, or, it seems, anything that's desirable by modern society. Instead, I'm living in this two-bedroom apartment with Anne, a fifty-one-year-old high school photography teacher, and our two cats. We even had three at one point, but her first cat, Poppy, sadly disappeared one day, and we had to assume it was something to do with the coyotes in the area.

Anne has lived here for over ten years already, which explains why she has so many things. The apartment isn't small, but it is stuffed with all the things she owns. I knew when I moved in that I would have my room, and of course would be welcome to use the common areas, but that there would be no space for my personal items in any of those places.

So, here I am in my room, stacking things on top of each other. I have a small wall closet that's filled so tightly with clothes that it's hard to push them apart or get a good overview of all the clothes I actually have. On the top shelf in the closet, I'm storing several boxes, duffel bags with things I don't need every day, and other miscellaneous stuff. Below the hangers on the floor, I lined up all of my shoes, and also managed to squeeze in my suitcase, my fan (which I only need in the summer) and my microphone stand. It's a mess.

My room has a really nice view of the courtyard with a fig tree right in front of my window. I bought bookcase benches that reach up to the bottom of the windowsill, and Baloo loves sitting there, watching what I call "cat TV." My queen-sized bed, with the most comfortable mattress I ever owned, is in the middle of the room. Next to it is my dresser (for more clothes, obviously).

The remaining two walls in the room aren't free anymore either. One wall is lined by my keyboard, which double functions as a rack for worn clothes. On the other wall I put a small desk, which took on the role of a vanity with all my makeup and a small mirror on it. And that's my whole life within four walls. I'm kind of proud of managing to get all these things in here and still have it look cozy, when everything is in its place. But I am longing for more room, and I wonder when I'll be able to have my very own apartment, or who knows, house. Living in LA, that actually might never happen. People have roommates until the day they die in this city, unless their roommate is their spouse, which in my case is non-existent. Hope dies last.

~

I'm helping out at work by subbing for another teacher, but I'm on a break. Might as well text that guy Nick from *Coffee meets Bagel*. He did give me his number on the app after we chatted about Pokémon cards, movies, and other trivial things. I start with a simple

"Hey Nick, it's Kathrin." 😬

His reply comes faster than expected.

Hey you! What are you up to now?

Waiting for my students at work. But it looks like they're not coming. Wbu?

Silence. He's not a fast texter after all, it seems. After browsing Instagram and wasting my break, and not hearing from him, I go back to the lobby to greet my next student and get on with work.

Even though I very much want to find lasting love and meet someone amazing, I don't expect too much from these dating apps anymore, or the people who come with them. I've matched with many seemingly nice and handsome guys, and it always ended with the other person ghosting me, being rude, only wanting something casual, or sending pictures of body parts I didn't ask for. Or, if an actual in-person date did happen, we just didn't vibe, and I maneuvered myself out of making plans to go on a second date.

As I very patiently go through the C major scale with six-year-old Sam for the tenth time, I see a text popping up. He's still there. He hasn't turned into a ghost.

Where do you teach? I'm finishing the workday at the gym here at the office. Just did the StairMaster before work.

I'm slightly confused by the term *gym at the office*, but I don't have time to text him back just yet. I have to finish these lessons, and hopefully, I can get him on a phone call, which we had talked about earlier. It's always easier to really get a feeling for someone when you talk to them. And it could save me a possibly bad date if the call reveals all the things I won't like about him.

After my lesson with Sam, I send him a text.

> Let's talk on the phone tonight if you're free.

I know it's a Friday, and he might very well have plans to be out and about, unlike me, who prefers to sit in her little room as a 29-year-old grandma. I pretty much gave up drinking when I gave the raw vegan diet a try a couple of years ago. Before that, I would only drink to get tipsy or drunk anyway. I always wondered if anybody really drank for the taste of alcohol. I can only bear it if it's mixed with something sweet that covers up the alcoholic, stinging, bitter taste. And if I really want to loosen up, that's nothing that a small chocolate edible can't fix. Going out just isn't as fun anymore when you don't drink. Or when you don't have twenty dollars to spend on a glass of wine. Or when you can't walk in your stiletto pumps for more than an hour and instead of having fun, all you can think about is getting out of them before your little toes die off.

My point is, I'm not a big fan of clubbing or drinking or spending any amount of my paycheck on any of those things.

~

It's 9:30pm. My shift at the music school was over 7pm. I haven't heard from Nick. It's been a little more than four hours. Oh well, I think he might have lost interest. A phone call might have seemed like too big of an investment.

I'm looking at inspirational quotes on Instagram as a text pops up.

> Just got home. I had dinner with some co-workers. Let's talk tomorrow. What's your schedule like?

OK, we're still doing this. I'm also quite impressed by the fact that he's using sentence marks and spells all of his words out. I shouldn't be impressed by that, but after so many 'What r u doin's and 'Hey's, I appreciate a man who can show some literacy and has the patience to type out full sentences.

~

The next morning, at work again, I'm sitting in my little cube room in between lessons and waiting for Nick's call. I gave him the option to call me after my shift which ends at 4pm or during my half hour break at 10:30am. He chose the half hour break, and part of me wonders if this is his way of making sure I won't talk his ear off. Regardless, I am very excited and quite nervous. I sit on one of the little piano benches facing the mirror wall, staring back at myself. What if he's trying to FaceTime me? It's OK, I think to myself, I'm at work, I look decent. I have makeup on. I just need to hold my phone at an angle that is flattering. I open my camera to make sure I not only look OK in the mirror, but also on my phone. As I'm holding my phone up to find the best angle, my phone starts ringing. It's a normal call. Phew. But I should let it ring a few times, so it doesn't seem like I was waiting for his call with my phone in my hand. My heart starts beating quite rapidly, which is so silly. I haven't even met this guy. I might not even like him. Here goes nothing.

"Hello?" I say.

"Hi Kathrin. It's Nick."

"I know. How are you?"

"I'm good. Just got back from the gym. How's work?"

I'm having somewhat of a hard time hearing him. Our connection isn't great, but I do hear that his voice sounds really nice and soothing, like that of a normal and nice guy. Fingers crossed. We exchange some more casualties and since his dating profile wasn't really clear on his job, I decide to ask what he does.

"I work for Homeland Security."

In my head I'm immediately transported back to Matthew, the guy I went on three dates with just a few months ago who also worked for Homeland Security, in the terrorism department. I find those jobs attractive, men in uniform, a real job, compared to mine. Matthew was tall, quite handsome, said working out was important to him, had his own place and made sure to pay the bill on our dates. But then our third date happened at his town house, that smelled like Grandma just a bit too much. He had the sports channel on his TV running the whole time I was there. We drank water and he casually asked me if I liked sex. But when it came to making a move in getting closer physically, he told me he doesn't ever really make the first step. He's afraid to overstep, and he'd rather be a coward and lose a girl than to be perceived as someone pushy or even molesting. So, I offered my bravery and leaned over to be kissed by him, which he did very reluctantly. I told him to lay on top of me to loosen things up a bit more. He proceeded to do just that. I laid flat on my back and he laid flat on top of me, just like that. I figured that was it. I gave up hope then. After two minutes of laying on me, he said he should probably get off me because he feels like he's too heavy. I agreed and went home a few minutes later. We never spoke again.

"Oh!" I almost shout. "What department in Homeland Security? Can I ask that?"

"Yeah, it's fine. I work for the Secret Service."

"Oh, OK!"

"Do you believe me? When I say that?"

"Say what? Why wouldn't I believe you?"

"Ah, I just meant the Secret Service thing. Some people are skeptical about that."

I definitely heard the term Secret Service before, and I was just going to go with pretending that I'm fully aware of what someone who works for the Secret Service does. I'll find out.

We continue talking about previous online dating experiences, and Nick tells me he FaceTimed a prospective date and she had so much attitude he didn't even want to meet her anymore. He tells me it's nice if someone looks good, but if the personality isn't right, then he doesn't *want it*. This conversation is making me confident that he could actually like me.

"I wish I could keep talking. I'm actually really enjoying talking to you. But I have my next student coming in, in two minutes." I say.

"I like talking to you too, Kathrin. We should definitely meet up some time."

"Definitely. Text me later?"

"OK. Bye."

It scares me a bit how well this phone call went. Because the longer it goes well, the bigger the disappointment will be later if it doesn't work out. But let's stay positive here. I have something to daydream about now.

Then

Eddie. Again. I just left his place about ten minutes ago. I mean, we had a good time, I just still don't know how to feel about his relentless enthusiasm about me, without really knowing me. And one thing doesn't leave my mind. When we went back to his car after my little bathroom break earlier, he asked me this really strange question no one has ever asked me, without any context or reason. We were just pulling out of the garage gate as he said, "Do you have any trauma from your childhood? Did something bad ever happen to you that made you the way you are now?" There I was, in his car, trapped in there with him and this question. "I don't really know," I said. "I think I had a pretty happy childhood. My parents were always good to me." Eddie said, "There has to be something, Bunny. There's always something. What's your bad experience that shaped you, that you still carry around, maybe?"

I knew he wasn't going to let this go without me giving him some kind of answer, so I decided to mention the fact that I was very clingy as a small child. Probably between the

43

ages of five and seven. I remember this very well. If my mom just left the house for five minutes, I would start to panic and look for her, call her back in, or cry because some weird part of me was scared she wouldn't come back. So, I held on to her as much as I could. And maybe, just maybe, that is something I still experience in some form, not with my mom, obviously—I'm the one who moved to another continent—but maybe in some other way.

Instead, I said, "But I think that might have been fairly normal. I don't think that's something that still follows me around."

And now he's texting me again. I liked how much he made me laugh today. I needed that. But I'm not interested in him like *that*. I thought if I went out with him and tried that French Toast, it would be done, and I wouldn't have to say *no* anymore. But now what's next? I might have started something that I don't want. More and more attention from Eddie James.

I'd feel bad if I didn't text back. And even if I didn't feel bad, it would be awkward to see him at the school knowing I ghosted him.

So as I park my car, finally back at my place in Pasadena, I start typing.

> *No, thank you!! I'm glad I came down there.*
> *I had a lot of fun. :) See you soon.*

It wasn't a lie. And because I happened to come across a nutritional fact sheet about figs on Instagram, I took a screenshot and sent it to him, since we had just talked

44

about it. I might not fall in love with the man, but spreading the idea of healthy eating is something I always like doing.

My phone croaks.

> *You can feed me as many as you like! I hope they'll taste good.*

And so, our conversation continues.

> *We have to be quick. Everything is almost out of season.*

> *I think there are not many figs left.*

(It's mid-September, after all, I think.)

> *Ok, well, let's get together and plan it. Tell me where to go, and I'll go get them. Or let's go together cause I have no idea what I'm doing, Bunny.*

> *Haha, we need a farmers market for them and see if they still sell some. Or Whole Foods.*

When I sent him the picture, I just wanted to further prove my point about fruit being healthy. But I should've known that it would lead to more than just that. A reason for Eddie to see me again. But it wasn't that bad the first time, so why not hang out with him again and get some more belly laughing in while eating my kind of food this time?

> *Ok, that sounds like the best idea! I go to the gym afterwards when I finish teaching. We should go visit that store. Wanna go??*

Is there anybody else in this city, except me, who doesn't go to the gym? I tried it, but I decided not to be a passive paying member anymore after three months. I started out going a few times per week and ended up doing cardio on the cross fit trainer, only because all the weight machines intimidated me, and all the muscular people there would find out that I have no idea what I'm doing if I started using them. Everybody would immediately know why I'm in the shape that I'm in, which wasn't horrible, but definitely not up to LA standards. I decided to go running again—which I manage to convince myself to do twice a month—and canceled my 24-Hour Fitness membership.

While we were driving earlier, I mentioned this vegan mecca store that I heard about, and have been wanting to visit. It's located about an hour from LA, in the Inland Empire, so I never went. But it's supposed to be the largest vegan store on the planet, and they have every vegan thing you can think of. A dream.

> *Nice. I'd love to! It's so far, though.*

I am aware that this would be another really long car ride with him if I say yes to this, and I'm not sure that I'm ready for that.

> *They have the same store in Santa Monica, just not as big.*

46

> *Bunny... Everything's far in LA. Let's go to the one you like the most! The further away, the more fun we get to have!*

Exactly my thought... The further away, the more time we spend stuck in a car together, and there's no way out if I wanted to shorten our second "non date."

> *When are we going? Why don't you come with me one Sunday, if you're not afraid of church? Then we could just go right afterwards.*

> *Oh, I see. That sounds good. :) I've never been to church here. What time is it at?*

It's true. I've never been to an American church. Not that I go to church much in Germany anymore, either. I think of myself as more spiritual than religious. But I heard churches here tend to be a lot more fun than where I'm from. So, I definitely am in for the experience.

> *Ok. I have to be there at 8:30am for the rehearsal, the service doesn't start until 10. Can I come get you?*

> *Pleeeease??!!*

Here we go again. Why is he so desperate to pick me up and spend all day with me? To give myself the option of an out, I say:

> *Yeah, let's talk again tomorrow night, and*
> *then I'll let you know for sure? :)*

OK!!!!

The next morning, I send him a screenshot of the Vegan Mecca Store's website with their address on it.

WOW!! I promise we can go there
afterwards! And it's even very close to the
church too! I guess we'll be having lunch
there!

Woo-hoo!

Now I'm actually excited. I can't help it. I've been wanting to go to this store for so long. And even though it isn't the Prince Charming of my dreams who is taking me there, somebody is. I don't even have to drive. This is starting to be a good thing. I hope I'm not going to regret it later. I tend to get excited about things too fast. Or tend to be too naive about somebody's intentions. In the end, they always seem to want something in return that I'm not willing to give.

Like William Krane. Production teacher at the music college I attended. He was never my teacher, but I got to know him through my peer, Jørg who is in one of his classes, and asked me to help him with a school project at Williams's studio in Echo Park. William got my number because he thought I was an 'exceptionally skilled singer ' and he might use me for something. Oh, the promise of work I'd actually love to do. Of course, I gave him my number. This was great. He has experience, he has a name in the industry, he has a studio. So, we started texting, about things very unrelated to music. And, slowly but surely, our conversations became very personal and intimately teasing.

Jørg all the while got wind of this and already wasn't William's biggest fan. He told the school that he was having inappropriate conversations with a former student. I should've known better at the time, believed Jørg about William Krane's real intentions, but I ended up defending him, listening to him while he told me his wife doesn't give him enough attention, or sex, for that matter. That he has to stay with her because of his five-year-old daughter, but that he's miserable. Countless times I met him on the couch in his studio, smelling his halitosis because he sat just a little too close to me. He said I'm a good friend, that I'm helping him. That if I was to record an EP, he would give me free studio time and help me.

One time, we sat on the couch in his studio, he took my hand, and he cried, saying how much he missed affection. That his wife is very cold to him, because of her culture. That he missed going down on women, how it's his specialty. Then he asked me to give him and his bike a ride home because it was too late, and he didn't want to take on the bike ride to Silver Lake anymore. Then he tried to kiss me and I didn't reciprocate. He said it wasn't a big deal to kiss him, but I insisted that I didn't want it. He didn't force me, but at the same time he didn't stop trying to get closer to me or kiss me either. And I don't know why I still haven't just cut him off completely.

> *Ok, I'm good to come tomorrow. What time are we leaving?*

It's a done deal then! I will pick you up at 7am.

> *7am??*

I don't fully believe that yet. I never even get up that early, let alone leave the house at that time.

> *I'm a bit nervous. I don't know what to expect.*

Yes, I wish I could get there later, but it's for the rehearsal. Good. A lot of people will be happy to see you! They will want to shake hands and give you lots of hugs. So be ready. :) That's it. You don't have to say anything. And I'll come out and sit with you.

> *Ok. I'm sure it'll be fine.*

And there it is. I just planned a second date with Eddie, the man I'm not interested in.

See ya in a little bit.

> *See you very soon.*

It's only 9:30pm, but I decide to head to bed, knowing I'll have to be up at 6am.

~

The next morning, I wake up dreadfully, seriously debating if I should cancel this whole going to church with Eddie thing and then getting lunch together. What was I thinking yesterday? But I figured he might already be on his way to me, and it wouldn't be fair to cancel at the last minute like that. I suck it up and step out of my queen-sized bed, which fills up almost my entire little room. It's October, but it's still so hot in LA. Except for my comfy Victoria's Secret thong, I slept entirely naked, with the sheets between my legs for comfort, the window open and the ceiling fan on high all night, and I still had a really hard time falling asleep. My neck feels a little stiff. I am everything but a morning person. Feeling motivated to do anything early is a myth to me. It happens to people in movies, and people who, in my opinion, must be lying about enjoying the early hours, and waking up ready to take on their day.

My roommate Liu has been up for at least an hour, I'm certain. She gets up so early every day and feeds Baloo. Hence, he never sleeps with me anymore. She's also blocking the bathroom right now, showering. Argh, I think to myself. Now I can't even shower before he picks me up. There won't be enough time to shower, dry my hair, put makeup on and eat a bite. Why did I get up? I should have known. Or I should have let Liu know last night that I needed to shower this morning. Oh, well. I'm not into Eddie like that anyway, I look decent enough. I'll just put my hair up, again.

After 15 minutes of reading and answering WhatsApp messages from my family in Germany, who started wondering why I was up this early, I resurge from the comfort of my bed once more and slide open my mirror closet doors. I decide to put on my secondhand dress from Rip Curl. More of a beach dress, but long enough to cover my legs and feet, including my shoes. Maybe it's a bit too long, actually. It was probably designed for someone with model legs. But considering the heat and my figure, this dress is my best bet today. And who am I trying to impress, anyway? I put up my hair in a tight (and this time not messy) knot and start putting my foundation powder on, as well as some eyeliner and mascara. For breakfast, I shove down a banana and some orange juice quickly and at 7:01 I get a text.

> *Ready to Rock'n Roll?*

I say goodbye to Baloo and Liu, explaining briefly where I'm going, and then step out into the Unknown.

I walk down the stairs of our small apartment complex and see him standing in front of his golden Honda on the other side of the street. In a white tank top. No. Undershirt? What is going on here? I thought *I* was underdressed for church. But then I see his whole attire hanging from a hanger in the back of his car.

"Good morning, Bunny," he grins. "Can I get a hug?"

Hesitantly, I walk over to him and hug him. His arms are big and muscular, with a few stretch marks drawing out diagonally from his underarms. His skin is so smooth for a forty-year-old, though. And he smells strongly of a citrusy cologne, that now seems to be stuck to me as well, thanks to the big bear hug he just squeezed me into.

Again, he walks me over to the other side of the car, opens the passenger door for me and heads back to the driver's side.

"Let's do this!" he exclaims in an upbeat tone that makes me wonder, once more, how people can be this awake, this early in the day.

"Alright," I say and squeeze out a smile. The whole car smells like perfume.

On the way to church, he asks me what my favorite movies and TV shows are. At the mention of "The Vampire Diaries," he starts making jokes about sharp teeth, and me liking vampires, and cracks up at his own jokes. I hardly think they're funny, but eventually, I have to laugh along with his infectious laughter. "He has *some* humor," I think, and just decide to go with it.

Finally, at the church, "Grace Haven," Eddie introduces me to basically everyone we run into. I'm having a hard time remembering any of the names, but everyone greets me so warm-heartedly, like I finally found my way back to a home I never knew I had. The church isn't anything like what we would call a church in Germany. It's a plain and simple building. No towers sticking out, no fancy medieval tiles or ancient portraits of saints, no statues. There is carpet. Carpet! It was one thing I had to get used to, all the carpet floors everywhere in America. Carpet floors in apartments, OK. Carpet floors in gyms, weird. Carpet floors at the music school, makes sense for the sound. But carpet floors at church? People walk on carpet with their shoes here everywhere.

"Where would you like to sit, Bunny? I have to go backstage and get ready for rehearsal."

Backstage? I think, but instead say "Stop calling me Bunny already," half jokingly, but also somewhat seriously. I chose a seat right by the aisle, halfway between the stage and the exit doors. Not wanting to stick out either way, the middle row seems like a good place to blend in.

"OK, Bunny. I'll be back in a few." He won't stop calling me that. Here I am, alone in a crowd of people I don't know. I'm here to embrace the experience, though.

Eddie checks in on me a few times before service starts. I got a welcome package from the church as a first-time visitor and as the pastor welcomes people, he asks all first-time visitors to stand up. No way in he... I can't even think of that word here. But now I'm being punished for coming to church? I have to out myself? No way.

From behind the drum set on the stage, I see Eddie motioning me to stand up. He smiles and mouths "Get up," and raises his drumsticks accordingly, for me to get his message. With people already starting to look, I get up and stand there stiffly.

"Welcome to Grace Haven," the pastor says again. I smile shyly. "Thank you for joining us today. We do hope you like it here, and we are so glad that your path has led you here. Everyone, let's give a warm welcome to our first-time visitors."

One other person further away in the room is standing as well. Just as I'm trying to find comfort in looking at my fellow newbie churchgoer, several people start walking towards me and cover me in hugs. People I've never seen. People I haven't been introduced to. "I'm so happy you're here," "Welcome to Grace Haven," "Eddie told me you're a special friend of his. Welcome." They all genuinely hug me, and I am sincerely surprised by this hospitality. I am starting to like church.

As the service continues, people stand up and dance, people sing with the modern Christian pop songs that are being sung by fantastic singers. People reach their arms and hands high into the air for prayers, and I'm very hesitant to do the same. This feels wrong. If I just accidentally stretched out one hand in my Catholic German church or chose to hug someone I didn't know, they'd probably never let me come back in, or refuse to give me communion. For a fact, I know the whole entire church would turn around and stare at me for being such a weirdo and for thinking that anyone but the pastor could raise their hands. I quietly chuckle at the thought of it and decide to go halfway. I face my palms upwards, but don't lift my arms, my elbows stay in place, so I can easily pretend I never moved. Just in case somebody looks.

Once the pastor wished everyone a happy Sunday, and people are slowly starting to empty the room—the service lasted almost two full hours—I stay in my spot to wait for Eddie. The same people Eddie introduced me to earlier come up to me again. Sandra, an older lady, takes my hands and shakes them up and down as she says, "Please come back, young lady. We love it when Eddie brings visitors."

I wonder what that means. How often does he bring people here? But instead, I tell Sandra, "Thank you so much for the warm welcome. I really did like it and I hope I can come back."

Another older guy named Henry who's responsible for the doors and ushering people in towards their seats says, "Thank you for coming to Grace Haven," and shakes one of my hands with both of his.

"Are you ready for lunch?" Eddie steps into my conversation with Henry, his drum stick bag in his hand. He's still fully dressed in his suit and the fancy dress shoes that replaced the old red Jordans that he had on this morning, paired with the sweatpants and the undershirt.

"Yes, I'm starving."

"OK, let's get out of here." He grabs my hand and walks me out of the building. Several people stop us and want to talk to Eddie, and I feel like I'm back in my childhood, walking through town with my mom, when we would meet people on the street who she would talk to forever. At least it always felt like an eternity because none of what they talked about made any sense to my five-year-old self. I kept tugging on my mom's hand saying *'Let's gooo. I wanna go home. You're taking too long.'* The only difference being that

I can't do that right now. This is Eddie's workplace and his people. So, I act interested and smile. At least another half hour passes by until we finally make it out of Grace Haven and back into the car.

After just a five-minute car ride, we arrive at the Vegan Mecca Store. That really was close. I can't believe my eyes as I walk in. This is a full grocery store with only vegan products. They have everything. I walk around the aisles and regret that I won't really be able to do much shopping. They have vegan salmon, vegan steak, vegan everything and I wish I could try all these things.

Eddie finds me in the cat food aisle and asks if I'm ready to eat.

"Yeah. OK. It looks like the bistro is over there."

We walk over to a counter with a menu on a wall behind it. I already know what I want. I've been hoping to come here for far too long. Their jackfruit is supposed to be outstanding.

"Helloou," Eddie says in a bouncy voice to the girl behind the counter, who seems to be ready to take our order.

"What can I get for you?"

"Good food, I hope. I've never been to a vegan restaurant and this one kept telling me about how amazing your food is, so it better be good. And how did you get so tiny, by the way?" I'm starting to realize that this is what Eddie does everywhere. Small talking and joking with people, trying to make them laugh.

Then he says, "What do you want, Bunny? What are we getting?"

"Um. I'd love to have the bowl with the jackfruit-carne."

"And I'll have what she has," Eddie adds.

While he pays, I head to the bathroom. Even though it seemed that people constantly got up throughout the two-hour service at church to go to the bathroom, I still didn't dare to leave my seat. Going to the bathroom during church is not something you do where I'm from. We don't even have a bathroom there. You only leave church if you're choking, if you or the person next to you fainted, or if you have a crying baby with you. And then, all the people stopped us after the service and I felt it would be better not to interrupt Eddie's conversations by announcing that I had to go to the bathroom.

As I'm walking through the clothing section of the store, I start thinking. This is weird. I mean, this just doesn't seem like me. Who is that guy and what are we doing here? Relieved from all the pressure that's built up in my bladder, and refreshed from the water running over my hands, I find Eddie sitting at a small table with four chairs, our food already on the table. Two big to-go boxes, filled with rice, beans, guacamole, pico de gallo and the most amazing looking Jackfruit Carne Asada.

As I sit down and get settled with my little purse, he suddenly looks me straight in the eyes and says, "God, you're beautiful." And he keeps staring for another few seconds.

58

I'm shocked for a moment and don't really know how to respond.

"I'm sorry, it just came out. It's just...your eyes..." Then he looks away and we start eating. I'm glad he's not looking anymore because otherwise he would see how red I'm turning right now. It's like I'm the opposite of a chameleon. The more I want to blend in, the more my face will start glowing. And the more embarrassed I feel about turning red, the worse it gets.

When we're done eating and walk back out of the store, the midday sun is burning down on the Inland Empire. It's fall, but it's still so hot.

"Can I keep you for a little longer?" Eddie asks me as we get settled in the car. He already had the motor on for five minutes to give it time to cool down. "We don't want your skin to burn up on these leather seats," were his words.

"I guess so." I'm still a bit shy around him. "What do you want to do next?"

"Let's go to the mall real quick. I want to show you something."

We park in a big parking lot in Ontario, quite a bit away from the entrance. It's crowded. When it gets really hot here, people try to get away from the outside. They go to the movies or the mall, where you don't feel the blazing sun. Nobody at home would understand that type of mentality. You go out when it's nice out. You have to take advantage of it.

As we walk through the mall, we pass the children's playground, in a fake jungle-like setting. I jump on the opportunity and ask Eddie the question that's been burning on my mind. "So you're 40, right?"

He nods. "Yes Ma'am."

"And do you have any kids?" My coworker already told me this, but I have no idea how old his child is or any other details.

"I have two kids, actually."

"Oh wow," I say surprised. Now that, I didn't know.

"Brandon is 19, and my little Smoochie is 13. Her name is Sasha. A boy and a girl. They're the best things I ever did. It didn't work out with their mother, but that's a story for a different day."

I don't know what to say. He's super upfront and honest about everything, but two kids who are, pretty much, adults already? 19? That's just a few years younger than me at 24. I was expecting the *one* child to be a small one. But this? He full-on raised a family. But that's OK. I'm not trying to date this man or be in a relationship with him, remember? And that's not what his intentions are either.

As we keep walking, our hands accidentally lightly touch as our arms swing back and forth. I automatically try to stay closer to my left, away from him. That was a bit awkward, but it didn't feel horribly bad. Eddie doesn't say anything. He probably didn't notice.

As we walk by the GUESS store, he stops. "This is my favorite store. Will you come in and try something on for me?"

"Try something on for you? Why? I can't buy anything today. What would I try?"

"I don't know. Let's just see, Bunny."

Hesitantly I oblige. We walk in and both look around the female section of the store. At this point, I'm already used to being surprised by how different this whole situation is from my usual experiences with men. As I'm looking through some casual T-shirts and some denim dresses, Eddie comes towards me with a long maxi dress, striped, dark gray and black, off shoulder, with a seemingly very long slit up the right leg.

"Will you try this for me, pleease?"

"I don't know. Why? What's the point?" I am uncomfortable, I don't even feel pretty in my body right now. We just ate. But also in general. This dress is a bit revealing.

"Just try it on real quick, and I promise I will let you be."

"OK."

"But if I don't like it, I won't come out with it," I add quickly.

"I'm sure you'll look beautiful in it, Bunny." He approaches the closest store worker. "Could we get a fitting room for this young lady, please? She'd like to try this dress on."

Two minutes later, I stripped off one dress and am wearing another. It's not bad, I must say, and it's comfortable. But that leg slit... I really don't like my legs. Pale and wobbly. Not something to show off. I open the dressing room door and walk out.

Eddie turns around and stops in his tracks. "Bunny!" he exclaims. "We'll have to get it!" The store worker turns around and says, "It looks perfect on you."

At this point, we have the attention of several other customers. Eddie is halfway hiding behind a table with men's sweaters, and keeps insisting that he wants to get the dress for me.

I change back into my own dress and walk out, insisting that he cannot buy it for me.

"I have to, Bunny. It looks too good on you. I want you to have it."

"I can't accept that, Eddie. I don't even know you, you don't know me like that. It wouldn't be right."

"Why would it not be right? I *want* to buy it for you. I'm going to buy it for you. I don't expect anything in return. I just want you to have it. You liked it too, right?"

"Yeah, it wasn't bad, but..."

"OK. Let's go to the register."

Even though I always dreamed of someone buying me clothes and spoiling me, and treating me like a little princess, carrying my bags even, like Eddie does right now, this feels wrong somehow. Like I didn't deserve it. Like there was something I'll have to do in return. Not sex. I feel

THE ONE I LOVE MOST

safe enough with him to know he wouldn't touch me without me wanting to be touched. But I can't shake the feeling that all of this isn't coming purely from a friendly feeling for me, and it makes me feel a bit uneasy.

Eddie agrees to bring me back home when we are done at the mall. It takes another hour before we pull into my apartment building's driveway. He backs his car into one of the parking spots and turns off the engine. We sit next to each other and look into each other's faces, which for the most part of the day, I realize I haven't done. I've been walking next to him, or sitting next to him driving, with his eyes on the road. We're awfully close right now. I see the big watch he has on his left wrist and the white shirt around his big, muscly arms. His cologne still fiercely clings to him and the whole car, really. And his piercing green eyes, which are almost the same color as mine, look at me intently.

"I had so much fun today, Kathrin! Thank you for coming with me. And thank you for letting me buy that dress for you."

"I had fun, too! And I'm glad I came. Thank you for taking me. And thank you for the dress, even though I still feel like it wasn't OK. You know the way I grew up, this isn't something we do, accepting things just like that. It feels wrong."

"I understand. Just know that I did it with no agenda. I like to make people happy and when I saw you in that dress I just had to get it for you. There are no expectations from me. I'm simply trying to be a good man. So, you don't have to worry about anything." He smiles at me.

"Thank you," I say again. "Really."

And for a moment, it feels like the atmosphere in the car changed. Did the distance between us just get smaller? Is something going to happen any moment now? What am I feeling? I feel protected, and cared for, but I'm confused by this.

"I should go now and prepare for my lessons tomorrow."

"Yes, you do that, Bunny. But let me get out and give you a hug first."

We both get out of the car, and he gives me a really tight but warm and good-feeling hug, and then hands me the bag with my new dress.

"Goodnight, Bunny Rabbit," he says.

"Bye."

Halfway up the stairs, I look back down and send him a quick air kiss and blow it over my hand. Why did I do that?

Now

It's Sunday. Fred, my boss, asked me to help out at the school because our receptionist, Sally, is sick. I just need to sit here and make sure everything's going smoothly, but since we just recently started accepting students on Sundays, the work-day isn't long, and it's very relaxed. I get to be on my phone and laptop when nobody needs my help. The only thing that's not quite optimal is that our heater doesn't seem to work, so I'm sitting here with four layers and a beanie covering my buzz cut because, even though it's always sunny in LA, it does get quite cold in January sometimes, and the buildings aren't the most insulated here.

After making some hot lemon/ginger tea for myself, I'm checking today's schedule to see which students are supposed to come in within the next half-hour. Two students. A guitar student named Raya is scheduled for 10:45am and another drum student, Michael, at 11am. My phone buzzes with a text from Nick. The phone call yesterday felt so refreshing, and we had texted a bit in the evening about football teams and his new fake down comforter. Not that I know anything about football. And for a second, I almost disqualified him when he mentioned the word *down comforter*, but he quickly told me that he

65

doesn't support animal cruelty and bought the fake kind, which made him even more attractive to me. He also told me he thought about me while shopping for it yesterday because I told him I'm vegan.

> *Good morning, Kathrin. What are you up to today?*

I would really like to see that guy in person, to not further waste my time daydreaming about him. I start typing.

> *Hi! I'm at work until 4 and the heat isn't working. >.< What about you?*

> *Sheesh! I hope you at least brought some layers!*

> *I need to hit the grocery store at some point. There are also a couple of games on today. And I either want to hit the gym or go for a run.*

He took this question very seriously I notice, amused. Many other people would have just given me something along the lines of "Uh, nothing serious." or "Just chilling." But Nick seems to actually want to have a real conversation, which I like.

I'm not sure how to respond to all of that information, though, so I ask:

> *Did you find a good running route down there? Do you hike sometimes?*

THE ONE I LOVE MOST

He happens to live very close to Palos Verdes, my favorite part of town, which I learned about only a few years ago, when I explored the area around Eddie's apartment. I'm a bit jealous of him getting to work out right by the ocean. The area is so clean and peaceful, and the best part is there aren't a ton of tourists, like in the other beach cities.

I'm new to running... I've been wanting to improve my mile-and-a-half time for work, so I'm just glad to finally start getting out there. I've found a good go to spot, but I'm sure there's a lot more.

Ah, ok. I always try to find the scenic running spots. ;)

And sorry to be so forward, but when you told me last night that you care about animals, that made you even more attractive to me. 😊

Haha!! Hush, that's not being forward at all.

Haha!

So when do I get to meet you in real life?

What are your plans after work?

None yet. ;)

Well, let's get together. I should be finished with this football game by 5. :P

Let's ;)

How about 6 or 7pm?

That should work. Let me confirm with you in a bit.

I have a date today!? That was sudden. But I'm excited.

As the day goes on, I'm starting to get more tired, and I still haven't heard from Nick by the time I get off work. He might have just disappeared. It wouldn't be the first time a man did that.

It's dark by the time I get home, and I almost settled with the thought of staying in and not going anywhere tonight. It doesn't feel good anyway to leave the house when it's so dark. I'm ready to just lay in bed for the rest of the evening.

But then, my phone buzzes again.

You off work?

Also, I'm not on your level, but I like to hit up my vegetarian dishes from time to time. :P Roasted corn and black bean burgers, kale and sweet potato gnocchi.

He adds a picture of said dish, which I have to admit looks pretty good. I also inspect the little kitchen space that's visible around the plate, and it looks neat and clean.

> *Yeah, I just got home.*

> *And if you're trying to collect plus points with me, it's working. :P*

I get a little GIF back of a happy boy smiling and making the winner pose. He sure does know how to charm me, and I haven't even met him yet. Let's see if he can live up to all this in person.

> *Would you still like to try and get together tonight or shoot for the week?*

> *I'm still up for tonight. ;)*

It's probably best to just get this over with. Waiting too long to meet him, and exchanging too many texts might have me build a romanticized picture of him, that he can't live up to in real life.

> *I'm thinking something simple. Coffee shop or something.*

> *Just not sure on location.*

> *Yeah, I like that idea. Would you mind coming up this way a little? Like somewhere in the middle, or around Downtown?*

KATHRIN JAKOB

Do you know any spots downtown?

*I don't go out for coffee much, but I can
check.*

I hate coffee. I never understood people who are
addicted to it. I don't judge, but I also don't get it. It's bitter
and if I have to put sugar and creamer in it, I might as well
just drink the milk and syrup only.

Lol! I'm more of a tea drinker myself.

We decide on a spot called *The Pie Hole*, that, compared
to most other places, doesn't close at 6 or 7. We agree to
meet there at 6:45. And this time, I'm more lazy than
nervous, having to make myself look pretty and drive when
I'm already tired. I know how these things go, but I tell
myself to just do it, so I don't have to be wondering later.

I put on the jeans I bought just about two months ago
for my birthday. I go with the blue jeans, even though
they're not quite as high-waisted as the black ones. I
combine it with the black, fuzzy cropped sweater I bought
the same day, that's off shoulder and also shows just a bit
of my belly. Then I add the blue and brown scarf my mom
just gifted me for Christmas, put on two sprays of my Kat
Von D Perfume and slip into my brown and glitter ankle
boots, which I rarely wear. Then I put on my makeup. Not
the lazy version like earlier today, but the full-on "I know
how to do make up now" version, including the liquid
eyeliner, contouring, eye shadow and extra mascara. I have

to say I look quite appealing as I'm trying to get a full view of myself in the mirror on the back of my door. It works.

As I walk out through the living room, ready to take off into the night, probably overdressed for a coffee, or in this case pie shop, Anne catches a glimpse of me and pauses her TV show, a bit surprised to see me this dressed up.

"You look fancy today. Where are you going?"

"Ah. I'm just going on a date with this guy, Nick, from *Coffee meets Bagel.* I kind of don't even want to go right now, and I'm not expecting much either, but oh well."

"It's good to get out of the house and even if he's not the one, it's still good practice, right? Where are you meeting him?"

"Just a coffee spot downtown. I shouldn't be gone too long."

"Well. Have fun! And you look great!"

"Thank you. We'll see what happens," I say as I make my way out through the kitchen and the back door.

I arrive at my destination right at 6:45pm, but then quickly become aware that I should've planned for some time for parking. This is Downtown, after all. Not the skyscraper part of Downtown, but still, restaurants and coffee shops don't come with parking lots here, and the street looks like there aren't any spots left. It's quite crowded. I manage to find a parking space two streets away pretty quickly, and I assume that walking back will take me less time than trying to find parking closer to *The Pie Hole.* I park my blue Prius "Hydie," check the signs to make sure

I won't get a ticket here on a Sunday, and then start heading back to the coffee shop in a hurry. I really don't like being late. Even though that's kind of a normal thing in LA. But I hate it when I have to wait for people, especially in a one-on-one setting, so I do my best to be courteous with other people's time. I hope Nick isn't waiting already. He hasn't sent me a text yet.

I manage to speed walk to our meeting spot in just three minutes and send him a text saying, "I'm here," when I'm across the street. Maybe he's already inside, waiting for me at a table.

> *"Just got here, too. Parking now. Be right there."*

Oh, well. I guess I didn't have to stress so much. If my thoughts had to be expressed in a single emoji, it would be the one with the straight line mouth and the two straight line eyes...

I linger around the coffee shop for a few minutes, going between trying to kill some time on my phone and wondering if I should just head in already. I'm feeling 'all dressed up and nowhere to go 'and wondering what the other people think of me aimlessly wandering around by myself. The weird girl with the buzz cut. When I had hair, I could at least hide behind it, now I always feel fully exposed.

Just as I shift the direction of my few steps again, I see a tall man walking towards me who looks like Nick. He does and he doesn't. I imagined him just a bit different, but I can clearly see that it's him now. I am almost immediately discouraged. I already know this isn't what I thought it was. *He* isn't. But I'm here now. I walk towards him.

"Hi! Nick?"

"Hey girl," he says and bends down slightly to give me a hug. He's tall, but not too tall. He has on jeans and a black North Face Jacket. I can smell his cologne, but it's not overwhelming. I'm not quite sure yet if I like the scent. It smells unfamiliar. He almost seems a bit too uptight, but my first impression is that he's nice.

"Should we head in?" I ask hesitantly.

"Yeah, let's do it," he says and opens the glass door to the rather tiny coffee and pie shop. There's a small line at the counter, and we add ourselves to its end. It was dark outside, so now we actually get to really see each other's faces. Nick looks me up and down and confidently says, "I see you, girl." I have to be careful not to start blushing like I do so often, but I'm hopeful that the makeup will keep that in check a bit as well. "I like that shirt, off the shoulder, *and* belly free. I *like* it."

"Oh, thank you. It's new." I answer.

Apparently, he's good at giving compliments. As I look in his face, I see what I saw in his profile pictures, but he also has that Cop look about him. He doesn't have any beard, very clean-shaven, but something about him just gives me that police officer vibe. Maybe it's just the fact that I know he actually was one before he took the Secret Service job. But I'm going to stop analyzing now and just get to know him, or talk to him, or have a good time, or whatever.

"Nice shoes, too," Nick adds and gives me a slight push, that was meant as a tease, but almost knocks me over. I'm glad my feet were planted hip wide and I didn't cross my ankles, like I do so often when I'm somewhere new, or when I feel nervous. Otherwise, I probably would have fallen over.

"Hey!" I exclaim and give him a tiny push back that doesn't make him move in the least bit. He's strong, sturdy. And that's something I like. Big arms and a strong build always make me feel protected, and like the small girl I always wanted to be. I always felt too big growing up, too heavy, not cute enough. With a man of his build, I always feel like I'm finally small and petite enough.

I'm trying to figure out what to order, while at the same time already getting to know him, and talking about our day. I usually just go for the Chai Latte, but decide to try one of their special drinks.

When it's our turn to order, Nick asks me what I want, making it clear that the drinks are on him. Quickly, I order the Pumpkin/Orange Latte, which sounds like it must be pretty similar to a Chai. I want to ask the barista a hundred more questions about the ingredients, but I try not taking too much time and be the girl who's 'extra. 'Plus, I figure, it will be fine. I made sure to order it vegan, what else can go wrong? Nick orders a Chai Latte with Almond Milk for himself.

We spot a rather big table right by the window, but decide to go for it, since it's the only available one. He thinks it's a bit too big, but I think it's nice not being glued to someone else's face sitting on two ends of an itty-bitty table.

We both put our drinks down, and I head to the bathroom. I'm not sure if it's nerves or the small glass of water I drank before I left the apartment, but I know I'd feel better if I didn't feel the extra pressure in my bladder.

I notice I'm quite sweaty once I'm in the restroom, I can even feel it in my socks. I don't even think Nick is a hit for me, but it's still a bit nerve wracking meeting someone you don't know, and sitting right across from them, having them observe your every flaw. The pimple I discovered this morning on my right cheek. Or that one canine tooth that sticks out a bit more because I had such a hard time ripping out that baby tooth when the second one had already come through. I never got braces because I felt like I was too old for that at sixteen. And while I feel pretty confident with that still pretty new haircut I have, it does also make me feel more vulnerable. If I have a bad face day, I can't make a 'good hair and distract from my face 'day out of it. I wash my hands after doing the small deed, that definitely wasn't worth going to the bathroom for—it must have been nerves. I check myself in the mirror and bravely walk back out to the drink and the man I don't know.

Nick smiles at me when I sit back down. I grab the waist of my jeans and pull it up over my belly. I know he can't see it, but it's a well-formed habit of mine. A belly is not supposed to flap over the top of my pants. I only notice that I'm doing it right now because I'm suddenly aware of every little movement I'm making that could potentially make me look stupid.

"How's your drink?" he asks me. I haven't even tried it yet for the fear of burning my tongue.

"I'm not sure yet. I think it might still be too hot to drink. Have you tried yours?"

"Yeah, it's pretty good. I usually get a Chai. I'm not big on coffee."

"Yeah, me too, actually. I usually get the Chai, but decided to try something different this time. I never liked the taste of coffee."

"But didn't you get a coffee drink though?" he questions me.

"No, I got this Pumpkin thing Latte." And as I'm speaking, it occurs to me that there might still be coffee in this drink. That's what I should have asked.

"Try it," he suggests.

"Yeah, I guess you're right. It does have a coffee taste. Oh well, it'll be fine. I do have a bit of caffeine once in a while."

"Are you sure?"

"Yeah, it's fine."

But really, I'm not convinced it is. I'll get over the taste, but I know how a little bit of caffeine sucks all sleeping abilities out of my body. But Nick already paid for this. It was at least $5, and I will drink it. I will also not embarrass myself right now by telling him I ordered a drink I don't actually want. I take another sip.

"It's pretty good, actually," I say and smile.

"So, what made you cut your hair? I noticed that you had pictures with both short and long hair on your profile. I actually think both look great on you, but I'm just curious as to what made you do it."

"Oh, well. There were actually a few reasons. I think most of all, it was a bucket list thing for me. I really wanted to have done it once, and I wanted to know what I'd look like without hair, or like, a buzz cut. But I also tried to do it for a good cause. I tried to save money for an animal rescue, and I said that I would shave my head if I'd get to 500 dollars, but nobody wanted me to do it. They didn't want to give me money because they didn't want me to cut my hair. My dad and his friend even wanted to give me money to *not* do it. I didn't make it to the full $500, but I decided to do it anyway. I set a date and I did it. And it's funny. After that, everybody started to love it and told me how good I looked. I planned on letting it grow back right away, like a fresh start because my hair was pretty unhealthy before, but I started liking it and it's so convenient. So, we'll see." What I don't mention is the wonderful fact that I no longer have to pull out ten or more hairs from between my butt cheeks, every time I shower.

Nick is holding his Chai and is listening, interested.

"Sorry, that was a lot of information."

"No. I think that's really cool. And you're rockin 'it. You looked really cute with long hair, too, but this is unique, and you can pull it off. You have a good face."

"Aw, thank you!" I smile. "So you said something in your profile about not liking women who don't take the shopping cart back?"

"Yeah, you remember that?"

"Yeah, I felt like it was kind of random, but I'm curious."

"I just think that's wrong, that it's not good manners. I don't like people like that."

"I agree with that. I always bring my shopping cart back. In Germany, we actually have to put a coin in them most of the time, so people definitely bring it back. I've been conditioned," I chuckle.

"Ha-ha. That's good then. I can see that you're a good human already."

"So, what are your short-term and long-term goals?" I've read this advice in a Steve Harvey book once, to ask this question. And it feels so weird coming out of my mouth. But I already said it. And Nick seems to be OK with it.

"Short-term and long-term. Let's see," he deliberates.

I still feel so silly having asked this textbook question. Literally. He must know....

"Short term, I want to improve my mile and a half. I think I mentioned that already. And I'm working on eating a bit better, too. And long term... I really want to make it into this team. So, I'm with the Secret Service right now, but there's this team, that's like the SWAT, but SWAT for Secret Service. It's not super easy to get in, but I think I can do it."

"Oh wow. That's cool. That's a good goal."

I don't know what else to say. I don't know anything about these things.

He continues. "But I've always been wanting to work with kids. I used to want to be a teacher. Obviously, I chose a different career path now, but maybe after I retire. I would love to mentor youth or talk to them. I did this youth sports program once, and it was amazing. I love kids."

"That's awesome. It's really great that you have those goals. And I'm sure you can make that happen."

"Thank you, Kathrin."

"I actually work with kids right now, and I wish I could love it. I mean, I love the kids, and I think most of them really like me too, but I never thought I would be a teacher. I actually told my friends back in the day to slap me if I ever become a teacher. And this is a bit different. I'm a music teacher, and it's not full time, and not in an actual school. But I said that because so many of our teachers just weren't good at teaching and took the fun out of school for us, or made it horrible. So many people who don't know what they should do, just become teachers and I didn't want that to be me."

"No, I hear you. That makes sense. And I'm sure you are a great teacher to these kids."

"Yeah, I really can't complain. And I like my workplace. I just don't think it's something I want to do for the rest of my life." Am I being too negative right now? Should I be talking about something that I like instead of complaining about my work which I'm not super happy about?

"So what else do you do when you don't teach? You said it's not full time. And to come back to your question. What are your goals?"

"Well, I sing. I just don't have a lot of gigs right now. I've been slacking." I'm being negative again. "But I just did a pretty cool New Year's Eve gig. With a German band, at a German venue. Lots of old people, actually. It was weird. I do German entertainment, and I yodel." What. Am. I. Saying?

"Ooh. That's so cool." he exclaims and takes another sip of his Chai.

My pumpkin orange whatever is still pretty full, and I'm so worried I won't be able to sleep tonight. I have to teach tomorrow, and if there's anything I hate more than teaching spoiled and lazy kids, it's teaching spoiled and lazy kids while I'm tired.

"That's unique. And I would love to hear your voice sometime."

I smile at him.

"Don't worry. I'm not gonna ask you to sing right now."

"Ha! Thank you! I wouldn't have done that anyway." I laugh.

So many people actually do that. Put you on the spot. 'You're a singer? Sing something...' It's really not that cool to be put in that situation.

"But anyway," I continue. "My short-term goals right now are to handle my visa situation and become a permanent resident in this country. It's been quite tricky. And also, I want to get my own place. I like the woman I'm living with, but I just feel like it's time to live by myself."

"I hear you."

"Long term, I want to do more with my music. Maybe get some songs placed in TV shows and movies. But I also love animals, and I'm hoping to have a small rescue myself. I'm not sure what that would look like. But it's always been music and animals for me. So, I want to do more of that."

"I respect that. It's great that you have such a big heart. And I hope you'll make that happen."

"Thank you. I hope so, too."

"But hey. You got something right there..." He starts pointing down to my chin. Or is it my neck? I start looking down, and he wipes up and gets my nose.

"Aah. I should've known better. Sneaky," I laugh.

He laughs way harder. "Got you!"

"Yeah, alright," I admit.

"So, hypothetically, if you and I were dating, and I had friends over for the Super Bowl, would you come and hang out? And I know you already said you're not really a football fan, but would you hang?"

'That's random, 'I think to myself. 'Is he girlfriend-testing me now? Is he actually looking for something serious and clarifying that for me with this question?'

"Yeah, I'm not really a football fan. And I did try watching it for my ex, but I never understood how people are OK with all the commercial breaks every minute or so. I'm more of a soccer girl, but at the same time, I like the fact that sports bring people together. That's what I've always loved most about soccer, and that's why I think I'd definitely want to come. I probably wouldn't watch it by myself, but I could see it being fun with other people, especially if there's a team to root for. When we were little, my sister and I always asked our dad when he watched soccer, "Dad, are we rooting for the white or the red jerseys?" and our dad would tell us which team to root for and that's when we were all in."

"That's cute. And I like that answer. That totally makes sense. Alright."

Our conversation continues and as we come to a halt between talking, sipping on our drinks and laughing, I look at Nick, and he smiles. At that moment, I know he's a good human. I like him. It just feels good. And not forced. It doesn't feel like I'm attracted to him, but I'm enjoying him. And he does have an adorable smile. He smiles like Trooper, the Golden Retriever I walk every weekend.

"Well, this was really nice," he says. "And it would be really nice to do this again. If you want that, too."

"Yeah, I agree," I smile at him.

"Are you ready to head out? Did you finish that drink?" He lifts my pumpkin caffeine and weighs it in his hand. "Girl, you have quite a bit left," he exclaims.

"I know. I guess I expected the small size to be smaller," I lie. But they did bring me a way bigger size than I expected. "I'll just take it home."

"Nah girl. This is almost cold. Ain't nobody gonna wanna drink that anymore. Let's just throw it." Before I can say anything else, he puts it in the bin. "Where did you park? I'll walk you to your car."

'A gentleman, 'I think so myself.

We get up, he opens the door for me and walks me back to my car. As we slowly approach Hydie I'm hoping that he's not going to try to kiss me. I like him, but more in a friendly way right now. I don't know how I'd feel about him kissing me. But as I unlock my little blue hybrid, he just opens the driver's door for me and tells me to get home safe.

"Goodnight. It was really nice to meet you," I say before he closes the door for me and walks off.

That went better than expected.

Then

> *Baloo is screaming at me for leaving him alone all day.*

This is not a lie, but why did I feel the need to text him right after he left? Wasn't I the one talking about how much *he* texts *me?*

> *Aww. Tell him I'm so sorry that I took his mommy away from him all day long. I promise I will be more considerate next time.*

> *Haha. He's all over me right now. Thanks again for today! I had a lot of fun!*

> *I should be thanking you, for once again you've made my day twice in a row.*

> *:)*

> *I think you are awesome and by the way, I must say you looked amazing today!!! Thank you for allowing me to be a small part of your life.*

So are you! And thank you. You already said that a few times now, but ok.:P

That's because it's true. I'm so sorry. I've just been wanting to tell you at least 15 times all day today, and sometimes it slipped out! I hope I didn't make you feel uncomfortable. I just wanted to tell you how I really felt.

After 40 minutes, my phone buzzes again.

I finally made it home... And I'm really missing my Bunny. I wish you were here with me. I'm working tomorrow at the school from 1:30-5:30 and I'm dying to see you tomorrow. Is there any way possible we can make that happen?

You didn't make me feel uncomfortable.

Am I deluding myself right now, or am I just saying this to him because I feel like I should? I did feel uncomfortable earlier. At least I did with the whole Guess store situation.

Hmm. I have work from 2-7:30 at my other school. But I'm pretty sure I'll have a big gap in there again...

Ok, I'll see what I can do, so I can hopefully see you before and after. I'll keep you in the loop.

Before *and* after?

> *Bunny, send me pictures, so I don't have to only look at the one you took for me.*
> *Pleease??*

A few weeks ago, Eddie had asked me to take a picture with his phone while we were at work, so he could use it for my contact in his phone. I begrudgingly agreed.

> *You should just have an Instagram or Facebook account, and you'd be able to look at all my pictures... :P*

He had told me that he was never a fan of social media and that he's not signed up on any of them.

I send him a picture of me blowing a kiss in my German outfit. A friend of mine took those pictures earlier this year in Hollywood. I put on a lot of eye makeup for that shoot. Who knew those souvenir shops around the Walk of Fame would be such good settings. It came out pretty good with my cleavage at the center of the picture, pushed out at the top of my *Dirndl*, just like it's supposed to be.

I also send him a selfie that I took two months ago, in a neon orange dress from Forever 21, lying down and slightly smiling with my hand in my blond hair.

> *You are so beautiful, little bunny. I want to know so much about you. You bring me new excitement and your smile makes the sun rise. You have the cutest little nose. And I want you to know that I am more than willing to share anything with you that you may wanna know. I have no expectations*

*other than hopefully you'll continue to allow
me to get to know you.*

If there was any doubt left about what Eddie's real feelings were, I think now it's clear. He keeps saying one thing, but it keeps feeling like something entirely different.

~

The next morning, I am barely awake when my phone croaks with another text. To my surprise, this time it's Liu.

*Bringing home a new foster cat tomorrow.
Hopefully, they'll get along better. It's a girl.*

Liu has been wanting to get a cat of her own for a while, and the last foster cat she had did not click with Baloo, or maybe more the other way around. He's the king of the house, and he will not tolerate a co-ruler in his kingdom, even though he might seem like the sweetest creature on earth when he cuddles up to you.

I'm about to send out my response text to her when my phone croaks yet again.

Can I see my bunny tonight?

Eddie...

*We can take a walk. I can show you Pedro
Vegas. And we can watch a movie.*

Pedro Vegas? I guess a movie sounds good.

> *I won't tell. You'll have to see it with your own eyes.*

> *What movie should we watch?*
> *1) The Notebook*
> *2) Love and Basketball*
> *3) Pearl Harbor*

Is he serious??

> *Are you serious?*

> *Yes, I'm serious. But ok, we can decide later. See you at 8?*

> *Ok. I will text you when I leave. I'm gonna wear comfy clothes. I hope that's ok.*

> *Of course. I can't wait to see you.*

How did it come this far? Me, actually wanting to see him again so soon? Going to his place? Watching a movie together? When just a few days ago, I didn't even want to go have breakfast with him. And when my mind is still made up about him not being my type, the age gap being too big and his kids almost being my age. But part of me seems to be too curious and intrigued. And maybe, just maybe, drawn to him a bit?

I go about my day like I always do, except that there's an added element of *feeling wanted* today. The kids are much the same as always. Ali plays a harder version of "Mary Had A Little Lamb," with both hands together, Anna sings a Colbie Caillat song and little Su hops around like a bunny when we sing warm up exercises.

At 7pm I say goodbye to Alfie, our front desk receptionist, and head home. I grab Baloo, tell him I'm sorry I'm home so little, grab a vegan cookie and change into my Victoria's Secret leggings and a loose shirt. American food has made me the plumpest I've ever been, and I know that even without a scale.

> *On my way to you. Should be there at around 8:30.*

> Ok Bunny. Drive safe.

I'm surprisingly nervous when I pull up into one of the parking spots on the street next to Eddie's apartment complex. I mean, I'm not trying to impress him, so what am I nervous about? All I brought with me is my small heart shaped Adidas purse. I walk to the front door and text him, to announce that I'm here.

> Ok Bunny. Push the door and come to my apartment.

The big glass front door makes a buzzing sound, I push and walk into the building that I now recognize from the inside. Last time we came through the elevator from the garage. I find Eddie's door, but still don't see him. The door is closed. I hear loud music coming from the inside. It's almost like he didn't expect me. I ring the doorbell. After about half a minute, the music quiets down and the door opens to reveal Eddie in black sweatpants and a shirt.

He looks at me intently. "This is what you call comfy? I was not prepared for this. Whoa." He halfway covers his eyes with one hand, pretending he's looking at something he shouldn't be. To me, they're just leggings, but I guess Eddie sees something else in my pants. "So let me show you the rest of the place. You weren't supposed to be here last time. My momma would've killed me. It was so messy."

"It really wasn't," I say.

"Well, as you can see. Except for the bathroom, I don't have a lot of furniture yet. I want this place to be perfect. So, right now, I'm sleeping on the most luxurious air mattress. Don't judge."

"I'm not," I say as I look around the sparse interior design, a few plants hanging around by the window. The airbed in the sleeping niche and some CDs piled up on the opposite wall. He does have a really nice kitchen island and three bar chairs to sit there. But that's it. This is a big studio apartment. And adjacent to the bedroom portion of the place is a small balcony overlooking a not so glamorous alleyway. He then leads me back to the bathroom that I, of course, have already seen. To the other side of that little hallway opens a door that turns out to be a walk-in closet. This seems to be the most furnished little corner of his apartment. Dozens of shirts are neatly lined up, hung on a horseshoe-shaped rail. The floor has a fuzzy, soft carpet laid out and against the wall there are at least fifty pristine-condition shoe boxes. Mostly orange-colored Nike boxes.

To the left and right of the shelf that's sitting on top of the rail are two small lion statues. The rest of that shelf is lined with about a hundred different perfume and fragrance bottles.

'OK, 'I think. 'This is definitely not my guy. 'I always liked clothes and shopping and of course I care for my appearance, but not like this. This is too much. Once I say my 'wows 'and express my being impressed, Eddie suggests he take me to Pedro Vegas now.

Ten minutes later, we pull up on the side of the street, next to what looks like a harbor. He comes around the car before I get the chance to step out, holds the door open for me, and closes it behind me once I'm out. "This is Pedro Vegas, Bunny. At least that's what *I* call it."

There are a number of huge, beautifully lined up palm trees that are lit up with string lights. These palm trees are thicker than the usual LA kind and seem well manicured as well. Next to the boats, the ground is paved, like a wide sidewalk or walkway. The boats are rocking softly with the waves. Some boats have their lights on. People live on them. I even hear someone play the guitar on a boat a bit further away.

"You know, I used to live on a boat for a while," he volunteers.

"What? Really?"

"Yeah, this guy I work for, Silvio, offered me to live on his boat, after he let me live in one of his houses in the Hollywood Hills."

"That's crazy. How do you meet these people?"

We walk along Pedro Vegas side by side, look down at the water, talk about some more random facts about ourselves, and at some point we stop walking and Eddie unexpectedly hugs me from behind. I am surprised, but I don't fight it. I lean in a bit, and I didn't expect how comfortable I would feel in this embrace. When we keep walking, we start to hold hands, like it's the most normal thing in the world, casually making fun of it by swinging our arms back and forth in an exaggerated way. He then tells me again that he didn't expect me to wear this type of outfit. "You said you'd be wearing something comfortable. And then you showed up in this."

"I'm sorry," I say, for the lack of a better explanation.

"No need to apologize, really," he chuckles. "OK, let's head back. Do you still want to watch a movie?"

I didn't see a couch at his studio apartment. Nor a TV, just a bunch of DVDs lined up next to the CDs and empty picture frames. When I check my phone for the time, it's 10pm already, but again I consent.

"Sure, if you want to."

"Of course I want to!"

Back at his place, he pulls out a small TV screen from somewhere that he puts on a cardboard box next to his bed. He grabs a DVD from one of the piles by the wall.

"Is 'Pearl Harbor 'OK? I don't think I'll be watching much of it anyway, but I want to make sure you'll like it."

"Yeah, that's fine. But you really weren't kidding about those movies, huh?"

I've seen the movie on German television before, but wasn't really paying attention and must have stopped watching about halfway through. I still can't quite get over the fact of how empty Eddie's apartment is. I wonder how long he's lived here. He must have just moved in.

"So, how long have you lived here?"

"About half a year now. I'm just getting started. I want to make this the sweetest looking apartment in Pedro. So that you'll come in, and your drawers will immediately drop."

"My what?"

"Your drawers. You know, your panties." He laughs and adds, "It's just a saying."

"Pff." I give out.

Half a year is a long time for that little furniture. But he has a plan. He doesn't just want to put random things in here. I get it.

We both cozy up on the tall queen-sized air mattress with the TV on the cardboard box to the left of us, positioned in a way that basically means we'll be spooning. I'm not quite sure what to think of this whole setup, but I feel comfortable with it right now, and decide to just dive into this experience. I am a grown up woman, and there's nothing wrong with this situation. I feel Eddie close behind me as we start watching "Pearl Harbor."

About twenty minutes into the movie, I feel his hand on my hip, then my upper thigh. At first, I'm hesitant to react. He keeps caressing the right side of my body, but I'm still

93

turned towards the little TV. This is not what I had in mind. If anything, I really didn't want things to happen this fast, but I feel unexpectedly drawn to him and the possibility of what's about to happen. I ever so slightly move and turn around a bit. He starts to softly kiss my neck, with his hand still around my general butt area. Then I turn over fully. I'm on my back and Eddie starts to kiss me, his lips on mine. He's going back and forth between my mouth and my neck and my ears, and then all of a sudden, everything goes really fast. He starts taking off my socks, then my pants. For a moment, I consider telling him to stop, that this is too much too soon. But then I don't. As much as I like what he's doing, I can't fully relax. I don't really know him. But he's determined while also being gentle. He takes off my shirt and takes off his own, revealing his slightly rounded stomach. Little by little, all of our clothes land on the floor. My mind is still fighting what's happening, but my body has long given up control.

Now

How does it always get this late before I actually get out of bed? I've gotten better. I signed up for the gym last September, after Derrick convinced me that lifting weights is healthy and necessary, and that running alone wouldn't do it. When I first met Derrick online, I was convinced I was going to marry that man. He is vegan, he's a doctor, and, hold on to your chair, he's a Prince, from Nigeria. Not one of the scam ones. I mean, he could have been. But it turned out he did tell the truth, mostly. He has three citizenships, lots of money and lots of muscles. It was almost too good to be true. And it was.

On paper, and in theory, he would've been perfect for me. I had even told Alana, just two days before I met him, that I'm sure my vegan prince will come soon. And there he was. Two days later I matched with a friend of his on Bumble and that friend said he was only visiting from out of town, but that his friend, Derrick, is vegan as well. He thought we should be vegan buddies, so he gave me Derrick's number. It was all very weird. And thinking about it, it also feels more like a setup than a lucky coincidence. But he was... different. Not a bad person, but also not a very loving one, and I quickly got frustrated and sad, and all the things I don't want to be. Moreover, he lied about his age, his last name, and his birthday, and he constantly referred to my ankles as "stripper ankles" because they're a bit thicker than most ankles. Not something I wasn't already insecure enough about.

But he did motivate me to sign up for the gym, and for that, I am still thankful to him. In the beginning, I managed to get up fairly early each day to make my way there before noon, play around with the weight machines for half an hour and then do my half hour of cardio. I'm quite proud of how consistent I've become with it. I just need to learn to not push it off so long in the morning. It's noon and other than a few private students in the afternoon, I have the day off. Anne gets up at 4am every morning to leave the house at around 6am. We basically run on opposite schedules.

I am really excited for later, though. Nick offered to take me to "one of my vegan spots" for dinner, and I thought that was such a sweet gesture for him to offer. We started texting immediately after our date on Sunday and decided we should see each other again. Soon. He called me during another work break on Monday, and we picked Wednesday evening, which is tonight, at one of my favorite restaurants Downtown, *Au Lac*.

He also mentioned he had a discussion with a friend about whether or not to kiss on the first date and asked my opinion. Presumably because we didn't kiss, and he wondered if we should have? I told him that I think it's good to go with what feels right. That it's totally OK to kiss on the first date, but not at all necessary. He agreed.

I'm just wiping down my cross trainer at the gym and throwing away the paper towel, ready to get on it, when his number pops up on my phone, interrupting my "Gym Cardio" playlist on Spotify. Should I answer now? It could be important. He might not be able to meet tonight. My heart starts beating a little faster when I push the green answer button.

"Hello?"

"Hi Kathrin, it's Nick. What are you up to?" Is he just starting a casual chat midday now?

"Uh, I'm just at the gym, about to do some cardio. What's up?"

"Ooh, look at you getting that work in."

"Oh, pff, trust me, it's not that impressive."

"So about tonight. Change of plans. I won't be going to work today, so I'm not going to drive up to Downtown. I was thinking we could take a hike or go on a walk around here somewhere this afternoon. What do you think?"

OK. Way to dampen my mood. Is this a red flag? Is he just changing plans without asking me? Without considering what my plans might be for the day? I should have known. It started off too good...

"Uhm, hmm. I don't think I can make it down there before it gets dark. I still have some work this afternoon."

"Oh. I thought you were free."

"No, I have some private lessons."

"What time are your lessons at?"

"They're between 3 and 5."

KATHRIN JAKOB

"OK, we'll figure something out. Why don't I let you finish your workout, and we can talk or text after?"

"Yeah, sounds good. I'll text you when I'm done here."

Man! He could have asked me if it was OK to just change our plans last minute. But he just decided on that.

On my way out of the gym, I start thinking about what to text him. I don't want to be that girl anymore, who is OK with everything and who cancels on all her other plans just to see a guy. Because I could do that. Canceling private lessons is easy, but then I'm also canceling my pay for the day, and who is he that I would do that for him at the last minute? I am somewhat annoyed but also frustrated because I did look forward to seeing him today. I just know that driving down his way would either be a major traffic situation right after my lessons, or it would end up being a really late date if I left later.

Once back home, I start texting, eager to sort this out and get it out of the way.

> Hey! I just got home. I was looking forward to seeing you today, but I'm not always flexible like that last minute, so it would have been good to know a little earlier. Do you just wanna reschedule for tomorrow? The earliest I could be down your way today would be 5:30, and I only know of one vegan restaurant in Long Beach.

Good job, Kathrin. Well formulated. To the point, respectful and getting your standards across.

He's typing...

I know... and I'm sorry about that. Definitely on me. I'm looking forward to seeing you as well, and I'd still like to shoot for today if that's ok with you. No pressure since I'm the one who changed things a little. So the spot in Long Beach later would be fine with me! But once again, no pressure.

He types again...

If we do the Long Beach spot, you'd be welcome to meet me at my place, and we could go from here, or we could just meet there. Not quite sure what would be easier.

Is that what he was trying to do? Get me to come to his place? Maybe he isn't interested in something serious as much as he let on last time. But in the end, I decide to go for it, hoping traffic won't be too bad.

As I get ready for my private lessons, I put on double the amount of makeup I usually do, so I'd just have to change into some different clothes before I make my way down there.

Eleven-year-old Mike and seven-year-old Roni aren't any more well-behaved than they usually are. Mike hasn't practiced all week and is farting and laughing about it, and Roni insists on playing only the songs she already knows and not the ones she actually needs to practice. But I get through it. Luckily, it's just two lessons, and then I get to eat. Almost.

It turns out the drive down to Long Beach takes way longer than anticipated. I decided to wear my super high-waisted black jeans that are now cutting my stomach in half pretty good while sitting down, so I decide to open the upper two of four buttons and relax. I might as well while I'm sitting in traffic. The longer it takes me and the more rerouting my Google Maps does, the more annoyed I get again by the fact that Nick just changed plans on me so last minute. It dampened my excitement a bit. I was looking forward to going to my favorite spot in Downtown. He better pay for this meal. I did text him that I will be going straight to the restaurant since Google Maps is sending me down the 710 instead of the 110, and going to his house would delay dinner even more.

This is just not a good time to go anywhere in this city. Not on a Wednesday night when everybody is going home from work. The app speaks to me: "We found a faster route that saves 5 minutes." I hit 'accept. 'Maybe for once, this is actually going to get me there faster rather than holding me up even more. Because that's how these things usually go. I take the off ramp, and now I am sitting in streetlight traffic. The app makes me turn left on a side street and as soon as I turn into it, I see that about a hundred other people were being redirected that way. I spot a stop sign about 20 cars ahead of me and can't imagine that this route is any faster. With both hands tightly around the steering wheel, I let out a scream. This was not how today was supposed to go. I am annoyed right now. This evening better be worth it. Driving in LA is just stressful. But driving to the other end of town during rush hour? Why do I climb mountains and cross rivers for people so easily?

When I finally make my way off the road, which actually looks more like an alley, a big truck passes me by. I can see ears and eyes through the slits and holes, and my frustration and traffic anger turn into sadness instantaneously. Knowing where these pigs are going reminds me of a harsh reality I'm mostly able to block out. I remind myself I'm almost there, and that at least on the way home, there shouldn't be any more heavy traffic. I text Nick to let him know that I will be there in 20 minutes, and he responds saying he just got out of the shower after a run. So, *he's* not stressed. There's definitely some sarcasm in that thought.

I am happy I find street parking right when I get there, and since Nick just sent me another text saying he just left and should be here in 10 to 15 minutes, I decide to go in to Seabird's Kitchen and ask for a table. I thought I might be the one today that gets there later, but he made sure not to leave early. Mentally noted.

After heading to the bathroom, I'm seated at a table that directly faces the door. At least he won't have to look for me long. Five minutes later, he walks in. I get up to greet him. He smiles, hugs me, and then places a kiss directly on my lips. I did not expect that. This was a "we do this all the time" hello kiss, not a "this is the first time my lips touch yours" kiss. But OK. I'll take it. He looks very sporty today, but still chic and not too casual.

"Thank you for coming all the way down here. I appreciate you being flexible at the last minute."

'OK. Good start, 'I think. "You're welcome," I say and smile.

I would usually say something like "Oh, no worries," or "No problem at all," but I have learned one thing about my worth and I don't have to act like I'm happy to do anything all the time. But I'll give him the benefit of the doubt.

He lets me know that with the current government shutdown, he decided to call in sick today, since he's not even getting paid for his work at the moment. And for the most part, he is still working, but didn't feel like going to the office in Downtown today and hence didn't want to be seen or make the drive up there. I get that. Now, it also makes sense that things were so slow at the airport a few weeks ago. I hadn't considered the shutdown.

We order two Mexican bowls with jackfruit and Nick makes sure to tell me that the food is 'on him, of course. ' We talk about what we looked like when we were little. He shows me a picture on his Instagram feed of him when he was in high school, with cornrows and a gappy smile, a gold chain and some white jersey. And then he swipes to the next slide and laughs. "Look, this is what I put in my yearbook as a life goal: Making money. Everybody else put something really inspiring, but I was always about that hustle." He laughs again. It is still a bit awkward sitting right across from him, eating. You always have to be so careful and aware when you eat in front of someone new.

"So, what made you want to see me again a second time?" He asks.

I politely swallow before I speak and then say, "I just thought it was really nice talking to you and I felt comfortable with you. And it was fun. So, I figured that it would be nice doing this again and finding out more about you."

He looks at me and smiles. He smiles like a puppy, actually, exactly like the Golden Retriever I walk. If Nick was an animal, he'd definitely be a smiling dog.

"What about you?" I ask in return.

"Oh, you know. I just felt kind of obligated." He stares me in the eyes, no smile anymore. I don't know how to react. I think he might be messing with me again, but he's too serious. So, I just awkwardly stare at him and think I'm making a sound, but don't really know what to say.

Then he starts laughing. "I wasn't serious, of course."

I think I'm turning red now. And I can't stop it. I'm starting an internal dialogue. 'Look away. Look at your food. This is embarrassing. You should have known that he was joking and reacted accordingly. 'Oh, well.

"But jokes aside. I agree with what you said. I just got a really nice impression from you and I had fun talking to you as well. And I do think you're very attractive, and I wanted to know more about you as well."

"Aw, thank you," I say, still blushing, hoping he doesn't notice.

"I got you there, didn't I?"

"Yeah, I mean, I was pretty sure that you didn't mean that, but you were pretty convincing." And then half jokingly I add, "Not. Cool."

Overall, the date is going pretty well. After about an hour, we're getting to-go boxes for our food, and while I feel like I could talk to him much longer, he asks me if I'm ready to leave. He does wrap up these dates rather quickly. But he insists that he walk me to my car again. Once there, he hugs me, gives me another small kiss and says, "I miss you already," which I find weird, given the circumstances of us really just having met. But it's also sweet, and a brave thing to say.

~

When I get home, I decide to send him another text.

> Made it home. :)

> It's really nice and easy talking to you. I appreciate that.

Good. I feel the same way. I'm digging hanging out with you so far.

What's your Friday looking like?

Woah. Is he trying to see me again that quick? He really IS interested. It's been a while since somebody was that consistent.

THE ONE I LOVE MOST

> *I have work until 7, but after that could work.*

> *Ok. We'll see if we can figure something out.*

> *You miss me already?*

Not sure what to say here. I barely know him. "Miss" is a strong word, but I do really enjoy my time with him and feel like it always goes by a bit too fast, which might partly be due to the fact that he does seem to end these dates a bit prematurely.

> *Haha. A little. Do you?*

> *I do. Kinda didn't wanna see you go tonight.*

> *Aww. :)*

> *Once again, I appreciate you being a little flexible today.*

> *No worries.*

There it is. I said it. He apologized enough to get out the 'pleaser Kathrin 'in me. That's not too much of a hard thing to do, though, to be fair.

We exchange a few more texts about ideas and things we want to do, like go for a hike, or him coming to my neighborhood to hang out during the day, and then we say goodnight. We'll see what happens next.

Then

I'm on my way home from San Pedro. Again. For the third time this week. Since last Monday, Eddie hasn't wanted to let me go. He said he would keep me locked in at his place and not let me go to work or anywhere else. He's a little obsessed with me, in a cute way. It's been a while since anybody has felt that way about me, and yet now that I'm back in the car, it doesn't feel quite right. I do enjoy his company though, the attention he gives me, the foot massages, the story times. Last night he told me a story, butt naked, about when he was still in the Army, and they were sleeping in a cabin in the woods, when he heard something that sounded like a bear.

He crawled on the floor to show me how he moved out of his bed to grab one of his swords, that he still has right next to one of his windows (in the case of anybody ever breaking in), and was ready to attack the bear once it came through the door of the cabin. He gesticulated so wildly as he told the story and moved around the floor so nakedly unashamed that it made me laugh. And then he said, "It wasn't a bear, and it turns out I almost decapitated one of our comrades who was just late for bedtime that night. But I was already asleep and didn't know what was going on. So don't ever scare me when I'm asleep, Bunny."

He also showed me an old photo album of his, with pictures of him as a baby, then as a little boy, teenager, some of his relatives, and handwriting that looked like a little boy's. He was so proud of all this, and I didn't know how to feel about that much information from someone I still wasn't fully interested in, in a 'more than casual 'way. But what am I doing? I've been here every other day and something keeps me coming back. I need to stop this. This is not what I want, and I can't make it seem to him as if I wanted this as much as he wanted it. This is wrong.

I'm still not fully over that personal trainer I met on *OkCupid* a while ago, even though that ship seems to have sailed. Just this morning, I saw a Facebook post of him and some girl at Disneyland. He posted them. He didn't post the pictures we took when Alana signed us in for free. I was so happy that day. My dream guy and me at Disneyland, with my best friend. We were all laughing and having fun, and I was so in love with this perfect human being. But here he was, cheesing in pictures with another girl. She looks a lot fitter than me. That's it. Of course, a fitness trainer would want someone who can keep up with their fitness and looks. I've lost. And here I am, receiving all the love I wanted, but from another guy, older, less Herculesey, less dreamy, but much more available. I will think about this and make a decision soon. But right now, I'll just go home and turn on some Ed Sheeran to lighten my mood from my strenuous overthinking.

I finally got to spend some time with Baloo again last night. He seems to get along fine with Princess, aka Alietta

(Liu renamed her). I'm at work at the North Hollywood school right now, and I'm in between lessons. My next student won't be here for another hour, so of course my first instinct is to grab my phone.

I have two text notifications from Eddie:

> *I'm so happy I get to be myself with you! Thank you for simply being wonderful. You take a little piece of my heart every time you leave me.*

> *I miss you so much already. I hope you have a fantastic day!*

Isn't that what I wanted? Somebody crazy about me? Who tells me that, and is all over me? Why can't I appreciate it?

He even told me to bring my laundry just a few days ago, and he washed it for me. Of course, I thought that was too much too soon, and yet I did it anyway. He takes care of me. Why? And why do I have to question it so much? I don't know what to tell him.

> *Oh, Eddie!. You're so sweet. I do enjoy our time together, but I almost wanna cry right now because of how confused I am with everything.*

It's true. This thinking back and forth really has taken a toll on me. I don't know what I want. And I can't continue like this forever, so I decide to be brave and start typing again.

I love the way you treat me. I don't think anybody was ever that crazy nice to me. I feel like a princess. It's just all so sudden, and it scares the hell out of me. Because I really like it, but it's not something I was looking for at all. I'm still figuring myself out, while you already did all that, it seems. I LOVE all of this. I'm enjoying it so much. But I'm also a free spirit. I always had a hard time being with someone for a longer time and not feeling like I was trapped or missing something. Every time I was with someone, I became someone that I absolutely didn't like. And it's even scarier because you know what you want, and I don't. You're older than me, and I was never with someone who was that much older, and I never thought about what it means to be with someone who has kids, etc. I'm scared because I know being with someone changes me. And I don't know if I want that. I don't know what I want, and this is soo confusing to me right now.

Phew. It's out. I did just send all that, and at least I'm not carrying it around with me only in my head anymore.

I decide to go to the Thai spot next door and order some lunch. The table I sit at starts vibrating as another text comes in. I immediately grab my phone and begin to read. What would he say to my "not knowing" confession?

It's ok. I understand what you mean and that it can be overwhelming.

He understands. Phew. I keep reading.

> *I'll tell you what... I'll just back off and give you your space and time. Maybe when you get it all figured out we can go from there, and if not, we can always be friends who shared a special connection at one time.*

I swallow hard and keep reading.

> *I don't feel any different based on what you've said, and you'll always be special to me and have a special place in my heart. You still mean a lot to me, and I'm glad you told me how you felt before you meant the world to me. That would be much harder.*

I swallow again. This time even harder. The waiter comes to take my order. I pause reading and ask for the usual. "Could I get the 'Pad See Ew 'with no egg, tofu and light on the sauce, please? And just water. Thank you!"

> *I will always be kind to you and treat you with the utmost respect. I will also always cherish our connection, and I will always honor our friendship as one of the best and one of my favorites. I still think you're awesome. Ok free spirit. Go get your life.*

A small tear runs down my cheek that I wipe away quickly because A) I prefer not to be the crazy girl crying in a restaurant, and B) I have to go back to work and need my makeup to stay where it is.

Then my phone buzzes one more time.

> *I'm sure I'm gonna miss you like crazy. :(But I'm still very grateful and thankful that I was*

THE ONE I LOVE MOST

*able to get to know you for a little bit and be
a small part of your life. If you ever need
anything, please don't hesitate to ask.
ANYTHING.*

Can I still call you Bunny?

Tears are rolling down both of my cheeks now, and I'm busy wiping them away carefully as the waiter sets my glass of water on the table and pretends not to notice my disturbed state of mind. I need to answer. This does not feel right. Throwing everything away? The whole last two weeks. I feel like I know this person, and he knows me. And as unsure as I am about what I want, just leaving it all behind now feels wrong. I'm crying, and I know I wouldn't be crying if he didn't actually mean something to me. Maybe this is my answer. It might not be what I was looking for, but maybe it's exactly what I need right now.

Woah! I feel even more like crying now.

No need to say I actually already did. It's embarrassing enough the way it is.

Is that not what you really want?

You, leaving me to myself?

*I don't want to. I thought that's what you
wanted. Is it not?*

Oh, my confused heart. What has he done to me?

How can you mean so much to me after only a few days??

And no, that's not what I want! I don't know what I want, but I know that right now I love being with you. I just also don't wanna mess it up, and I would understand if you can't be with someone who doesn't know what she wants and can't promise anything. Because I know what you want, and I don't wanna keep you from getting just that.

I want to sit in the car with you for hours and go places and hold your hand and your arm. I want you to make me laugh. And I wanna work out with you. I just don't know what's gonna happen and how it will make me feel. I'm scared that the same thing will happen that happened before. But I guess you can never know...

Ok, Bunny. I'm just happy you still want to see me. There's no pressure. We will let things happen naturally. I just love being with you, and we will take all the car rides you want. I can't wait to see you again and squeeze you really tight and fall asleep with you as my little spoon.

Now

I pull up to the little checkpoint, roll down my window and am greeted by a police officer. "I am here to visit someone," I say hesitantly, just like Nick told me to.

"Can I see your ID?" the officer asks.

"Yes, of course." I pull out my California Driver's license and show it to him.

"OK. Please pull over here until they come and get you."

Nick already explained this to me. Since he and his colleague are renting a house in this military housing complex, I can't just come to his door. This is a secured area and nobody can just come in. Nick actually has to come to the gate and confirm that I am visiting him, and only then am I allowed to drive my car to their house. He really does live right by the ocean. I can't believe it. This is the very area I want to be in, right next to Palos Verdes, and he lives here! I did a great job manifesting this one.

As we were trying to make plans to see each other again, we didn't seem to be able to find a time that really worked. He went to a wedding of a colleague yesterday, and he initially had plans tonight as well, but he ended up changing them. For me. And he said he wanted to cook for me and looked up several vegan recipes. He is really making an effort, and he does make me feel appreciated and special.

After about a minute of waiting by the officer's little guardhouse, I see a dark blue Honda come around the corner, and in it, Nick dressed in a tank top waving at me, smiling. He parks behind me, confirms with the officer, comes to my window and tells me to follow him. We drive down a winding road and after just a minute I can see the ocean stretched out in front of me. We stop at the third to last house before the coast, and I am in love with where I am.

The house is modern, with a garage, upstairs and downstairs, an open living room and adjacent kitchen/dining space, and I feel ready to move in immediately. I am aware of course, that I don't know him that well, but this just all seems very promising. And this man is making a real effort for me. When we're done with the tour of the house, he sits me down on the sofa in front of a huge TV and tells me he will start cooking dinner now. I ask him if he needs help.

"You just relax. I got this," he says, and puts a blanket on me.

"You're pampering me," I grin.

He leans over to me from behind the couch, I tilt my head back, and he softly kisses me. All of a sudden, I feel like there's nothing missing in my life anymore. Not right now. Everything I need is right here, right now, and the comfort I feel in this very moment makes me realize what it really was that I have been missing these last few years.

Nick recently recorded "Surviving R. Kelly" on his TV, and we decided to watch it. Me, relaxing from the couch, him cooking a surprise dinner in the kitchen. I hear him cutting things, putting something in the oven, he's taking quite a while. I'm just enjoying the occasional princess treatment I haven't had in so long. Could it be that he actually wants to do this right? That he wants to take things slow? That he's not like most other LA guys? There are things about him that I consider not perfect. I'm almost uncomfortable with how comfortable he is in his world and with himself. But this might just be something good.

He steps out of the kitchen and comes to give me another kiss, then another one. And another one. This almost turns into a little make out session, but he stops before it gets too intense. He's a good kisser. I can probably count on one hand the people I've kissed who've done it in a way I actually really enjoyed. The kind of kiss you don't ever want to stop. The kind of kiss that doesn't have to lead to anything else because it feels so good in and of itself. The kind of kiss that makes your heart beat faster and faster while your lips dance with his so perfectly, and you melt into a little trance together. A shiver runs down my back. This almost feels too good.

Nick's attention wanders back to the TV, to one of the women confessing what happened to them. "This is just crazy. Did anything like that ever happen to you? I hope it didn't, but I know there are a lot of guys out there who take advantage of women."

"Yeah, there are. Luckily, I never had to go through anything *that* crazy. I've had my fair share of problems, but I don't want to get too deep into that. I'll tell you more about it another time."

"Fair enough. But hey, dinner's ready," he says.

"Ooh. OK. I'm excited to see what you cooked up there."

Nick serves me a red plate with tofu and a mélange of quinoa and veggies. He introduces it with, "This is Honey Sesame Tofu, which is why I asked you if you eat honey, obviously, and the quinoa is from Trader Joe's."

"Mmm," I smile at him. I don't really care so much about what exactly he made. It's the effort he put into this that makes me happy right now, and that makes me feel special.

"I first drained the Tofu with some paper towels, and then I marinated it with soy sauce, the honey, vinegar, and oil. Then I put it in the oven, and after that, I marinated it again in a pan and added the sesame seeds. I found the recipe on Pinterest."

"Aah. Well, it looks delicious."

The portion seems a little small for my usual hungry self, but with all these butterflies in my stomach, I already know that there isn't as much space today anyway.

"You did really well. Thank you for cooking for me. That was really nice," I compliment him.

"Of course. I had a lot of fun doing it, and I'm glad you like it." He smiles his great dog smile again, and his eyes are smiling, too.

"Are you allergic to any oils?" Nick asks while he's putting away our plates.

"Uh, I don't think so. Not that I know of. Why?"

"I was thinking I could give you a massage later, if you want."

"Ooh, that kind of oil." He is either the sweetest person I've met in a long time, to spoil me like he is tonight, and he is really into me after a very short time, or... he just knows exactly what women want and is making use of that knowledge.

I did tell Anne that I was going to come home tonight and that I definitely wouldn't want to have sex with him. That it's too early, and I finally want to start taking things slow for once. That this one could actually be something real. I also said, "You never know," but most likely I will be coming home.

He guides me up to his bedroom, where he lights two candles, one on each night stand. He turns on soft R&B music and has me lay face down on his bed. There's no way that this won't go any further now that I'm already laying here half naked, but I will just go with the flow from here.

He is extremely thorough in kneading and touching my skin and does it all in a super gentle way. My body has his full attention, and he added another level to my being pampered tonight.

"Why are you so sweet to me?" I ask while I'm lying face down in his bed.

"I just like being this way. I wanna say that's just how I am, but I also don't want to sound cocky. I enjoy doing this." His big hands are kneading my back thoroughly.

"OK," I smile into the pillow. "Thank you."

Nick massages me for at least twenty minutes and while his hands are pretty rough I love how they feel on my skin, how carefully he uses them.

"All done," he says eventually. I roll over onto my back and reach out my hands, motioning for a hug, knowing good and well that my naked chest is pointing right at him. He leans down, hugs me, and then his lips are on my neck, my ear, my mouth. I hold his head with both of my hands and let the one thing happen that I thought I wasn't going to do today.

Then

My mom has caught wind of what I didn't tell her just yet. To me, the situation with Eddie is still just that. A situation. Which I've been enjoying very much, to be fair. But it wasn't anything I was going to put out into the world any time really soon. My friends from music college did ask me what gave me that glow, and so I told them. And they all seem to think that it's totally OK to be with someone older if it feels right. However, I didn't mention anything to my family, and they aren't here. How could they tell the difference? Well, my mom can. She feels it, and she detects the slightest change in my online presence algorithm.

"Who have you been seeing all this time?" she sneakily asked me just a week ago.

"No one?" I said hesitantly. "Why would you think that?"

"Oh, Kathrin-y, don't you know by now, that I always know? You haven't been on your phone as much lately, and you're always busy. Is there someone?"

So I told her. And now all of my family knows. And then Eddie asked me if he could call me his girlfriend. I voiced one of my main concerns, apart from him being so much older than my almost 26 years. My wish to be with someone who shares my love for veganism and animals. It might not

119

seem like such a big deal to most people. But all I see, instead of just a meal, is what that meal used to be when it was still alive. And it can be a hard cross to bear at times, when the person you love doesn't share that compassion.

Eddie said, "Of course I'm aware that this is something that's really important to you, and I am also aware that eventually one of us would have to change the way they eat to make it work. And I know that someone won't be you. So, I have no problem going vegan if this is something that lasts. If we make it to two years, I will be vegan by then."

I don't want anyone to change their diet for *me*. I want them to do it for the right reasons. Because they believe in the cause and possibly also the health benefits. But the fact that he offered to make such a big change for me, made my heart grow even fonder of him. It was the last little piece I needed to finally commit to being Eddie's girl. So now I have a boyfriend. That sounds so strange. It's been so long. I wanted to be loved for so long, and now there is someone who calls me his, and he is mine. It still feels surreal.

~

On my birthday, he agreed to join the Skype call with my family. It's a Tuesday night, and we're sitting on my bed in my small room, with Baloo constantly asking for our attention. The Skype app on my MacBook starts to ring. As I'm pushing the green answer button, I'm not only excited to have my little online birthday celebration with my family, but also scared and nervous about what they are going to think about my older boyfriend. Eddie is as much of a surprise as he could be in how different he is from all my previous boyfriends.

But immediately after everybody sings me a Happy Birthday, Eddie runs the show and wins them over, just like he did me. He is just being his silly self, and entertains us all, until my Dad randomly, and with his German accent, just says "Approved."

"Approved?" I ask.

"Yes, I like you, Eddie. You're alright. I approve." Eddie looks content and proud, and I'm relieved.

We finish by unpacking presents they sent me, which I waited to open until they could watch me. I miss our birthday traditions at home and wish they could be here and spend it with me.

~

On Friday, I invited all my music college friends to a Local Pub we go to for get-togethers and birthdays, and Eddie agreed to come to this gathering as well. This is the first time any of my friends are going to meet the new boyfriend. Again, I'm wondering how they will react. I'm worried about what they might think, and also curious about how he will be around them, if he will make them all laugh, and if they will take a shine to him just like I have.

Like every pub in America, this one also has several TV screens positioned all over. I never liked this kind of distraction, especially when I come here for the conversations and not whatever sports game might be on. After saying hello to some of my friends who are already sitting at one of the tables, Eddie's head almost immediately tilts up, and his eyes are glued to the screen. I'm convinced this will change. He knows these people are my friends, and they're important to me.

But it doesn't change. The whole evening, he seems to show no real interest in my friends or in the conversation around the table, except for a few short conversations about drums he's having with my friend Lucas. I start to feel the weirdness in the air, the awkward and unspoken truth. The thought that nobody wanted to turn into a spoken phrase. "Why is he being so rude?"

Instead of feeling celebrated and enjoying my birthday, I feel strange, and like I did something wrong by bringing Eddie into a group of people who are all way younger than him, and who he probably can't relate to. Even when we leave, and he seems to be content, the weird feeling inside me lingers.

Now

I'm trying hard to think of what I could be writing for this month's song prompt. The assignment is to write a fun summer anthem because that's what agencies are going to be looking for. I was never the type to write happy-go-lucky, upbeat songs. Whatever I write usually comes more in the form of a ballad or some sort of love song. I can't help myself. Growing into my adult self as a teenager, I used to listen to Dido and Sarah McLachlan on repeat. I just felt like they got me. But this is different. I'm in this course to learn how to write songs for TV shows, movies, or commercials, and it's all about meeting a demand, writing for what's needed, and staying up-to-date with what is currently being licensed. I put about ten songs in a Spotify playlist to inspire me, but simply can't come up with anything *hot, sunny, fun, summer-related*.

My mind is too immersed in lovey-dovey feelings and thoughts about Nick, who will come over to my place today. I'm nervous, but excited to see him again. My living situation isn't perfect and doesn't show that I have it fully together. I'm worried what he will think about me once he's been here, in my small room, and the non-adult living space that's hardly comparable to the house by the ocean he lives in. He does have a roommate too, yes, but I still feel like I'm living a student life when it comes to my housing and financial situation. But hey, this is LA after all, and as a non-immigrant, my options of what or where I can work are limited as well. This just really has been off to a good start and I don't want to jeopardize it by not being good enough for this great, hot man who happens to work for the government.

We had texted back and forth this whole week, deciding when to meet and what to do, with Nick recovering from a slight cold. We decided we were just going to hang out at my place and take things easy.

I had also sent him a recording of me singing a Sara Bareilles song that he mentioned he liked. I'm a good singer, but I'm usually shy to sing in front of people or send things. But I knew he'd like it, and I thought it would be a sweet gesture for a sweet guy. He immediately called after I sent the recording. I couldn't answer because I was in a lesson, but he left a voicemail.

"Kathrin! That is one of the coolest messages I have ever received. Um, I am, ha, uh, I just got out of the office, and I'm heading back home. I'm probably gonna play that the whole way home, um, the whole way through. Hehe. I can't even talk, but that was so cool. But give me a call when you get a chance. That was really cool, and honestly, I want more, like I'm trying to get the whole song. Um, you sound awesome. You sound amazing. Alright. I'll talk to you later. Bye."

I just had to grin when I listened to his message. And so I listened to it a second time, and a third time.

THE ONE I LOVE MOST

Singing hasn't been that much fun for me in a long time. Nobody has reacted like that to my singing in, I don't know how long. Especially here in LA, great singers seem to be on every corner. It's nothing special anymore. I love singing, and I do it well, but I don't think I stick out anymore. The way he got so excited about it brought back my own excitement, and honestly, I want to send him more recordings now.

Then he texts.

Good morning!

I've got a proposition for you.

Let's hear it.

I'm gonna call you in 25-30 minutes.

I wonder what that proposition is about. Is he about to mix up our plan again and change it? I was excited about today.

"So hear me out," he says once we're on the phone. "Since I'm still not feeling back to 100 percent, I was wondering if you could come down here one more time, and I know I already mentioned the MMA fights are on. We can grab pizza and maybe watch that, and then next time I will definitely come up your way."

He did mention those MMA fights before, but he previously said he'd 'survive 'without watching them. Again, I feel somewhat unimportant. Even though he asked me if all of this is OK with me, and he didn't just change the plans without first confirming with me, it still makes me feel like I'm already an option to him and not somebody he's trying to win over anymore. Did we have sex too soon? I should have not given him everything he wanted so soon and been so available right away. Men like a good chase. If it's too easy, it's not interesting anymore. But I want to see him. I already planned on seeing him today. I deep-cleaned my room, making sure it's somewhat presentable, and already shaved almost all of my body hair. What is my option now? Say 'No, I don't want to come down there. See you later?'

"Hmmmm. Fine, OK. But then you do owe me. For me driving down there again, last-minute, and watching sports with you."

"Yes, OK. I owe you."

"When do you want me to be there?"

"Like around 2? That way we have some time to sit outside and talk for a bit. And we can grab the pizza before the main fight, during the break."

Oh, Lord! The main fight? How many fights are we about to watch? How much do I like this man to willingly watch sports and drive all the way down to San Pedro again for a casual 'hanging out at home 'date? A lot, probably. Quite a bit.

"OK, I'll text you when I leave."

~

THE ONE I LOVE MOST

Once more, I roll down my window as I arrive at the little guard house at the entrance of the military housing community. As we both pull up to his house and park our cars, Nick comes out of the garage to take the two bags I brought with me. I already texted him ten minutes ago, saying I urgently needed to use his bathroom, and so he clears the way for me.

I use the downstairs bathroom and decide to remove my panty liner. You never know what is going to happen when. We already made that first step and now things could happen at any moment. He also doesn't seem to be under the weather too much anymore, despite his request for me to come down here, so he can recover a little more. As I open the little trash can to throw my female waste wrapped up in toilet paper, I see something that looks like it couldn't possibly be a man's trash. It looks like some sort of beauty packaging. My chest starts to clench just a bit, but then I tell myself that this could be from before Nick knew me. I haven't even known him for more than two weeks. Also, this is the guest bathroom and who knows how often they actually empty this trash can. Furthermore, he does have a roommate who might have female company once in a while, who throws away beauty product packaging. I take my foot off the lever and let the trash can close, and with that, my wondering and worried mind also comes to a halt.

Nick asks me if I want to sit on the patio for a bit, to talk before the fights start. He opens the sliding door that leads from the living room to the garden and patio area, and the most beautiful view greets me. The ocean is right there in front of us, with Catalina Island clearly visible in the not so distant background.

"I envy you so much for this place. You got really lucky," I sigh.

"I know. I love it here. We did get lucky, thanks to Mark. He used to be in the military and knew someone here. I'm pretty sure this is also cheaper than normal LA housing."

"Not fair." I playfully punch him in the arm. His very firm arm. He unfolds two camping chairs and puts them next to each other, facing the ocean.

"So, is this weird, coming down here to San Pedro? I mean, with your ex and everything?" He inquires.

Last time I was here, I told him just a few things about Eddie and how things went, but I felt like it was too soon to go into too much detail. But he's considerate. I am surprised he brought it up.

"Umm," I say. "I did think about that too, if it would be weird to come down here again, but honestly, this isn't even the same area of San Pedro he used to live in. And it's also been a while, so it's not weird. And I love the area. I'm glad I'm here." I put my hand on his forearm as I say this. He looks at me and smiles. More so with his eyes than with his mouth.

"I'm also glad you're here. Thanks for coming down here again. I don't like to keep tabs on things, but I do want to come up to Pasadena as well. And I will."

"It's all good now."

THE ONE I LOVE MOST

We sit for a while longer and talk about some rather trivial things and some stories I share, but nothing really life revealing is coming from his side. The talk is over much too fast. I'm enjoying him. Time flies. Before I know it, he says, "Let's head in, the first fight is about to start." He picks me up and throws me over his shoulder, carries me into the living room, and then slowly lets me back down and kisses me.

Safely back on the ground, I confess, "You know, this is kind of my weakness."

"What is?"

"I love to be picked up, carried around, and that kind of stuff."

"Oh yeah?" He smiles.

I don't know if there is anything that turns me on more than a strong man who can lift me up without an effort. Maybe kisses on the neck, but that's not relevant right now.

He picks me up again. This time not over his shoulder, but in a way that I can wrap my legs around his body, and then he starts kissing me as he holds me there. He walks into the kitchen with me, his hands supporting my butt and thighs, and then he squats down. We are still kissing while I'm now sitting on his thighs, and I'm equally impressed as I'm turned on. Without trying to sound cliché, I feel like I'm in a dream. Who is this man, and where has he been all my life? In Georgia, I know. That's where he grew up. But I mean: I have no words.

As we settle on the couch, I have no idea what we are watching, but at least Nick doesn't exclude me. He explains exactly how it works, in between his loud exclamations and conversations with the TV. "MMA stands for Mixed Martial Arts." I didn't even know *that* much. He comments, "So, he just called a foul because you're not allowed to hit the other person on the back of the head. These are the lightweight fights right now. The main fight is going to be the last one. We can get our pizzas right before that one."

I'm learning something new again. And while I was afraid that I was just going to sit on the couch while Nick gets sucked up in these fights, this is not the case at all. We are cuddled up under a blanket together, with me sitting between his legs or laying on him for the most part. And the way he reacts to the fighters makes me laugh more than just a few times. I might not be a fan of this sport, but I think I could watch him watch this for quite some time, especially when we're cuddled up like this.

In one of the breaks, he starts giving me small kisses. It's playful at first, but then we can't stop. He puts his hands around my face, and before we know it, we're kissing like we've known each other for a lifetime, but haven't seen each other in forever. My heart is beating fast and all needs for anything else just fly away from me. Eventually, we manage to pull ourselves apart and stop.

Finally, the main fight is on, and we are readily sitting up, with our pizzas on two folding tables in front of us. The two main fighters are introduced. 'Dillashaw vs. Cejudo, ' the TV channel announces. Both fighters jump on the spot before the first round begins. After just about 30 seconds Cejudo beats Dillashaw in a knockout and while his opponent is lying on the floor, cowered up, he jumps up on the railing and beats his chest with his boxing gloves, triumphantly. I look at Nick for an explanation of what just happened, but he stares at the TV, unbelieving.

"What?" He half laughs, half screams.

"So what now?" I prompt.

"Nothing. It's over. He won. That was a knockout."

Wow. So, that was the big moment we waited for today. Even the commentators on TV seem to be surprised about what happened, and are calling it one of the shortest fights in UFC history. Oh, well. Now Nick can focus on me. But as soon as we finish our pizzas, he starts watching the replay of everything we just watched live already.

"Really? You're watching the summary of all the things we just watched?"

"Yeah, I just want to hear what they have to say, see the highlights, you know. And we did miss a fight when we picked up the pizzas." He's serious about this, but not condescending to me.

"Tsss." I don't know how else to respond.

All of a sudden, he gets up and holds out his hand towards me.

"What?" I ask.

"Come here." He pulls me up, and we stand face to face, belly to belly. "Step on my feet," he commands.

"Really?"

"Yes, come on."

I giggle and step my little feet on his size 13 ones. "We used to do this with my dad," I remember.

"Let's do a little slow dance," Nick suggests, and then he starts singing. "When you watched Cinderella, you wished that it was you, and then you asked your Mama: Do fairy tales come true?" As he sings, he's slowly making us step in circles, clumsily dancing. It's been so long since I've done this. I have to giggle. This is so sweet, and yet his uneven pitch and dedication to this impromptu romantic action make me laugh.

He keeps going. "You love romantic stories, and you cry time and again, when Allie and Noah see each other and are kissing in the rain." And then he raises his voice and shout-sings the pre-chorus to this song that I never heard before. "I know it feels like it's hopeless, you've been lonely for so loo--oohohoo-ohooong."

I'm full-on laughing now, leaning my weight into him, not prepared for the big chorus.

"Let me be there for you, I can be your ma-a-an, love you with all that I ha-aa-aave, if you give me your hand. My heart is yours to keep, you're aaallll that I need, and everything to you is what I want to be. Please let me sho-ow yo-oo-ooouuu, that love can be true." I'm not sure if he's just enjoying himself, or if this is a message to me through a song. But more than anything, I'm amused.

"Hey, that was not bad," I say as he stops.

"Oh yeah?" He proudly smiles. "You know, I love my Old School R&B."

"Well, thank you for the dance!" I'm still smiling.

We sit back down, and shortly after he falls asleep on the couch, which is cute, but also disappointing. He must still be a little sick after all. Eventually, I manage to convince him that we should go to bed.

We make love. This time without the candles, and without the sexy rhythm and blues. Then he turns off his lamp next to the bed and immediately falls into his next slumber. As I return from my routine-after-sex bathroom visit, it seems that he is fast asleep.

"Um, Nick? Did you just decide we're gonna sleep now? Without even saying goodnight?"

He doesn't seem to fully react, but says, "Just give me a few minutes. Just five minutes." It doesn't sound like five minutes will bring him back, though. It sounds like the opposite. The day is over.

A few more times I remind him that the five minutes are up, that I'm not ready to go to sleep yet, that it's not even that late yet, but he gives me the same answer every time. "Just two minutes. I'm not sleeping."

Eventually, I give up. I turn over to 'my side 'of his bed towards the window and can't help but feel stupid. How was this time so different from last? Did he get all he wanted, and is the time of him making an effort and pursuing me over now? It all started out so good, and now it's turning into what it was with all the other guys I've dated over the years. Everybody pretending to care, but then treating you like a disposable object.

For a minute, I try to sleep, but the tightness in my chest won't allow that. I've gone through too much to allow myself to stay in this situation. I'm trying to make him realize how I'm feeling with my heavy sighs, shifting around constantly, but he's happily in dreamland. I can't allow a situation like this again. I agreed to drive all the way down here, again, a 45-minute drive. I watched a sport with him all afternoon and evening that I had no interest in whatsoever, and let him substitute that for a real date. I had sex with him, and he didn't insist on satisfying me. And now I'm laying here, used, like the condom he just pulled off. I hate to pop my dream bubble, but I have to leave. He's not what I thought he was.

I start putting my clothes back on and pack my bag. I don't do it super quietly. I want him to hear me, I want him to stop me. When none of that wakes him up, I speak.

"Hey Nick? I'm leaving now."

He finally wakes up. Sleep drunk. "Oh. OK."

That hurt even more. He doesn't seem to care. "Do you want me to leave?" I ask. *I* clearly don't want to leave, or I would long be gone. The good thing is I don't need him to escort me out of his fancy military block. Leaving is allowed.

"Do you *want* to leave?" he asks in return.

"No, I don't want to leave."

"Then why are you leaving?"

"You just decided to go to bed. You didn't even say goodnight. You just turned off the lights, and you were

134

gone. And I've been in too many situations where I was ignored. I came down here for you today, and I was hoping we could talk a bit more, but now I just feel stupid."

And then he does something I didn't expect. He says, "Come here." And for a second, I think he just wants me to shut up, and he'd fall asleep again with me in his arms. But he sits up and hugs me. He doesn't get mad. My anxiety level is pretty high right now. I look into his face and see one of his eyes drooping down. He's having a really hard time keeping it open. The other one is doing alright. He had turned the lights back on.

"It's OK," I say. "You're super tired. Just sleep."

"No no. We are staying up now. And we'll talk."

"Look at you. You can hardly keep your eyes open."

"Don't worry about me. I'm fine. I'm catching a second wind right now," he slurs.

Again his right eyelid falls shut, and I can't help but giggle. "OK then. Tell me something about you," I request.

"So when I was five," he starts, "I was adopted. My mother was an alcoholic, and she died when I was a teenager."

"Oh wow. I'm... so sorry." I really didn't expect this. Not from him. Not at this time of night, not casually told like this.

"Your turn," he says.

"I really don't know what to say now. What do you want to know about me?"

"Anything." And as I begin to tell him about my family, both of his eyelids fall shut again, and this time I let him sleep.

Then

I'm anxiously waiting in the Arrivals Hall of Terminal 2 at the airport in Munich. Everybody else that came with the flight from LAX seems to have come out already. Where is he?

I'm so excited to see Eddie after almost two weeks, and to introduce him to my family. I've spent almost every day with him since we decided we're a thing now, and not having seen him for so long definitely made my heart grow even fonder.

It's New Year's Eve. My parents paid for Eddie's flight when I was booking my flight to come home for Christmas. I was going to leave right after New Year's, but the flights were twice as expensive compared to the ones with the returning flight a week later. So for the same price of one flight we got two and Eddie gets to spend the last week here with me. Eight days to be exact. And my parents are happy because I'll be home longer. It's still quite hard for them with me being so far away and not having the opportunity to spontaneously come home once in a while. I do wish that living my dream wasn't so hard on them.

I've been waiting for a good 40 minutes now, and nobody else seems to be coming out through the automatic glass door. I text Eddie. Another five minutes go by, and I'm starting to get nervous. Where could he be? Maybe they lost his luggage? What if something happened, and he didn't even get on the flight?

But I got him an Uber to the airport last night, and I know he got in it.

Then he finally comes out. "Bunnnyyy!"

"Baby!" I run towards him ready to jump, but he's too tired to catch me, hold me, or carry me. "Where were you this whole time? I started to get worried."

"Ya boy needed to freshen up a bit. I was in the restroom to make myself smell good for you, and I brushed my teeth."

"Aww. But that still took you quite a while."

"Nothing compared to how long that flight was, Bunny. Are we ready to go home?"

"Yes, we are," I exclaim, excited and nervous all at once.

~

Eddie is the same clown with my family as he is with me. He gives my mom the biggest hug when we get home and says, "Hellooo Mamaa." Not one of my other boyfriends has ever called my mom 'Mom, 'or 'Mama 'for that matter. She laughs, but I can see that she doesn't know what to think. He then shakes my dad's hand and greets my sister with "Hi, Bunny Junior." I did pick a special kind of boyfriend. I am aware of that, but I wouldn't want it any other way. Gone are the days when I wished for some dreamy personal fitness trainer, who didn't know what he wanted. According to Eddie, most guys, especially the younger ones my age, don't know how to treat a woman, or how to keep a woman. He says they make the effort to win her over, but then they just let it slide and are surprised when she becomes unhappy. I can definitely agree that that's true. That's kind of how my first three relationships here in Germany went. It was exciting in the beginning. Then it was just cozy, no excitement, and little passion. When I told them what I had been needing for so long and then still didn't get any of those things, I started to resent them. And by the time they finally realized that they were about to lose me if they didn't change anything, it was already too late. Eddie is different. He has made plenty of mistakes in his life. But he's learned from them, and he does know how to treat a woman.

~

During our one-week winter vacation, we go on small trips together. We take pictures, cozy up with my family at home, buy our home team's soccer jerseys, visit my immediate family and even convince my not so open-minded family members to accept and even like my American boyfriend. We have brunch with my girlfriends one morning, where he, once more, makes me horribly uncomfortable by being quiet, almost the whole time we're there. And while I was hoping that my new boyfriend would make a lasting good impression with my closest girlfriends, I feel like the opposite is happening. They're not fluent in English, and obviously, he doesn't speak any German. And even when one of them tries to engage him in some conversation, he gives very short answers and I feel so uncomfortable that I decide to leave early.

After a week, when we get to the airport, my parents tell us goodbye. My dad tells Eddie, "Take good care of her. It was nice to have you here."

Eddie hugs my mom and then my dad, and says, "You've raised an amazing daughter. You did a great job. Thank you for having me." A tear rolls down my dad's cheek, and then both he and my mom hug me tightly before we walk through security. Saying goodbye is still so hard every single time. It's not that I don't want to leave to return to California, but I love them, and I wish that there was a world where Germany and Los Angeles could be right next to each other.

Now

The day has come. Nick is finally coming over to my place tonight, and we will get my favorite vegan street food. And tomorrow morning we will go on a hike. It's all perfect.

I still can't believe that he thought it was 'cute 'when I woke him up in the middle of the night last weekend and demanded attention. Every other guy I met in LA thus far would either have had me drive home or just kept sleeping, or asked me what was wrong with me and why I was so attention hungry and insecure. But Nick texted me the next day after I had left and said that it was 'cute. 'That he liked the fact that I was standing up for myself and communicating what I needed and how I felt. He never told me any more details about the story with his mom.

Work is almost over, and I can't wait to meet him immediately after. We worked it out so that he would meet me at my place when I get home. I already put on extra make-up today and dressed a little nicer than usual when I go to work. The kids don't care so much about how nicely shaped my butt looks in my jeans or how well I did my make-up. Au contraire, my seven-year-old student asked me what those weird lines on my eyes were just a few hours ago. I guess I still need to get better at putting on my eyeliner. I also *really* cleaned my room. This time even better, and I tried to clean some of the common area a bit as well, but I'm hoping to just lead Nick through the dark living area, and straight into my room.

As I'm finally leaving the school and getting into my car, I get a text from him. We've been texting throughout the day about random stuff as usual, but also about tonight's dinner plans.

> *Baby girl... on another note, tho, I've got some not so great news.*

Oh, my. Not again. He's going to cancel on me tonight, for real. He hasn't done it so far, but there's always something, and I'm afraid that's the only thing I can think of that could possibly be *not so great news.* But then I read the text again. He called me *Baby Girl??* I hope that's not just a distraction tactic to make me less mad about what he's about to tell me. Just as I am about to start typing, my phone rings.

"Hellloo?" I answer slowly.

"Hey girl." He sounds run down. "When will you be home?"

"What's the bad news? I'm just leaving now, so I should be home in fifteen minutes. Are you OK?"

"Not really. I just threw up on the side of the street. I guess I still have a little bug. I'm close to your house. Do you have any juice at home, though? I don't think I can eat anything tonight. I'm sorry."

"Oh nooo. Oh, you poor thing. I don't, but I can run to Whole Foods on my way back really quick and buy some.

And I'll also get us some wellness shots with ginger and lemon, OK?"

"OK, how long will that take, though?" He really sounds beat down.

"Not much longer, it's on the way home. I'll hurry."

Despite his weak condition, and even though he just threw up half an hour ago, Nick gives me a kiss and compliments my look. He then lays in my bed and covers himself with all the blankets he can find. I eat the rest of my lunch that I didn't finish at work and by request cut up an apple for him which I bring him together with a big cup of tea. Despite feeling horrible, he is somewhat cheerful and grateful.

"Thank you so much for this. I'm sorry that I ruined our date night. Hopefully, I'll feel better by tomorrow, and we can still go on that hike."

"I'm actually surprised you stuck around and came here after work, feeling the way you feel."

"What would you have thought if I had canceled on you today or not come over? Would you have believed me?"

"I don't know. I guess I would have worried and asked myself if maybe you just don't want to come over, knowing my thought process. And also keeping in mind that you already changed plans on me twice."

"Exactly," he says. "That's why I came over. I didn't want you to think that."

Something in my heart warms. He somehow always manages to say the right thing. As disappointed as I am that I can't show him my amazing food spot, this is kind of sweet, and taking care of him comes naturally. There's still a chance he'll feel better tomorrow.

~

Nick is still in bed by 11am. He asks me to put my hand to his forehead. He thinks he has a fever. I don't have a thermometer. My mom has been telling me to get one. I need to get my life together. It doesn't look like anything will happen today, let alone hiking up a mountain. Nick asks me if he can take a shower, and while my insides cringe at the thought of him having to use our bathroom the way it is, I willingly and understandingly bring him a towel and wash rag. He immediately returns to the bed when he's done and again covers himself with both my duvet cover and an extra blanket. I make him more tea and bring orange juice and decide to hop in the shower myself.

When I come back in the room with just underwear and a towel on me, I slowly drop the towel to put clothes on. I am starting to like my body more and am not as shy as I used to be, but I'm still not someone who likes to rub it in someone else's face. But just at that moment, Nick looks at me and his jaw falls open. I always think that the 'open jaw' analogy is an exaggeration, but that's really what describes best what I'm seeing right now.

His eyes open wide, and he says, "Kathrin!"

THE ONE I LOVE MOST

I feel myself turning red. "What?" I hastily try to cover myself again with the towel.

"Those undies. Kathrin," he repeats. "Stop, stop. Let me see it."

I reveal just a little more again, for him to see my underwear, feeling like a deer caught in the headlights. I'm wearing my black Calvin Klein thong that I bought when I was trying to impress the vegan prince, Derrick, last year. Strangely enough, it never worked on him. He didn't really care about my underwear. But Nick is eating me with his eyes right now.

Not long after I dressed, we lay cuddled up, his arm around me, my head resting on his shoulder. I prop myself up and find him looking at me. He looks me straight in the eyes and smiles a brighter smile than all the cute dog smiles he's given me so far. And it's not awkward. I'm not turning red. Ronan Keating's song "When You Yay Nothing at All" would describe this situation best. We don't have to say anything. It's all being said just like this. We kiss. Despite him being sick and feeble. And all the clothes I just put on come off again. He is alive again, and so am I.

~

Despite us having spent all day in bed, it wasn't a bad day. Nick thanks me for taking care of him the whole day, but announces he wants to leave. I'm not ready for this day to end. "Don't leave. You don't have to go yet. Just spend one more night here. I'll make us some food."

"It's OK. I don't want to overstay my welcome."

"You're silly, you're welcome here as long as you want," I say. "I want you to stay. Really. Don't go. I'm enjoying this too much."

"I do have to go, Kathrin," he insists.

We bounce back and forth like this for a while until I finally understand that he won't stay, and I won't be able to convince him to. Anxiety gets a hold of me again, and all of a sudden, I can't take the thought of him leaving. It feels wrong. And there's something that's been pressing on my mind, and I need to tell him before I fall for him even more. This might very well be a dealbreaker and if it takes another week to see him, I need to get it out now. I tightly hold on to him. "There's something I want to tell you about what happened with my ex, and I'm afraid you won't look at me the same way anymore. I'd understand if this changes how you think about me." And then I let it all spill out. And to my horror the tears come out with this truth which might be a bit early to tell, but I just needed to know that he can love all of me, and my past.

When I'm finished, he still hasn't let go of me and I carefully say "Do you think differently about me now?"

"No. Bad things happen and we learn from them. You're fine."

"Ah, I'm sorry, I'm crying. You wanted to leave, and now I'm being super clingy and this is all a bit much. I'm so sorry."

"You know what Shrek says, right?"

"No," I sob.

"Something like 'Better to get it out than holding it in.'"

I laugh. And then I hold on to him as more tears come out.

"And for the record. I like it when you're clingy."

"Really?"

"Yes. It's cute."

How is suddenly everything I do cute? But I'll take it. Finally, I collect myself and Nick feels comfortable leaving. The bed still smells like him, and I miss him already.

Then

"I can pull over the car right here, and you can get out and see how you get home."

"No, please! Stop it!" I'm screaming. Tears are rolling down my face. My chest is tight, and I still don't understand what's happening. How did all of this escalate so fast?

"But I think that's what I'm gonna do right now. I can't have you in this car anymore, and you're annoying the living hell out of me."

"No, I'll behave. I'm sorry. Please don't do that."

Eddie is beyond angry. We got into an argument about something really stupid. It all started with him saying I need to stop living my life like I'm on vacation here. That I'm living like a little girl who gets things from her parents. Yes, maybe that might be true, that I don't fully have my shit together with my 25 years, that my mom and dad are still helping me out. But I'm just getting started in this country. I'm an immigrant. Not even that. I am a "non immigrant," an "alien."

I don't even have a visa yet, and that alone scares me so much. I'm on a work permit right now, that's basically an extended student visa, and soon the year they gave me will be up, and I'll have to apply for an artist visa. Those visas aren't easy to get, and I haven't even been putting myself out there. I studied and partied, and now I'm teaching. What do I have to show? How am I going to prove that I am an artist of 'extraordinary abilities? 'And why does Eddie judge me so much all of a sudden? Didn't he know what he was getting into? What was he expecting from a 25-year-old girlfriend who isn't even from here?

I ended up being just a bit pouty after that snarky remark of his. And on the way to his health Guru—who sells plant medicine for people who want to eat crap, but be healthy nonetheless—I might have made a remark that the man on the cover of the catalog he showed me doesn't even look so healthy. He had what looked like a beer belly. Granted, the man isn't the youngest, but he doesn't look that much healthier than my dad, and they must be about the same age. That's what made Eddie furious. "Oh yeah?" he said. "And you think you know it all, huh? You have no idea about what this guy does, and you're just making smart remarks now?" I opened my mouth to strike back, but I didn't get to it because he was on a roll.

"You don't know anything. You're young. And none of your friends know anything either. You all think you know it all and are so smart, but you don't know anything." He snorts. "And now you're trying to tell me about something you don't know anything about. It would have been smarter to just be quiet. I know what I'm talking about. I'm 40 years old, and my life has come full circle."

We yell at each other until Eddie says he wants to have me out of the car and I can find my way home. We're on the 405, on our way to Marina del Rey. I'm sure I could get an Uber somehow, but I can't let him treat me that way. So I apologize, for everything I didn't know I did wrong, and somehow the beast retorts to his cage. I say that because Eddie calls himself a Lion, because he's a Leo, and he identifies with his sign very much, even though he doesn't believe in astrology.

We buy Echinacea tincture and a bowel cleanse, vitamin C and a big jar of superfoods, all the highest quality possible. Then I agree to the fact that I was wrong and that this is indeed a good natural pharmacy.

~

We're back at his apartment, but I'm still exhausted from the day and our fight earlier. He is on his phone, texting. "Who is it?" I pry.

"It's Ines."

"What does *she* want?" I ask, a little too snappily.

He has been telling me some things about Ines, but in his earlier stories she was always the girl he worked with at Silvio's studio, the guy who let him live on his boat and in his Hollywood Hills house. But right before our plane landed at LAX just two weeks ago, he casually mentioned that Ines used to be his girlfriend. That they were together for years, that she knows his kids and his ex-wife, and met his mother, and that she's been trying to get back with him. So naturally, I'm having a hard time being happy about the fact that they're texting now.

"She dropped her phone and her screen cracked. So stupid. I've been telling her to get one of those screen protectors made from glass. It would have saved it."

"But why is she telling *you* that she dropped her phone? What are *you* going to do about it?"

"Relax, Bunny, she just asked me for advice."

"Fine."

"I used to be responsible for her, and we are still friends. Do you have a problem with that?"

"I guess not. I just don't understand it, but that's OK."

It's clearly not OK. And Eddie catches my tone. He now not only screams at me but does a full-on angry dance in his kitchen telling me how insecure and how young I am, and how much I don't know 'shit about anything. 'And again I cry and ball myself up on his stupid air mattress.

Now

Baloo meows as I grab my bag with my laptop and put my shoes on. "I won't be gone too long, Boosi. But Mama needs to work. Go play with Ziggy, and I'll be back soon."

My nicknames for Baloo range from Baloosi, Booboo, Boobsi, Boosi, Mausi to Mow-Mow. How is it always our pets who end up with the most names? Probably because they're the ones who are always around. They're loyal, they deserve a variety of names.

"Meooooow."

I kiss him goodbye and head to Highland Park for my co-writing session for this month's song prompt. I'm looking at it as a valuable experience. Maybe I'll finally get better at collaborating and co-writing, if it just wasn't so awkward.

Once there, Eian and I come up with several lyric ideas in his studio. We brainstorm "wind in your hair, feeling free, living in the now, rooftops, brand-new day" and similar ideas that are supposed to convey a carefree feeling. Somehow, it just all still seems forced. At the end of our two-hour session, I'm happy we came up with a full idea called "Live Out Loud." I'm not in love with the song, but it's a song. And I did it, and survived a co-writing session. It can only get better from here. But still, I feel like a big fat failure in the world of sync licensing, of creating unique hits that have the potential to make a lot of money or even get my name out there.

It's 6pm when I get back home. I unlock the backdoor to our kitchen and two hungry cats greet me there, ready to eat.

"Meow. Meow. Meoow."

"OK, OK." I take one of the already open cans out of the fridge and give each Ziggy and Baloo a scoop full into their bowls. They're happy. Time for me to relax. But then my phone rings. It's Nick, and I'm positively surprised. He's called me a few times during the weeks so far, and there hasn't been a day when he hasn't texted me. He's consistent and that is so refreshing in a world full of serial casual daters.

"Heyy," I answer.

"Hey Kathrin. What's up?"

After our nurse and patient date in my room, he thanked me for taking care of him several times. Even though he was sick and really not feeling his best, we both enjoyed our time together.

"Not much. I just got home from a songwriting session."

"Ooooh. That's so cool. What did you guys write?"

"Uh, we had to write a summer song. I'm not loving it. I'm still growing into the whole co-writing thing. It's different from writing just by yourself."

"I see."

"How about you? How was your day?"

"It's been good. Work has been busier again, now that the shutdown is finally over. And I might be going on a trip this coming weekend."

"A trip?"

"Yeah, a work trip. A protection assignment."

"Aah. I guess I still don't really fully understand what exactly you do and where and when," I admit.

"So, basically the way it works is that every other month we are on what's called ROTA. That's our travel month, and they can send us on trips at any point during those months, usually with a few days' notice in advance," he explains.

"And so the other months you're off!?" I ask, trying to make sure I'm getting it right.

"Well, no. We're still in the office, working on investigations and stuff, but you're correct, in that we won't be sent on any trips out of town."

"Ah OK."

My answers are short because I'm still processing this information. Until a few weeks ago, I didn't even know what the *Secret Service* was. And I feel like I'm still in the dark quite a bit.

"I'll tell you a bit more next time I see you."

He wants to explain it to me. He wants me to understand, and he wants to *see* me again! I'm swooning in my head. But then I remember there's something I never asked him, that actually maybe I should have asked a while ago already. I'm always assuming people live here and stay here because why wouldn't someone want to stay here? But knowing he's not from here, I decide to ask.

"By the way, are you planning to stay in LA long-term or what's your plan?"

There's a brief silence on the other end.

"So, the way this job works is that we had our training in Maryland for close to a year, and then we got to choose a field office anywhere we wanted to go. I'm going to be here for about three years in total, and then I'm transferring to Washington, D.C. for what we call Phase Two, which is usually six or seven years long."

"And then after that?" I carefully ask.

"After that, I can go anywhere I want."

Why have I not asked this question sooner? This should have been a first date question. Actually, *he* should have mentioned this.

"Oh. And since when have you been here?" I'm trying to calculate how much time he has left here, while I'm trying not to sound too disappointed and let down.

"I've been here since summer 2017, so I'll have another one and a half years or so here."

"OK." I'm a bit at a loss for words. This is pretty clear now. I have to let him go. Or at least the idea of this finally being 'the one, 'that will stick around, the one I'll want to stick around. But I think it's already too late to make those butterflies fly in reverse. I don't know how to feel and what to do, but I know no part of me wants this to end.

Then

I can't believe I'm being filmed for TV. I used to watch this show years ago, when I still lived in Germany, and when moving to another country for any reason seemed like the most idiotic idea anybody could ever have. Maybe not idiotic, but I just couldn't understand why anybody would want to leave their family, their friends, their whole life basically, for the Unknown. Germany is great. We're safe there and for the longest time I never questioned my original intent to stay in my little village, get married, build a house, have children and live the same life everybody else does there. Until one day, when the idea to study abroad in America crept into my head. And then that idea became a reality, and from merely studying I went to never wanting to leave again. How can a person change so quickly?

The show airs every Sunday on a major German TV channel, and follows German expats who want to realize their dream in foreign countries. And while I was trying to collect evidence for my upcoming visa application, which by the way scares the crap out of me, I applied online to be a part of this docuseries. So now I'm showcasing my life in LA and the process of applying for a visa. Any media exposure should be helpful for me, in getting one of the

156

highly sought-after visas for 'the greatest country in the world.'

But it seems like the producers want to make this a love story. Eddie's type is so popular with the producer, Annika, and the camera guy, Sven, that they keep engaging him. They are staying for six days, all of which are tightly packed and planned with different shooting locations. There's a script. They scripted my life. This is supposed to be reality TV. However, there's only one week to get everything filmed. So, my story changed from merely having to apply for an artist visa as a singer, so I can stay here. Now it's more like 'Girl from Germany who's pushing her visa deadline, tries to gather all the documents at the last minute and can't get it together. She's also in love with her boyfriend, who's her mentor, and her biggest fear is losing him.'

Eddie is enjoying all this attention. He told me how proud he is of me for making it into a German TV show. We've been going solid the past few months. We're having our arguments here and there, but I know that's part of any real relationship. And he *is* quite a bit older than me, he *does* see things differently many times, and I decided that I will trust his guidance. I've been spending almost all my free time with him at his apartment and only really go home to switch out the clothes I bring to his place, say 'Hi ' to Baloo occasionally, and go to work. Sometimes Eddie works for his uncle and asks me to go to my place on those days. But overall, we are getting closer and closer, and we're starting to really know each other. He mentioned how he has his way of determining how he knows if he wants to stay with someone. He says, 'after two years, that's when you'll know. 'So if we make it to the two-year mark we'll start thinking about marriage, and obviously, he'll also go vegan then. I can't wait to be someone's wife. I can't wait for the day he proposes to me. While I was so unsure about all of this in the beginning, I couldn't be more certain now. He might not have been what I was looking for, but he *is* what I need.

"Ok, we'll have you arrive again, just like you did, but this time we'll film it from inside Eddie's apartment. And then we'll do it one more time filming you from the outside," says Annika, the producer of the show, who they sent all the way from Germany.

I have the little mic attached to my clothes again, the receiver attached to the back of my pants and the cable wrapping around me beneath my clothes to the mic on the neckline of my shirt. Seeing how this all works makes me wonder how I never questioned any of these reality TV shows. How could it not be staged when they are filming everything from two different angles, but you can't ever see a camera in the background?

I climb back out over the balcony railing to the alley. This is how I enter Eddie's place. I stopped using the front door since he told me it's best to park in the alley and then just climb up the balcony to his first floor apartment. Way easier. Sven, the camera guy, is filming as I call Eddie's name and then climb into his apartment over the balcony, through the patio doors and into his arms. He grabs me, then puts me on his back, and they film us running back out together, piggyback style. 'How silly, 'I think, but it *is* fun. And I always wanted to seem fun to other people, instead of just showing my usual shy and introverted side.

They also film me while I'm filming my music video to a silly yodeling cover I did. They document one of my teaching days, they fake a visit to my lawyer's office, where we pretend I haven't prepared anything, and that I'll need to submit everything in a week. Additionally, they have me fake-call someone on the phone and pretend that I get rejected asking them for help with my visa. They tape it when I get my recommendation letters signed, and they do tons of interviews with me, mostly about my visa, my fears around that, and Eddie. They even film him at his weekly rehearsal with Silvio, the weird Hollywood guy. And in the end they film us going to the beach together, sitting arm in arm watching the sunset. Eddie doesn't even like the beach. We've never done anything like this, but it looks good on TV.

I really like Annika and Sven, but I'm starting to feel like my life is just becoming a cheap story to entertain some bored couch potatoes, which essentially is exactly what is happening here.

The one thing I still can't get out of my mind though, in the middle of all of this, is the email I should have never read. I've never gone through anyone's phone or emails before. It was so out of character. But a few weeks ago, when I was at Eddie's place alone, and he left his iPad, I couldn't help it. The constant texts with Ines started bugging me more and more, and I wanted to make sure there was nothing I'm missing, or even worse, something he could be hiding on purpose.

I went into his mail app and used the search bar to look for 'Ines. 'Only one email came up. A good sign, I thought. But when I opened that email, my heart started beating faster and faster and brought back that tight feeling in my chest. Nothing about this felt good, but I had to know. There was a picture of a pretty, but not 'cute 'pretty, brunette girl with green eyes by a Christmas tree and the text read something like 'Remembering all the good times we had, like this one under the tree. Don't you wish we could have that again? I'm sorry I wasn't ready to try again when you were, but I am now. Please take me back.'

I was shaking. Even though he had told me before that she tried to get back with him, seeing it with my own eyes made it so much more real, and in a way it made me feel helpless. I reminded myself that I am the woman in his life and that he is with *me* and not with her. I kept reading.

'... I know you are seeing other women, too, but the biggest trigger to me is still Carina.'

Who is Carina???

Now

> Just made it home. I appreciate you taking the time to hear me and hold me and let me cry. I hope you won't be in too much of a rush now.

Of course, Kathrin!

I'm terrible at packing (I always over pack) so that got a little interesting. Hope the drive wasn't too bad. 😂

> Haha, uh-oh. I'm the same. I always pack too much or too little. Drive was ok. 🐠🐚 was much worse.

Lmao!!!!! You ain't lying! That smell was horrid! Glad you got that smell off your hands last night. *Crying laughing emoji*

> I guess I won't be touching any more shells soon. I can't wait for bed tonight...

Was someone up late last night? :P

> *Haha, no, but somebody else snored pretty loudly. And I think I've exhausted myself today.*

Judging by our text conversation, you wouldn't think last night or this morning was anything worth mentioning. But that's probably because I am a master of concealing when I feel like I need to be. And since I let too many of my thoughts and emotions spill out last night *and* this morning, I decided it's time to dial it back a bit and act 'normal. 'Like I'm not a crazy girl who can't live without somebody she just met a month ago.

Yesterday started out normal. Nick and I decided—pretty last minute—that we should see each other last night, since he's leaving on a work trip to Northern California today and will be gone for the weekend. Everything started as usual. I drove down to San Pedro, and showed my driver's license to the police guard. Nick picked me up, we parked our cars, we went inside, and put my stuff down. Then he picked me up into a big, long hug during which we kissed and confessed that we've missed each other. Then he said he wanted to take me to Palos Verdes, to his favorite spot. I was curious because I have a few favorite spots there myself, since I've elected it to be my favorite part of town. He wanted it to be a surprise, but as we pulled up to *Abalone Cove Shoreline Park,* I knew where we were, and was happy that he likes this spot as much as I do. He called it *his spot*.

We parked his car and walked down the narrow path, to the rocky beach part and into the cove. It was close to sunset. California doesn't have real winters, but the days are much shorter during this time of year. I will never get enough of this view. The ocean stretched out before us and around the peninsula we're on. A beautiful scene with cacti, trees, plants. Even the rocks that make the cliff are of the most beautiful orange and tan colors. We sat on some of the bigger rocks that were half out of the water, and just watched the sunset finish its wonderful show of colors for the night.

Before it got really dark, we slowly started making our way back up to the car. Ever since the phone call about Nick's non-permanent living status, I've carried around this confusion with me. Was I, once more, running into a maze of feelings, that it would take me forever to get out of? A maze that I was hoping to find some valuable treasure in, but that even if I found it, I wouldn't be able to take it with me? I had to know. I already have feelings, but I couldn't keep running around like a chicken with its head cut off, just pretending everything is fine when there are facts I might be ignoring, or purposely trying not to find out.

"So, I have a question for you, Nick," I said on our way back to the car, halfway through the rocky beach.

I never felt so comfortable calling someone by their name all the time. Not somebody I was dating. They were always *babe* to me, or the German *Schatz* or some other pet name. It has always felt awkward to me calling someone by their actual first name. I don't know why that is and where that came from, and if I'm the only one who's developed such an awkwardness around that. But Nick has been using my name so much. In texts, when he calls me, and in

163

person. He doesn't just say "Good night," he says "Have a good night, Kathrin." He says, "Good morning, Kathrin." And when we shared our middle names, he said my full name out loud several times. "Kathrin Simone Jakob. (He pronounces it as close to the German way as he can, but with a clear accent. 'Kuddrin Simoné Yuhkobb.' He said, "I really like it. Kathrin Simone." So, I started using his name too, Nick. And it started feeling natural and normal and good.

"Ask away," he said.

"I was just wondering... What was your intention when you signed up on the dating app, knowing you won't be staying here long term? Like, what are you looking for exactly?"

It was out, but saying it made me only more nervous. It was hard to even enjoy the magnificent scenery and the beautiful atmosphere, having the answer I might not want to hear hanging in the air.

He paused. He clearly needed to think about that one. Eventually, he answered.

"I guess I just wanted to meet good people while I'm here."

"Oh."

"And you know, even if I can just show someone that there are still good guys out there. That would make it worth it."

I didn't get it. What did that mean? I was too afraid to ask what I really wanted to know and swallowed my need for clarity on where this is going. And then I picked up something that further ruined the night. A beautiful snail-like shell. And as I held it in my hand, I noticed something dripped out from its top. And then I noticed the smell. I tried to wash it off, but the smell was still there. Nick advised me to 'wash 'my hands with dirt, and for a second, it seemed to work. But once we were back in the car, we noticed that I had become a nasty sea monster with that smell on me, and there was no escaping it until I could finally strip myself of everything and shower. I brought the smell to Veggie Grill with me, where we ate, and then back into the car. Finally, I showered at his place, finding that I was able to rid myself of this embarrassing accident. I should have known.

And then my self protecting mechanism came back in, and I asked Nick if I was setting myself up for a heart break with him. We talked for about half an hour about how he thinks he wouldn't want me to move away from here, since I love California so much. How I ultimately want a relationship, and how he ultimately wants the same. How I am so scared of getting hurt, and how he doesn't know what he wants right now. And I let that be OK. It had only been a month.

Then, when he asked me, "What would you have said if I said I didn't want a relationship?" my answer was clear.

"As hard as that would be, I think I'd have to distance myself and protect myself. I've been hurt too many times, and knowingly going into a situation like that would be plainly stupid." He nodded.

He did snore, but that wasn't the only reason I barely slept. I didn't get the answer I was hoping for, not even close. All I got was more mysteries and more questions.

I was already in my car and driving away from his house the next morning, when I decided that his vague answer wasn't enough for me. I turned around before it was too late, i.e., before I was outside the gate, and called his number.

"Can you please come out again?"

Without a question, he just said "Yes."

I parked and got out of the car, and we stood on the sidewalk in front of his house, facing each other. His neighbors were getting ready for work and the kids were on their bikes and scooters. "I just can't leave without getting a clear answer. I didn't really get one last night, and I know that thinking about this will eat me up. We don't need to be in a relationship right *now*, but I need to know if this is going anywhere."

He looked at me with a sad and sorry face. "I don't know, Kathrin. I just don't know."

"How can you not know what you want?"

"I don't know."

"Are you seeing somebody else?"

"No, Kathrin, I wouldn't do that." He looked me straight in the eyes. "We might not be in a relationship, but I know we respect each other enough to not do that to each other. That wouldn't be fair."

Well, that was new to me. A man assuming that being exclusive *outside* of a relationship is what's natural and fair.

"OK, but then what is it? I'm starting to really fall for you, and I can't go through another big heartbreak right now. Just tell me. I can take it."

"I don't know what to tell you, Kathrin. I'm sorry."

Once the question had finally left my lips, I couldn't stop anymore. I kept asking one question after another. When I still didn't have anything close to a clear answer after ten minutes of hugging, asking and crying, Nick asked me to come into the house again. We sat down on the couch and I kept doing the same thing for at least half an hour. I felt embarrassed for how I was acting, but I couldn't seem to help it. He assured me that it was OK, that we both developed feelings for each other fairly quickly, that sometimes connection *can* really happen that fast.

"So what is the problem then?" I asked again.

And again Nick just looked at me with sad puppy eyes and couldn't seem to say much. The only thing he told me was that his relationships with women are tricky due to what happened with his mom, and that while he knows he probably should seek a therapist, his pride won't allow him to. I want to fix him. There's nothing more I want to do than fix him, show him the love he needs, heal him. But my rational side knows that it is an illusion so many of us girls have, from watching all those romantic fairy tale movies. Talk about "Cinderella" and "Let me show you that love can be true..."

"If I had to give you an answer right now, and if I really thought about it, I would say I'm not ready for a relationship."

There it was. He said it. But he said it in a way where there is still hope. *Not ready* just means he's not ready *yet*. At some point, he has to be.

"I don't know what to do now," I said, half to Nick, half to myself.

"I think you have to go. You said it yourself last night. You have to protect yourself."

"I know. But I can't. I can't leave. I can't do it. Why do I like you so much?"

Tears kept rolling down my cheeks. He started to get in a hurry to pack for his trip, and consequently, I had to leave. But I made him promise that we would see each other again, and therefore broke my promise to myself, that this time I would protect my heart.

~

And now here I am, happily texting with him, almost as if nothing had happened, as if everything was fine, collecting dopamine from one text message after another. I will see him again soon, and I will show him what true love is. And with just a bit of time, maybe he will change his mind.

Then

"You thought what?" I scream, laughing.

"Yeah, I really thought that adult women would constantly give milk, all the way until I was thirteen," Isabella responds.

"But... what about your mom? You must've known she wasn't constantly giving milk," I protest, then cackle again.

"I thought she was hiding it."

"Oh my god. I can't with you."

We proceed to shout-sing the whole 4:52 minutes of *Fergalicious* with the windows down. I sing, while Bella still doesn't know how to break down the words into single letters like Fergie does, even after all these years. Even though she is a teacher. In Germany, I should add. In elementary school. So, I guess I can forgive her for her choppy English skills.

"It's the word *delicious* spelled out," I yell over the loud music in my small Toyota Scion. She just laughs through the rest of the song, and *Rise* by Gabrielle comes on. It's her turn to start singing. This was always one of her songs, ever since our school band days.

'Why did we even put sad songs on this road trip CD mix, 'I silently ask myself? My good mood from just moments ago is replaced with immediate sadness again. It never takes too long these days. She notices.

"Aw, babe. It will be OK. Let's just try to have fun. Don't worry."

Bella's visit might be distracting me, but it can't make me forget what happened. When she landed at the airport just a few days ago, everything was still perfectly fine. We planned this whole fun road trip along the coast and I couldn't have been more excited that one of my high school besties came to visit me. The crazy one of the bunch, the loudest and funniest one, and the one I could count on to get the most laughs out of me. So much so, that I'd A) actually feel like I did a belly workout or B) peed my pants. I always preferred the former one, but I can't say the latter hasn't happened.

The night before we left town to head up to San Francisco, I told her that I read Eddie's emails. I told her how confused I was by what I've read. That Carina actually called his phone one time when we were in the car together, and as I asked who she was, he simply replied with "Just work." And while I have been pretty good with suppressing all these thoughts and telling myself that I should have never read his emails in the first place—that he can never find out—I brought all the doubt back into my head by talking about it to her.

I just couldn't shake the feeling that there was a puzzle piece missing, that something wasn't adding up, and that Carina wasn't 'just work. '

"Well, maybe you should just ask him then, if you can't let it go. It's not good if this is eating you up so much," she said.

And so, on a whim, I drove down to San Pedro to see Eddie and tell him what I did. He first listened calmly and didn't really say a word. He just looked at me as I confessed that I read his emails and apologized and felt stupid. Then he started pacing back and forth, from his window where the living room should be, to his kitchen island, and back, still not saying anything. Eventually, he just said, "Let's take a walk."

We walked, and he told me that he's feeling a very heavy feeling in his chest, and he doesn't know what to do. 'I know that feeling, 'I thought. Then he told me that I had really hurt him by breaking his trust, that it was not my place to go through his emails, even though he gave me the password to his iPad. And then, as we were back at his place, he told me that he needed to think about how we should keep going. That our differences were something to consider anyway. That I shouldn't expect to hear from him much, that I should be focusing on my visa anyway, and that I should enjoy my time with Isabella while she's here. And that we'd talk, but that he needed to process what I did. His look was stern and so different from the one I get when he loves me, when I'm 'the love of his life, 'that 'he wished he met sooner. '

Also, I didn't really get an answer to my question. Carina was still 'just a work acquaintance. 'But he did add that they know and like each other, but that it was silly of me to worry. I can't believe what I did. Even Eddie said, "Why were you stupid enough to even tell me? You could have saved both of us a lot of hurt by just keeping quiet." And I asked myself that same question that night as I drove home.

In San Francisco, I lose a few more tears as we come by all the hearts at Union Square. Everybody seems to be coupled up here, and I'm about to lose my boyfriend, who I, quite honestly, really don't think I can live without anymore. I need him. But right now, for Bella's sake, I pull myself together and tell myself to enjoy this vacation which we've been planning and have been excited about for months. We take the trolley car, walk what feels like 20 miles, and go to Pier 39. We also find Janis Joplin's old house in Haight-Ashbury, drive over the infamous Golden Gate Bridge, and then decide to drive back to LA that same night, so we don't have to spend money for a place to stay. We already stayed in a small hotel in Santa Cruz last night on our way up the Pacific Coast Highway, and we were both trying to be as good with our pocket change as we possibly could.

On our way home, in the middle of the night, I'm having a hard time keeping my eyes open. But when "The Story" by Brandi Carlile comes on, my vision isn't obstructed by my falling eyelids anymore, but by rivers running down my cheeks. I manage not to sob loudly as all of my emotions come spilling out of me. I've been waiting for Eddie's texts for too long now. He's still giving me the cold shoulder, and it's my own damn fault. I hate myself. I hurt him.

Now

> Daddy is on his way.

I don't know how this whole 'Daddy 'thing started, but it did, and at this point it's an inside joke. I would never seriously call anyone 'Daddy, 'especially not in intimate moments, but now I think it's funny. Nick is picking me up from LAX. I went home for the weekend for my sister's wedding. An awfully short time to go all the way to Germany. But I was there, and that's what matters. It was a small and intimate wedding, with Natalie being at the peak of her pregnancy and nobody caring about a huge party with a hundred drunk people.

Nick voluntarily offered to pick me up. Who does that? Nobody in LA voluntarily drives to the airport, not even on a Sunday. Things have been going pretty good between us after our *almost goodbye* two months ago. We've seen each other almost every week, except for March, when he went on a two-week work trip to Mar-a-Lago in Florida. I didn't think I could dislike the president even more than I already did, but his leisure golf trips, which are the reason for Nick's absence, definitely made me despise him even more. We're still texting every day, we FaceTime when he's on a work trip or when I was in Germany, and I just wish I could be showing him off to the world as *my* man.

Ten minutes later, he pulls up in his blue Honda, hops out the car, pulls me up into a hug and then grabs my luggage for me. He opens the passenger door, so I can climb in while he stows everything in the back. "I'm loving these pants. How come I've never seen them?" he asks.

I'm wearing my flared pants from Forever 21 with a red and white hippie pattern that my mom had to shorten for me, but still make a long leg and accentuate my round booty quite nicely. On top of that, they're super comfortable. "Thank you. They're just more of a summer item. So I haven't really worn them lately."

We turn right on Sepulveda Blvd and Nick puts his right hand on my thigh. I love it when he does this. I grab his hand and start to relax. Just a few weeks ago, it was me who picked him up from the airport, but I still feel special that he's picking me up today and driving me all the way to Pasadena. Not everybody would do that, and he really doesn't owe me anything.

"Smiiile." I decide to take the first selfie of us ever. There are no pictures of us together. It's kind of sad. We're just always too lost in the moment when we're together. He grins and looks way cuter than me and my tired double chinned selfie-self.

"You must be hungry!" He inquires.

"Uh, I'm not sure, actually. I'm more tired than hungry right now."

"OK, just let me know. We can grab food. We could go to Veggie Grill. But you don't have to know just yet. We have a little way to go." Nick has developed somewhat of an obsession with the bowls at Veggie Grill, and I'm equally amused and attracted to his new love for vegan food.

"Are you going to stay the night?"

"No, unfortunately, I can't."

Immediately I feel sad. I know I'm going to want him to stay. I'm even clingier when I'm tired, and I haven't seen him in almost two weeks. Thank God there's some traffic, which usually isn't something I'm particularly fond of, but if it means I get to spend more time with Nick chauffeuring me around, I hope that the whole 110 freeway is backed up. But traffic is not on my side today, and so I decide I want to go to Veggie Grill to buy some more time with him. I grab his arm with both my hands and lean over to him far enough so that I can lean on him. I love these arms so much. I don't even know what I would do if it doesn't work out between us. Spend my whole life searching for perfect arms like these, that come with a cute dog smile and a great personality?

"Baby girl is tired." This is the only nickname he ever gave me, and my heart immediately jumps and does backflips at the mention of it. He's been using it quite a bit lately, too.

"I love it when you call me that."

"Oh yeah, baby girl?"

"Yeeess. I wish you could stay over tonight."

"I know. But I have to prepare for that training we have this week, and I need all these guns in the morning. I couldn't have brought all of those to your house."

I'm not a fan of guns, or even the police or military or any institution that has to do with guns or war, but for some reason Nick's job makes him even hotter than he already is. The first morning I woke up at his place, he told me I could stay in the bed and leave when I wanted. Since my workday didn't start until the afternoon, I took advantage of that offer, and while I rolled around in his bed he was getting ready for work. He pulled out his handgun from the nightstand to put it in his holster and said, "Are you comfortable around guns?" He was so sexy to me at that moment. Not because I love guns, but his attire, the fact that he so casually puts a gun on his belt and isn't the least bit cocky about his profession. He had me then. And he has me now.

Once we're at Veggie Grill, we order at the counter and Nick pays for both of our meals. We talk more about the wedding, his upcoming training and his birthday in a week, and then he drives me home, where I fall asleep as soon as I lie down in my bed and grab Baloo.

Then

I hysterically cry to *Iris* by The Goo Goo Dolls. My mom just told me to get off the phone because she doesn't like it when I'm on the phone in any way while I'm driving, especially not when I'm crying. I assured her I'm fine, but decide that a good cry to my *Sad Songs* playlist will also be good right now. Tears roll down my face and cloud my vision, while I scream the lyrics, sobbing.

I'm on the 110 freeway right around Downtown. This all seems like a bad dream. Things with Eddie seemed to be almost back to normal. He was mad at me, but he let me come over again. We hung out, we made love. And then today, out of nowhere, he told me we should take a break. That he is still hurt over what I did and that I should focus on getting the papers for my visa together first, and that we can reevaluate our relationship then.

I panicked. "Does this mean you're going to see other people?"

Without really answering my question, he said, "It just means we're not boyfriend and girlfriend right now."

I tried to make him change his mind. This hurt too much. It was too painful. What happened? He was the one who wanted to win me over at all costs. The one who constantly said he had to have me, even though he might have not admitted that in the beginning. And now he is taking all my girlfriend privileges from me, including the key to his apartment.

"You can have that back later, maybe, when you've earned it."

"When I've earned it??" I yelled desperately. "What does that mean?"

"When you show me that you have what it takes. You don't even have a visa right now."

I tried to call two of my work colleagues to see if they could take over my lessons for me today. Teaching and putting on a happy face would be horrible today. But none of them can do it. So now I am on my way back to Pasadena, one big mess on the inside and outside. The next song on my playlist comes on. *The Wings* from the Brokeback Mountain movie soundtrack. And this one always gets all the heavy sobs and snot out of me when I'm already in a sad mood. My vision blurs up again, I scream in my car. Who can hear me anyway? With both hands tightly around the steering wheel, I let my voice express all my desperation, anger, sadness, everything in a high-pitched cry. And then I see it, the traffic is doing its thing, where you don't see it coming. All of a sudden, all the cars stop, fast enough not to crash, but slow enough to not make it seem like you have to abruptly hit your brakes. But that's what I have to do. Shit, shit, shit. I have to hit my brakes. My right food presses the gas pedal like never before. My car makes a screeching noise and then' …Crash. '

I just caused an accident. I can't believe it. Didn't I just tell my mom I'm OK to drive? I'm shaking. My face is puffy from all the crying. Luckily, I haven't put on makeup yet, but I don't even care right now. What did I just do??

~

Four hours later, I'm at Alana's apartment in Anaheim. She picked me up from the repair shop, where currently my AC is being fixed. The damage to the body of my car will be something I'll have to live with for a while. The mechanic can't fix that, and I also don't have the money for it. The engine hood is slightly bent. I still feel bad for the guy I crashed into. He looked fine overall, and luckily, my last-minute break action prevented the worst from happening. But I probably ruined his day, and definitely his trunk.

I bailed out of work, since the mechanic I go to is all the way in Riverside. I think Fred, my boss, thought I was just not coming because I didn't want to. And I really didn't want to, but I wouldn't just have cancelled without having a substitute teacher in place, if it wasn't for the accident. I just feel bad all around.

Alana manages to make me laugh at least a tiny bit. As we both are sitting at her kitchen island working on our visa documents, creating flyers for events that might or might not happen, just so we have something to show, Eddie finally calls me back.

"What happened now, Bunny?"

"I had an accident." My voice starts to shake again. "I was crying, and I didn't see the traffic build up right in front of me."

"Oh, Bunny." All of a sudden, he sounds so caring and loving, and it gives me hope that maybe things aren't all bad. Maybe this accident will make him reconsider things.

In the evening, Alana drives me to pick up my car and then the two of us meet up with Eddie to get pizza and ice cream over the shock. I feel cared for, and he makes me laugh by being his usual silly self. He's asking the girl who takes our order 'how she got so small 'and makes jokes about me and my best friend, and my car's brand-new bent metal style. But then he leaves me again, and nothing, not even a little bit is OK.

Now

First things first. I'll start the day by writing my morning pages. Maybe whatever mood I'm in will pass, and I can live my day unfazed by possible horror scenarios in my head.

April 14, 2019

It's Nick's birthday. I haven't heard from him since 7:30pm last night. I tried calling, but he didn't answer. I texted, he didn't answer. He did mention he was super tired in the afternoon, but usually, if he falls asleep early, he at least texts me in the early morning. I swear to God, if that man is lying to me... I don't know... He's going to break me. It would be even harder to trust after that. But really, it wouldn't make sense if he was. I don't see how he would have had time to meet someone else the past few weeks and then spend his birthday with them. But he also hasn't been on his WhatsApp since 7pm on Thursday. Oh, well. Maybe I'm overthinking. I hope I am. I just hate feeling this way. I'm going back and forth between thinking he would never do that — he knows how much he'd hurt me if he lied to me — and being scared that that's exactly what he's doing. But let's just list some things that make it unlikely that he's lying to me:

— He calls me baby girl / his girl.
— He picked me up from the airport. He cares.

THE ONE I LOVE MOST

— *He told me we respect each other and wouldn't be seeing other people.*

— *So far, he always did what he said he was going to do.*

— *He always leaves his phone lying around face up.*

— *He seems like a good guy, and he knows how much he'd hurt me if he lied.*

And just why can't I let go of that thought? Maybe because it's been a fear for over a month? That he just doesn't <u>want</u> to spend his birthday with <u>me</u>? But then he wouldn't have waited so long to tell me that, right? I wish I could just 'snap out of it'.' I wish I could just feel secure. I miss him a lot. I need him to text me or call me. I need him to prove he's doing what he said without me asking. I have no idea when he's leaving today. Maybe he had to leave early. And really, all those thoughts come from my past, I think? From my insecurities, constantly fearing I was being lied to. But when has Nick ever lied to me? And why would he? There's no real way to use my intuition when I'm this scared. But maybe there's something. Maybe it's not awful. Something he didn't tell me, just like the other time I felt so anxious? When I was so worried about the European chocolate and his weird reaction when I asked him where it was from. And when I finally had the courage to ask, he said it was from an old girlfriend who sent it as a Thank-you.

But really, it would really hurt me if he lied to me about anything. If he thought he had to lie to me, I don't know what I'd do. And look what a shit show this journal has become. All about him because I can't relax. He texted! Right now. Relief! He wouldn't be lying. He told me in detail what he did last night and this morning at his training. I need him to hold me and tell me he'd never lie to me about big things like that. I'm emotional, scared, insecure. I need help!! I hope those people will call me back soon. Having my sister and Alana tell me he sounds like a good guy and like I am overthinking also helps me. Nick tells the truth. He does.

I close my notebook and get ready for my meditation, but my thoughts are persistent today. I started writing these morning pages half a year ago when my songwriting group suggested *The Artist's Way* by Julia Cameron. A book consisting of 12 weeks' worth of exercises to bring out the artist in you again. And part of that process is to take yourself on an artist date each week and to write morning pages every day. Morning pages aren't necessarily a diary, they're more like a stream of consciousness. You write down whatever comes to your mind, even if it doesn't make sense or add up. These are not to be read again, it's a pure writing exercise. It seems like my morning pages are increasingly becoming a diary, though. And it's all about Nick. I almost want to throw up at myself. How am I so cliché? Don't I have something more important to fill my mind with and stress over than a boy who doesn't make any effort for me?

I called the school for psychology this week, which Anne recommended to me. I never had therapy, but I think there are things that I still need to work on, and with my state of mind lately, I do feel like I should vent to a professional. And who knows, it might help. The good thing about this clinic is that they have affordable options, for example, if you choose a counselor who's still in training. They said they'd call me back soon, and I am more excited than I thought I would be, to get started.

~

THE ONE I LOVE MOST

I'm on my way to San Pedro, once again. I've been looking forward to this. I bought whale watching tickets in Long Beach as a birthday gift for Nick. We are finally celebrating his birthday together, a week late. The boat is leaving the harbor at 11am, and we want to be there early to pick up the tickets and make sure we get a good spot on the boat. We decided to meet at his place at 9:30am. I wouldn't have minded coming down here last night. I don't know why he seems to be unable to spend more than one day or one night in a row with me. I've been wanting that so bad, and after three months it still hasn't happened.

But then again, I got to see him more often this week than any other week before, except maybe our first week of dating, when he was still pursuing me. Now it feels like I've become the chaser, always trying to plan something, asking for his time, calling him more often than he calls me. It's exhausting. On Tuesday, he said he missed me though, and since I finished work early that day, I decided to spontaneously drive down to see him and give him his birthday present. He's been growing a mustache recently, and I gave him a little set of beard balm and oil to groom his little manstache. A day later he texted me saying *Guess what? I decided I don't want the mustache anymore. I just shaved it all off.* Knowing it couldn't have been my present that made him decide against it made me just take it lightly, and I laughed at the timing of it all.

He also spent Thursday night with me. We were trying to go to my favorite vegan restaurant again, after three months, and they ended up having an event that night that made the kitchen too slow to accommodate more guests. There was tension that night, but we spent the night, him snoring, me awake with feelings of unease. There was something in the air, but at the same time everything was fine.

I really have been looking forward to today. We've been talking about this whale watching day for a while, and I'm so happy he finally was able to make time on a weekend and agreed to go with me.

Nick is rapping along to one of the songs on his playlist, driving his car, alternating his attention between the road and me, almost performing. I'm trying to get into it, but I've never heard the song before. I look at him and laugh. Even though I still feel a little slow today—the weather isn't all 'sunny LA 'yet—Nick's enthusiasm for this song is making me smile, and then laugh. He knows every single word, and there seems to be a lot of them. He's moving back and forth, getting as much motion into his upper body as possible. After four minutes, the song is over, and he turns the volume down. We're on the big bridge that crosses over from San Pedro's harbor to Long Beach and with his hand still in mine he looks at me again. I can't help but smile. He's such a sweet human being. He smiles in return.

"You have such nice teeth and a gorgeous smile, Kathrin. Did I ever tell you that?"

I didn't expect that. He meant it. "No, I don't think so, but thank you!"

And just like that, he gave me my special boost for the day.

THE ONE I LOVE MOST

Before we commit to standing in line for the boat, we decide to run to Starbucks for a small breakfast and a restroom. We each get an oatmeal and as we eat, a very committed punk rock-styled kid with a huge green Mohawk walks by us.

"I hope that my kids won't be running around like that one day," Nick remarks. "Not that I wouldn't love them either way. If they're gay, too. I don't hope they'll be, but I know I'll love them and support them. But yeah, I just don't get how people want to run around like that."

I'm surprised. That's the most futuristic talk he has ever engaged in. Talking about his *own* children.

"I wouldn't want my kids to be that extreme either, but it could just be a phase," I respond. I decide not to say anything about how weak my knees just turned when he unpacked the '*I'll love my kids no matter what*' talk. I wasn't even fully aware he wanted kids. He doesn't even know if he wants to be in a relationship.

"Mark always says I'm going to end up like him some day." He laughs, clearly denying such a thing, that he could end up like his roommate.

"What do you mean, like him?" I ask.

"Well, you know, he's 40. And alone. With a roommate," he adds.

"I don't think that will be you either. You're still eight years younger than him."

But in my mind a silent question forms itself. *Maybe that could be him, if he keeps saying no to love because he's afraid he'll get hurt?*

Again, he shrugs off the idea. "Nah. That won't be me."

We found good seats on the boat. I'm glad we brought all these layers because it is chilly today for an April day in LA, and the wind that the ocean brings isn't helping either. I'm freezing, even with my shirt, sweater, and vest jacket on.

"Come here, baby girl. I got you." Nick hugs me tightly against him, with his right arm around me, grabbing my forearm.

I really hope we'll get to see some whales today. I've done this before. Numerous times. I was somewhat of a whale and dolphin freak when I was in fifth grade. So much so that I wanted to join Greenpeace, and then I wanted to become a marine biologist, just so I could go out on boats and meet these beautiful ocean mammals. But then I found out that studying such a thing involves more taking dirty water samples and analyzing them, instead of any interaction with wildlife. Especially if I had done it in Germany. Nick, on the other hand, hasn't been whale watching before. It's his first time, and it's his birthday present, so I strongly hope the two and a half hour trip will be worth it.

Once out of the harbor, the boat starts speeding up, and now we are jumping waves. Every time we jump especially high, everyone on the boat goes "Woooo," and we all laugh in delight. Nick is still holding on to me tightly. He looks at me and smiles.

"We haven't even seen a whale yet, but I'm already having so much fun, Kathrin. Thank you for this. This is amazing."

There it was again, that glint in his eye. That happiness that everything we need, is right here, right now. And just with a simple statement, he makes me relax about the outcome of our little cruise and helps me to just enjoy this moment.

A school of dolphins comes out of seemingly nowhere and accompanies the boat for a few minutes, jumping happily alongside us. Everybody stands up when they first start showing off. Nick squeezes me tightly. I am happy. I am so happy. I love the ocean. I love California. And I love him. But I couldn't possibly say that. And then the announcer/wildlife expert uses the speaker.

"Eleven o'clock. It looks like we have a humpback whale right in front of us."

Everybody on the boat runs to the bow of the boat, holding on to the railing, to see this majestic ocean giant. The captain turns off the engine of the boat, and now we wait and see.

"It seems like this young whale is sleeping. Whales sleep floating right beneath the surface and will breathe out every few minutes."

Everybody has their phones and cameras propped up and as the whale finally exhales a happy murmur goes through the small crowd. Something so simple, yet so magical, is taking up everyone's attention.

On the way back to the shore, Nick falls asleep, and I sneakily take a selfie of us. I might be able to use this later, to make fun of him. There's no scenario this man can't sleep through. He slept through a whole movie in the movie theater just a few weeks ago, cuddled into my lap. He also doesn't seem to have a problem falling asleep sitting up or talking mid-sentence. Midnight is usually when I'm most entertained, when we sleep next to each other, because he will tell me stories that don't make any sense whatsoever, but crack me up. I recently started recording them, and we've been having a blast listening back. I can't even be mad at him anymore. At least he made it to seeing the whale.

Back on solid ground, we grab dinner at Yard House and then make our way back to his place with a detour to the mall to grab new workout pants for his upcoming work trip.

"I might have a surprise for you," he says.

"A surprise? Really? What is it?"

Could this day go any better? He never surprised me. Nobody has surprised me in a while. I wish that would happen a lot more often.

"You'll see. But I can't promise anything."

Fair enough. At least he thought about how he could surprise me. That's as far as anyone has made it in the last three years.

Once we're out of the mall with just one new pair of pants, I am in dire need of a dessert. My lunch was so salty.

"I wish I had something sweet to eat at your place, like dessert."

"You want to go by Whole Foods really quick? It's on the way." He knows me. And that fact alone makes me feel special.

"Yes, let's do that." I'm exhausted, but I'm loving this day. I can't wait to cuddle up with him and enjoy the rest of the night together.

When we finally make it back to the house, I put my lunch leftovers in the fridge. And just as I grabbed a small fork out of the silverware drawer to start eating my tiny gluten-free apple pie, Nick starts watching me with a rather concerned look on his face.

"What?" I ask, not thinking anything. The pomelo and my favorite veggie puff chips I brought are laying on the counter between the kitchen and living room. I love bringing him my favorite things. He usually loves them, too. And I love introducing him to new things we can devour together.

"Would you mind it if we didn't spend the rest of the evening together?"

Would I mind?? It must be one of his really convincing jokes again. He doesn't admit he's messing with me until I absolutely buy the lie.

"Are you messing with me again?" I ask confidently with a smirk on my face.

"No, Kathrin. I kind of just need some me-time."

He is so convincing. And I start feeling horrible. He knows he can't do this with me anymore. I'm too sensitive with what has happened with Eddie, and all. We had that discussion. It's really not cool if he's doing it again. But his face is stern.

"Are you serious?" I'm hesitant to believe it. In just a minute he will laugh at me and say "Gotcha." And then he will apologize and hug me.

"Yeah, I just feel like I need to be alone."

And then it dawns on me. He is not joking this time. He looks at me, ashamed, knowing that he's letting me down. But that doesn't change the fact that he wants me gone. I can't believe this is happening. Panic mode takes over, trying to fix what I can before it's too late. What happened? Didn't we just spend the most perfect day together? Wasn't there still something he wanted to surprise me with?

"What's going on?"

He's quiet. More regretful looks on his face.

"We've talked about this. You said you would never send me home like that." My voice is getting quieter.

"I'm not sending you home."

"You're asking me to leave." I slightly raise my voice. "So yeah, you are sending me home. I can't believe this."

I jump up from the table, where I was peacefully starting to eat my dessert just moments ago. I grab the pomelo I brought, as well as my veggie puffs and fire them both into my bag which is still laying on the foot of the stairs, where we left it this morning. Then I grab my pie and my leftovers from the fridge, and also add it to my pile of things. I'm angry and hurt, hoping this will make him realize that he's not clear in his mind right now, and that we can figure it out. But he just watches. I am too distraught, too upset, my chest is hurting more than it has in the last two months combined, and I can't get myself to leave. But obviously staying isn't an option either. I go into desperate mode. I *so* wish I could be the self-assured, confident girl, who knows her worth and doesn't fidget long when presented with a clear situation like this. But I can't. I am not her and this situation shows it.

"I just don't understand. Everything was fine. When did you decide that you didn't want to spend the night together anymore?"

"I don't know."

The infamous Nick answer. How is it he's so smart and then all of a sudden, can't answer the simplest of questions?

"I thought today was good."

"It was. It was amazing," he insists.

"So what's the problem? Can you at least try to explain what came over you all of a sudden?"

I cower into the smallest possible ball on the couch and am too upset to even cry. I can't think clearly, this is throwing me off so much. He stands next to the couch looking down at me, obviously feeling like the bad guy, but not doing anything about it. So, I keep throwing things at him.

"You know, I've been feeling something this whole week, maybe longer even. I feel like we have this great connection, but it's just not going anywhere, and I don't know what to do anymore." He sits down on the couch next to me, still quiet. "And I even signed up for therapy. I'm going to therapy next week. I think I need it. Obviously." Why am I telling him all this? Then he finally speaks.

"Kathrin, we had a conversation on this same couch a few months ago. I told you I don't want a relationship right now."

Now I scream. "You said you didn't know what you wanted."

"I did, but then I said I didn't want one. I just don't think I'm the one."

"Oh, you don't think *you're* the one?? How can you just determine that? Why don't you just say what you really should be saying? That *I'm* not the one for *you*." Silence. "If you keep talking around it, I'll never get it. Just say it to my face, Nick."

I slide off the couch onto the floor, sitting down there with tears in my eyes. I am aware of how dramatic I am, what a scene I'm causing, but I can't help it. Finally, I am letting all of me come out. I guess there's no more reason to be careful now, to worry what he thinks about me. It looks like that hasn't served me so well all this time, has it? Then he says it.

"I just don't think you're the one, Kathrin."

"Thank you," I answer.

I am not feeling grateful towards him right now, but I am glad he finally said what the actual problem is. And then he adds. "I just never thought that far ahead. I'm moving away. I think we should stop seeing each other."

"Why?" I'm sobbing.

He calmly says, "I don't want us to hurt each other anymore. I think it's for the best."

Whatever last piece of emotion I contained, it's untangling itself from my grasp and I break apart, right in front of him, with Mark, his roommate, probably hearing me from his room. I am ugly crying in front of the man of my dreams, the man who now goes back to being just that, a dream, never more.

"Come here." He grabs me by the shoulders and pulls me up. "Let's go upstairs."

What? Is he trying to have some sort of weird break up sex now? While I'm crying my heart out, panda eyes included.

"Just come." He must be ashamed of Mark hearing everything. He brings me to his room and closes the door, sits me down on the bed, and then just holds me while I cry into his sweater. I cry and I cry.

"I feel silly asking this again, but I just have to. I'm sorry, but is there somebody else?"

"No, Kathrin, that's not why."

I keep crying. My heart is heavy when I finally grab my bags and walk out the door, back to my blue Hydie. I can't believe this is happening. Again, Nick hugs me tightly as we say our goodbyes.

"Promise me that you'll always tell the truth to the next girl, no matter how hard it is." He nods. "And if something cool happens in your life, I want to know, OK?" He nods again.

"OK. And if there's ever a concert I can come to, you'll let me know, too?" he asks. "You know I'll be supporting."

"OK. Take care Nick. You're a good guy."

"Bye, Kathrin."

Knowing I'll cry the whole way home, I connect my phone and hit play on my Sad Song playlist. I might as well get the most out of it. I don't know how I'll survive this yet. I must have forgotten how much a broken heart can hurt.

Then

He makes me want to write. I finally found my muse again. It's Saturday, and I'm at work, passing time, playing with chords on the piano in front of me. I saw this quote the other day. Or was it a random song title generator? Either way, it came to my mind on my way to work again. I drove past a building with a piece of wall art that showed a black and white painting of a lion with a woman on it's back, against a blue wall. And crazy enough, the woman, or girl, was holding a banner that said *She Rides The Lion*. The exact same line. That is my sign to finally write that song.

I start sketching down lyrics into the notes app on my phone.

He's a beautiful monster,
And he wants to control her.
He's out to get what he wants.
He doesn't shy the hunt.
He wants things his way,
Doesn't accept nothing else,
His roar sometimes scares her,
But she learned to live in his world
She rides the lion, She is not afraid
The wind in her hair is strong

But she knows where she belongs.

She rides the lion, She's made to be brave.

The sun is hard on her skin

But she knows with him, she wins.

Eddie is so hard-headed. We went to the gym the other day. He told me he can train me. He trained many people during his time in the military, he said. In the beginning, he was very patient with me, but I simply couldn't do some of the things he instructed me to do. When I was too tired, after two hours, to do 30 burpees, he left me standing there by myself. I tried really hard, but other than jogging I have never really worked out, and I've never done burpees before. My spine kept on bending every time I jumped back into the plank position, and I was worried I was going to hurt myself.

"I can't. I'm exhausted, babe," I said.

But he didn't want to hear it. "You're just giving up. 'I can't 'isn't an option. I'm going to do cardio. Don't think we're going to do anything else together today."

I felt like I had disappointed him, especially when at the end of our three-hour gym visit, he said, "I'll never come here with you again. You're on your own from now on."

Maybe I have another verse in me, I think as I snap back from my recent memory.

Just as I put some chords and a melody to my new rhymes, my next student waves at me through the little window in my door, and I have to put on happy teacher mode again.

THE ONE I LOVE MOST

~

It was a long day. Seven hours of teaching can hardly be compared to seven hours of office work, even though I wouldn't want to trade. Saturdays are also tough because, as a renowned morning sleeper, I have to get up earlier than I usually do and start teaching when my brain isn't fully awake yet.

I get to Eddie's place at 6pm. He's already busy organizing things, so we can clean the place. It's already clean in my opinion. Quite frankly, with little to no furniture, all we have to do is swipe through once and wash the bedsheets. But Eddie wants it shiny, spanking fresh and clean for when my mom comes.

My visa application wasn't denied, but I got a *request for more evidence* from the Immigration Services. Even the fact that I was featured in Europe's biggest Sunday newspaper and got a whole page to myself, apparently didn't help. Or the other two TV shows I was asked to be on, since my 'Bavarian Yodeler in Hollywood 'act has gotten more and more attention. That means I had to add further evidence and material I didn't have. I thought I could get by, but it turns out people weren't lying when they said it's a hard endeavor to get an artist visa.

Eddie is going on tour with his band in just a few days, and he'll be gone for the 4th of July and the whole week that I am off work. I can't go home to Germany because, while my waiting status allows me to stay here, it wouldn't allow me to come back into the country without a valid visa. All of these things have really taken a toll on me lately. The constant visa worry, fights, and break-ups with Eddie, and me being away from home. I asked my mom to come visit me and knowing how I felt, she agreed. And Eddie agreed to let us stay at his place while she's here and he is gone. Much more space than at my place, shared with Liu and two cats.

"I'm so tired," I tell him.

Eddie sighs. "We have to get this clean-up done, though. No excuses. I want this place to be tip-top for Mama Bunny."

"I know, I know. What should I do?"

"You can start vacuuming."

"OK, babe." I grab the little vacuum cleaner I bought for him recently, and start making my way around the living and sleeping space and then around the kitchen island.

"Bunny!" he yells.

"What?" I mumble absentmindedly.

"What are you doing?"

"Vacuuming the floor. Like you asked me to?"

"You didn't even get everything out of the way first. You can't just be vacuuming around things. Take the floor mats and put them somewhere else first," he demands. "Otherwise, it'll still be dirty afterwards."

I sigh loudly. I can never do anything to his liking. He always has to teach me everything.

"I know you never had to clean at home, but let's do this right," he adds.

"I'm just exhausted. I had a long day. I told you."

"OK, you know what? Why don't you start cleaning the light switches instead?"

"The light switches?"

Never in my life have I cleaned light switches. Not on purpose, not when I didn't accidentally get something gnarly on them. And now I got demoted to cleaning the light switches. Fine. Less work for me.

"Yes, the light switches," Eddie repeats.

I grab one of the rags and start cleaning the switches by the kitchen counter. They're the long and flat shaped type and as I start cleaning it the light starts going 'on—off—on—off. '

"Bunny. Stop it. You have to clean it the other way. This is bad for the light bulbs."

"I'm sorry. I didn't think. I'm just tired." I keep cleaning them the right way and then move on to the light switches by the front door and the ones in the bathroom. And just for two seconds my mind blanks and I continue to clean brainlessly. Again the light, now in the bathroom, goes 'on—off—on—off. '

"What did I tell you?" Eddie yells. "This is bad for the bulbs. Can't you ever listen to what I say and do something the right way?"

He seems like he's had it with me, but his tone is so rude. I just look at him. I would apologize, but the way he's talking to me is beyond what I can accept right now. He continues. "You're not good for anything."

I snap. "Why don't you do it yourself then?" I know how pouty I sound, but I can't help it. I roll my eyes at him as I say it and throw the rag on the kitchen island next to him. He's angry.

"You're done for tonight. You can lay on the bed and be on your phone again. But you're not touching anything else."

"I *want* to help. Just don't speak to me like that."

"No. It's OK. You told me you're tired. I should have believed you. I don't want to hear anything anymore. Just get out of my way."

Am I supposed to just accept the way he's talking to me? The way he's treating me right now? I am so angry, but I know snarking back at him is only going to make things even worse. The lion in him is coming out again, and I need to just get out of his way for a second. I grab my little black purse and hastily walk through the front door to the outside.

"Where are you going?"

"Out," I say and disappear from his sight. I'll come back in a few minutes. Things will have cooled down by then, I can pick up the rag again and start cleaning the right way, and we can sleep next to each other and be loving. I will rub my booty on him while we spoon, and he will say, "Oh Bunny, I love it when you do this. Come here, little one." I go to the back of the building, get in my car, roll the windows down and drive. I'm just going to get some air here at the harbor and go right back, and we can apologize to each other and tell each other that we overreacted.

THE ONE I LOVE MOST

There's a dog running straight through the middle of a four lane road. What is it doing? Then I hear fireworks going off. I heard them earlier too, I remember. Why do people have to do this, weeks in advance? I pull over as soon as the road is clear and as I call the dog it comes right to me and is more than happy to jump into my car. It's a girl. A pit bull girl. And she's all into me right away. My heart hurts. From the anxiety my fight with Eddie just gave me, but also because of this dog who is so sweet, and lost. I drive to a parking lot with her in the back of my car and try calling the local animal shelter. But nobody answers.

After ten minutes of waiting on the phone for nothing, we start heading back to Eddie's place together. I park the car, grab my new friend by the collar and walk her to the front of Eddie's balcony, where I call him. "Babe. I need your help with something. Babe? Eddie?" I am so nervous and tired and confused right now. He doesn't react. He must have not heard me.

I see him moving things out onto the balcony. And then he says, "I can't help you. Figure it out, Bunny," as he closes the door. He is still mad. This is worse than I thought. But I have to help this dog now. Then I can come back and talk to him. I remember where the local shelter is and decide I could at least try going there with her. As we pull up, there are several other cars in the parking lot and a light in the main office. Thank God. It is after 10pm already, after all. They can help her. She jumps out of the car, but she does not want to go in. I try to pull on her collar, but she doesn't move.

Again, my heart breaks just a bit more. She looks at me like she's saying, 'But I want to stay with you. '

"I can't, sweet girl. I'm going to bring you to these people now, and they will help you. I hope your owner will come find you here, or that you will find a wonderful new family. You deserve nothing but the best. I wish I could keep you, but I have a cat and no space for you. You deserve an amazing home. And maybe somebody is looking for you already." I almost cry as I tell her all of this. Then I grab her and start carrying her in. I fill out a form and say goodbye, this time with actual tears in my eyes. Why is this so hard? I just met her.

When I get back to the alley by Eddie's place, the balcony doors are locked. I park my car and head over there to climb the railing, so I can knock on the window. And then I see that all of my things are sitting on the balcony right in front of the door, in Ikea bags. All the laundry I brought that we were supposed to wash together, my razor, that he took out of the shower, my big purse, my tooth brush, even the frozen food I had in his freezer. All thrown into three fully packed Ikea bags. He is really trying to make a statement. He is going to be really mad at me when he lets me back in. I start to panic. I knock on the door. I yell his name. No answer. I knock again. This time harder. "Eddiiie. Babe. Please let me in. You can't lock me out here."

Then he answers, from inside. "Yes, I can. Go home, Bunny. You have all your things there."

"I can't. Please let me in," I plead and knock again.

"Stop it, or I will call the police. Heck, the neighbors might call them if you keep making noise like that."

"Please," I whimper. He is serious. I'm left out in the cold. "You can't just treat me like a dog."

"Go home, Bunny."

"The bags are too heavy. I can't lift them over the balcony." They are. The ground is pretty far down, and I don't know how to get the weight up and thrown over there without spilling everything into the filthy alleyway.

"You'll figure it out," he says coldly.

I try to lift one of the bags, but I fail. I lay down between all of my things and type Eddie's best friend's number. Archie. "Archie, it's Kathrin, Eddie's girlfriend. We just had a really silly fight that escalated. He just locked me out on the balcony. I don't know what to do." I'm sure he must be able to talk some sense into Eddie, or at least give me some advice.

"Look, I don't know what to tell you. That's between you and him. I'm sorry you're feeling that way, but I'm sure he had a reason. If he told you to go home, just go home for now."

"OK. Thank you." I cry all my sentences and am fully aware that the neighbors might exactly know how crazy I am now. Then I call Alana.

"Bueno?" When she picks up, all that comes out of me is a heavy sob. "Kathrin? What's wrong?"

I try to speak. "Whua ham hia, sobsob, hand Heddie locked me oooouuuut."

"OK, you need to slow down. Where are you right now?"

"On Eddie's balconyyyy. He locked me ouuuut."

"He locked you *out*?" Her tone just switched from calm to upset.

"Yes, with all my things, and I cahahan't lift theeeeeem."

"Can you drive?"

"I'm scared to driiiive because I already had an accident because of this, remember? And the bags are too heavy. I'm just gonna stay on the balcony until he lets me back in."

"No, Kathrin. Send me the address, and I'm going to pick you up, OK?"

"OK, Maus. Are you sure? OK, I will send you the address. Thank youuu. I love yoouu."

She picks me up half an hour later. Together, we heave my bags over the balcony and into her car, leaving my car behind in the alley parking lot.

We watch "The Fox and the Hound" when we get to her place in Anaheim and I sob my heart out. I cry for about two hours and when I'm finally exhausted enough to go to bed and sleep, despite everything that happened tonight, Eddie texts.

Where r u?

"Is he serious right now? He told me to go home. And now he's acting worried."

"Just ignore him. He doesn't deserve an answer right now. He doesn't deserve *you*. Period. What he did is not

OK." She leaves a space between the last two words when she says it to emphasize how *not OK* it is what he pulled off tonight.

"But he could be worried," I say. "My car is still there, but I am not."

"Well, then let him fucking worry. He deserves it."

~

Eddie is mad at me the next day, for disappearing. He makes me apologize for worrying him, for not telling him where I was going. I don't think I'm wrong, but I agree to the fact that I don't know how to communicate. I agree that I was wrong. I just want things to be right again. I just want him to love me. We can figure the rest out later.

Now

I am worthy. I am loving. I am peaceful. I am rich. I am wise...

I am listening to the 55-minute affirmation audio I found on YouTube. I've been listening to it every morning while walking Trooper, the poop-eating Golden. I took my life into my own hands again. From now on, I am going to manifest everything that I deserve and want, and more.

This is just one of my new habits which I started after Nick 'broke up 'with me. Technically, I can't call it a break-up because we were never together, but it definitely felt like one, even after just three and a half months. I spent the whole first day cowered in bed, crying my eyes out, loudly. Anne heard me and brought me a vegan consolation cake and a calming lavender candle, which made me cry even more. I wished the cake or the candle could have made me feel better.

It didn't help that Nick forgot his Secret Service badge in my purse and had to pick it up the next day. We hugged for about 30 minutes in the courtyard while I cried into his chest again. He didn't want to lift me up because he said my shorts were too short. Everyone would see my butt. He also didn't want to come in. "Why aren't you upset at all?" I asked him.

"Oh, I do feel it, Kathrin. Just because I can't show it in the same way, doesn't mean I don't feel it."

What did that mean? It doesn't matter. All the analyzing him has never actually brought me any good. Even if I was spot-on with my speculations, it wouldn't change anything about the fact that he doesn't want to be in a relationship with me. This is for the best. At least I get to 'not worry' about having to move away from California.

Last Wednesday, I had my first therapy session with Cindy. The moment she closed the door and I started telling her why I came in, I couldn't hold my tears back anymore. It made it hard to even talk, sobbing and trying to keep myself from hyperventilating. Cindy just looked at me understandingly, and let me tell my whole story and all of what, I think, is wrong with me, while handing me the tissue box. This was long overdue. I can't wait for her to analyze me and tell me what's wrong with me exactly, and how to fix it in our future sessions.

I am silently repeating each of the affirmations that come through my earphones when Trooper finds a slice of pizza in the park. "No, no, no." But he already has it in his mouth, determined to devour it. "Give it here," I demand. I grab the pizza slice by the crust and pull. I end up with a tiny little piece, while Trooper devours the rest of it with one big swallow. "Fine. You win. Again. At least this time it wasn't poop."

I've been asking myself a lot lately what it is that I want. I didn't come here to be a teacher, and at the same time, I am not at the point where I don't have to be a teacher anymore. But what do I want to work toward? What is the one thing that's going to make me get out of bed when I don't have to walk Trooper in the mornings anymore? What will actually make me *want* to get up? If only I knew. At least now, I am not distracted by trying to make some imaginary relationship work anymore, even though it's hard. I've been trying hard to find reasons not to like Nick. But even the way he broke it off between us was rather kind, looking back at it now. In one of my morning page entries, I wrote a list of *things I don't like about Nick*. This is what I came up with:

— His right big toe nail is not pretty.
— He has flat-bottomed feet.
— He has the TV on too much.
— He doesn't have enough time for me.
— He doesn't want to be in a relationship.

The last one is kind of 'duh. 'But since I really struggled with finding things to put on that list, I thought I'd add that one, too, just to show myself that there are plenty of reasons not to like Nick Eric Watts. But somehow, half of those things make me realize how much I really like him. Because I don't really care how crooked his toes or how flat his feet are. I fell in love with that man. Knowing that the only way out of this was to stop speaking to him, I forced myself, two days after that horrible day, to ignore him for three weeks. Twenty-one days. That's how long it takes to form a habit. And either he would realize how big of a mistake he made during this quiet time, or I'm going to have an easier time moving on. According to Matthew Hussey at least, the YouTube dating expert, who sold me his *'Get Him Back in Two Months '* program. The only action I thought I could take. No amount of goodbye texts or singing videos seemed to make him change his mind. I knew that if I paid for this program, there was at least a chance I'd stick to the three week no contact part of it. And so far, so good. I'm proud of myself. It's been almost two weeks. I made a little sheet for myself. Every day I get to cross out a day.

When I get back home from our walk, I cross out Day 12. Nine more days and I can send him that casual *'I thought of you* text. I walk to the kitchen to blend up my daily calorie bomb smoothie with frozen raspberries, peach, banana, pineapple juice and spinach. Anne is preparing lunch already. She had the day off today. The school year is almost over. "So, how are you feeling? You seem to be getting better?" she asks.

"I think I am. The three week no contact thing is good for me. And I started listening to all these affirmations, and I'm getting better with meditating in the mornings again. And thank you again for recommending the psychology school. I really like Cindy so far." She seems content with my answer.

"Oh, I'm so glad that worked out. And I'm happy you're starting to feel better. He really did you a favor by ending it. As hard as it was."

"Yeah, you're probably right. It was like a bad addiction. I just wish there was an actual reason to not like him. It would be easier if he was a dick, like Derrick, the vegan doctor prince, or Ian. But I still like him a lot. It's just going to take time, I guess."

Ian was another guy I dated just two years ago. He was tall, dark, and handsome and prided himself on a really low percentage of body fat, which in turn made his muscles pop. He had a nice car, a steady job and a two-bedroom apartment all to himself. But he could only see me on weekends. One day per weekend, to be exact. We would sleep in his second bedroom with a mere mattress on the floor. His actual bedroom reminded him too much of his work routine, he said. I was expected to go home in the mornings when he made breakfast for himself. And sometimes he would take me out, but only when he had a Groupon deal. Because he only went to places if he had Groupon deals. When he told me his last name was James, I should have run, but I didn't. When I asked for a serious talk, he told me he doesn't believe in relationship labels. He did, however, believe in a flat earth and that the Illuminati are influencing people to become gay. Looking back, I don't know why I stuck around for three months.

"Ah, forget those guys!" Anne says and then adds "Nick might not be like them, he was a good guy, but he wasn't good for *you*. You drove yourself crazy, and unfortunately, you guys just don't want the same thing right now."

"I know." The hopeful part in me will always die last. With every consequential action I take, there's still always hope left. Why am I such a fairy tale chaser?

My phone lights up on the counter. I gave up hoping that it would be Nick. It's probably my mom. And expecting it to be her won't make me resent her when it actually is. But it isn't my mom. It *is* Nick. "Oh my god, he texted!!" With my pulse doubled, I unlock my phone, holding it to my face, and the body of the text appears on my home screen.

> *Just for the record Kathrin, I think about you every day.*

My heart pounds, my fantasies are being reignited. He misses me. He's having a hard time. The freaking plan is working. But then I catch myself and bring myself back down to the ground of facts. This doesn't change anything. He didn't declare his love for me, he didn't say he changed his mind, he didn't say he wants me back. None of that. So, what's the point of this?

For the rest of the day, I think about how to answer that text, if I should answer at all. I go back to the rules of the '*21 Day No Contact*' program. If they reach out, you are allowed to answer. But what good is it, if it's that easy for him? In one of my work breaks, I decide to simply react to the iMessage with a heart. I didn't ignore it, but I also didn't respond. He will have to work harder if he wants *any*thing from me at this point.

Then

Mom and I are spending the day at home today, meaning at Eddie's place. We went whale watching yesterday. While the announcements were made that it's best to take any hats off, my mom decided to simply tie her scarf around her head to secure her favorite hat. It was sunny, after all. Wearing one of Eddie's prized hats, I decided I should be doing the same. I asked my mom to help me do it and just at that moment the boat started picking up speed and my mom's hat went in one high bow and became one with the ocean. I took off my hat right away because Eddie might kill me if I lost his Raiders hat. And then we both cracked up over how her hat didn't even stand a chance.

Once we're back in the car, I started noticing that my face felt really warm. I looked into the rearview mirror while driving to our lunch destination and saw that my whole face was red, except for a sunglasses-shaped area around my eyes that was my normal cheesy pale color. Once we got home, the red intensified, and while my mom didn't get burned as much as I did, we both still had way more sun than our usually freezing German selves can handle.

So now we're here, just taking it easy and recovering. It's 7pm already. The day went by fast and my mom just passed out on the bed, after we attempted to watch today's episode of 'Sturm der Liebe '(Storm of Love), one of the cheesiest telenovelas you could come up with. It's a family thing. She's still jet-lagged, and so here I am, left with my phone. There are so many pictures of Eddie and me on here. And I'm itching to post them. I want to show my man to the world. Our cute pictures together. But he doesn't want to be posted online. He doesn't have any social media either. Except for an old Facebook account without a profile picture, that he doesn't use. He also doesn't have any bank accounts. He wants to avoid being traceable. Somewhat understandable in this day and age. And I also know that his ex-wife still tries to make him pay for things he doesn't owe her. So, he figures, not having anything on paper means she can't come for it.

But being my Millennial self, I am pretty bothered by the fact that I can't engage him in any sort of social media posts. I can't put a mark on him. At least his band has a Facebook page. I decide to go on there to see what they are up to. I see a video of them playing a pub, a picture of them posing with fans and then scroll down to another picture of them, on the road, posing with Starbucks drinks. I keep scrolling. Wait. Is that...? It can't be! I click on the list of people tagged by the lead singer. Carina!

Carina is not in the band. Carina works for a real estate agency in Orange County. She has no business being on tour with them, halfway across the country. My breathing accelerates. I want to scream, I want to cry, but I don't want to wake my mom. Instead, I take all my anxiety and direct it inwards. What is happening? This can't be true. I walk to the bathroom and close the door behind me. This place doesn't even have any freaking rooms. I dial Eddie's number. He doesn't pick up. I know it's at least two hours later there, but they must still be up, so I send a text.

> *What is Carina doing there? Please explain.*
> *Call me!!*

The half hour that passes before he calls me back nearly kills me. I thought we were through this? I thought this was settled. I made him promise me he would never cheat on me, like he did on Ines, with this girl he worked with, for a year. He said he's learned his lesson, and he is a better man now. But he also said, "The only reason I'd have to tell you I'll never cheat on you is because you're insecure. You shouldn't have to ask me that. You should just be confident." I knew what he meant, but I still needed to hear it.

"What's wrong, Bunny?" he says when I answer the phone.

"What's wrong? I just saw your guys 'picture. What is she doing there?"

"No need to worry, just stay calm. I'll answer your questions."

"So is she there or not?"

"Yes, she is. She had to be somewhere across the country and instead of taking an expensive flight, she came with us."

"Uh, and everybody is just OK with that?"

"Yeah, they know her. She comes to our gigs regularly."

"Oh, well, *that's* good to know..."

"Yeah, well, now you know. Nothing to worry about."

"But wait. You guys have already been on the road for a week now. So, where does she sleep when you guys stay with friends of the band?"

"Ah, she doesn't stay there. She takes hotel rooms."

"So, it's cheaper to be on the road with you guys for two weeks and take a hotel room every night, than just taking a simple flight? They're not that expensive."

"Bunny, yeah. She wanted to go with people she knows and likes. And she's not coming back with us. She will take a flight back from Springfield."

"OK. This just doesn't make sense."

"It makes perfect sense. But you know... if you really don't trust me even that much, maybe we shouldn't be doing this anymore. I can't talk to you every night like this, having to convince you about something I didn't do."

"No, it's OK. I believe you," I hastily say.

When we hang up, after he tells me he misses my bunny bubble booty, my chest doesn't want to let me sleep. Something is eating away inside me and is bringing more and more questions. It doesn't make sense. Why is she there? Why would anyone go on a business trip like that? She must lose at least a week's worth of work that way. But I can't ask any more questions. I need to stop being paranoid. *I* am Eddie's girlfriend. Not Carina.

217

Now

I still can't believe I made out with Lukas, and a little more. I also can't believe they put me in one of the middle seats in the middle row, surrounded by sleeping people in a dark plane, with nowhere to lean my head against. Good thing flying back to the States is always easier than going to Germany, with it being a day flight. Nonetheless, I'm tired. I had to get up at 4am to make my first flight from Munich to London. And that after a somewhat crazy weekend.

One of my best friends got married on Saturday. The last one out of our group of five, except for me, that is. They are still my best friends, but things have changed. Except for our rather wild days of the past, there isn't really a lot of common ground anymore. With all of them married now, three of them having children, and all of them building or already inhabiting their very own huge house. Houses that would cost about 5 million dollars in LA. And still, I wouldn't want to trade. I envy them sometimes for their loyal husbands, their families, the security they chose over the thrill of a big city or unstable career. At almost 30 I can see how appealing that is now. But I also know how bored I would get. I just have to sit things out a bit longer. The next big move will be my very own apartment. It almost happened just a month ago, when one of the big one-bedroom apartments opened up in our building. But my credit score wasn't good enough yet, and then Trooper's dad cancelled all our walks for the summer. So, I'm still living at Anne's.

The wedding was fun. I made it fun. I decided to stop being an outcast for a day by drinking as much as everyone else did. These days, I rarely drink, but I knew if I didn't want to feel like the odd one out again, I'd have to adapt at least in one way. And it wasn't going to be by eating meat, the rich, dairy-infused cakes, or by wearing a bra under my light blue, tight cocktail dress. So, I drank wine and then some. And while I tried to hold up the conversation with my girls, who had their kids with them, I got tired of resting my chin on my palm listening to conversations about bedtimes and funny poop stories.

Instead, I joined my younger cousin, by seven years, and her friends, celebrating and jumping on the tables just like we were a few years ago. Luise, my cousin, and I have just gotten back from a tiny vacation to Austria and Italy. We are both very hard-headed, each in our own way, and definitely butted horns a few times, but the few days of rest we got from each other gave us the distance we needed. She kept pouring wine in my glass, and before I knew it, I had to force myself to only drink water and nothing else. And then I made out with Lucas. I finally felt like I had taken back some control of my singleness, since Nick. I had given him every part of me, every privilege, without him ever even asking for it. This was proof that I am free. And yet, it wasn't overly amazing. I definitely won't get hooked on this man. That wouldn't have been a good situation anyway. Me in LA, and him in a small Bavarian village.

I text Sarah, my best friend since we were teenagers. I bought myself the crappy plane Wi-Fi, knowing I won't be able to sleep between two strangers, and she's the one friend I was always closest to and still am. Being one-on-one with her is great, it just doesn't happen a lot, and meeting all the new moms together at once just results in a big discussion about husbands and baby stuff.

> *I made out with Lukas.*

> *That's where you went? Omg. How was it?*

> *Yup. Lol. It was ok, but definitely not amazing. I'm good now.*

> *Haha. Well, I'm glad you got it out of your system.*

> *Me too.*

> *I miss you already. I wish we weren't so far apart.*

> *I know. Hopefully, I'll be able to come back soon again.*

I do believe her, but at the same time, it doesn't seem like they all miss me so much. Things are just not the same as they used to be, and that is OK. We all grew in different directions. At least I grew in a different direction than all of them. I'm excited to go back to California. It always takes me a few days to readjust, but I do feel at home in Pasadena.

I text all kinds of friends, but getting closer to the end of the flight, it's already early morning hours in Germany and everybody there is in bed. Nobody responds anymore and that's all this in-air internet is good for, texting. Try to load a picture on Instagram, and you will have used all the 250 MB in just two minutes, without actually ever having seen any part of the picture. I tried this more than once, unfortunately. The now sleep-drunk part of my brain is thinking of another round of people I could text. The "not go tos, the ones you only text when you are desperate and don't have enough self-control. I already texted Lukas. Why not? But how did I get home from the airport last time I landed at LAX? Nick! Ooh. Well, that's a *no no*.

'Remember that Katy Perry song you were listening to just an hour ago again, Kathrin? 'I mentally ask myself. Once you dip your toes in again, you might as well drown yourself. I quietly start to sing *Never Really Over,* 'hoping nobody will hear me over the engine noise of our Boeing 767.

The last time I texted him was almost two months ago. I waited three weeks and then sent him that very casual text. A screenshot of Mexican loaded fries, that I knew he'd love, telling him it reminded me of him. And he must have felt like he needed to get back at me because all he did was react to my message with a heart. And then he was generous enough to send a bunch of emojis. My attempt at reeling him back in failed. There was no 'I'm so glad to hear from you, I missed you so bad. 'And no, 'we should get those fries together and have a talk. 'All that anticipation build-up for nothing. He did text again the following day asking how I was doing, but at that point I felt like it wasn't really all that important to him, and our very shallow conversation came to a rather quick end. I can't text him. That would be so weak. Another one of the songs on my 'Break up with Nick 'playlist comes to my mind. Lizzo's *"Soulmate."*

Oh, but it's so hard right now to love myself, all by myself. Fuck it. I need a ride. And he won't even reply fast enough anyway. He takes half an eternity to reply to my texts. This is drunk Kathrin texting. Sleep drunk. That counts. I am delusional right now, and I feel like I need to send that text right now, or I won't think of anything else until we land.

I start typing.

> *Hey you... How have you been? I'm just on the plane coming back from Germany. It would be*

DELETE. Let's keep it simple.

> *Wishing I had amazing Secret Service LAX pickup service again right about now.* 😊

I put my phone on the tray table in front of me, on top of the book I have been too tired to read. I texted everyone

I could think of. The $30 for this internet was a waste. Oh, well. I turn back to the little screen in front of me to gently select another movie with my index finger. (I hate it when people hammer on those screens and make my head shake like I'm one of those wobbly head dogs in a car.)

My phone lights up. My mom must have woken up again. I almost go into cardiac arrest when the name that lights up is none other than Nick Watts. I don't think he's ever responded this fast. And I don't remember the last time my heart beat felt quite so violent. I feel like I just drank 10 cups of coffee, and I'm not a coffee drinker. The anticipation of what the text is saying is giving me sweaty hands. It could be, '*Now you're texting? When you need a ride? Call an Uber.*' or '*Sorry to disappoint, but I'm out of town.*' That sounds about right. He's never available at the last minute. Always working or working out. Or he could be with someone else now. He must have met someone within the last three months. Not expecting too much, I open the text.

> *Why didn't you tell me earlier, Kathrin!??*

> *Are you there now?*

Oh my god. Is he actually considering picking me up? No, he can't be. The last thing I expected was for him to actually text back in time, let alone pick me up.

> *Hahaha, what do you mean? No, I'm landing in half an hour and then customs.*

> 🧑 *This is how I feel.*

> *Lol!!! What do you mean, what I mean?? I mean, you could have at least asked me.* 😫

Wait? What? Am I in the wrong movie? Is he complaining right now that I didn't ask him to pick me up from the airport?

> *Really?? We haven't talked… People I talk to on the daily don't even want to go to LAX for me.*

That is definitely not a lie.

> *Lol! That doesn't mean I don't still think about you and, like we talked about, having to take an Uber/Lyft home from the airport is not cool. How long do you think customs will take? I can probably make it to you.*

My heart. I'm trying to stop myself from feeling all the excitement that's trying to come out of my body like hot steam. My sleepiness is gone. I'm cured. But I am afraid I might have catapulted myself right back into my own bottomless fairy tale.

> *Wow. Really?? That would be amazing!! I'm assuming at least an hour or two. I'm not expecting to get out before 7, but you never know.*

THE ONE I LOVE MOST

> *While you're at it, you should just come in and escort me out, too.*

Nick knows about my airport hold-ups. It would be nice for someone to just show up and make the process shorter.

> *But hey, don't stress it. I'm used to the Lyft rides.*

I'm gonna come and get you. Let me know when you land.

> *You're the best.*

~

> *Just landed.*

Ok, cool. I'm going to leave in a few. I cut some mangoes the other day. Do you want me to bring you some for the ride?

What? Why is he doing this? He hasn't texted me for months, and now he's acting like he found an old childhood treasure of his that he values dearly.

> *Ok, great. Hmm. That sounds good. ;)*
> *Maybe, if they're ripe.*

I almost forgot about you and your weird fruit preferences. 😂

KATHRIN JAKOB

> *Today is my lucky day. Yes! Because you
> know who's already been bloated for the
> last 11 hours.*

It must be the airplane food, but I'm pretty much guaranteed to have gas sitting among 500 other people, high up in the air.

> *Omg, I'm through already! That was so
> quick today! We landed in Terminal 2.*

> *Sweet. The 405 was actually a breeze!
> Almost there.*

And then I see him, pulling up in his blue Honda. It's only been three months, but it feels like forever. He pulls up to the curb, walks around the back of the car, gives me a hug and plants a kiss right on my lips. I'm having déjà vu. Hasn't he done this unexpected, almost inappropriate kiss thing before? What is going on here? Slightly taken aback, I shyly step back. I don't know how to behave. Obviously, I want him to kiss the living hell out of me, but what is he thinking?

"Let me do that." He opens the passenger door for me and grabs all of my luggage and stows it right behind me on the back seat with two swift hand movements. He is so strong. "I like that suitcase."

"Oh, really? Thank you. I've had it for a while now." And no other male person ever liked it. It's a colorful suitcase made of hundreds of Mickey Mouse comics. Eddie hated it. It was 'too childish. 'But I still like it. And it's so easy to find

226

on the conveyor belt between hundreds of boring uniform ones.

I sit in the car, feeling more awkward than in a random Uber. Not knowing what the unwritten code is just yet. Did he think we could just pick up where we left off?

"Oh, here's the mango. I also brought utensils. They're in the same bag." He hands me a bag with mango slices in a Tupperware box and neatly packed silverware.

"Thank you. That's really sweet of you. And thank you for picking me up."

"Thanks for texting me. I'm glad I could come give you a ride."

As we make our way out of the airport circuit, he very casually puts his right hand on my left thigh, just like it used to be. It feels so good, but I can't be happy about this now. I can't make it seem to him like it's OK that he just acts like nothing has happened. Not knowing what else to do, I lightly pat his hand with mine, sitting so naturally comfortable around my thigh.

"What was that?" he asks.

"Uh, nothing, I guess I just don't know how to react just yet. I haven't seen you in so long, and I wasn't sure how it was going to be."

"I know," he thoughtfully says, and then adds, "I've missed you."

"Really?"

"Yes, and you know what," he says as a blue Prius just like mine passes us, "every time I see a Prius I think of you. Wondering how you're doing. Yodelstar."

I chuckle. Yodelstar is my custom license plate. I can't believe he really missed me that much. Every time he saw a Prius? About every third car in LA is a Prius. So, he basically missed me constantly. I have a hard time believing that. He never really texted me.

"Are you hungry? Should we go pick up some food for you?"

"I'm not sure yet."

"OK, just let me know."

At Veggie Grill—I decided I wanted to drag out our 'reunion'—we finally sit face to face. "So what's new?"

Then

Early October:

Eddie walks into his apartment. He had to go return his uncle's car and I waited at his place, hiding his special gift for our one-year anniversary. We definitely had our ups and downs, but I love him, and we're still going strong. I still didn't get my visa. After re-submitting everything two months ago, USCIS is taking their sweet time in sending me a decision, and my anxiety about the whole thing is skyrocketing. I try not to think about it, but I'm not always very successful at keeping myself calm.

"Happy anniversary, baby! Go and find your gift!"

"My gift??" Then he sees the bread crumbs on the floor. "Bunny! What's with all the bread crumbs?"

"You have to follow them. They might lead you to your gift."

"Bunnyyy!!" He follows the pieces of cheap bread that we bought to feed the ducks, and stops in front of the pantry closet. "Now what?" He asks.

"Well, where do you think it could be?" He opens the doors and sees the Jordans box. Hastily but carefully he opens it. "Are these...?"

229

"Bred 11s. You get it now? Bread?"

"Yeesss. Bunny. How? My Bunny got me Bred 11s? Those are so expensive."

That is true. At $500 for a pair of shoes, which didn't cost more than $20 to make, that is quite the price. And quite honestly, I don't have the money to do this. But Eddie has given me so many things, and I wanted to see him happy like this.

He's making a happy dance in his living room space, crawling on the floor, holding one shoe right next to his face, posing with it while I am filming him. Then he comes and gives me the biggest hug. "Bunny, this is the best gift you ever got me."

Most of the gifts I gave him over time weren't really his thing. He rejected a shirt I gave him and told me to send it back. He didn't like the socks I bought and told me to return them, and generally always lets me know when I did a bad job at choosing a present for him. But this time it's all different. "I'm so happy right now." Eddie is gleaming. "I love my Bunny." And that makes me happy, too. For once, things seem to be right again.

~

Mid-October:

We pull up right next to the main door of Eddie's apartment building. "Ok. Hop out Bunny. I need to pick up Uncle's car. I'll be back in a little over an hour." I didn't even know he had to pick up his uncle's car again, and I don't feel prepared to spend all this time at his place by myself. I do have my laptop and my phone, but I've been sitting and lying on that air mattress way too much.

"I'm going to come," I say decidedly.

"No. You can't." That came out a little fast, almost panicky.

"Why not? I don't want to be alone for that long right now," I whine.

"You're sick. And I might have to help him with something in return for borrowing it. Come on, Bunny, I'll be back."

"So that means you'll be gone even longer? And why do you need the car again?"

"Silvio wants us to go to this party in the hills, remember? That's why he rented that tux for me. And I wanna go home when I wanna go home, so I wanna drive there myself tomorrow. I don't know yet when I'll be back, but the longer we sit here debating now, the longer it's gonna take me in the end."

"Fine. But text me when you're on your way back, OK?"

"Yes, Bunny. See you later. Let me see that booty." I open the car door and step out while stretching my butt towards him. He squeezes it and says, "Love you, babe," then drives off.

I just can't shake the thought that something isn't right here, with this car, with Carina. Didn't he drive the same car months ago, and didn't he say it's a 'client's car?' And then he drove the very same model months later, saying it's his uncle's car? It must be a coincidence. I googled this woman's name so many times already, and I haven't found any evidence that suggested Eddie was lying. Why can't I just let it be? I'm going to ruin this relationship with my mistrust. But something in me keeps nagging, so I google her name once more, back inside Eddie's apartment. I find a car sales website that states Carina bought a Mercedes in 2013. Eddie's uncle's car is a Mercedes. Gray. It shows a VIN on the car sales website, but there's no license plate. That would have been too easy. I still think I'm probably wrong, but I know I won't be able to let this go until I rule this possibility out. I google again: *Where to find VIN number of a car.*

... The most accessible place to see it on a car is from the outside at the base of the windshield on the driver's side. Another place to look is the pillar of the driver's side door jamb. Open the door and look at where the door latches to the vehicle body. The passenger side doorpost often displays the VIN...

I hate myself for this sometimes. Why do I always have to play detective? Why can't I just trust my boyfriend? He's picking up his uncle's car, who is a mechanic, who he helps out from time to time. But I'm doing this for me. I will do it, and then it's over because I'll know there's nothing to worry about anymore. Eddie falls asleep before me anyway, and he usually sleeps pretty tightly. I just need an alibi in case he does wake up and look for me. I have another hour before he comes home, so I have time to think.

THE ONE I LOVE MOST

A few hours later, we're both in bed and Eddie is starting to talk crazy stuff to me again. This is how I know he's falling asleep. But I must wait about half an hour to make sure. There's no way I would fall asleep right now anyway, my adrenaline level is up quite a bit and my heart is pounding loudly in my ears. I am so stupid. If he catches me and I don't know how to justify what I'm doing, he's going to be so mad at me and then send me home. Oh, God! I will first go without the keys. Just in case he does wake up. I don't know how to explain myself if he sees me with his uncle's car keys. If he *does* notice I went out, I will say I forgot something in my car that I have to get. Hopefully, the VIN will be visible from the outside of the car and I won't have to unlock it. Worst case, I'll come get the keys and find the VIN by the door. It has to work. I'll be fast. He can't wake up with me gone.

I take a deep but quiet breath and carefully get out of the bed without pushing too much air his way. Air mattresses aren't very gentle when it comes to movement reduction for your sleeping partner. I grab my car keys, so I can verify my alibi, just in case, and slip into my shoes, quietly open and close the door and head down to the garage via the stairs. There it is. Do I really want to know this? I can still turn around. I still have the option of not knowing. But I could also calm my mind right now, right here, just by reading two different VINs.

I pull up the screenshot on my phone that I took earlier and walk around the car to find the number. I really don't know much about cars. I look in the rear window and can't find any number. I need to be fast, but I can't find anything. Oh, no. Am I going to have to go back up and get the keys? And then I remember. It said 'windshield,' not 'rear window.' Duh. I walk to the front of the car, and there it is, right under my nose. My hands are shaking, and I read the first few letters and numbers and compare them. 3Y5WV. They match. And so do the rest of the numbers. It's her car. It's Carina's car. He didn't go to his uncle's. He went to her place. He lied.

Shaking, I make my way back up. It should be clear what I need to do next, but once I'm back in the apartment, I can't move. I sit on the bed. I can't wake him up. What would I say? I can't lie back down. There's no way I can sleep now. I sit cross-legged, rocking back and forth, in an effort to calm myself, I guess. It's dark, but everything is blurry. I start breathing, heavier. In. Out. Louder, and louder. Until. "Bunny?"

"Hmm?" I keep breathing, rocking back and forth.

"What's wrong?"

"I don't know. Umm."

"What's WRONG?" Eddie sounds alarmed now. He jumps up and turns on the light. He sees me sitting there, anxious, small, out of myself.

"Bunny, what is wrong? What happened?" He didn't notice that I went out. My plan worked. But what now? He lied to me about *her*. Aren't I supposed to just leave now? What am I even doing back in the bed? It's too late to leave. But is it ever too late to leave a liar?

"I can't," I stumble.

"You can't what?" He's getting impatient now.

"I'm too scared. I'm scared."

"Don't be scared. You can tell me anything. Just say it."

"I, I...." I breathe again, almost hyperventilating, rocking back and forth, holding my feet with my hands.

"Bunny, dammit, just say it."

"I don't know how."

"Please, god. Speak."

"I know it's Carina's car." It's out. His eyes open wide. "I checked the VIN. You lied to me. I, I don't know what to do now."

Now it's his turn to look nervous and struggle for words, but he collects himself quickly. "I told you it's her car, and you didn't believe me."

"What??" My anxiety turns into anger. "Are you serious? You're just gonna talk yourself out of this now? You never told me that. You always said it was your uncle's car. Why would I not believe you? You keep hiding things. Why?"

"I'm sorry, Bunny. I must have made a mistake then. It wasn't you. But Ines had a problem with me driving her car, and so I just wanted to avoid you being upset, I guess."

"Well, great job."

"I know, I'm sorry. I shouldn't have lied." I almost can't believe he just apologized. "You're right, baby, it's all on me. There's nothing with Carina. She just sometimes lets me borrow the car when she's out of town. We're friends."

"But why did Ines have a problem with her in the first place then?"

"She ran into us at a business meeting at a restaurant once, and she made a whole scene. She thought I was having another affair."

"But you didn't?" I clarify.

"No, I didn't."

"Do you know how much this stressed me out? I *felt* that you weren't being truthful. You'll definitely have to make this up to me." And I think I'm being generous right now in believing him and forgiving him.

"OK, now, don't make a bigger deal out of this than it is, OK? You had me worried here for a good ten minutes, rocking back and forth like some psycho, like some terrible shit happened. And you couldn't open your mouth and talk? Grow up, Kathrin. A grown woman knows how to say things."

I'm small again. How did this turn around so quickly?

"You can apologize by buying me dinner tomorrow," he adds.

"I'm sorry, babe." And then we sleep. *I* was supposed to be mad at *him,* and yet again I ended up being the last one to say sorry.

~

End of October:

"It says my visa application was denied."

"Are you sure?"

"Yes, Ronald emailed me. It's over. What am I going to do now?" I thought the waiting phase was tough, but what I am feeling right now doesn't even compare. I feel like I can't breathe. Somebody took my dream and ripped it into little pieces. And all the money my parents paid to help me stay here. I feel like such a big failure. I have an adult boyfriend and I can't get my life together. Not only that, but I can't even manage to stay here. "I don't know what to do now, babe?"

"It's OK. We will figure it out." How can he be so freaking calm? Does nobody care but me, if I'm here or not? I know my parents would be happy if I returned. But I don't want to. I want to be here. A tear starts rolling down my face, and Eddie walks over to the high top chair I'm sitting on in his kitchen, and puts his arms around me. And then the waterfall starts.

After two minutes, I start hyperventilating, just like when I was a little kid, and I can't get out a full sentence without taking a hasty breath between each word. "I. Just. Don't. Know. What to. Do now."

Eddie tries to calm me. "Right now we're just going to throw a pity party, and you get to feel bad for a few days. After that, we'll find a new solution. How long do you have before you have to leave?"

"Six months, I think."

"See. You'll be fine. That's plenty of time."

"I know, but I wanted to go home for Christmas." At the thought of not being able to spend the holidays with my family for the first time, or as a second choice not being able to come back into the country if I do, I let out another loud cry.

Eddie takes the reins. "Come on, let's go to the store."

He takes me to the store, and he tells me to throw everything in the cart that looks slightly good. Vegan ice cream?—Yes. Chips?—Yes. Frozen vegan burritos?—Five of them. Expensive coconut water?—Yes.

We come home with bags full of groceries and as we empty it all out on the kitchen island, Eddie says, "We are celebrating. Those suckers just don't know yet. You're still going to win. But tonight we're celebrating this shit day of yours." And with that, he put a smile on my face and I can't help but laugh.

"Thank you. I love you."

Now

> *Any more trips coming up this week?*

Nick and I have rekindled our texting game but, so far, have failed to meet in person. The day after he picked me up from the airport, we decided we should go on the hike that we've been planning since the day he ended up lying sick in my bed. But he seems to have been busy with work or going to beaches in Orange County. And my mind has taken me to all kinds of places wondering who he could possibly be going to the beach with. He must have met someone new after all.

We're texting, trying to figure out when to meet, with him having a potential work training coming up soon. But as always, he's slow to respond, so I send a follow-up text.

> *Honestly, I just don't want this to become exactly what it was... And it feels a little bit like it right now.*

Ok. :(

> *Ok?*

> *You can call later if you want, in case there's anything to talk about. I would have much rather talked in person, but I had a feeling I won't see you for another few weeks.*

> *I'll call you.*

The following day, after I get home from work and just before I head out to my movie date with Alana, my phone rings. Nick is calling, on FaceTime video. I position myself on the bed with the help of my FaceTime mirror before answering. I wonder what he wants to talk about. I'm sure he didn't just suddenly change his mind about wanting to be with me. I gave him another out, and he's not taking it? Really, I shouldn't be nervous, but I am. Finally, finding an OK cross-legged position, I hit the green answer button and my carefully practiced serious face immediately turns downside up at the sight of Nick smiling at me. How does he do that? I can't even be mad at him, or at least keep a straight face.

"Hey girl? What's up?"

"What's up? *You* called *me*." I try to sound snappy, but I'm failing.

"I know. How was work?"

"It was good, actually. How was your day?"

"Busy. Work has been a bit hectic, but I can't complain. I did get assigned to go on that trip, by the way."

"Oh, OK." I'm trying to sound like it doesn't faze me.

"So, what movie are you guys watching tonight?"

"The new Lion King. Have you seen it?"

"I have, actually, when I went home to Georgia. You'll have to let me know what you think afterwards."

"OK."

Then there's silence. He didn't call to just make small talk again, did he? That is the very thing I can't deal with anymore. A casual 'Hey how are you? 'text every day, the small talk that lacks the depth, exchange of feelings or real thoughts. And the absence of actual dates or meetups. Meanwhile, my heart is getting attached to the idea of us finally being together again. It's like I have him dangling right in front of my forehead, like a donkey with the carrot on the stick. That's how I feel. Still silence. He wanted to talk about something. Do *I* have to start the serious talk again?

He looks at me with longing eyes, surreptitiously, then smiles.

"What?" I ask.

"I miss you." Oh, really...

"Oh yeah?" I say unbelieving.

"Yeah, and I miss your legs. They look good."

"My legs?" My legs must be my least favorite body part. I started to accept the idea that my butt was welcome in this country, but my legs and I still aren't the best of friends. I am sitting with one of my knees up, he can see them, but that was random.

"Yes. I like your legs. They're good legs."

241

"OK, thank you. I don't really like them that much, but I'm glad you do." Silence again.

"So," I start. "You called. What is it you wanted to talk about?"

"I don't want to lose you, Kathrin. I still want you in my life."

"But how is that gonna work if we never even see each other?"

"Could we just be friends?" He offers.

"Like friends with benefits?"

"There doesn't have to be any benefit. You're one of the really good people in my life and I don't want to lose you." He looks just a tiny bit desperate. Or more like he's sorry. It's just hard to believe all of this when he didn't even reach out to me for months.

"I don't know, Nick. I don't know if we can just be friends. And if anything, I want to be around people who can talk and say what they think, and I feel like you're always just scratching the surface and doing casual talk. I feel like I don't even really know you. I don't know anything about you. I would need you to try to change that. If I'm friends with someone, I want to know them and be able to talk to them and have them talk to me."

"OK."

"And if we're friends," I add, "I think we shouldn't meet at either of our houses because we both know what that would lead to."

"OK, I agree." He is so composed and doesn't make any jokes right now, which is unlike him.

"OK, I have to go now, or I'll be late for my movie date."

"Who are you going with?" Did I detect a hint of jealousy there?

"With Alana."

"OK, have fun, girl. And text me after and let me know what you thought." He's back to his usual carefree and happy self. He doesn't doubt that I'm going with a girlfriend, and he wouldn't care if I didn't.

~

> *Simba became an R&B singer.*

> *And I really could have used someone to throw my legs on.*

I am doing it again. When will I learn??...

Then

"Yaayy, birthday month!"

"Birthdaay moonth!!" Alana and I yell after each other. We're in the car to San Diego on a secret mission. Secret only because Eddie can't know about this. He basically forbid me to go skydiving. *"You're not going! It's dangerous. And if you do, you better make sure I don't know about it."* But it's on my bucket list, as is shaving my head and going to Hawaii. So, I have to do it. Might as well get all the life in while we're young.

"So Eddie always celebrates the whole month of his birthday?" Alana asks.

"Yeah, he's seen that somewhere years ago. Some celebrity doing it I think, and since then, he has lived by it. And he suggested I do the same."

"I mean, why not?" She laughs.

Eddie is out of town this weekend on another trip with the band. And who knows, Carina might be there. But I can't get so riled up about it anymore. I'm starting to feel like I'm a bit paranoid. I wish I could just relax a bit about the whole thing.

"We're gonna have a blast today. He doesn't get to tell you what to do. Or not to do, in this case."

"Yeah, he just can't find out."

"Whatever, Kathl, if he's mad at you for living your life, why do you even want to be with him? After everything he's already put you through..."

"I know. And I appreciate you, always being there. But he's not a bad guy. He just has a different world view sometimes. He's older, and he's lived through more stuff. And I do love him. I haven't felt like this in a long time."

"Ok. You have to know what you're doing. But today we're enjoying *us*. I can't waaaait."

"Me neither. I can't believe we're actually going to be jumping out of a plane. Aaaaah!"

~

Two hours later, I am stretching my index finger far back into my throat. Hopefully, this will relieve some of my nausea. The pull of the parachute opening definitely made me sick, and I figured that knowing how to make my insides come out when I'm nauseous is a good thing this time. Of course, I feel horrible about my choice, considering I was bulimic for a good number of years as a teenager, but desperate times require desperate measures sometimes. The jump was all worth it, though. We flew in a little plane that had the door open the whole time. But once we jumped out, into nothing but air, all the nerves were gone and replaced with pure bliss. We fell so fast. There was so much wind in our faces. It was over so quickly, and when we made it back down to the ground safely, Alana and I both hugged our guides and then ran into each other's arms. What a wonderful experience.

As I come back out from the tiny restroom, several people are gathered around the instruction area, where they also have a computer to put music to the video recordings of our jump. I hear everyone laughing and when I get closer to the screens I see why. Alana's nostrils are displayed on three big screens, wide open and flaring, while her mouth is also stretched wide open, exposing her teeth and making her tongue flop back and forth from one side to the other. All of that is happening to the soundtrack of John Mayer's "Free Falling." I know I just came back from the restroom, but I have a hard time not peeing my pants. It's especially funny because the instructors told us to smile while we were up there and to not open our mouths because the wind would do its thing, and it would look especially horrible in the pictures. Alana is not a rebel usually, but she sure was today, and it just made the start of birthday month even better.

~

Later that month:

I find an A4-sized piece of paper on the kitchen island. Scribbled on there, not very prettily, it says, *'Happy B-day month Bunny!!'* There's also a gift bag. It's still two weeks until my birthday, but I guess since it's birthday month, Eddie is spoiling me early. I look into the gift bag and see a box with golden headphones. I pull them out. Bluetooth headphones.

"What? Babe! Are these for me?"

"Yes, who else, silly? Happy Birthday Month!" I didn't even wish for headphones, and they look expensive.

"Thank you!! Wow! You're crazy."

"That's just the beginning, babe. But a musician needs good headphones, and you don't have any. I hope you'll like them."

"I dooo. Thank you. They're so pretty. I'll have to try them after we get breakfast."

"Yes, let's go."

We take my car. Eddie got into a multiple collision accident last week and his trunk won't fully close anymore. When we get to the juice bar in Long Beach, to get our açai bowls, he stops me from getting out of the car. "Hold on, babe. Can you put these in the glove compartment for me?" He hands me his house keys.

"Sure." As I open the little glove compartment, another A4 note falls into my lap, again saying *Happy B-Day Month!!!* Behind it is a white box with an Apple logo on it. "What?? Something else?"

"Look at it," he prompts me.

I turn it around. It's an iPad Mini. Golden, matching with the headphones. "What? Babe? Are you crazy?? This is too much!"

"You don't want it?" He grabs it from me.

"No, I do." I quickly take it back and keep looking at it. "It's just... Wow! I didn't expect so much."

"That's how birthday month works. I told you. Now you know."

I grin at him, a big smile. Has he always been this sweet?

"Now, put that back in there. Let's get some food first. And give me these back." He motions for his keys.

"I thought you wanted me to put them in there?"

"I just needed a reason for you to open the glove compartment because you wouldn't do it during the ride, silly."

~

One week later:

I sit on Eddie's toilet with the fluffy white bath rug between my toes when I notice there's no toilet paper in the holder. "Babe, there's no toilet paper," I yell. "Could you bring me some?"

"I'm out, Bunny," he yells back. "Just use the wipes."

"Nooo, I'm peeeing."

"Well, I don't have anything else. Just use the wipes."

"I can't wipe wet with wet. I'd rather just shake it off."

"Babe, just use the wipes, I'm telling you."

"I don't want to. Do you have any paper towels left?" Even those are gone. He usually has a big roll in his bathroom.

"I don't have those either," he shouts back.

THE ONE I LOVE MOST

I shake most of the moisture off and with my pants down wobble over to the cabinet under the sink, which is too far to reach from the toilet. Empty. How? He always buys a year's supply. After wobbling back to his ceramic throne, I sit back down, and grab the box of wipes. I don't use these a lot regardless, but if that's the only option right now, so be it. I open the top lid, but no sheet sticks out. I take the box apart and instead of a package of wet toilet paper, another Apple box greets me. "Aaaaah, babe."

Eddie storms into the bathroom with his phone in his hand, filming me, pants down on his toilet with a brand-new iPhone in my hand. "Finally! She found it."

"How long has this been in here?"

"For a while." He rolls his eyes. "Now I can finally put my toilet paper back in here. I thought you'd never find it. I was waiting for you to use the wipes, but apparently you never do. So, I thought if I took all the toilet paper away, you'd have to use them."

I laugh heartily. "Oh my God, I'm not as obsessed with wipes as you are."

"What do you think? Do you like it?"

"Do I like it? Of course!! You're crazy! And it matches the iPad and the headphones. Everything in gold. I love you. Thank you!" I hug my new possession.

I did tell him that I needed a new phone because my old one was starting to act up. But after he already gifted me the headphones and the iPad, I really didn't think a phone was still in there. And how did he do all of this anyway? It's not like he swims in money. I ask him, and he just says, "Don't worry about that, babe. Let that be my concern." And then he slips me another item in gold.

"Oh my gosh, what? What is this now?"

"It's a Mophi, a rechargeable phone case. It's like a portable charger, but you don't have to carry it around separately."

"You're the best. You know that, right?"

"Of course I do. I told you I'm not playing around."

Now

Dear Nick,

I hope your trip home was good!

There are some things I haven't said yet. Half of them simply because there wasn't the time, the other half because I was afraid of your reaction. At this point, I feel like there's really nothing left to lose. I don't know how long this letter will be, and I don't expect you to read it. I'm writing this for myself. I just want it all said because I feel like I never got enough time with you. Having you in my life, the way things are right now, seems to just not be good for me. I want so much more from you than you are willing or able to give me. I am, of course, still working on myself, my life, my goals, and hopefully that'll never change. At the same time, I have so much I want to give and so much I want to share, but I can't do that with you. You are simply too close to what I want in a man. It's like the biggest tease. And I keep my expectations low, but somehow I still get disappointed.

Right now, there's already plenty of uncertainty in my life. Never really knowing for sure if I'll get to stay in this country is one of them. Not knowing when my living situation will change is another one. And my career itself is ever-changing, too. Deciding to keep you in my life as a 'friend,' who, as far as I know, I might not get to see for another few months, just adds one more of those things that I can't predict, but I am hoping for. I need more certainty. People, things, and events I can rely on. Right now, I am not strong enough to handle this all at once. So if you don't

251

know what it is you want from me or if I get mixed signals constantly, I can't do this right now. I am very stubborn, and I don't give up easily, but I have to choose myself first.

Having you in my life (by text, on the phone, in person) reminds me of all the things I want so badly but can't have. I was always a fan of your kisses! So good! And the way you pick me up. The way you look at me when I have certain underwear on. The way I feel when we're together. I was so sure in the beginning that you were falling in love too. I could feel it. And I could see it in the way you looked at me. But now I'm not so sure. I'm not sure anymore if my gut feeling about this was ever right. Because the thing is, if you really want to be with someone, you'll make it happen. Despite all the baggage or little time or other priorities. I know I am talented, I am pretty, I am kind, I have a big butt, I'm funny sometimes, I have good taste in food... And I know you mean those things when you say them. But the bottom line is: I am not enough for you. Because if I was, you wouldn't have let me go. I understand there might be other things you haven't told me. And I always wanted to know more, or dig deeper, but I can't make you open up, nor can I make you want me in ways that you do not. The two of us can't be friends. It doesn't seem to work. I want more, and I can try to convince myself otherwise as much as I want, but I always end up back here, hurt. I feel like I'm chasing you, and it makes me feel stupid and like I don't respect myself enough.

I don't know why you're 'not ready' or what exactly you're not ready for, but I'm sure you'll be when you meet someone who just makes you forget everything else. Because anything can be done if you really want it. But it takes two. I know we could have figured things out, if it would've ever gone that far. I wanted that challenge, but I think you've made it clear that I'm wasting my time trying to make something happen that only I want. I can't give away small pieces of myself anymore. I want *someone to want all of me. And I would have wanted it to be you. That's all, Nick. I wish things were different, but there's always a lesson in everything. I'm sad I don't get to keep you, but you were never mine to begin with.*

Much, much love,

Kathrin ♡

Tears are rolling down my face as I read through my letter out loud, sitting in my car, before I put it in the envelope. I will actually send this letter. I need to say these things and I need to find closure. And it finally all needs to be said.

Then

My last two fake lashes are hanging on by a thread, and honestly, I want them gone. Having the lash extensions in the beginning was pretty great. They had a deal in a town close to our village and I decided to treat myself, to be sparkly for Christmas, even though Eddie wasn't there with me this time. Our plan was to not spend another Christmas apart, but his gigs in LA around the holiday time, and on New Year's Eve, kept him from traveling all the way to Europe. That, and his budget. He hasn't even bought furniture yet, let alone the car he was boasting about last year when he met my parents, talking about all the money he was saving. Somehow things seem to be taking a bit longer than he anticipated.

It's been a week now since I've been back home in Pasadena. For the first time in a long time, on a tourist visa. Since I didn't want to miss the holidays with my family, the travel visa was my only way of coming back right now. Roland, my lawyer, resubmitted all of my documents, in the hopes that this second time, another officer would judge my case differently and grant me an artist visa after all.

Eddie is currently rocking his brand-new green soccer jersey for the German team. He asked me to bring him one, and even though it really wasn't within my budget, I couldn't help but get it anyway to see the happy dance that he's performing right now. And yet something feels weird. He was excited when I got back. I almost drove to see him in Las Vegas on New Year's Eve, the day I got back. His mom was there, too. But I had a feeling he wouldn't have liked it, me showing up unannounced. And I was tired and jet-lagged. When I saw the pictures a day later of him posing with the fans, then him and the band, and then him and his mom, and... Carina, my stomach turned around quickly. We have talked about this so many times, and he has reassured me countless times of what I've wanted to hear. That there's no reason to worry. She's simply a friend of the band and a person he knows through work somehow. Still, it stings. I return my attention to him shuffling on the floor with the socks my mom knitted for him. "Buunnnaaaay," he yells. "Dance with me."

"You know I don't dance." I retreat to the bed. Maybe I'll be normal again tomorrow.

I'm looking up at the ceiling as I'm lying on the air mattress, waiting for him to brush his teeth and join me. We just bought a new one a few weeks ago. There was a hole in the old one. We did try to fix it, but we woke up on the floor the next morning. After trying to fix it a second time, and almost sinking immediately, we both laughed so hard I almost got a cramp, followed by a Walmart visit, where I was chosen to pay for the new lux air bed. I wish he would just buy a cheap mattress for now.

I remember having a horrible dream last night. There was something he wasn't telling me, and more than any action, the dream consisted mostly of a feeling. A feeling of loneliness, being scared, and the lack of love. I really don't feel loved by him anymore on most days. I feel like lately I've been chasing the person he showed me in the beginning, the very loving man who would have done anything for me, but now he makes me work so hard for his attention. I don't pray a lot, but right now, I need guidance. Keeping my ears alert to him returning from the bathroom, I keep my gaze facing up and interlock my fingers on top of my chest as I whisper. *"Please, God, Universe, if there is somebody else out there that I am supposed to be with, let me know tomorrow. But also, please give me a sign if Eddie is the man I am supposed to be with, within the next day. I just need to know, and I am so tired of being insecure and wondering. Please just give me a sign. Thank you!"*

I hear Eddie's footsteps and light switches clicking, and I quickly unlock my hands and grab my phone to act like my normal self. He doesn't need to know how I feel or what I'm thinking right now. He would just call me sensitive again, and we might end up having an argument, and I really want to sleep well tonight. Without saying anything, he grabs his iPad and puts it on his chest while I'm scrolling through my Instagram feed.

"Can we watch that documentary I've been wanting to show you, babe?"

"Tomorrow, Bunny," he answers absentmindedly. "I'm almost knocked out. We'll make it an us-morning, OK?"

"OK."

I do want to make love, I want his attention, and his affection. But I know how tired he is today, after all his gigs, and I let it go without even trying this time. Five minutes later, I hear him snoring.

It's 7:56am when we wake up the next morning. The first thing I do is grab my phone. Eddie didn't even hold me last night. He always spoons me and asks me to 'put the booty on him.' Not last night.

"I'm gonna brush my teeth, and then I have to go, Bunny. I'm getting my rims fixed, I have an appointment. You can come if you want."

"Mmmm," I mumble. I'm still not quite awake yet. I'm grumbling while trying to decide whether I can get myself out of the bed and ready fast enough to come along. But before I can make up my mind, he already answers the question for me.

"But you're not ready. Just stay in bed, and I'll be back."

With the hope of getting our movie time in a little later and the possibility of a little romantic time then, I doze off again, and let him leave to get his car looked at, and fixed. With a quick kiss on my forehead, I transition back into dreamland.

I'm in a hotel room. I'm not sure what I'm doing here. There is another room attached. I open the door and walk in. I see him on top of a curvy, older lady. They are both naked, now spooning. It's Carina. I hear them moaning. It's disgusting. I'm appalled. I'm shocked, I don't know what to do. I am panicking. My heart is starting to beat faster, and

I want to scream, but I can't. My heart feels like it wants to stop. I hear myself making a sound, loud breathing and painful groans are finally coming out of my mouth and I wake up.

Finally. It felt too real. This was the worst dream in a very long time. I feel horrible. I try to fall back asleep and get my mind off of it, but even after half an hour I can't. That movie my brain created gave me too much anxiety to be able to relax again. I take my iPad and decide to watch an episode of my super cheesy German telenovela. Maybe that will take my mind off this crazy dream and make me feel somewhat normal again.

The fact that everybody on that show is lying and cheating actually doesn't really help either, but at the same time, it makes me feel a bit like 'home 'and reminds me of our little afternoon family ritual. Right before the dramatic, climactic end of the episode, Eddie calls.

"Babe, this is taking longer than I thought. I have to go somewhere else to get the bolts of the rim fixed, but first they're going to do a little more work here. So, why don't you get dressed and come up here, so we can get some food together?"

"OK, that will work, but give me like 15 more minutes before I leave. I'll let you know when I'm on my way."

I finish the episode and quickly get dressed, brush my teeth and comb my hair. Just enough to look presentable. I make sure to wear the black Levi's jeans he bought me, though. The ones he loves because they make my butt look even nicer and rounder. I feel like I am constantly working to get the affection from him that I know I got so many times before. There has to be a way to make him love me like that again. Like in the beginning. I'm almost out the door when I get a text.

> *Bunny, sing the pancake song.*

> *Why?*

But knowing he doesn't like unnecessary questions and wouldn't answer anyway, I just hit the record button in WhatsApp and start singing the song from Adventure Time that's become somewhat of a joke online. I end on a high note with '*pancaaaaakes.* 'My voice is still raspy and sounds like I woke up the minute before I started singing.

> *That was horrible, I couldn't even get in my lil 'groove because you sounded like you were pooping.*

> *I'm leaving now.*

Knowing now that the work on his car is taking longer than expected, I scrap the idea of any romantic or sexy time between us this morning and replace it with the idea of enjoying lunch together. We'll both have to leave for work in the early afternoon, him to go practice at Silvio's studio in Hollywood, and me to the school. He's already waiting at America's Tire when I get there. "What do you want to eat, little bunny?"

"An açai bowl. I haven't had breakfast yet."

"OK, here's some money. Go get your bowl and meet me at Chipotle after."

"OK." We're so romantic these days.

As we're eating, he's talking about Seattle. He won't stop researching and talking about it. I just wish I had been there before, or that we could go there together, so I'd have a chance to share his excitement. If he's so serious about moving there, I'll have to get on board sooner or later. His phone rings for the third time now, but he's not answering. I'm curious, but I decide to hold off from asking. "Commercial calls," he says as he pushes the decline button again.

"Is it OK if I come back tonight? We didn't really have much time together at all, or get to do what we wanted to."

"Of course you can."

"OK. Cool. Let's go to Sprouts real quick. It's sushi day and I want to grab something to go, for work," I suggest.

"Sure."

"I'll just also run to the restroom real quick while we're there."

"OK, Bunny, but don't take too long."

With my pack of sushi in my hands, I find him already standing in the line at the register. He's on the phone when I approach him from behind. I catch a quick glimpse of his message thread and one of the first four names on there, again, is Carina. But we've been through this. Nothing to worry about, remember Kathrin? But did I just see a heart emoji? Or what was that? Was it yellow? *Was* it a heart? Am

I tripping now? It's too small for me to possibly see. He didn't have the message opened, it was just the preview of the last message she sent him. I am completely off today. It is not a heart. It's probably just normal 'happy emojis.' Stop being crazy and paranoid. I know this wouldn't end well if I started asking again right now.

After reading his emails I have no right to demand to see his texts, and I try to avoid risking not being able to come back here tonight, so I decide to let it go. My heart is pounding. Actually, I feel quite light-headed. "I need to get some water, I'll be right back."

"OK, babe."

As I make my way towards the water aisle, I don't feel like I'm in my body. And my thoughts seem to be an entity of themselves right now, spinning and making theories and asking questions. I probably just need some space and a good meditation and once I'm back later I'll be fine. That horrible dream is probably still affecting me.

I drive Eddie back to American Tire, ask for a kiss through the window and tell him 'See you later. 'It's not the most loving goodbye we've shared, but I will come back later and then things will be alright. We will finally cuddle and make love, and I will feel secure again. I have his keys, I can come back anytime I'm done with work.

~

I'm five exits away from the end of the freeway. Almost there. I can't wait to be there with him and have everything be back to normal after this somehow weird and crazy day.

I just want to be held, and I just want him to tell me he loves me. We'll make love and everything will be the way it always is, or the way it is when things are good.

I haven't heard from him all day, which feels weird but is not unusual. He does turn his phone off when he's at rehearsal, but usually the rehearsals aren't that long. It's 7:30pm already. I went to Whole Foods to grab two slices of pizza. Nothing else looked appealing with their never-changing buffet. And even though I picked off the garlic pieces which looked like eggplants at first, I'm still worried that Eddie will accuse me of 'stank breaf 'again and use it as an excuse not to kiss me. This has been happening quite a bit lately, actually. He's also called it 'dragon breath 'or 'spitting fire 'and I'm honestly worried at this point that I do have a serious case of halitosis. Just the thought of it makes me cringe.

I remember William's breath, thinking of it, and a quick shudder runs down my back. In hindsight, I can say I'm happy that he got so mad about me dating Eddie and not telling him about it right away. We haven't spoken since, and I finally see the situation for what it really was now. He was never really going to help me with my EP or give me free studio time. Not if he didn't get something else in exchange first. I'm pretty sure he wanted more than an open ear or a ride home.

Apart from that, I'm also worried I have serious mental problems. I always knew I'm somewhat insecure, but what I experienced today felt like paranoia. At least that's what I imagine it to feel like. When I got home earlier, I immediately searched YouTube for a guided meditation that would help me. After 20 minutes of "guided self-healing for anxiety and paranoia" I felt a slight relief that lasted for about five minutes. Then that underlying feeling of something being horribly wrong came right back. It was overcast today, though. And I am pretty sensitive to that. But either way, I can't be like this. Maybe it is best to talk to a therapist after all. The closest I got to therapy was when my mom sent me to a guided self-help group for eating disorders back in my bulimia days. But I didn't last long there.

When I told Alana how I felt, she just said, "Oh Kathrin," which is what she always says when I'm making life harder for myself. I told her about my dream and my fears. "You're probably just being a bit paranoid," she said. There it was. It's clear to everyone, including me. *I* am the problem. And as much as I don't want to be seriously paranoid, I do hope she's right. I can fix *me*, but if this was intuition and there's something *to* my doubts, I don't know what I would do.

My phone rings. Eddie. Finally. "Hey! I was wondering where you were. I haven't heard from you all day."

"I'm sorry, babe. I actually went out to dinner with my old friend Pong. And guess what? He offered your boy a regular gig, starting in May."

"Oh wow, that's great. I'm happy for you, babe! I also ate as well, I wasn't sure if you already had dinner."

"Yep. I'm on my way home, passing Downtown right now. You can go in if you want. You have the key."

"OK."

I pull into the alley parking lot, and he continues talking. "So Pong has this situation with a lady. They've been together for five years now, but they don't even like each other, and she's just using him for the money. I mean, there's always two sides to each story, but man, he just doesn't know how to break up with her. He told me they sleep with a pillow between them. And now he has this other lady coming from Korea, and he's planning to be with her."

"Wow. That's crazy. That sucks. But at the same time, you know, no matter how stupid she is and how much they don't like each other—and of course I don't really know the whole story either—but no matter what, he should just break up with her. Because whether she's in love or not, it hurts to be cheated on. If a man feels like he needs to sleep with somebody else, then please just break up first with whomever you're with. Everything else is just asshole behavior and not necessary."

"Yeah, and now he has this other lady coming and doesn't know how to handle the situation. But let me get off the phone, babe. I'll be there in 20 minutes."

"OK, see you very soon." I grab my things from the car, including the pecan tart I bought for him, which I know he loves, lock my car and walk around the building to get to the front door.

With my hands full, I manage to also get his mail out and walk into the apartment, with a strange thought popping into my head. *What if this was the last time you*

came in here like this? Not minding my crazy thoughts all
too much, as they come and go constantly, I put my things
on the floor and start eating the rest of my pizza, at least
the not so garlic tasting parts of it. As I'm humming along
to Spotify, playing Adele's new album, the door opens and
startles me. I didn't expect him just yet.

"Hey. You scared me."

"Sorry babe."

"All good. Hey. Are you gonna shower tonight?"

"Yeah, I'll have to."

"OK, let's do it now. I wanna shower with you."

Eddie is in the bathroom turning on the water in the
shower while I take off my clothes in the hallway, still
singing Adele's *"All I ask."* For some reason, I can't get this
song out of my head. And still, I don't feel quite relaxed,
even though we're both back here. But I know everything
will be fine again soon. It's just that there's something in
the air.

In the shower, we keep discussing the situation Pong's
gotten himself into. That he just can't get himself to tell his
girlfriend that he wants to leave her. With one half of my
brain tuned in to the conversation, the other half is still
trying to figure out what's wrong with me and how I can
calm myself down.

"And that's why you should never move in with your
girlfriend until or unless you get engaged. Because these
things happen, and then you have a dumbass situation that
you don't know how to get out of."

"But shouldn't you live with somebody first to actually find out if you wanna marry them and if it can work out?" I ask in return.

"You can figure that out like this as well." *So much for moving in. I'll probably be driving from Pasadena to Pedro and back for at least another year.*

Then an idea pops into my head, which I've had several times before, ever since I promised Eddie not to go sniffing around his phone or iPad again. What if, while the phone was charging, I could just go in and open things without the passcode? It always looks as if it doesn't lock while he's charging it, and he just put it out there to charge. *If I shower fast and get out, and he'll clean the shower, there'll be enough time for me to go and check if, possibly, I have access to his text messages.* I just want to know that I have nothing to worry about. I need to relax my mind, and apparently his words don't do it for me anymore.

"I'm done. You can finish and clean it," I say with some sass to make it believable. I usually stay in the shower longer than him. I wrap my hair in the smaller, still way too big towel and wrap the 'big 'big towel around my body, rub back my cuticles and clean my ears with some q-tips. At the very least, I have to do the usual. I don't want it to seem like I'm up to something. After that, I feel confident to leave the bathroom and I nervously approach his little window pane where he puts the phone for charging.

My hands are shaking. My whole body is, really. Just like I thought, the phone is lit up and when I touch it, I have access. No passcode needed, nothing is locked. My heart starts pounding ten times faster. Do I really want to do this? I promised him I would stay away from this and if I ever did it again, he could just break up with me. That was my own deal. But he doesn't have to know. I'll find that text I thought I saw earlier. Then I'll see with my own eyes that everything is alright, and then I'll leave the phone alone. By the time he comes out of the bathroom, everything will be back in its place and will look like I never even touched it.

I open his messages. I don't have to scroll down to see Carina's. I see exactly what I thought I saw earlier, only this time I'm certain. A heart, a kiss emoji and another heart. I open it. Words are sticking out of these messages, jumping right at my eyes, like sharp blades. *"Babe "Thx babe."* *"Goodmorning babe, could you...?"* My heart is sinking, way below where I ever thought it could fall to. It feels similar, but way worse, than the time I found out he lied about driving her Mercedes. I try to scroll up further to read more but stop at a text that says, *"I'll be in Pedro at 10/11 the earliest tonight."*

What is this??? What the hell is going on here?? I was right the whole time, and he made me believe I was paranoid??? I start breathing heavily. I don't know what to do. I am naked, wrapped in two towels at a man's place who promised me the stars in the night sky, who I thought I wanted to spend the rest of my life with, who said he was done with all the bullshit he has done in his life. I feel too weak to scream, but not able to hold it in. I am breathing in and out heavily, making a noise that, even to myself, sounds like I am suffocating. I am hyperventilating.

Then I hear his voice. "What is going on?" He's running out of the bathroom, still naked. He's coming towards me and looks from me to his phone in my hand, back to me. There's nothing I could possibly say. All these questions. I asked them before. And he always gave the same answers. He is unscrupulous. Is there anything I could say that would get him even close to understanding how I feel right now? He's an arm's length away from me and I decide to do the only thing I haven't done yet to show my desperation, disappointment, and anger. My right arm lunges out, and with a swing, my hand lands on his cheek. *Smack*. For a second, I lose my sense of orientation. He's stepping towards me and just for a moment I'm sure he's about to hurt me, but then he falls into his own step and holds me with both of his hands.

"Why are you calling her babe??" I am too upset to cry, and too confused to move or talk normally.

"I call everybody babe." That must be the most stupid excuse I've ever heard.

"You call everybody babe? Her? And how come I don't know about that?"

Then he grabs his phone, still naked, unplugs it and starts dialing.

"What are you doing? What are you doing?" I demand to know a second time, but louder.

"I'm calling the cops." Panic starts to replace my anger.

"No, don't. I'll leave right now. I'll leave you alone, but don't call them." I start talking faster. "It's all good. I'm already leaving." I start putting on clothes, even underwear. I usually don't put on underwear at night, but I need to be ready for the worst case.

"Yes, my name is Eddie James. I'm calling because my girlfriend hit me in the face and I want to press charges."

Again, I reiterate, "I'm already leaving. You don't have to do this."

"Kathrin Jakob." Pause. "26." Pause.

I can't believe this is happening. I actually hear another voice coming out of his phone. He isn't just playing. I remember him telling me before he would call the police if I ever put my hands on him. He said: "That's just the rules of this country. If you damage my property or hit me and I call the police, it's my word against yours and depending on whoever calls first, the other one will be arrested. So don't think it's not possible. You'll see. You'll see if you keep it up. You were lucky nobody called the police on you when you were hammering on my door and screaming in the alley in the middle of the night." That was the night he locked me out.

He hangs up the phone and walks out the front door. What is happening right now? I made a mistake. I should have trusted him. He could have explained, if I asked first, instead of just hitting him in the face. He already called them. I have to face this now. But first I have to apologize. In my Victoria's Secret pajamas and a vest, I follow him outside. "What are you doing here? Why are you outside?"

"I'm cooling off my cheek. It hurts."

"I didn't even really hit you that hard. I was just so angry. I'm sorry, babe. It just doesn't make sense."

"Go home, Kathrin."

"Please. No. Please just, let's be OK."

"Go home, Kathrin."

"Why are you calling me Kathrin? You never call me that."

"That's your name. Kathrin. Isn't it? I told you that you'd ruin this relationship with your insecurities and trust issues. You did it."

I don't know what to do. I squat on the pavement outside his apartment complex, crying. Quite hysterically. But I can't go. I need him.

"Take your car and go home."

"But you already called the cops on me, I can't disappear now."

"Do you really think I called the cops on you?"

"I don't know. Didn't you? You were on the phone with someone."

"I'm not gonna say anything anymore. Just go home."

But I can't. I know what happened the last time I drove after he broke up with me, and I won't have another accident with this car.

Then they pull around the corner. Two police officers step out of their car, slowly walking towards us. "Are you the one who called?" One of them asks Eddie.

"Yes, Sir."

"OK, we will be asking you questions, separately from each other."

I know that if I just tell them the truth, everything will be fine. I will admit that I made a mistake, I will promise to never do it again, and that I will go home right now. They will understand that Eddie's ego was hurt and that was the only reason he called them. He's not hurt. I face one of the officers.

"Can you tell me what happened?" he asks.

I answer calmly. "I read his texts, I know I shouldn't have. And I saw something that made it look like he was cheating. And I didn't know what else to do, so I smacked him on the cheek." I feel so humiliated.

"And did this ever happen before?"

"No, never," I am shaking.

My mind still can't grasp what's happening. Not only did Eddie just break up with me, I also just found out he probably cheated on me this whole time, that he was lying to me all this time, and then he called the cops on me? Despite everything, I am surprisingly calm. Calmer than you would think you'd be in a situation like this, at least. Officer Martinez asks me to stay where I am. He walks over to the officer who questioned Eddie, and they talk to each other in low voices, discussing something.

When they come out of their little bundle of two and lift their heads towards us, the other officer asks: "Mr. James, do you want Ms. Jakob arrested?" I look at him, still searching for the man I loved so much and who promised to love me just as much. He has to say 'No.' He can't possibly do this to me. This is enough to make me leave. Enough for me to never do this again. I look at him desperately, hoping he'll save me from this situation he created. I just want to get my things and go home. Of course, he won't actually have me arrested for slapping him in the face. Before I can say anything to him, he has already opened his mouth and says, "Yes!"

"Please, don't do that. I'll go home. I'll leave you alone. You can still take it back. Please!"

"He can't take it back anymore," the police officer says. "We have to take you with us now."

The policemen guide me to their car. "Please face the car, we will put you in handcuffs now." Eddie is watching, from the same spot, right outside his front door. Just standing there, as if one big problem is being removed from his life. I hear the policemen talk: "We'll need somebody to search her, call somebody." Then into their walkie-talkie, "Yes, we have a female here, and she needs to be searched."

Now

"Jump up." Nick positions himself in front of the two stairs leading up to Anne's apartment. He doesn't have to tell me twice. I jump on his back, and we run through the courtyard, just two doors further, to my new apartment, my very own place. I still can't believe it actually worked out. I got my dream apartment. Even when there seemed no hope, with Eddie messing up my credit score, and me not working on fixing it for too long. I convinced them to make me a sole tenant. It's still hard to grasp.

"Woah, Kathrin. This is you?" Nick says as we walk in.

I nod proudly. "Mhm."

"It's big."

"I know. That's why I wanted this place so bad. Everybody else always kept saying 'you'll find something else, something better, 'but they haven't seen this place yet."

"I love it."

"Thank you. I really do, too."

"So what should we get first?"

"I think the bed will be the most important. Especially the mattress."

"OK, let's get it."

He is going on a work trip tomorrow, but he agreed to help me move all my furniture and the heavy things. It's in the same complex, but up the stairs, and I definitely can't move these things alone. His Herculean strength is perfect for this.

~

After I actually did send the letter to him by mail, he sent me a text. He thanked me for the letter, but said he understands that I wrote it for my own sake, and he said he's sorry, and that he can understand my frustration. I thanked him for letting me know that he received it. And then the confusion continued.

> *So do we not talk anymore, or how does this go?*

> *Oh boy, idk. I'm not gonna ignore you, and I don't want you to ignore me. But since we're not on the same page, it's probably better if we don't communicate daily and flirt and try to make plans that we can't make happen.*

> *Understood.*

> *Are you tired of this/me?*

> *Kathrin, no. I'm not tired of you. I won't ever get tired of you.*

THE ONE I LOVE MOST

Felt like it.

I feel like you would if I actually constantly said what I wanted to say. But that's ok. This is not the time, and I respect you not being ready.

You can say whatever you want to me. I know that's easier said than done, but you've earned that right with me. :)

Side note: Tell me what you think about this cover...

He sent me a link to a cover by Lianne La Havas. Nick is infatuated with music, especially good covers of songs. He could spend hours listening to good acoustic songs, and he always picks the most romantic ones. In the beginning, I thought that this was him trying to send subtle messages, but he said it's not.

I love Lianne La Havas and I like that cover.

And it's not the telling you part. It's the fact that I don't seem to get much back. I'm trying so hard to figure you out, but you won't let me. I don't see a point in saying everything anymore if it's not for actually finding a solution. I can express myself in therapy or with friends. But saying things to you makes me hope that I'll get some kind of answer I haven't gotten before... And I don't think I will. So rambling on like this

> *(which I can do a lot of) makes me feel stupid at some point. Because I'm the only one of us two who does it, which means I'm over-investing for no reason, and therefore I shouldn't.*

He basically asked for it. I finally started voicing all of my thoughts.

> *But when we talk, I give you my thoughts. I know we don't talk a lot or haven't often, but I feel like when we do, I express myself. I don't feel like you ramble for the record, and just because I don't overly express myself doesn't mean that I don't care about you and think about you. For example... I looked at your IG story last week and saw that you were in the studio recording. Then I saw you sitting on the lap of some guy. I didn't like that and actually got upset. But then I had to check myself because I don't have a right to get upset. But I felt how I felt.*

I didn't know he watched my stories. I was hoping, for some reason, that that day he would. Sitting on my friend's lap when I had a bad day was not a setup for him to see, but it might as well have served a double purpose. And somehow the jealousy he expressed gave me so much hope and made me feel special, after I had already started to draw a finish line with my letter.

> *Yes, you're not a stone and I appreciate that. You validate my feelings when I share them, and you express things that seem to be easy enough to share for you. Except for last time when I actually got you upset and you more or less ignored me. I am in love*

with you, Nick. All I ever wanted was to know where I'm at with you, but it seems to be this limbo. Because when I do try to pull away, something brings me back, and then you tell me how much you like me or that you got jealous. It's very confusing. I appreciate you being a good and nice guy. But you don't have to do that for me. You can be upset. I would be upset too if I saw you with another girl. I get jealous just thinking about it. But it doesn't make sense to me. You want me, but you don't want me. Experience is telling me you just don't care 'enough.' while I can sense that to some degree you do.

You're right. I care about you and have feelings for you to a certain extent... not to the extent that you feel for me, I know. For a while, I thought about you and asked myself if I was falling in love... because those feelings were very present and real. Kathrin, I pushed you away. And I did some self reflecting. I pushed you away because we were getting closer and closer... And I got scared. For the record, it was a natural 'closer.' Anyway, I realized that my issue is with commitment. I know it stems from what I experienced during my childhood, but that's something I need to deal with. I don't know how just yet (one of my good friends says I should talk to a counselor, but the pride in me won't let me). I don't know Kathrin. This is me, and I'm flawed, and I have things to work on before I begin to allow someone in. Fully in.

*I knew that all this time. I had a feeling.
THANK YOU for sharing this and saying this
because it helps me trust myself more. Even
though I was thinking this could be what's
happening, I still wasn't sure because you
said you had girlfriends before. So I
convinced myself it was something that had
to do with me. We're all flawed. Most
people are just too afraid to show it and say
it out loud. My female nature wants to
cuddle you and love you and help you
through whatever it is you have to work
through. But I can't do that, not without your
permission. And I can't force you to let me
in. I don't even need to be let in all the way
right away, but because of my issues, I'm
scared to be dropped again and left behind.
My biggest lesson in life seems to be
patience, and I'm slowly getting better at it. I
seem to like tricky situations and honestly if
I knew that at least part of you wanted to
try I'd be there in whatever capacity you
could allow. Just know this: You are so very
strong (not just physically ;)) and you are so
hard on yourself. So much discipline, so
much devotion for your job and health and
being a happy person. But showing what's
inside and admitting that you're scared of
something or whatever you think your
"flaws" are shows that by just expressing
that and allowing that part of yourself you
will move through it, and eventually past it.
But the only way is through. I have so much
love for you, and sometimes I'm hurting just
because I can't express it, not because I'm
not getting it back.*

And just like that, it's like I never wrote that letter. He confirmed what I thought the reason was for him letting me go earlier this year. I know he's just broken. Like we all are. More than I thought, maybe. But I know the feelings are there, and I can't ignore that. I can run from this all I want, but I always end up in the same place again, so I might as well stop resisting.

~

After just a few trips between the old and my new apartment, everything is in my new place. All my furniture and all the heavy bags I couldn't carry alone. I'll still have to put things together, but I've done that by myself before. We also planned to finally get that hike in together today. It's my birthday month, and I'm so happy with how it is starting out.

"You know we'll have to do a housewarming, right?" I say cheekily.

"Kathrin, you know I'm leaving tomorrow. I think this might have to wait."

"OK. Let's go hiking then."

Echo Mountain is one of my favorite trails. It's a good workout with an astonishing view on top. Almost all the way to the top, Nick reminds me of his time restriction.

"We're almost there. I promise we'll be back in time," I assure him.

We finally walk around the last little curve and straight up the trail, where the familiar rusty wheels and remnants of an old railway greet us. There was a huge house up here once. We walk around and take in the view.

"We should take a picture," I suggest.

"OK." He doesn't seem very eager, but he also doesn't have any objections. I think, so far, there's only one picture of us together. The selfie I took in the car when he picked me up from the airport after my sister's wedding. He never once took a picture of us, and thinking about it makes me sad. Maybe the signs were there all along, and I really just didn't want to see them. I ask another couple if they could take a picture of us and hold on to Nick, like I wish I could every day. I wish I could post these pictures with a simple #mancrushmonday hashtag in two days. But he's not mine, and I'd only make a fool of myself, virtually drooling over a man who doesn't want me.

"I need to pee," he announces on our way back down.

"OK, we're almost down again. It might be hard to find a spot here." The trail is very narrow and there aren't any bushes to hide behind.

"It's OK. I think I can hold it... Actually. Stay there and watch out."

"Oh my god, you're gonna do it?" But he already pulled out his instrument and starts tinkling down the hill. I look the other way, making sure no other hikers are close enough to see him. Then I look at him and can't help but laugh. "I hope this won't land on anyone's head."

"Girl, you're supposed to watch."

"Sorry," I giggle.

"Too late now. All done." He inhales sharply. "Huh? Did you hear that?" He alarms me.

"Hear what?" I answer, sharpening all my senses at once. He looks off to his right, then lifts his right leg and lets out the biggest fart I have heard since I sat on the living room couch with my dad the last time. He immediately laughs, and the whole situation cracks me up so much I almost pee my pants. "Oh boy, you are something."

On the way home, Nick plays DJ in the car, while I drive. "Oooh, I love this song," he exclaims. "Beautiful Soul" by Jesse McCartney starts playing, and he doesn't miss a single word. It's a karaoke party in the car and once the chorus comes on we both sing loudly with the music. Next is "I don't care" by Ed Sheeran and Justin Bieber, and Nick is in his element. He sings all the ad-libs including the main melody lines. I don't know when the last time was that I enjoyed someone's presence this much. We sing and laugh and I know I love this person, friend, or boyfriend. He has a beautiful soul.

Back home, I prepare myself for Nick leaving any second. He still has to pack and wanted to be gone by 1pm. I can't believe we moved all of my things and made it back here from our hike, all within four hours. But then he starts kissing me. He takes my shirt off, then my pants, and I stand naked in front of him. "Should we take a shower first?"

"No, we can do that after."

"OK, as you wish."

He stops. "Kathrin, can I ask you something?"

"Yeah, what is it?"

"Did you have sex with anyone while, when, um, while we were..."

"While we weren't seeing each other?" I finish his question for him.

He nods and says, "Um yeah, did you?"

I hesitate for a moment, but there's no need to lie, and I wouldn't want to. I'm thinking of my little drunken escapade after my friend's wedding and George, of course.

George, my special friend, who I met on Bumble years ago. He barely makes an effort, and he's an actor, but he's a good person and once in a blue moon we share that special connection, but we frequently get mad at each other. Him because he always has to make the drive to me, and I because every time we actually try to have a deeper conversation, he so vehemently adheres to his already formed opinions of whatever it is we talk about. He also barely has time, and thought he could boast of the fact that he takes enough time to send me ten-second videos on Instagram that were only for me and no one else. We just don't go well together, except for those few special times, that is.

"I have, but it was protected. Have you?" At least I know he won't lie now. I already admitted I saw someone else.

"No," he says, short and crisp.

What? All this time I was so sure he must have met other girls. How could he not? He must be popular on those dating apps. I've swiped across him at least once during that time. I'm shocked. In a good way. He continues to grab me and kisses me with both of his hands around my head. My hair is a little longer already than it has been the whole last year. I decided to grow it out again. He grabs one of my legs and pulls me up into my favorite hug, then walks me into the bedroom and throws me onto the mattress that we threw into the middle of the room earlier. He pulls off his pants and gives my new apartment the housewarming I was hoping for. It had to be him.

~

My birthday:

Good morning, birthday girl.

"He texted."

"What did he say?"

"He didn't even wish me a happy birthday. He just said, 'Good morning, Birthday girl. '

"Lame. Forget him. Let's have fun today."

If that was so easy. He was supposed to be here, with us. My friend Elena and her boyfriend Tobias are doing their west coast trip right now, and we decided to spend the day on Catalina Island for my birthday. Of course, I already caught her up on the whole story already. Nick said he wanted to come, if he has time. But then he blanked and scheduled a bike tour in San Diego with his colleague and his wife. I don't know which thought hurts me more. That he forgot about my birthday and scheduled something else instead, or that maybe he just didn't want to come with us.

We talked on the phone two nights ago, and I asked him if maybe it was just too much pressure for him to spend a whole day with me and another couple. He reassured me it wasn't that. That he'd love to spend time with my friends, and he wouldn't have a problem with that. But he also said he'd like to spend more than a day in Catalina and that we should go another time. That thought consoled me a bit. However, it's hard to believe he'd want to take a two-day trip with me, considering that even a whole day with me seems to be too much for him. "I thought about driving back early, so I could maybe still join you, but that might be a bit rushed. I'm sorry, Kathrin. I'm really not proud of how I handled this," he said.

I sent out a quick reply.

> *Good morning.*

> *You'd be proud to hear that I just dropped the kids off at the pool right now.*

>

I am really not in the mood for casual morning-poop talk. I can't believe this right now. I want to say I'm not mad, but I'm very disappointed. It's my 30th birthday. My family can't be here because we have a bedridden dog at home, and here I am like a 3rd wheel on my own birthday. Not that I don't enjoy my friend and her boyfriend, it's just that

I pictured my 'Big 30 'a bit more exciting and show-off worthy, or romantic. But at least we're about to go zip lining, and I'll be able to post those pictures. I know that will make Nick regret his decision.

As we check in for our activity, Tobias looks a little worried. "You guys might have to go alone."

"Stop saying that. You're coming with us," Elena persists. Tobias has a fear of heights, but assured us he's OK to do this. But as we see the zip lines up in the air, he changes his mind.

"I'll watch you guys from here."

"Noo," Elena exclaims. "We came here to do something together."

The lady who checked us in is waiting for our German discussion to be over. "You could also go to the aerial park. It's not as high up."

"Yeah, why don't we do that?" Elena chimes in.

Noooo, nooo, nooo. It's my birthday. This was the one thing I looked forward to the most. I paid money for this. I don't want to be jumping or climbing from tree stump to tree stump.

"We should let Kathrin decide. It's her birthday," Tobias says.

"It's alright," I say. "Whatever you guys want to do is fine." It's not fine.

"OK, then let's do the aerial park," Elena chimes in again. "That way we can all do it together."

I want to cry right now. For several reasons. I don't want it to be my birthday anymore. That way I wouldn't be so disappointed. I feel like the biggest loser right now.

~

I'm finally in bed. It's barely after 9pm, but the student concert yesterday and the early and busy day today have gotten to me. I'm exhausted. And I'm ready for this day to be over. My guests are still jet-lagged. Nick didn't even call. Just when I turned off the lights and grabbed Baloo my phone rings, and it's him. I'm reluctant at first, but then answer anyway.

"Yeah?" I say quietly.

"Hey girl, I just wanted to give you a call and wish you a happy birthday in person."

"Thank you." I can't even be excited about him calling right now.

"Did you make it home already?"

"Yep." I sigh heavily. "You made it home, too?"

"Yeah, I got home around six."

"OK, cool. You could've come to dinner with us then." No answer. I told him we'd be having dinner in LA, and it would be nice if he could join us.

"I'm sorry, Kathrin."

"Are you, though?"

"I bet you wished that I wouldn't even have called today," he says and keeps going. "That way you could have been really mad at me, right?"

"What?" I say, unbelieving. But he's right. I don't know what to do with this call right now. I can't be happy about it, but can I really be mad? What did he really do? He doesn't owe me anything. "I'm just so mad. You really hurt me. You not being there, or forgetting my birthday, or preferring something else over it and then not even coming to dinner. And then you sent me some stupid morning text. Sorry, that I can't be grateful right now. I'm just really frustrated. And I can't even really be mad. You're not my boyfriend. I just wish you would talk."

"I'm sorry, Kathrin."

I keep pouring my heart out and voicing my frustration in the hopes he would explain what's going on in his head, but instead he says. "I got an early flight tomorrow, so let me get off the phone, so I can finish packing."

"OK. Bye."

I hang up the phone and cry. Why do I always set my expectations so high? Why can't I just be content with a non-special birthday, with love from the people who *want* to give it to me? Why do I hold on to people who don't want to be held on to? I know I'm not, but I feel alone. I hold on to Baloo tighter and close my eyes. Hopefully, I'll be over this tomorrow. I'm done with being 30 already.

Then

"I know this sucks. But we're just following protocol. I'm sorry this happened. This actually happens more often than you would think. And between us, what he did wasn't really OK."

I'm sitting in the back of a police car while one of the officers is trying to console me. It must be because I'm crying like a little girl, with my hair still wet from the shower and dressed in Christmas pajamas that look like a onesie. I wasn't aware that the back of a cop car doesn't even have real seats, but plastic ones instead, kind of like those that auto scooters have in them. They're shaped so that your butt will fit in, but apparently nobody put in enough thought to make sure you can sit comfortably while having your hands cuffed behind your back. Or maybe that's exactly the point.

This still feels surreal. Between my sobs, I manage to get out a question. "Where exactly are we going now?"

When the female officer, who they called to the scene, searched me, they took away everything I had on me, which wasn't much. My phone and the guardian angel necklace my dad gave me. They did tell me they could write down three phone numbers of my choosing from my phone on a piece of paper. I knew Eddie's by heart, but there's no point in calling him now, is there? I had them write down Alana's and Liu's, as well as my friend Helen's, in case I couldn't reach my roommates. I really didn't know who else I could even tell what is happening right now. Completely at the law's mercy, there's no other way but to go along with whatever has to happen next.

"We're taking you to the police station in San Pedro, where we have to check you in, and then we'll have to bring you to the county jail in Downtown. But we got another call that we have to take care of before that."

"OK. And how long will everything take?"

"We really don't know, but we hope it's going to be fast." They park the car not too far from Eddie's place at the local police station. Officer Martinez opens the car door and, grabbing me by my arm, guides me out of the car and into the building where they chain me to a metal bench and take my shoe laces.

"Why do you have to do that?"

"We're required to take out shoe laces because those can be a hazard, or used as a weapon. Some people hang themselves with their laces."

"Oh. I see." I can't even be mad at them. They're just doing their job. Luckily, I'm wearing my slip-on Converse and the laces are really only for decoration anyway. "How long do I have to wait here?" I'm calm. The shock of all this has made me submissive and small, and nice at the same time. I will just follow orders and be my usual kind self, and then they'll notice that they can let me go.

"We should be back in half an hour, and then we'll take you to the next facility where they can process you."

"OK. Thank you." *Thank you*? I'm thanking them now? Well, I guess I'm just grateful they're nice to me. There are also cells in here. But I am not in one. I am alone on a bench, facing a wall, my wrists starting to hurt already from the cuffs and the way I have to hold them.

I start singing. Maybe that'll calm me down. A tear rolls down my face and creates a ripple effect for the whole damn to break again. And then I remember. I asked for this. I asked the Universe for a sign. I couldn't have gotten a clearer one. And God knows I needed it to be obvious. I had my signs before, and I didn't listen. There's no way back now. Eddie was lying. The song "*When You're All Alone*" from the movie 'Hook 'comes to my mind and another flood of tears washes down my face. I don't care how crazy they think I am. I am already an outlaw now. And I'll most likely be sent back to Germany anyway, after this. I'm sure I can forget about my visa. At the thought, my heart breaks even more. I lost everything in one night. With one sudden hand movement, I lost my boyfriend and my life in the States.

I wonder how much time has gone by already. It feels like more than half an hour, but it could be ten minutes for all I know. I'm not used to not having my phone on me. All I know is that it has to be at least 2am by now. I keep alternating between singing and crying, until finally, I see the two officers coming through the door again, with another handcuffed suspect. I was never happier to see two cops before. And they've been nice.

" Sorry it took us so long. We thought this would be a quick one."

"It's OK."

"We'll take you to the Twin Towers now."

"Twin Towers?"

"Yeah, Twin Towers Correctional Facility, that's the county jail. Downtown LA."

"How long do I have to stay there?"

"We don't know. They'll process you there."

Again they put me in the back of their uncomfortable car with my hands behind my back. I can't believe how much I've failed. I've failed my parents, they are going to be so disappointed in me. They've raised me to be better than this. They spent so much money on me. Only for me to end up here? And now I'm going to have to call them to bail me out?

"I can get bailed out, right?" I ask when we finally arrive at the destination, and they get me out of the car again.

"Yes, you can. But honestly, see if you can just stay. I know it sucks, and you want to get out of here as soon as you can, but it would be better if you just sit it out here. That way you'll see a judge, and you'll be done." I have no idea what that means.

"OK, I have no idea how any of this works, but I'll see then."

"I know it doesn't feel like it right now, but you'll be alright."

"Thank you." I don't feel soothed at all, but I'm polite. Once we enter the building, the two officers hand me over to the prison staff.

"You're on your own from here on. Good luck." I know they mean it.

"Thank you."

"And what did you do this time?" A big man asks me while I'm going through yet another inspection.

"This is my first time here."

"Won't be your last one, though."

"I'm definitely not going to come back."

"That's what they all say. You'll be back," he says coldly, but is clearly amusing himself, and moves me along.

I see the plastic bag with my phone, necklace, and shoe strings in there and the lady behind the glass asks me if this is mine. Then she checks my name off a list. A female officer guides me to a small cell. "This is temporary. It's your holding cell. Somebody will come to get your ten prints soon."

"When can I make my phone calls?"

"There's a phone in there that you can use."

She opens the door to a small cell with three other women already in there. There's a metal bench to the left, fixed to the wall, and a tiny wall with a toilet behind, right in there, for everyone to watch. The telephone is right by the door above the bench that has things carved in it. How people managed to do that is a riddle to me. They took anything from us that is sharp or could potentially be turned into something sharp. A blonde girl is on the phone, crying. "Fuucck," she yells, smeared mascara around her eyes. I give her a sympathetic look. I think I know how she feels.

Another girl is sliding her hand into her panties and when she pulls it back out says, "Fuck! I'm starting my period." With her fist, she knocks on the door that locks us in this tiny cell. "I have my period. I need a pad!" Girl number three doesn't say much, but doesn't have a problem pulling her pants down and peeing in front of all of us. I try not to stare, but I am not sure that I am successful. This is like a movie to me.

When the blonde girl finally lets go of the phone, I ask everyone if it's OK if I take my turn. Everybody looks at me, but nobody speaks. Nobody objects either. The cable is barely long enough to get the receiver to my ear without squishing my face to the wall. I try calling my parents' number in Germany. But it doesn't go through. I must have gotten the country code wrong. Alana's next. It rings. Thank God it rings. *Please dial 0 plus the area code and number you wish to call. Please state your name clearly after the tone.* "Kathrin Jakob," I try to say loud enough, but not too loud. *Your name has been recorded as "Kathrin Jakob." Please hold while your call is being connected.* It rings again. But it keeps ringing. She's not picking up. She's also not picking up the other 7 times I try. Neither is Liu. It's at least 4am. But I was hoping I would wake them up. I feel bad for occupying this phone for so long, but there's a big poster right above the phone with about a hundred numbers of bail bond companies.

I don't know much right now, but I do know that I have to get out of here. I look at the yellow piece of paper they gave me. And now I see it. *Bail: $20,000.* What? That can't be right. I barely did anything. I try several of the bail bond companies in the hopes that they could communicate with my parents. They tell me they need ten percent of the bail, and they will get the rest from court when I appear for my court date. But with me not being American they don't have any guarantee that I will actually do so, and with the risk of them losing that money they can't help me.

"I know this sucks. I'm so sorry. I know you must feel horrible. But just hold on. It's actually better if you just sit it out right now and get through it. Much less trouble in the end." The lady on the phone is nice. And she says the same thing the cops told me. After half an hour on the phone, I'm defeated. None of my friends answered. I give up.

The girl that just peed takes her turn on the phone and when she's asked to state her name she says, "It'sKeritheyarrestedmeIgotaDUIIjustwantyoutoknowI'msafe," all within 2 seconds. I look at her.

"Ain't nobody gonna pick up the phone, it costs too much."

The girl on her period chimes in. "These collect calls are ridiculous, they're making a fortune with this."

The door rumbles and opens. "Jakob." It's not a question. It's a demand.

THE ONE I LOVE MOST

"Yes," I answer.

"We're doing your ten prints and pictures."

And here I am, in the hallway of a prison in Downtown Los Angeles getting my mugshots taken. One from the front, one from above, one from the side. Followed by prints of all of my fingers, including my palms. I'm a little surprised they didn't make me take my socks off to get toe prints, or take DNA samples.

"So, what do you do?" the officer asks.

"I'm a singer."

"Oh, cool. So, where do you sing? Do you work anywhere right now?" He might be genuine and just trying to calm me down, but I have a bad feeling, so I tell him I'm here on a tourist visa and that I'm currently not working. "Are you on YouTube?"

"Yeah, I have a YouTube channel." *Keep it short. Don't tell them more than you have to.* He wipes my hands clean of the ink and puts me back in the cell with yet another new girl in there.

So now we are five altogether. A few minutes after that, the little slit in the gray door opens, and we are apparently being fed. Plastic-wrapped white cardboard trays with food. I take a brief look at it, everybody else is eager to eat, but I stop when I see that the meat patty they are serving us is green. Not that I'd eat any meat anyway. "I'm not hungry. Does anyone want mine?"

"Sure, I'll have it. I'm hungry as hell," the girl who peed earlier, volunteers.

Another time, the heavy, thick, gray metal door falls shut with the sound of two tons crashing into the strong door frame. It's even louder than the fully-turned-up TV echoing in the little hallway which I can see, looking through the little window, built into the massive door. The TV is hung up on the wall in a way where you can only see it when you bend your neck backwards and stare up straight. There's a setup of sterile benches and stools fixed around a table in the hallway that we get to roam during afternoon hours, all made from cold, gray steel. A few of the empty small orange juice cartons are left on the table from dinner. Phone hours are after lunch for the whole afternoon. TV hours are also during the day. The telephone cables, all out of hard silver material as well, are still not longer than in the holding cell, about 8 long. So while we're allowed to make calls, we have to lower our head down and glue it to the phoning device. All while using the left hand to shut the left ear, to at least *try* to drow out the constant television noise.

They moved us up here shortly after the first meal. That was last night. According to the clock in the hallway, it is already 10pm the following night. All of my cellmates, who were in this cell with me, already got to go on the bus to the courthouse. That's the next step, apparently. I don't know why I'm still here. They've moved me in and out of here two times already, for the cell to be cleaned. Each time, we have to take our blankets with us to whatever cell we sit in while they mop and clean those thin, nasty mattresses. I haven't really slept. I also haven't eaten anything, except for orange juice, if you can count that. At first, I was excited about the apples, but once I took a bite, I knew those apples came straight from the evil Monsanto Queen. They tasted so bad that I figured it had to be healthier to eat no apples than those.

It all still seems like a horrible dream, and even though I am fairly convinced it all feels like real life and not blurry like a dream, I've been trying to wake up several times. I just want to get out of this nightmare.

At 3pm, they called another round of names. I was eagerly waiting to hear mine. I want nothing more than to get out of here. But another round of girls got to go home or at least to see a judge, while it seems like I have to spend another whole night here. I finally reached Alana earlier. She said she didn't answer the phone because it was a Texas number. And when she finally heard my voice on the voicemail, she thought Eddie took me somewhere far away and did something to me. In a translated sense, I guess that's true. I still haven't figured out how to call my parents. But Alana did. "Your parents said that you didn't do anything wrong. They're not mad at you, Kathrin. Eddie is the monster here. They are so worried about you. And your mom wanted me to tell you that she lit a candle for you."

All I could do during phone hours was to cry. Alana also called Roland for legal advice. I then talked to Liu on the phone because she wants to pick me up when I'm out, whenever and wherever that might be. And I just feel horrible for causing everyone so much trouble and making them pay enormous amounts of collect call fees. How do I always end up costing everyone so much? Why am I such a liability? Why can't I just be normal? I'm reading the paper they gave me for the 15th time. It tells me to bend one of the corners if I'm sexually assaulted. Thank God that hasn't happened. It also told me that I can ask for a Bible, which I did, just so I'd have something to read. I've never seen a Bible so small in my life. It's not even the size of a travel dictionary and, not really being religious, I'm fighting hard with the psalms that were written in a time when English seemed to be a different language. My deliriousness didn't help.

I'm alone in this cell right now. I felt comfortable using the toilet in here. I haven't pooped, but then again, I also haven't really eaten anything. There's a sink, but the mirror isn't a mirror. It's more like a steel plate that almost shows you your reflection. Everything is a hazard, so we have nothing in here. I start singing. Loudly. Nobody is in here, but me. I know the guards can hear me if they want. But maybe I can entertain them. This must be a pretty horrible job. Again Adele's song comes to my mind and I start crying. I cycle between singing and crying for a while. If, at least, I could have my phone... I would be OK if I had my phone. That's all I need right now.

The door opens, and another five girls are ushered in, occupying the remaining bunk beds. Two of them, I don't know why, decide to put their mattresses on the floor instead, and make camp there. They aren't shocked, they seem comfortable here.

"When did they pick you guys up?" One of them asks the others.

"I just left the house at 2am, and they found me, said they were doing a raid," another one answers.

2am? Who leaves the house that late? LA doesn't party that late, especially not on a Thursday night.

"Same. I barely even started, but they were coming for us today."

A girl with a long blond wig gets up from the floor and pushes the gray button that makes the guards hear us. "Can I have some underwear, please?" She apparently wore something a bit too revealing and they gave her different clothes. She's also holding a thick period pad in her hand, which is probably what she needs the underwear for. Her shoes are boots that would usually be laced up to the top and now are just collapsed around her ankles. I'm so glad I'm wearing the perfect shoes for this occasion right now. And I came in my pajamas. I'm so glad I'm not wearing jeans. God, that would be quite awful right now.

"I really like your onesie. It's so cute," yet another girl says to me. She's older. She looks slightly wild. Definitely like she came from the street.

"Oh, thank you. It's actually not a onesie, but it kind of looks like one."

"So, what are *you* doing in here?" She puts a heavy emphasis on the 'you,' while eyeing me up and down, clearly deciding that I don't belong here with them.

"I slapped my boyfriend in the face because he cheated on me. Or ex-boyfriend now, I guess." Again, I can't hold back the tears.

"Aah, I'm sure he deserved it. So, this is your first time?"

"Yeah."

"You'll be fine, girl. They'll just release you, especially if you've never done anything before."

"Really?"

"Yeah, you'll see."

"I hope so."

Everybody around here keeps telling me I'll be fine if I just wait. It's hard to believe, but I pray to God they're right. Meanwhile, the two girls on the floor are still talking.

"One time, while I was giving this guy a blow job in his car and tried to get some of his money, he ended up putting a gun on my neck while I sucked him."

My eyes shoot open wide. I'm not involved in the conversation, but it's clear to me that everybody is going to react in the same way to this statement. But then the blond girl says, "Aaah, I hate it when they do that."

What?? What actually did these girls do?

"I constantly have fights with my baby daddy, but I'm glad he never threatens me."

"I always try to pull out more money from their pocket when they don't notice it."

These girls are prostitutes. This weird experience just became even more interesting. I can't believe this is happening. I'm in awe.

~

"Nah, ah, I'm not going. They're gonna have to carry me out of here." The more run down older woman turns around on her mattress facing the wall when her name is called, snuggling deeper into her blanket. "This is just as good as a motel, and it's free, including food." She's snored quite a bit not too long ago and my ear plugs, made from toilet paper, only helped so much to dampen that noise. I might have gotten a few minutes of sleep in last night, though.

"There are three times per day when the bus goes to the court," she explained to me earlier. "9am, 11am and 3pm."

"I've been in here so long, I just hope I'll actually make it out before the weekend," I worried.

"Honey, they can't keep you longer than 72 hours. They have to let you go today."

"Really?"

"Yeah, trust me, I know this place."

Again, all of their names are called for the first bus ride, and I'm sure I will be left in here once more. Even the guards couldn't tell me why, or when I'll finally get out of here. In the beginning, I was sure it was just going to be a matter of hours, just like in the movies. Somebody would come bail me out, and it would've just been a stupid mistake. But I feel like I live here now. I'm part of the gang. I'm going to have so much to tell when I get out of here.

"Jakob." The last name they call is my name. Is it really? "Did they just say Jakob?" I ask the others.

"I think so," the blonde wig girl says. Suddenly, my energy is back. I'm getting out of here. I'll see daylight again. My bed, Alana, my parents, Baloo. But I have to see a judge? In my pajamas?? And my hair is a mess. I slept on it when it was wet. I have to fix what I can. I could braid it, but I have nothing to fix it with. No hair tie, no shoe laces, nothing.

Then I have an idea. I grab a few sheets of toilet paper and roll it up. Then I go in front of the fake mirror and do my best, combing my hair with my fingers and dividing it up to make two braids, one left, one right. I tie the toilet paper string around the bottom of each braid and as I look in the mirror, I almost have to laugh because I look even more like a little girl now than I did before.

As we line up for the bus, a tall and handsome police officer with a tattoo sleeve eyes me up and down. I don't know if I look especially pitiful and ridiculous or if there's actually a bit of sex appeal left in me, even after sleep deprivation and not brushing my teeth or showering for two days.

~

THE ONE I LOVE MOST

"You guys are good to go. Let's get you out of here." I can't believe it. The girls were right. We didn't even get to see a judge. They dismissed us just like that, after a day of sitting in another cell, this time in the courthouse. With different girls, mostly also prostitutes, but different ones. One of them told me her mom was already selling her body for money, and that she has five kids, all of which she managed to get back from Child Protective Services. She cried as she told the story. She also talked about someone who burned all of their fingertips, so they can't identify him by his fingerprints.

This world they live in is beyond me, but it seems so normal to them. Another girl, I hadn't met before we got onto the bus, cried because she had to leave her dog behind when she was arrested. And she was afraid they'd put him in the shelter and give him to someone else. I could feel her pain. At least the food was slightly better. We got peanut butter and jelly sandwiches and something one girl called 'Jesus Bread.' They gave us each a plastic bag with all of that after they lined us up on the wall and strip searched us, like we could have conjured up something while being tied up inside a prison bus. Once in the cell, I called Liu a few times to tell her I'm at the Long Beach Courthouse, but that I had no idea when I'd get out.

I collect my belongings in a small plastic bag and a police guard opens a door for me. I find myself on the side of the courthouse. Not where 'normal 'people would enter. It's dark already, the clock inside showed about 6:10pm. I am a free woman. My phone still hasn't turned back on, but I must have battery left. I walk around to the big stairs in the front of the building, and then I see Liu. She comes towards me.

"Thank God, Kathrin. I tried to find you." I fall into her arms and tears fall down my face again, but it seems like I've already emptied all my reserves. I'm just exhausted.

"Thank you so much for being here."

"Of course. Anyone would do that."

"No, actually, they wouldn't."

"I can't believe he did that to you."

"I know. How did you get here?" I wonder.

"I took an Uber, and I'll order us one to get home."

Liu doesn't own a car, she walks everywhere or takes the train. "I'll pay you back."

"Don't worry about it."

"OK, but let me just check my phone. My car is still in San Pedro, and so are all my belongings." I see the Apple logo lighting up on my phone and then countless notifications pop up on my home screen. 27 missed calls from my mom, 11 from our home phone, three from my dad, five from my sister. Five texts from Eddie and three voicemails. What could *he* possibly want?

> *Your car is parked in the alley. I gave the key to the people in the sports bar, all your things are in the car.*

> *Call me when you get out, so we can talk about it.*

THE ONE I LOVE MOST

"He can't be fucking serious."

"What did he do now?" Liu asks.

"He wants to *talk* about it. He's the last person I'll call."

"Yeah, I'm gonna make sure of that."

"Can we just take an Uber to San Pedro, though? My car is there. I can drive us home."

"Are you sure you're OK to drive? You must be exhausted."

"I am, but I don't want to have to come back here. I'll be fine. But first I'll call my family really quick."

"Kathrin, Maus?" My mom answers. She cries. "We were so worried about you. I thought you were lying dead in some ditch on the side of the road."

"Oh, mom, of course not. I'm so sorry for what happened. I shouldn't have..."

My dad cuts me off. "Don't you be sorry for a thing. You hear me? I'm so angry at him. I'm going to sue *him*."

"Dad!" my mom explains. "That doesn't help right now. We had a candle lit for you. I didn't sleep either the last two days. I'm so glad you're OK. I've never been so worried."

~

We successfully retrieved my car and are on our way back home now, Liu in the passenger seat. My phone rings. "Who is it?" I ask Liu.

"It's him."

"Hit decline."

Now

> Hey Kathrin. Are you free tonight?

> *Hey. I am, after work tonight. Why? How was it? Are you in?*

Nick just finished tryouts for the team he told me he wanted to be in. His ultimate goal.

> Finished the day early, so moved the flight up to today. I get in at 8:45pm tonight. I'd like to see you, of course. I don't necessarily need a ride.

He didn't answer my question.

> *Ok. Call me when you land. I'm not sure why you're asking me to hang out tonight instead of this weekend. I'm sure you're gonna be exhausted?*

We never hang out on weekends anymore. I just get a few hours here and there, and it's mostly when he's tired. And that means he falls into a sleeping spell he can't escape until the sun rises again, while I lie next to him, frustrated and unsatisfied.

Cause I may have to work. 😞 And there's a good chance I might be gone for work for 15 days... But yeah, I'll hit you up when I land.

Ok, wow. I just want you to be aware that I'm still mad. I do want to see you, too, but if I end up seeing you tonight and something rubs me wrong, I'm gonna be really mad, and I'm not in the mood for that. But yeah, just call me when you're back.

If that's the case, Kathrin, we can just scrap it and I can see you another day properly. Or, depending on how I'm feeling, I can drive to you after I get home. But I gotta Uber to the office and then drive home.

We end up postponing because he's too tired, and I'm still mad, and I don't feel silly enough to make the drive again, just to watch him unpack and fall asleep. I still only ever had one orgasm with him. I just don't feel like I can really let myself go during sex when I'm with him. I feel like a burden when he has to go out of his way to satisfy me, and it doesn't seem like it's really that much fun for him. We have great chemistry. But compared to the beginning, when he wanted to make sure he could pleasure me, he seems to have just given up after the few times I told him, that it takes time for me to feel comfortable enough.

On Sunday morning, while walking Trooper the Golden, I decided to just call him. There's still too much to say, and I'm tired of this whole back and forth. I want this out of the way, whatever way it has to be. I'm frustrated enough to just give up this time. I can't seem to let him go, no matter what he does, but it also doesn't seem like anything will go anywhere anytime soon. I can't just hang out again today, acting like I'm not mad. The birthday thing was too much. And then for him to say he's sorry, but not really acting like it... It's just not enough right now.

He picks up. "Hey Kathrin." He doesn't sound like his usual perky self.

"Hey," I return quietly.

"How's Trooper doing?"

"Oh, he's OK. Just his usual poop-eating self."

"Ew, OK. How's your morning so far?"

"It's OK. I can't complain. How are you? You never told me if you made it into the team?"

"I did this time. And you know what? I'm actually glad I didn't make it the first time because I wasn't quite ready. This time I already went into it differently. I knew what to expect."

"That's awesome. Congratulations. I'm really happy for you," I say, and I mean it.

"Thank you, Kathrin."

"So what's next then? You said if you make it in, you'll move to DC sooner, right?"

"Well, yeah, maybe like a month or two earlier than normal. But first we have a seven-week training. That should be in March, April. And then I'd probably start phase two in the summer."

"OK. That will be hard for me, you know. Seeing you go."

"Kathrin, it won't be easy for me either. I thought a lot about it, and it's gonna be tough. You mean a lot to me."

"You keep saying that, but your actions don't really always line up with that. You really hurt me on my birthday."

"I know, and I'm sorry for that."

"You know, sorry just doesn't do a whole lot anymore. I just always had this feeling with you that we work together, we're good together. It just fits somehow, but I guess I'm the only one who sees it that way."

"No, I do agree with you. We would be a good fit. You're not imagining that."

"Trooper, no!" I interrupt him. "Sorry, but he's trying to eat poop again."

"All good."

"All of this doesn't help me, though. Like, I just don't know what to do with that anymore, Nick. You know, I'm thinking that maybe if you met the right woman, somebody you really like, then it'll just work and all of these things I hang myself up on won't be an issue."

"Kathrin, no. It's not that. You are amazing. And I do have very strong feelings for you. I just have commitment issues. I know I need to work on that, but I haven't figured out how yet."

"Oh you..." The line is quiet for a moment. "You know as much as I want to be with you and want to have you for me, I really want you to be able to have what you want. I know you want a family at some point. You're going to have to let someone in. And I know you feel like you can't go to therapy. But I like to compare it to working out. Nobody would expect to go to the gym once, and then have a super toned body and muscles right away. Also, you can't go there and get your dream body and just stop. It's the same with our minds. You have to constantly work on it. One step at a time. We all need it." I can tell he's listening.

"You're good, Kathrin."

"Yeah, I'm good... But this can't keep going the way it has been." I know I need to set some boundaries with him, and he can sense it.

"I really don't want to lose you, Kathrin. I wouldn't want that."

"I'm not trying to break up with you right now. Not that you could actually call it that, we're not even together. But I need you to try harder. If you say I'm important to you, then show it. Show up."

"OK, I will."

"Are you sure?"

"Yeah, I don't want to lose you."

"And what about that trip to Catalina? You said you wanted to go longer than a day?" I laugh, unbelieving, at that thought again.

"Yeah, I still want to do that."

"Are you sure you can stand me for more than a day? Last time we did that, you broke things off with me."

"Kathrin, it's not like that. Stop saying I am putting a time limit on seeing you."

"OK, then let's plan it. And come over today, or I know I won't see you until after Christmas, probably."

"Kathrin, it's a lazy day and football is on."

"Oh my God, OK. You just said you wanted to try harder."

"OK, I could be there around 6pm."

"Six?? Nope. You're coming at two."

"Kathrin! That's pushing it!"

"3pm and not a minute later."

"Yes ma'am. I'll do my best." — "Just be there."

~

It's 2:25pm and my phone lights up with a text.

I'm here.

I open the door and find Nick standing in front of it with his duffel bag, packed for the night.

"Wow. Look at you. You're early!"

"I kind of like it when you're bossy," he grins.

"Oh yeah?"

"Yeah." He gives me a hug and pulls me up, so I can wrap my legs around him while I give him his hello kiss. "Could we watch football, though?" He carefully asks.

"Fine. Because it's you."

We turn on the football channel and ten minutes later he says he wants to watch something I want to watch. And because it's almost Christmas, and it's my personal tradition I pick 'Love Actually,' surprised he's never seen it before. We laugh, and he holds me while we're snuggled up together on the couch.

When the movie is over he says "I really liked it, Kathrin. That's a great movie."

"See? I told you. I'm glad you liked it. I watch this every year before Christmas and since I won't be able to go home to my family this year, this was perfect."

I'm still waiting for my visa renewal to go through, and that's why I can't really leave the country. I won't be able to come in and work here without a valid visa. So for the first time ever, I'm spending Christmas here in LA, away from my family.

Of course, we ended up in bed and the way we connected today makes me think I can't hold back much longer, from telling him how I feel. The way he holds me just does it for me, even if I still don't seem to be able to fully let go and forget everything. I love this person. I know it'll scare him. Maybe it won't scare him *away*, but I know his phases by now and if he was a snail, that would definitely make him retreat into his house.

"You didn't just agree with me on all those things I said earlier, just so I'd be quiet, right?"

"What? No, Kathrin." He seems appalled. "I wouldn't just agree, to shut you up. You know I meant that."

"OK."

We lay there quietly for a moment. The urge, to say those three words, comes back. A few times they almost come out, but then they don't. It feels like jumping off this big cliff, never quite ready. Scared of the big fall, the silence, the impact, waiting for someone else to push you instead, so you don't have to be brave. But I know I won't say it if I keep waiting.

OK. 5,4,3,2,1..." I love you." I turn my head and look at him. "It's OK, though," I add hastily. "You don't have to say anything back. I just needed to say it."

He slowly turns towards me and looks me in the eyes. This is where insensitive people say 'Thank you 'or 'Aw. ' He knows better, he won't say anything. I gave him an out.

And then he says, "I love you, too. Even though you're a bit annoying at times," he grins. *What?*

"Heeey," I complain.

"Annoying, but cute, and I don't mind it." He smiles.

~

Two weeks later:

"Why can't you just be my boyfriend?" My heart is pounding hard. I've been so brave lately, with the things I've told him and the things I requested, and honestly, it's worked quite well. But now that the question is out of my mouth, it feels like I went too far. Nick looks at me through FaceTime, from his hotel room in DC, not saying anything.

It's Christmas Day and we both don't get to spend it with the people closest to us.

"This wasn't a joke, it was an actual question," I add. "I just don't see why."

"Kathrin, we've talked about this. I'm not ready." But I can't let it go. Not today. I've been patient for too long, and I know this is more than a 'friends with benefits 'situation. He's moving away soon, and once he's gone, there's nothing I can do.

I tell him I love him and that I don't want to hate myself later for never having tried, that I'm confused because he's had a girlfriend before. He tells me he pushed her away, and regretted it later. He tells me he loves me, but that he's not *in* love with me, that I'm just not *the one*. Then he says he doesn't think there's only *one* person for each person, and it just doesn't make sense anymore.

"By the way, who was that guy you had sex with last summer? When we didn't see each other." He randomly asks.

"What? Why do you want to know that now?"

"I just want to know."

"You don't make any sense. You're telling me you don't even want to be with me, but now you're jealous of someone I slept with last summer?"

"Well, that's just how it is. That's how men are sometimes. I still don't like the thought of you with someone else."

"His name is George. He's an actor."

314

"OK."

I keep asking questions to understand him, or to maybe change his mind. I take it too far. It's too much for him. He says, "If I were to move away tomorrow and knew that I would never see you again, I think I'd be completely fine. And I think I am ready. If I met the right person right now, I'd be ready."

There it is. I've asked him this before, and he always denied this theory. He's ready to hang up. "Maybe you need some time," he says.

"OK, enjoy your Christmas. I think *you'll* need some time, but it's OK. I'll be out of your hair for a few days."

"Merry Christmas, Kathrin."

I'm ready to sleep through the remainder of this year. I just destroyed the little bit of Christmas spirit I had left. Unpacking Amazon presents that my family sent, and watching movies with Anne, just aren't the same as the last 29 Christmases I've had.

Then

Today might be the first day I feel empowered again. I feel like what happened might be good. '*Single Ladies* 'by Beyoncé is playing on the radio, and I'm dancing to it, at least with my right hand and my upper body moving left and right, while driving back home on the 710. I am wearing a new shirt and did my hair and make up. I know Eddie would like it, but that won't be a thing anymore. He won't get to see me.

I just had an appointment with the city attorney in Long Beach. Since I wasn't seen by a judge that day, I had to go to his office to sort things out. Apparently, Eddie was supposed to appear as well, but he didn't, which made it easy for the attorney to settle my case.

"No charges have been filed against you," he said.

He made me tell him what happened. After I gave my truthful rendition of what happened that Wednesday night, three weeks ago, he said "This guy is 41 years old, has two kids, and thinks this is the best way to teach you a lesson? Considering you've never been arrested before, and how ridiculous I think this case is, I won't give you any community service hours or anger management classes. I just don't see that it's necessary. Your case will be closed one year from the date when it happened. But nothing can happen in this time, or you *will* go to jail for six months. You understand that?"

I nodded and assured him I won't do anything that would jeopardize the 'get out of jail free 'card he just gave me.

"And I would stay away from him. Just a personal recommendation."

"Yeah, I'm done," I assured him.

I asked if he could tell me how this would affect my visa situation. And while he couldn't tell me exactly how immigration would handle this, he told me he was pretty sure I'd be fine. He wrote me a letter stating that no charges were filed against me, and that my case will be closed next January.

So now I'm in my car, ten pounds lighter, ready for a fresh start. The last few weeks were hell. I've never been so heartbroken in my life. And I have never been so thankful for my roommates, Baloo, and most of all, my family. Liu didn't complain when I woke up in the middle of the night, screaming and crying both at the same time. The pain was so bad I almost couldn't stand it. I thought about all our memories, the ones we made and the ones we still wanted to make. All of our shared jokes and insiders, the way we fell asleep together almost every night, the way he called me 'Bunny 'or 'silly rabbit', or 'bunny rabbit, ' or 'rab*it. '*

Alana would sleep in my bed with me when I needed her, and Baloo slept right on my chest. He knew I wasn't OK. My family constantly checked in on me and when I blocked Eddie, they were the ones taking care of any communication with him. My sister told him to delete all pictures of me, to which he replied that nobody could force him to do that, that they were his memories to have. He was rude to them. He might have said sorry once, but he still thinks there was a lesson he needed to teach me. When I refused to talk to him, he emailed me, telling me he'd try to get a restraining order against me. That he would tell them I took off my clothes when we went to the desert one night, to prove that I'm crazy. He told me that he knows that I looked up Carina and her son on my iPad through Facebook, and that he'd have to protect himself and his friends. But, he said, if I would meet up with him to 'get closure, 'he'd think about it.

I had no other choice. So, with Liu as a guard in my car, I drove to the Korean friendship bell in San Pedro to meet him. And contrary to what I thought he would do, which is drag me through the mud even more, he told me he still wanted to be with me. He also told me he was sorry, but that I had to learn my lesson and that that's how things work in America. I let him say all he wanted to say and then returned to the car, shaking. It's not like it didn't move me, but there was no way back.

"I have to write about this one day," I told Liu.

"Yes, you have to! What a psychopath."

When I get home, I push the ten new attorney letters I received to the side, and take a bite of my leftovers from yesterday. Immediately after I was released from jail, one letter after another arrived with appraisals for lawyers and attorneys that wanted to help me with my case. It was crazy. The jail gave out my information to all these cheap lawyers who were hoping to make money off me. I sit down on one of our bar chairs and put my phone on the counter, which serves as our eating table. My phone lights up with a WhatsApp message, from Eddie. I had unblocked him yesterday, just in case he tried communicating about the appointment today. I haven't re-blocked him yet, and now it's too late. It's been two whole weeks since we last spoke.

> Hey Kathrin, I saw you unblocked me. How are you doing?

There he is, being casual again. And yet, I can't help but type back. Anger, curiosity, and missing his familiarity don't leave me a choice.

> I unblocked you because we had an appointment at the city attorney's office today that you didn't show up to.

> I didn't know about it. Why didn't you tell me?

> Because I'm not talking to you, and you got a letter in the mail.

> I must have missed it. I actually just moved.

> Ok. It's ok. Probably better that you didn't show up anyway. Bye.

> *Hold on. Can we talk tonight, just for a little?*
> *There's something I want to tell you.*

Am I finally going to get the confession I've been waiting for all this time? The reassurance that I wasn't crazy or paranoid, but that he, indeed, did have an affair with Carina? Hard to believe, but somehow there's hope in me that he will tell me something he hasn't before, and that it will clear things up in some way.

> *Ok.*

When I answer the phone, he says, "I miss you so much, Bunny."

I tell him the truth in return. "I miss you, too. But honestly, I'm doing much better now, and I don't think what you want to tell me is going to change my mind."

"Just listen, please," he pleads.

"OK, so what is it?" He's quiet. "Hello?"

"I don't know how to say this."

"Just say it, will you?" I've run out of patience for him. I can feel him struggling to say whatever he wants to say, but my empathy isn't moving towards him any bit. He starts again.

"What I'm about to tell you, I've never told anyone else before, not even Ines."

"OK, keep going," I say impatiently.

"This could get me in big trouble, so I need you to promise me not to tell anyone else, OK?"

"OK."

"No one, not even Alana."

"OK." My tone is monotone and I'm still unimpressed.

"Bunny, this is really important. Please!"

"Yes, I won't tell anyone. Promise."

"OK, so." He sighs. "This is hard, but here it goes. The reason I couldn't tell you about Carina and the car is because we've been doing something that's not very legal. I told you I met her when I was working, right? I was playing with the band at this doctor's house in Santa Monica, and that's when it all started. They started talking to me and told me they're involved in money laundering. Do you know what that is, Bunny?"

"Kind of, I think so. I know it's not legal."

"You're right, yes. I'll send you a video later, so you understand better. I just don't want to keep this a secret from you anymore. I've lost the most valuable thing. You."

I'm quietly listening, not saying anything.

"I made a terrible decision and decided to get involved. I can't back out now. But I want to promise you that I'll be done with it soon. I just want to get a certain amount of money, and then I'll stop. They can't know that I'm telling you this, or I'd be in big trouble, so you can't tell this to anyone. But that's why I kept Carina a secret because that's what we're doing. And that's what all those envelopes are, in the trunk of her car. I'm sure you've seen them before."

"So, what do you do?" This is all a bit hard to grasp and to believe.

"I'm just a middle man. We just deliver these envelopes. But sometimes we have to drive all the way to Arizona or Nevada, and that's when I'm gone for a few days. And when I said I was staying at my uncle's, that's really what I was doing."

"OK, so you never cheated on me?" Somehow, this is still the most important thing for me. He just told me he's a criminal, but all I care about is if he cheated on me with someone who's over 50, and could easily be my mom. Heck, her children are even older than me. I know that because I'm good on the internet.

"No, Bunny, I never cheated on you. This is why I lied to you. And I regret it so much. I hate myself for losing you, for doing this to us. But I hope that in the end it brings us closer together." I let out a derisive chuckle. "Don't laugh. I'm serious."

"OK, sorry. You just have to understand this is all coming a bit late."

"I know. I hope you will forgive me, but even if you don't, I wanted you to know this. And there's something else I need to tell you."

At this point, we've been on the phone for an hour already. "Remember when I told you about those masked parties Silvio was taking us to?"

"Yeah," I say hesitantly. "The ones in the hills?"

THE ONE I LOVE MOST

"Yes, exactly. They weren't just networking parties like I told you, they were sex parties."

"Excuse me, what?"

"Please listen. You know, Silvio is a bit crazy and weird. There are these secret societies in LA. They organize orgy parties, pretty much. It costs like $500 to get in, and people just have sex everywhere. But I didn't, Bunny. I hated them. That's why, the second time, I wanted to drive there myself, so I could leave when I wanted to. I just stood on the balcony for the most part. I didn't want anything to do with that."

"What? That is crazy. That is horrible, and disgusting." I'm appalled.

"I'm telling you, this place is bad. That's why I want to move away from here. Do you understand me now? It's full of people like Silvio and even crazier ones."

"But I don't understand. Why did you go then? I mean, if you didn't know the first time what kind of party it really was, OK. But the second time?"

"Bunny, I didn't want to. But Silvio would have gotten so upset. He's already bought the tickets for us and ordered the tux rental. I make too much easy money from him every week. I can't risk that. He isn't someone you want to upset."

"I don't know what to think. I hate the thought of you being there."

"Bunny, I promise I didn't do anything. The whole time I was there, I was just wishing I could be home with you instead. I hated every second of it. And Jen, she became one of them. She started to enjoy these parties." (Jen is one of the other musicians, hired by Silvio.) "All these people... I don't belong there."

"No, you don't," I say. "Thanks for telling me that."

"I miss you so much," he confesses again.

Instead of a short phone call, we end up talking all night. We talk about everything that happened over these last few weeks. I tell him what happened in jail and cry and laugh at the same time, about the prostitutes that I didn't know were prostitutes, about the guard that flirted with me after I braided my pigtails. Then Eddie tells me about the time *he* was in jail. I tell him how hard it was to get over everything, and how most of all, it was hard to want to share everything that happened, with him, when I couldn't, how it broke my heart. And by 5am, I feel closer to him than ever before. I am still heartbroken, I still feel left and abandoned, but he acted out of desperation. I was about to find out about his illegal activities by snooping around so much, and he couldn't allow it. Too many people are involved. He did lie to me, but he really didn't cheat.

That night, I barely sleep. When I go to work I take a five-hour energy shot, which doesn't make me any less tired, but makes me shaky on top of that. I just want to get through my lessons. And then Eddie asks me if he can see me after work, and says that he will come to meet me here. And I agree. I need someone to lean on, and even after everything that happened, he still somehow feels like home.

We sit in his car, and he lets me cry. Finally. He doesn't tell me I'm a cry baby for it. He doesn't tell me to go home or ask if I'm on my period. He just lets me cry and holds me. And then we kiss. Harder than ever before. And every piece that shattered inside me these past few weeks suddenly and magically is in its right place again. This can't be the right thing to do. I was determined to let it all go. I was certain that what he did wasn't something I could, or should, forgive. But when tears roll down his cheeks, I comfort him, and hold on to him, and tell him it will all be OK.

"I never want to treat you that way again, Bunny. I know I haven't been a good partner. I put you down, I took you for granted. If I'm even close to doing that again, please tell me, but please give me another chance. I want to do better. And I will. I promise."

"OK," I whisper and know that by choosing him I'm betraying everyone who was there for me, really there for me, these past few weeks, including my family.

Now

I look at the pictures Daniela secretly took of Nick and me, when I took her to San Pedro just two days ago, to show her the beautiful ocean view. I had double intentions for coming down here. One of them was a quick meet up with Nick, to surprise him with an extra large bag of his favorite popcorn that I buy at my local farmers market. He agreed to meet us, and when I saw him walking towards us, on the lawn of the Korean Friendship Bell, I ran towards him and jumped right into his arms.

I've barely seen him since Christmas. I went to see a psychic in early January. Just because I wanted her to confirm that I'm barking up the wrong tree, and that he's not the guy for me. Sometimes I just need a little outside push. I was already on the fence after the last disastrous call we had.

But without telling her much at all, she read my cards and told me about someone special in my life, but that it's a triangle situation and that another person was standing in the way of our happy ending. I assured her that the problem wasn't anyone else, but rather his fear of commitment. The only person I could see creating a conflict was his late mother, who supposedly was one of the reasons for him having such a hard time letting love happen. She said, "I see marriage and children with him, the whole deal." I knew that this was a setback to my almost fully-formed decision of letting it all go. But my heart bloomed and did a happy dance when she told me about the future with him that she saw for me. She also mentioned that my aura is orange and that she sensed that I could be a teacher or a writer, and that my creative time of writing will probably start around spring-time. I'm well aware that there are many imposters out there when it comes to supernatural abilities, but I am equally impressed about the things she seemed to know about me.

So without getting the necessary push I needed, quite contrary, I told Nick that I wanted to keep seeing him, despite everything, but that I would start dating other people again, since we aren't looking for the same thing. I just can't give up on him completely, not when there's even just a glimmer of hope left. Not when I think everything he said was to push me away and run from his fear of commitment. It's OK. My big life lesson is patience. It comes back to me in all forms, whether it be love, money, or my visa, which, by the way, still hasn't been officially renewed this time around. (I've been waiting since last August, when we, my lawyer and I, submitted all required documents to Immigration Services, and it's almost March now.)

Meanwhile, my lawyer also sent out the application for my green card, which will go through the music school and Fred. He will hire me full-time, which will give me an immigration benefit, when the process is through and everything is approved. I am so grateful for this, and I almost can't believe we are making such big moves. Moves that would allow me to not have to worry about my visa for 10 years. Moves that would give me so many more options in this country. But until all of that goes through, I need my previous visa to be renewed, to be able to stay and work here.

I think I'm getting better at being patient and accepting the Universe's way, even when it's not always exactly what I want. Not even the fact that Nick confessed that he, in fact, *didn't* want to take a two-day trip to Catalina Island because he felt it was too 'couple-like,' could deter me. I felt horrible when he told me, but I regrouped within just one day and accepted the fact that he's not ready yet, and just needs more time. Whatever happens, at least he isn't Eddie. He's a good person and in the worst case I would have had a good time with an amazing human being. Whatever is meant to be, will be. I look at a picture of Nick and me hugging, and then another one of us from the side, walking, our stride in sync. We would be such a good team. Maybe the psychic was right. Daniela said she took the pictures accidentally, but I know she took them for me, after I wouldn't stop talking about him the whole time she was visiting.

Daniela is someone I met 3 years ago on a TV job during my longer stay in Germany. She finally decided to come visit me, pretty last minute, and after just six days she left to go back home today. I was sad to see her go. We had a great time. I woke up to a clean place every morning, and had breakfast made by her as a 'thank you 'for letting her stay here. We had good talks. She listened, and she understood. But no matter how good the last few days were, one thing isn't letting me go: Mila, the girl who randomly followed me on Instagram earlier today.

I wouldn't have thought much of it, but I noticed that Nick follows her. While I hoped, at first, that he finally told his friends about me and that's what was happening, I had a feeling that wasn't it at all. And it just seemed... off. So, I decided to ask him. I just come straight to the point.

> I get so jealous sometimes!!

> Jealous of what??

> Girls, who know you. Mila followed me today. I think you know her? She's probably super nice, but for some reason my inner lioness came through for a second...

> Oh, yeah? I'm liking this inner lioness! You sound like me when I saw you sitting on that dude's lap. 🖤

> You do?? And I remember. I like it when you get territorial! But why did she follow me?

> She told me it was an accident. She claims she was doing two things at once and your page came up as 'suggested people to follow 'and she accidentally clicked 'follow.'

> *Oh, you asked her? I didn't mind her following me, I was just curious. She's a friend from home? Or was it more? I'm upset that I can't claim you and write my name all over you. Just the thought of someone else having had something special with you...*
> *Aaaah!*

I don't get an answer anymore. It's past 9pm, and he must have fallen asleep again. Somehow this is just weird. If she accidentally followed me, why didn't she just unfollow me again? I would have never seen it. But OK.

The next morning, I check my Instagram again and saw that she, in fact, did unfollow me. She must have felt bad about it. Me asking Nick about it probably made it seem like I didn't want her to follow me. I don't want to come off rude, so I send her a brief message just to clear things up.

> *Hey girl. Sorry. I hope it didn't come across like I didn't want you to follow me. I asked Nick because I was curious. I get a little territorial with him sometimes. Have a great weekend.*

I don't expect an answer. Most of the time, I'm way more invested in conversations than other people, even if it's people I don't know. I've found that most people don't even care to answer. They just like or 'heart 'the message and that's it. But ten minutes later, a notification pops up. A message from Mila.

> *I'm so sorry. I didn't mean to follow you. It was a stupid mistake.*

> *May I ask what kind of territorial feelings*
> *you have for him? Are you two together?*

Strange message. This is starting to sound like not 'just a friend. '

> *No, not really. We just have a special*
> *connection, but it's not serious.*

> *Oh, ok.*

> *What about you? How exactly are you guys*
> *connected? If you don't mind me asking.*

> *Nick is someone very special to me. But I'm*
> *happy for you two, and I wish you all the*
> *best.*

Didn't I just tell her we're not together? I'm starting to get more and more curious. Especially when Nick finally texts me back at almost noon, when I'm about to leave for work.

> *We've been friends for at least 7 years. And*
> *yes, from Georgia. She just told me*
> *yesterday, voluntarily, before you texted me*
> *about it. Did you talk to her?*

Why is he asking me if I talked to her? I have a gut feeling, and it's not a good one. I just want to get to the bottom of why I feel such strong discomfort about all of this, this harmless little situation. So, before I text him back, I message her.

I tell her that I can't have him, and while I'm very much in love with him, he doesn't want to be with me. She tells me she has very strong feelings for him, which she's been having for a long time, and that she will probably always have, but that she doesn't hold it against me that he's in my life now. I can't believe how nice we are to each other, when, according to the circumstances, we could have already scratched each other's eyes out, virtually, or something. I'm already in the middle of my lessons and I know I should let it go. I'm not even supposed to be on my phone, but while my student is playing the *Super Mario* theme, I keep typing hastily.

> *Can I ask you something? Since I've been seeing him, last January, have you guys seen each other at all? Have you been intimate?*

I know he didn't lie to me. I told him that was the one thing that would break me, for someone to make me doubt myself. And Lord knows, I asked him. I just need her to confirm all of that.

Then she replies.

> *I'm sorry, Kathrin.* 😔

I start shaking. How am I going to teach for another seven hours? I just want to cry. The one thing he promised me, that we wouldn't do this to each other, that he wouldn't be like my ex, that's the exact thing he did because he thought I wouldn't find out. Mila continues.

THE ONE I LOVE MOST

> *I saw him last March when he was in Mar-a-Lago. I drove two hours and spent the night at the hotel with him.*

She might as well stab me with a knife while I'm trying to contain it in front of my student. I have to go home, but I can't. I can't let this affect my work.

> *And then right after Thanksgiving, we had sex, unprotected. I'm so sorry, Kathrin.*

I didn't even ask for any details. I don't want to picture them, together, in the hotel bed I always wished I would be sharing with him. I am so angry. While I am praising my student for her good work and let her play through the chords of the next song, I text Nick.

> *You know that if one thing breaks me, it is when someone I deeply care about lies to me about something major... I expect you to call me tonight, I don't care what time, I know you're working. I don't care. I am working, too, and trying to stay calm. So please tell me you will call TONIGHT. And don't come with your 'I don't know what to say, Kathrin'...*

I just need to make it through this day. And then I can take the whole weekend to fall apart like I want to right now, already. I never thought he could hurt me this way, or that he would. I always thought that the one noble thing about him was his honesty. Never making promises he can't keep, never saying he'll give more than he can, never lying. But this is worse. This is worse than just being a straight-up asshole. I will get through today, and then I will let the tears flow, as much as I need to.

~

I can't believe I made it through eight hours of teaching, with only two small breaks. All of my students showed up, and that might have actually been better than having many breaks. I would have fallen apart. And while we do have a small teachers' lounge for private time, there's a camera, even in that room. I barely ate any of the food I brought. Usually, I'm starving by the time I have my first break. Today, every bite made me more nauseous.

Mila and I have been texting back and forth all afternoon. I even planned to call her, but she just sent me a voice message, saying she is at a small get-together and can't talk, that she just stepped outside. How is she so calm? Probably because, like she said, Nick never promised her he wouldn't see other people. Heck, she doesn't even live here. She must have known he had to see other people. He's lived here for two years. She admitted that she's a bit crazy about him, that she knows every new girl who follows him on Instagram. That she's checking their stories periodically, that, while none of them post pictures of him, she knows when they're together. And she told me that he went bike riding with a girl named Rebecca on my birthday. It wasn't a colleague.

I'm so hurt and broken by all of this, angry and disappointed. I want to yell at him, I want him to explain everything. At the very least, I wish he would man up and tell me how sorry he is, and that he realizes he messed up, and that we should just be together already. But the longer I listen to Mila's messages, the more I become aware that I'm on the way to becoming just like her. And that's the last thing I want. I just need to get home. I need some rest. I need Baloo. When I get home, I see that there are five more voice messages from Mila, and I know that our conversation is far from over.

All night we send messages back and forth. She sends me screenshots of text conversations and tells me when she saw him, how they met, and that she hoped one day he would return to her and give her babies. From some of the text messages she sent, I learned that he lied to me on more than just one occasion. That, unless paddleboarding counted as training, there was no work training he had to attend on his birthday. That 'falling asleep early 'was code for 'at a comedy show with someone else, 'and that random girls from the internet become 'colleagues and their wives.' That commitment issues aren't something that happens to him, but that he chooses. The only thing that's holding me together right now is talking to her. She knows exactly how I feel and why I can't let go of him, even after he told me several times that he can't be with me.

When it's 10pm, Nick still hasn't called, and I know that means he won't. It's 1am when Mila says she has to go to bed. She's on the East Coast. It's 4am there. I always thought I was the crazy girl, but now I know that might not be the case, as much as I thought. Just like I thought I was a huge Disney fan, until I moved here and met Alana, who knows every single movie by heart and can speak along to every ride's instructions at Disneyland. I ain't shit. And in this case, that might be a good thing.

Then

Hi Mausi, send us a picture of you, so we know you're ok. You've been so quiet lately.

Shit, shit, shit. I'm at Eddie's new place, and they can't know. It would break their world. I take a selfie against the naked wall and send it.

All good. :)

Especially since the jail incident, my mom has been worrying even more. She checks when I was last online, and if it's been more than half a day, she definitely worries. As for me, I thought that I already digested everything that happened, but sleeping in on the air mattress this morning, I dreamt that the police came into his new apartment to arrest me, and I woke up screaming. Eddie came to sit on the bed and told me that everything was OK, and that it won't happen again. I want to feel safe so badly, and trust him, but it's hard. My heart is on guard and while I feel at home with him, I also still feel anxious every time his phone rings. Or every time I have to let him out of my eyesight, even if he's just in the bathroom.

"Let's take a walk, Bunny." It's dark already, and lately, we've been walking to one of the 7/11 stores in his

337

neighborhood to buy some vitamin water, or just to have a reason to take a walk. Eddie grabs his spray can of Raid.

"Are you seriously doing this?" I ask disbelievingly.

"Yes, Bunny Rabbit, I told you. There's too many roaches out there. The streets aren't clean."

"You're crazy."

"Whatever. Come on, let's go."

Out on the pavement, Eddie starts spraying every single roach he sees, heavily. They are big and there are many, but somehow this just doesn't seem very feasible. He's out here with sweatpants, a tank top and his old raggedy Jordans, that don't even have laces in them anymore. Good thing he doesn't care what people think. There aren't too many people walking here anyway.

I get impatient. "Come on, babe, let's go." But he's committed to the task.

"I'm not done, there's still so many."

"Please, I want to enjoy the time I have left here with you. I'm only here for a few more weeks."

"Two minutes."

I sigh. Since I'm here on a tourist visa this time, I have to leave within three months. My visa still hasn't been approved, so I don't even know when I'll be able to come back here. I'm just glad that our arrest and jail incident didn't make it completely impossible for me to do so. Things have been fairly good, and Eddie has been taking more time for me. He also promised to take me to Seattle, so I can finally experience his favorite city for myself. He really wants to make it right.

"OK, two minutes are over. Please."

"Alright, alright." He tosses the empty Raid can in the trash bin by the bench, and we finally continue walking.

Now

I didn't do anything this weekend except for talking to Mila, texting her, to be exact, and sending hundreds of voice messages. I barely ate and we both went to bed super late, her always three hours later than me, of course. I already knew Nick was working in Beverly Hills the last three days, but given the severity of the situation, I thought he could take some time, once he was off his shift, and call me. But he didn't. Neither did he call Mila. She's convinced, however, that he will call me, and tell me that she's crazy, and that he and I will be happy together.

I told her that believing either one of us will have him is a waste of time, ridiculous. I don't even want him anymore. My heart is still very much broken by this situation, but more than anything, I'm angry. And I'm glad about that anger because it makes it easier.

"I just wanna show you that there are still good guys out there." Ha. I laugh at the memory of his statement from a year ago. I let him see all of my flaws. I told him my weaknesses and revealed my deepest fears, one of which was being lied to. And here I am again. I always knew he was a good liar because he had to do it for his job, when he was undercover. He told me many stories that were made up, just to laugh at me five minutes later. But I thought he

was good enough to not lie to my face about any serious questions. He told me I'm special and that I'm the only one, when in reality it was just something he said to make me stick around. I feel so very stupid. All the times I tried to understand him, tried to fix him, wanted to hold his hand while went through what he had to go through, until we could finally be together.

And I still have a hard time believing that Nick Watts is not a good guy. He is sweetness in person. But even more so, he is an addiction, my addiction. Not only mine, but Mila's too. And if I learned one thing these past few days, it's that I don't want to be like her, and I see myself on the way there. It's time to listen to him when he says he doesn't want a relationship, and walk away with the little bit of pride I still have left.

~

I got to sleep in today, which is nice, since I have a full afternoon of work. Baloo is cuddled up next to me, and I'm checking my emails, which I know I shouldn't do first thing in the morning. Suddenly, my phone starts vibrating, and Nick's name lights up.

He's calling. He's actually calling. What is he going to say? Should I answer? I waited for his call all weekend, and he decides to call now... What does it say about me if I'm always so readily available when he calls? But I know good and well that if I don't answer his call now, I might not reach him for who knows how long. My heart feels like it is up in my throat. My morning anxiety is at its peak. I just woke up. It feels like my body went from zero to 100. One minute relaxed, and the next pumping adrenaline, breathing like I just ran up ten flights of stairs. Calm down. Compose yourself. Be mad at him. Don't forget that you are mad at him. Nick is one of the people who I can be mad at and once I see him, my face just opens into a big grin, like a dumbass who just forgot who she is and what she's doing. It's the same on the phone with him. He says, "Hey girl," and I'm immediately giggling. Not today. This is way worse than before. There's not a single thing to laugh or giggle about, or be happy about, when it comes to him. I push 'answer.'

"Hey," I say, with as cold of a voice as I can muster.

"Hey Kathrin." He is not his jumpy self. He knows this is too serious. I can hear he's in the car. God, I hate the fact that he always waits to call until he can do it to kill time while doing something else. Kind of like 'In the car? Might as well call Kathrin.' But rarely does he just take time to call me anymore, uninterrupted, not even when I just found out about the other girl, and many other things, for that matter.

"You took an awfully long time to call," I muse sarcastically.

"I was working," he states.

"I know that. But you didn't work through the night, did you?"

"No, but I didn't wanna end the weekend like that." The audacity.

"Oh, neither did I, believe me. I actually had more fun things planned this weekend. You're an excellent liar, Nick."

"Kathrin, I'm not lying to you."

"Yes, you are. And now I also know who you really went on that bike tour with, on my birthday."

"You talked to her, didn't you? Mila. You shouldn't believe her. She always does this, taking things way out of proportion. She's irrational."

"Oh, is she, really? Only thing is, that I've seen screenshots. It's hard to deny that."

"You shouldn't believe her. I wish you would have talked to me first."

"Talked to *you* first? She gave me more information about you these last three days than I got from you in over a year. And I tried talking to you, but you wouldn't answer my texts, or call me."

"I was at work."

"Yeah, so you said. I know what I know, and honestly, I don't know what else to say. This was all a lie."

"No, Kathrin. It wasn't."

"So did you sleep with her when you went home for Thanksgiving, or not? And last March when you were in Florida because Trump was playing golf? And did you, or did you not, do it unprotected?"

"Oh, it doesn't even matter what I say? You already believe her."

"And you don't even deny it. You couldn't even say 'no ' right now, because it's true."

"Kathrin, please."

"What do you want? I don't get it. Tell me you see a future for us."

"I do."

"OK, and what does that future look like?"

"I don't know."

"Oh, come on."

"You know that I always wanted to sing a duet with you."

"A duet? Really? Fuck that. You know that that's not what I meant by 'future.' Be my boyfriend."

"No."

"Why not? What do you want?"

"Just no, Kathrin."

"OK, then I don't see any point in this anymore."

"Mila, please, just..."

"Did you just call me her name?" He laughs. This is too much.

"I'm sorry. Kathrin. Let me get off this phone. I actually wanted to call her too, and I'm not saying this to impress you, but I probably will stop talking to her after this. She's gone too far."

"Yeah, you should. I thought *I* was crazy, but not after talking to her."

"But yeah, call her. Bye."

If I thought I was mad before, I'm furious now. Clearly, this doesn't really affect him that much. He probably has other girls lined up already. I'm so mad, tired, and exhausted, that I can't help but cry. I need to get this all out before I have to put my happy teacher face on for the day, so I do what helps me best. Putting on my sad song playlist on Spotify.

~

Two days later:

I'm sitting on the little brown leather couch in Cindy's office. I spot the box of tissues on the little table next to me. Lord knows, I'm going to need them today. I spent the past five days being angry, more than anything else. When she asked me how I was doing when she walked me in, I just said, "Alright." I know the tears will come today. And oh, do I feel stupid. All the tales I told her about 'Nick, the Great,' 'Nick, the Honest,' 'Nick, Prince Charming,' the poor soul with commitment issues who treated me so much better than Eddie. And I'm about to pop my own bubble by telling her what happened.

"So, you're just alright today?" She asks, after I settled on the couch and put my bag to the side. My lower lip is already trembling.

"It's just, that..." I take a deep breath. "It turns out that..." Deep breath, I can get through this sentence without crying. "Nick lied to me all this time."

A tear rolls down my cheek, then another one. I use the sleeve of my shirt wiping them off, pretending that I didn't know a whole storm was coming with what I'm about to tell her. Cindy looks at me sympathetically and just listens while I tell her who Mila is, and what she told me these past few days. I don't mention the fact that I saw a screenshot of Nick asking her if he could '*cum inside of her*' the next time she'd come visit. But I do tell her about the Christmas card I found in his room not that long ago. How I was wondering who would write such a thing. *You'll always be my favorite person in the whole world.* How I remembered just a few days ago that it was signed *'Mila.'* That she visited him in LA right before he met me. And that the plastic wrapper of whatever cosmetic article that was left in his guest bathroom trash can was left by her, on purpose, so the next girl would find it, and know that she wasn't the only one. How he called her on her birthday last year when I was in the car and how I remember the exact date because it was 'Pi Day,' and we were going to get pizzas, but the line was too long. And how he told me she was just a friend.

I tell her that he went to a comedy show one night, when he told me the next day he fell asleep early. I tell her that Mila told me that she was sure he's having a sexual relationship with me when she saw he liked one of my posts on Instagram. But she never thought it was serious because Nick doesn't like girls who show too much skin, and in that post you could see my thighs and my belly, and I only had a sports bra on.

I mention how he told her that 'Kathrin Jakob is a good person 'and he 'likes supporting me.' That was his answer to her asking about me. I also tell her that I'm proud of myself for not playing detective this whole year, that I didn't want to drive myself crazy, while Mila searched every Instagram story of every single girl that Nick followed. She knew who he could be with every day.

What I don't tell her is that I went to see a psychic, even after realizing how insanely accurate the whole triangle situation was that she told me about. But I'm too embarrassed already, as it is.

"I decided to trust him. I really believed him. I thought he was the last person who'd ever lie to me. All I ever asked for is the truth. Tell me anything, I can handle it. But don't lie to me. That's what I told him. He knew that."

And that's when the flood starts. Cindy looks at me shocked. "I'm so sorry, Kathrin. I didn't see this coming, and usually, I'm pretty good at reading situations." And then, I see the tears in her eyes. She manages to swallow them back up, but they are there, and knowing how much this moves even her, destroys my composure even more right now. This wasn't a simple lie Nick told me. This was mean, and weak, and cruel. A while ago, I always said it would be so much easier if he was an asshole, like Ian, or Derrick, or Eddie. Be careful what you wish for... because I think my wish just came true.

"Maybe I needed this to happen to let go. But man. He's so much more messed up than I ever thought. And here I was thinking I am the one with the issues."

"You are amazing, Kathrin. And I mean that. You've come such a long way, and I so admire how hard you work on yourself and how honest you are with yourself. I know you will be OK. But I also know how bad this must hurt. He really betrayed you."

"He did. And I don't think there's any coming back from this."

"So, what do you want to do?" Cindy asks.

"I'm not sure yet, but I think I might have to block him. It hurts, knowing he doesn't care enough to get in touch."

When I get out, I decide to text him again to get it all off my chest. I just want him to admit it.

> *The unfairest thing of all is that you make it look like I just don't want to believe you, and that I'm wrong. You're teaching me not to listen to my gut, you're challenging my ability to use my logic and gut feeling, and you know damn well I'm gonna need both of those things with the kind of men that are out there. For you to get so upset about what my ex did and then gaslight me and compromise my health, and not, at least, giving me peace by admitting the things you did lie about... I never expected that from you. I wish you could do that for me. If you truly loved me (as a friend, as a lover, as a person) you could show the integrity to admit things. Or if really none of that is true, to talk me through it, so at least I don't feel so played. It's not fair what you do. In no way.*

And for once, he replies.

Kathrin, I'm sorry for everything I put you through. I'm sorry for placing you under this stress and making you feel like you can't trust me. I apologize for being so stubborn and not accepting love when it's right in front of my face. I don't want you to feel like you can't trust me or men again. I haven't treated you great every time, I know this. But you need to know that I honor you and I respect you. I admire you, Kathrin. Your strength, your openness to be vulnerable and express yourself. Your willingness to tell me what's on your mind, even when it may be uncomfortable, like you did the second time you stayed over at my place. I'm sorry.

That's all I'm going to get. He won't admit anything. He's too afraid of being the bad guy. And that is exactly what made him one. Saying the things that sounded good and hiding the ones that didn't. Telling me what he thought I wanted to hear. He won't man up and tell me what he did. He only apologized for how he made me feel, not for what he did. I wish he gave me a choice. I wish he would have let me see him for who he really is. A man who likes to play, instead of a knight in shining armor whose only fault is that he can't be committed. But being stubborn, I send him another 5 novel texts asking for his honesty. When he doesn't deliver, I draw the last straw.

You won't be able to contact me for much longer. It's not like you're gonna tell me anything you haven't said before. I'm breaking my own heart and I don't want to

> do this, but I have to block you. I love you
> too much and this hurts too bad. I need to
> do this for myself. If you want to say
> Goodbye, call me before tomorrow morning.

Again, tears fall down my face while I'm typing this.

And after 12 hours without a single call or text, I finally push 'block contact.' That is how this fairy tale ends. I thought I finally knew how to trust my gut. Turns out I was wrong.

~

3-4-2020:

He kept my voice message. He didn't call. I had to block him. And I'm finally sad. I'm finally feeling the heaviness. I don't know how to feel anymore. It's so confusing. I feel like one of many girls now. Also, apparently I'm not important enough to call and/or fix this. It's been shit already. What would I be getting from this, if it would keep going the way it was? Really, the Universe did me a favor. But it's hard to accept that I won't be looking into those eyes anymore, or kissing those lips, or being held by those arms. And that I have to throw all of those future hopes with him out the window now.

That's probably what hurts the most. How far I went in my head and how none of that is ever going to happen. In my mind, I'm still wondering, if this is the part where I absolutely let him go, and if I'm convinced of this, then this would also be the part of the movie where he'd finally realize the truth, because I'm not doing this anymore to get his attention. How silly of me.

It also really bugs me that Mila still wants to stay friends with him. I understand her reasoning, heck, she's basically me, but ten times everything. But I think that neither one of us can throw our hopes with him away. Even if he was just a friend, I need more than that. I need people around me who can talk and open up, because the more he doesn't, the more I feel like I can't either. And you become who you surround yourself with, and as much as I admire him for his discipline and kindness, I don't want to become closed up like that. It's time to invest all that time and energy into something worthwhile for me. Baloo's hungry. I need to go. I love me. 💕

Then

I can't believe we're actually on our way to Seattle. My feet are propped up on the dashboard of our rental car. Eddie is driving, and I'm so excited I finally get to experience the city he loves so much. If things work out between us, I might have to be OK with moving there. The trip wouldn't have happened though, if it wasn't for my one American credit card, which I accidentally signed up for at Banana Republic last summer. Eddie promised to take me on a trip, but he doesn't have the money right now. So because I wouldn't stop bugging him, we decided to pay for the car and the hotel with my credit card, and he said he'll pay me back when he gets paid.

Eddie's playlist is on blast, and I'm just a tiny bit disappointed that I don't get to listen to Ed Sheeran, but instead have to listen to Tank and Frank McComb. It's not that I don't like that kind of music. It's just that he has it on repeat all day, every day. I even know a bunch of these songs by heart now. I just want to be singing harmonies to my songs. But it's OK. He agreed to drive all the way up the coast without a break, and I get to just relax in the passenger seat, taking in the scenery.

As we pass Portland, I decide to take a picture of the view. The city sign on the freeway, my toes on the windshield and the greenery surrounding us. It's beautiful. I take a happy selfie and send both of the pictures to our family WhatsApp group. I just want them to know I'm OK, and maybe they can just be a bit excited for me, that I get to take a trip for four days. But I'm aware that mostly, they hate the fact that I am with Eddie.

When I was home, I dropped the bomb. Eddie took some pictures of me in Palos Verdes, by the coast, right before I left LA. I showed my family the pictures the second day I was home, and when my mom asked who took them, I didn't lie. We've had a few family dramas before, but I don't think any of them were ever as serious or loud and tearful, on all sides, as this one. I had promised them I wouldn't go back to him, that there was no way back, and that I was aware that if I chose him, I'd decide against them, because of the amount of pain that situation put us all through.

My mom was quiet at first, but I saw the shock on her face. Then she said, "No, Kathrin. No. Please tell me that's not true." Then my sister started crying and my Dad, at first, was watching from the sidelines. When they all tried to talk some sense into me, I started crying and told them they don't understand, and I ran to my room and locked myself in.

I FaceTimed Eddie and told him what was happening, and he said it's understandable how they feel, but that I have to do what feels right to me. I never thought I'd be in a situation like this. Where my family, and friends, for that matter, hated the person I was dating, literally didn't want me near him. But here I am. I just need them to see that he can prove himself to be worthy of my love. He promised me that he will be better, that time will show that he can be all that, and treat me the right way from now on. My family wasn't the only challenge while I was home, though. Eddie got quite jealous over an old male friend I hung out with a few times. He said he wasn't jealous, but that he's not stupid, and he sees it when there's some flirting going on, even though he only heard me talk about the person.

But luckily, all that is behind us. I'm back here with him, and from now on, things should be *smooth sailing*, like he says. The car alerts Eddie of a text message he just received, and he pushes 'read.' The computer voice starts reading it out loud.

"Thank you so much for sending Carina my way. I can't wait to work with her."

Immediately, my blood freezes. I try to stay calm. I know the nature of their connection now, and what it's all about. I need to learn not to get so upset about it. I look at him. "Can you just tell me what this is about?"

"Oh, it's nothing," he tries to calm me. But noticing that I'm not ready to let it go, he adds "Carina mentioned to me that she wants to get better at choosing makeup, and how to put it on, and just create a better look for herself. And I happen to know this girl, Tina, who does hair and make up, and I sent Carina her way. No big deal."

"OK." I know if I don't let it go now, the atmosphere in the car will become very toxic, and we still have another three hours to go. But my mind is already spinning again.

I know how he rearranged my wardrobe. This might very well have been his idea, and not hers. Who talks to a guy about makeup anyway, as a colleague? I close my eyes. Time to zone out. I want to continue being excited about this trip, and I can't wait to have sex in the hotel bed. Probably because Eddie still doesn't have a real one, and I feel like I basically live there.

~

10 days later:

I'm still in awe of these ancient giants. I am so happy we spontaneously drove through the Sequoia forest on our way back. I'm looking at pictures of me balancing on one of the fallen trees, me posing in a tree trunk, and me meditating on another tree. I'm trying to decide which one to post first. My family must see how happy I am, because of Eddie.

I can't believe it's already been a week since we came back. Honestly, the trip to the National Park was probably the highlight of our vacation. Seattle was... OK. We didn't get out of the car much, and Eddie used a lot of the time to look at houses and apartments, driving to different neighborhoods that didn't have much to do with sightseeing.

We took one of the famous ferries, which was impressive. Driving the car onto the boat and getting off at another dock, just like a scene out of Grey's Anatomy. But there was no hotel sex, and no walking around in

Downtown. Eddie got sick the moment we got there, and while he was OK to drive and get out of bed, the romantic and sexy time I had been looking forward to so much became another distant dream. I also didn't get to try more than one vegan restaurant there, which is something I look forward to everywhere I go, because Eddie only wants to eat at places that have three-star ratings on the Michelin guide, and many new vegan places aren't even listed there.

I find the video Eddie took of me while I sat down between the trees to pee while he is narrating the scene: "Bunny, the rabbit. Doing what she does best. Marking her territory." He starts filming towards my butt and I see the tanning lines from the spray tan that I got a few days prior to our trip. I have to laugh. Who else could I be silly with like that?

I decide to post the picture of me in the tree trunk and then put my phone away, now I'm browsing through random things on Eddie's new kitchen island, when a *Guess* receipt catches my attention. "Guess is my favorite store for women," he always says. There are quite a few items on this receipt, and as I look at the bottom of it, it reads: Customer name: Carina Blevit. Oh God, not again!

I have to say it. It's only going to get worse if I try to suppress it. "Why do you have Carina's *Guess* receipt here?" I yell because he's in his closet, where he's hanging his new shirts. Hold on a minute. He just got new shirts.

"It was in the car and I must have brought it up with all the other papers," he shouts.

But I'm already scanning the receipt for items that could be his. "*Stripe mans*" sounds suspicious, and I type in the article number into Google and find the exact same shirt he just showed me. With my anxiety turned all the way up, I walk towards the closet to confront him. "Did you guys go shopping together?"

"Yeah, we had some time to kill between two jobs, and we went to the mall. We paid separately, though."

"Then why are your items on her receipt?"

"Well, I gave her the money. It's not a big deal."

"Uh, you just told me the receipt was hers, and it was in the car."

"Duh. Because it is, and it was."

"I really don't like the idea of you guys going shopping together."

"We didn't go shopping together."

"You did."

"You know what? If you don't trust me, why don't you go home right now? I don't have time for this. Here we are again. I told you, we're just not a good fit. There's no point in this. I already told you what it was, but you choose not to believe me," he fires at me.

How did this turn around so quickly again? Am I *that* wrong? "No, I'm sorry. It just didn't make sense, and you have to understand that this is a huge trigger for me."

"Are you on your period?"

"No. I'm not."

"Well, you better get with it, or I can't be doing this anymore." I retreat to the kitchen island with a horrible pit in my stomach. Then his iPad lights up with a text from Carina.

~

Six weeks later:

It's almost August and I still haven't heard back about my visa. This is the second time I applied, and the second time they asked for 'more evidence.' Let's just say things aren't looking that great. I wish Eddie would just finally marry me. We've been together for almost two years now, and after two years you know. That's what he always says. But I don't see that happening anytime soon. He hasn't even given me back the key to his apartment, after he took it from me when I told him I read his emails. Or I should say, given me one of the keys to his new place. He sometimes gives it to me, but he always makes me give it back. I know I can prove to him that I can be the woman he needs and wants in his life. I am determined. We've already been through so much together, and we're so close.

But if this visa doesn't come through, I'm honestly going to be a bit lost. I'll definitely have to go to Germany. The officer at the airport in secondary inspection told me she'd give me another three months on my tourist visa. "But don't come back this year," she said. I had to heavily argue what I was going to do here all this time, and tell her who's paying for my trip, and what my ties to Germany are, on top of explaining my arrest. I have always been nervous coming back into the country, but this time must have been the most nerve-wracking. They have the power to turn me around at any point. Being an indefinite tourist with an arrest record definitely doesn't make me look good. I know that if I wasn't a somewhat petite white girl, with long blonde hair and green eyes, I might be treated way harsher than I am. Most airport officers already aren't really what you'd call nice or kind.

There is one more possible option that I could go for if I don't get this artist visa. A visa for culturally unique performers. A category that, as a yodeler, I definitely fall under. So, not all hope is lost either way, but I just really hope I don't have to start over, after all the painful processes and money my parents put into this to help me.

"Bunny, I don't have my rent money yet. Silvio hasn't paid me." I'm at Eddie's place again, the fifth consecutive day. I barely see Baloo anymore, and I feel bad. I wish I could just move in with Eddie. Everything would be so much easier. But he doesn't think I'm ready.

"Oh, why hasn't he paid you yet? And when is rent due? It's only the 25th."

"I don't know. He's just all over, and I can't really complain. It's not due until the first, but I really want to build a good relationship with these people, so I've been paying early every month." He's seemingly irritated by this.

"How much would you need?" I carefully ask. I just made about a thousand dollars from three recordings I did for a producer, but I'm going to need that to pay my half of the rent, and I don't really make any other money currently.

"Like a thousand bucks. Could you help me out?"

"I'd love to, but I have to pay rent, too, in a few days."

"Your rent isn't that much, Bunny."

"Yeah, but I still have to pay it."

"But you're not trying to pay early like me. I'd give this back to you by then. I'm gonna get about five grand next week."

"Oh, what? Wow." That sounds like a lot, but given the fact that he told me he was doing a special side business, I have a hard time judging what's normal and what's not. "OK, if you promise to give it back to me by the 1st, then I can help you out."

"Yes, Bunny, I promise. Thank you! You're the best, Bunny Rabbit."

"Yeah, yeah. OK, just pay me back. I can't afford to gift you half of your rent just yet."

Now

3-16-20

It's going to be an interesting time, that's for sure. Maybe I've wanted this in a way. It's like that song 'If The World Was Ending' by JP Saxe and Julia Michaels. Everything shutting down always sounded somewhat romantic. Finally, there's time for the really important things, each other. But it looks like I'll be sitting here alone, and it does bother me. For days now, the only thing people are talking about is Covid-19. I want to call Nick. I need a quarantine buddy. Not that he could even stay this long. Ha Ha! Gotta go...

4-13-20

It's Nick's birthday. I know it, I think of it, but I'm not going to text him, or call him. I think I'm really done. I'm very proud of myself for getting so much done yesterday. I went shopping for Peter, then walked Trooper, then took a nap, I worked on my visa papers and got almost everything done I wanted to get done. I recorded some yodeling for that brief, I worked on our new work material, I made food, I watched Outlander. Late at night these days, I ask myself all these existential questions. Like, what do I want? German men? American men? Living here? Living there? My life is already unconventional, at least for German standards. So I might as well keep living it. Keep working on the big stuff. I don't have to know how exactly I'm going to get there. I just have to keep doing things, trying things, finding a way. Writing, singing, being creative. I still think my story should be heard. I will write that book. Once my P3 visa renewal application is sent out, I will take time to write every day. This can be done. I think I might have to poop, but that has to wait until after my Zoom work meeting. I still have 5 minutes left, though. I'm so good. I can do everything I put my mind to! I have it in me and I can bring it out! I have to remind myself that it is OK to feel good and carefree, even in the midst of uncertainty. My visa petition will also be approved. I have to give myself some credit. OK, till tomorrow.

4-18-20

It's been almost two months since I ended the whole Nick thing, once and for all. I'm proud of myself. I'm also proud of getting up right now, half an hour before I had to. My day is a bunch of half-hour tasks today. Walking Trooper, teaching Susan, going to the post office for Peter, writing a song, changing my sheets. Oh yeah, and I want to work on my book. It's actually really fun to do that right now. I know what to write. It's not too hard. It's just going to take a while.

If I were to write a letter to my ten-year-old self, I would say life is harder than you think, but you are also much stronger than you think. The most important lesson you'll learn is how to love yourself. Your tears won't stop just because you get older. But there is so much to see, so much to learn. If I wrote a letter to myself right now, I'd say: Know that you're doing everything right. Nobody has it all together at all times. Give yourself credit where it's due, be honest with yourself when you need more discipline. Follow the feeling of living carefree. Follow what makes your heart light up. Live one moment at a time, but don't abandon your dreams, for with endurance and joy, you will get where you long to be. 💟

THE ONE I LOVE MOST

God, what cheese ball did I swallow last night again? But anyway, this was just brainstorming for the song I'm supposed to write. The key word is 'letter.' Talking about: I got an RFE letter for my visa application, which, with this visa, never happened before. And everything is so freaking weird right now with this virus, which doesn't seem to be in a hurry to go anywhere anytime soon. No one knows when normality will return. Everyone says they're sure it's still gonna work out with my visa, but I'm scared. Whatever officer got assigned my case this time around seems to be overly strict and doubts that Bavarian Yodeling, my specialty, is any different from all other kinds of Yodeling. So now I'll have to put more work in, to deliver the evidence that will satisfy her critical eye. I need this, to be able to smoothly transition to green card status. If I had to leave now, coming back would be tricky, with all the travel bans. But I just gotta have faith. I got this.

4-29-20

Nick texted me this morning. I just thought about him and the whole situation last night. How he lied to me. I don't have to text him back. He didn't really ask me a question. Also, what would I possibly still want from him at this point? More lies? Sex that won't make me happy? Hope for something? The prospect of him moving away? Falling in love all over again with someone so broken that they don't even bother lying to you? And it's not like he'd help me with my status here in the States, either. How? I'm doing that by myself. I am loving myself, I'm satisfying myself when I feel like it, I'm handling my visa situation and everything that comes with it. I live in LA, I worked hard for this, and still am, and I have no intention of anyone playing with that again. I'm good. I'm a powerful woman. I know that if I just text back like nothing happened, the conversation would keep going like nothing happened. So I'll tell him I'm not OK doing that. Does it bother him that I'm not running after him anymore? Is he running out of lady friends during quarantine? Does he feel sorry for what he did, but can't admit it? The perfect thing to text back is NOTHING. I'll do my therapy first, then a workout, then finish my vision board. Maybe write for my book today. And that sounds great. :)

~

It was my own fault for opening this Pandora's box again by unblocking him and sending that casual text. But it was really just that. When *"I Don't Care"* by Ed Sheeran and Justin Bieber came on the radio, I had to think of him sitting in my car shouting every single word and every single ad-lib out the open window. He's really not the greatest singer, but he doesn't lack confidence, and it's quite charming. I couldn't help but chuckle at the memory of it, and I sent a text, telling him.

And apparently he thought it was OK to pretend that the whole Mila fiasco didn't happen. But it did. And I'm angry. So angry. I know that I am PMSing. I'll get my period in a few days, but now I just want to be angry at him. I never got the chance to be angry at him in person about this. And really, I'm angry at all of 'malekind 'right now. Yes, I'm one step further in my green card process, and I'm happy about that, but I'm still worried about maintaining legal status until all that is through. And I feel alone right now. All the rather horrible dates with people from Hinge and Bumble were so frustrating and made me feel even more alone. Going on walking dates hasn't been the worst thing. At least I still got some exercise in if the date sucked, but it's still a bummer meeting one weird guy after another. Or people who don't look like their profile picture. Or guys who just aren't into making an effort whatsoever. Or men who tell you straight up that they just haven't had sex in a long time and that's all they want. With every failed date, the belief that the right guy is out there somewhere shrinks.

My ceiling fan is broken and so is my dresser. I must have been high last weekend, when I texted Nick and asked him to fix it. But here he is knocking on the door, while I'm sitting on the couch with a casual glass of wine. I rarely drink, but tonight I'm making a statement. I just don't know what that statement is yet.

"Door is open," I say as I get up, and there he is with a big tool box standing in my door frame. He looks just as always. It's weird seeing him, and I don't know whether we should hug, for two very obvious reasons. If I was worried about the virus that much though, I wouldn't even have asked him to come. I know he gets tested for work. Really, I don't even expect him to be able to fix anything. He's not the handyman type of guy. I just wanted to see him in person and, even if nonverbally, load all my anger off onto him. I know it's stupid, but sometimes you do stupid things, even when you know they're stupid.

"So, I can't turn the light off when the fan is on. I think that one chain isn't working," I say, leading him into my bedroom.

"OK, let's see." Without saying much else, he climbs onto the bed and starts fixing my fan, or at least tries to.

After an hour, he almost electrocuted himself twice, but still hasn't fixed a thing. If anything, my fan is now less usable than before. We barely exchanged any words so far. I start poking. "How's Mila doing?"

"I don't know."

"You're not talking to her?"

"I'm not *not* talking to her."

"OK."

I listen to music while he continues to fix what he apparently can't fix. He points out my Hinge notifications when I hand him my phone to use it as a flashlight, and he has a weird tone while he says it. Like he has the right to be upset about it. We go on like this until a more sad song by Katie Buxton comes on. And somehow the lyrics are just very fitting.

I wanted steady, I wanted you. But I loved deeper than you asked me to.

So you flew, and I chased until my feet turned blue.

What is love if you have to beg for it? Nearly killed me just waiting for it.

So I watched as you flew.

The wine has gotten to me too, by now. I never drink much, and a little bit goes a long way. I'm in my feelings, sitting on the opposite edge of the bed from where Nick is standing. But he notices, and steps down. "Come here." His arms are open and he looks sincere.

"Why?" I ask dryly.

"Just come here," he says again.

"You haven't even apologized yet." I'm tipsy and pouty.

"I'm sorry, Kathrin. I really am."

"Say you lied to me. Admit it."

"I did. And I'm sorry. I should've handled everything better." That's an understatement.

I get up and accept the invitation. He hugs me tightly, but comfortably. Both of his arms wrap around me like I just found my harbor. My head against his chest, his cheek resting on my head. He doesn't make any movements with his arms or hands. He just holds me. It's a real hug, the kind Nick gives. I've missed it. Finally, we loosen up.

"I wish you would have just told me. We could have been friends. But now? You ruined it."

"I'm sorry. I know." We go back into our hug for another two minutes, until I decide to take a step away, and he directs his eyes back to the ceiling fan. "Look, I think I've tried everything in my power, but I guess you'll have to call someone to fix this," he apologizes, still looking up to the fan. "For now, you can just unscrew the light bulb if you need the fan at night. I'm sorry I couldn't do more."

I take his hand and pull him onto the bed with me. I just want to lay here, and feel what it feels like laying on his chest one more time. And then we kiss. Why do I feel so much like I'm home with him? Why does this feel so perfect? And why does it feel like nobody else could give this to me, even after two months of going cold turkey? This could easily lead to more, and he's trying, but I won't go that far. When he starts to slide his hand under my shirt, I make sure he knows that his quick apology doesn't get us back to where we were. "The door is closed for you, sorry."

As he leaves, and I sit on my couch, fairly tipsy, we stare at each other, like we're saying goodbye forever, yet again. I can't take it. I don't want him to leave. I know I'm drunk, I know I'm cranky. He sits down and holds me, again. And then he leaves, again.

Then

Eddie still hasn't paid me back. My rent is due tomorrow. Things are pretty good between us today, so I just ask again. "Hey Babe, I kind of need my money back. I need to pay rent tomorrow." I'm sitting on one of his bar chairs, facing him on the opposite side of the kitchen island.

"Can't you just pay it with your German credit card?" He casually suggests. He's sorting out coffee pods. He doesn't like coffee, he just likes to have it, in case someone visits and needs to be impressed.

"No, I can't. And you said you'd pay me back this week." I'm getting impatient. He notices.

"Yeah, I can pay you off soon." What does he mean?

"Pay me off? You said you'd give me the money back last week already."

"Where do you think I would get that much money from so fast?"

"Babe, you said you'd get $5000, last week!"

He shakes his head vehemently. "Five thousand? Where would I get that much from? I never said that."

I blow out air. "Carina? You said you'd get five 'G.' Those were your words. I need to pay rent, too."

"Maybe I said I'd get $500, but not five thousand. And I still have to pay off other things. I can give it back to you little by little."

"Seriously? I need that money."

"I know your parents will help you out if you need it."

"Yeah, but right now, they wouldn't have to. And I can hardly tell them that you owe me money. You know they already think the worst of you."

"Exactly, so why would it matter? They're not gonna change their minds about me anyway."

"I can't believe you... I know I remember that you told me '5G,'"

"I know that I didn't."

He can't tell me that I'm imagining this anymore. This one I know for sure. Just like I knew that the receipt was Carina's, and they went shopping together. And just like I knew that panty liner paper in his trash wasn't from 'his cousin's car.' This time he's driving his family's car for real, and it's not some brand-new Mercedes, it's an old Camry. I didn't go looking through his trash two days ago. I think I have enough dignity left not to do that. But his bathroom trash can is always emptied neatly when I get there, every time I stay at my place for a few days. And the white trash bag by the door was transparent enough to catch my eye, with the pink Carefree paper shining through. So, I pulled it out and confronted him. He asked what it was, and that he must have brought it upstairs, out of his Cousin's car, when he cleaned it. Of course there's a small chance that could be true, but it doesn't really make sense, especially since the parking garage has several trash cans. But I wanted to believe him.

The next morning, I see that I received an email from Roland. "*I'm so sorry, but your case was denied again.*" I cry, but it feels just a bit like routine now. But this means I don't know when I'll be coming back here just yet. I'll only have 12 more days until I have to leave the country, and I will have to clean out my room. And Baloo? He'll have to wait. I am breaking on the inside. Leaving Eddie, leaving Baloo, not knowing when I'll be allowed to come back?

Luckily, Eddie put me in touch with another lawyer, two weeks ago already, for exactly this case. She told me that I never had enough evidence to get approved for an O-1 artist visa, but that she's confident that I could be approved for a P-3 visa, as a yodeler. It's only for a year, but it also costs less. Since I don't have the money Eddie owes me, I pay the lawyer's fee with the remaining allowance on my Banana Republic credit card, and continue to fight. If I want something, I don't give up easily. I am not done here. There is always a way!

~

10 days later:

Eddie and I are sitting in the park by the ocean, close to the Korean Friendship Bell. We brought a blanket, and the fact that I'm leaving in two days lessens my ability to fully enjoy how beautiful it is here. It actually makes it harder.

I sold almost all of my furniture, and put the rest of my things in bags and boxes which I stored in Alana's garage, who now lives with her boyfriend. I have two suitcases packed, mostly with clothes and my microphone, and they're already at Eddie's place. I said goodbye to Baloo last night, and my heart felt like it was being tugged on from all different directions. He was so clueless, and I felt like the worst mom ever, to leave him behind like this, not knowing when I'll be back. I know he's in good hands with Liu, and it's best for him to stay in his familiar surroundings, but man, this hurts!

I lean against Eddie and tears start running down my cheeks. I don't want to leave this place. I don't want to give up my dream that I fought so hard for. And this relationship. Am I going to lose him now, after everything?

Eddie doesn't seem to be bothered. Somehow, he has all the faith in the world that things will work out the way they are supposed to. But I have a problem with the fact that it doesn't even seem like he'll miss me much. My parents don't understand how I still haven't given up on being here, after all the hardship and all the setbacks. And, most of all, they don't understand why I'd still want to be with Eddie. Quite honestly, right now, he's the main reason I'm here. I don't really do much, other than spending time with him and my phone. But I also haven't been allowed to work.

Back home at his apartment, he tells me to lock the door.

"Done."

THE ONE I LOVE MOST

"Are you sure?"

I double-check the little button, and it's pushed in and turned so that it's locked. The door can still be opened from the inside, but not from the other side. "Yeah, it's locked," I say confidently.

Five minutes later, Eddie walks to the door with a bag full of trash that he decides to take out, and without unlocking anything he opens the door, just by pushing down the door handle. "I thought you said you locked it."

"I did. It was locked."

"Clearly it wasn't." Does he really still not know how his front door works, after months of living here?

"It was locked, nobody could have opened it from the outside. But when you push down the handle, it will unlock. It's completely locked from the outside."

"Are you really too stupid to lock the door? I gotta do everything by myself?"

"I told you I locked it." I'm getting frustrated now, and we're escalating into a full on argument. Tears start welling up my eyes again.

"I can't wait for you to be gone. It's gonna be so peaceful here, when you're not around." He walks out with the trash bag, and when he comes back, neither of us says a word. I just want to be home now. He's said many hurtful things over time, but this one probably hurts the most.

Now

It's Memorial Day, and it's so nice to have the day off. Part of me feels like sleeping in again. But there's a lot to be done. Most of all: writing my book. I need to put in a lot more hours, if I want this to be done anytime this year. If I used all of my TV time to write instead, I could actually get somewhere. I need this book, even if it's just for myself. I need it, and I need to write the ending to it so that I can manifest it. I'm feeling so mellow and relaxed right now. I'm missing something to look forward to. A trip, a date night with someone I love... And I have to trust that those things are coming. Right before all of this started, I wanted to mingle more, get out more. Now I'm in my 'staying home' element. I do manipulate. I did it this week. I didn't get what I wanted, and I started a tantrum. Drunk on my couch. I wanted him to stay over, and he said no. I knew it the very moment it was happening. But it's all about accepting what God gives us and working with it. The best way I can work with it is to make art from it. I just have to actually DO it. I wonder what I'm going to do today. Writing. I feel lonely. Sometimes having the closeness we want to feel makes us feel even lonelier when it's gone again. It's like a bad drug. I'd do so much to get it back. It really is an addiction. How can I give myself that amount of dopamine? That's what I'll need to figure out. I will figure it out.

THE ONE I LOVE MOST

I decided to really pack my bag and, despite it probably being busy, to go to one of my favorite places by the coast, to write. I grab sunscreen, water, a book to read, my laptop, my phone, sunglasses, and my yoga mat, and say goodbye to Baloo. "I'll be back, baby. I just need to get out a bit."

Once parked, I find a spot in the grass, with a big enough radius around me to be able to take my mask off. It's not even sunny down here. What a bummer. But at least it's a bit cooler this way, and it actually makes it easier to see the screen of my MacBook. I read two chapters in the romance novel I got from one of the little libraries in my neighborhood, and then start writing on my script again.

This chapter is about Eddie, and somehow those are harder to write than the Nick ones. Especially after Nick came over the other day, writing about our first date just happened naturally. I didn't even have to think about it. I sigh. Why do I still like him so much? Why do I still love him? We did talk on the phone a few days ago, and I asked him what advice he'd give me, as a friend. Should I let him go? And he was clear. "I would tell you to let me go, Kathrin." And he also told me he didn't know if it was a good idea to keep seeing each other. I texted him two days ago.

I still want to give you that guitar lesson.

Kathrin, that would be a dream to learn that. I just struggle with not being sure if it's a good idea for us to be together.

You struggle? I think you say that so that it's not your fault the next time I cry. You were selfish with me for a year, stringing me along and keeping me around. I was stupid and naive with you, for a year. We're still the same people. We feel good together. I want more, you want less, I start asking too many questions, you pull away, I promise myself to never talk to you again, I miss what we had, you miss me and come back to get more and the cycle starts over. Until you move away, or until one of us finally finds the love of his/her life. Maybe that's just my perspective. But it's ok if you don't want to hang out.

*Imagine me saying this in a nice tone. I know it might have come across a bit bitchy.

I catch myself getting tangled up in thoughts about Nick when I'm supposed to write about Eddie, and get back to my task. I write another page, then read another chapter in the novel, then write a bit more. I'm starting to feel that my skin feels a bit warm in my face when my phone rings. It's... Nick? I haven't even texted him today. This is unexpected.

"Yes?" I answer.

"Yes?" he repeats. "Do you always answer your calls like that?"

"I actually do. That, or I say 'hello. 'Why?"

"It just sounded kind of harsh. Like you're mad at me."

Maybe I did come off a bit too empowered. Maybe I am slightly mad at him. But I'm aware that I don't have a reason. "No, I just answer like that sometimes."

"Oh, OK," he says, unbelieving. "What are you up to?"

"I'm actually very close to you. By the whale museum. Just reading and writing."

"What? You are?"

"Yeah, is that so hard to believe?"

"No, I just didn't know. Why didn't you tell me you're coming down here?"

"For obvious reasons, I guess? What are *you* up to?"

"Good point. And I'm about to go to the park. But I thought about your offer with the guitar lesson, and I'm tempted. I wanted to see what you're doing later."

And just like that, I have a date for when I'm back home. Nick has to come here because they don't allow visitors at his military housing complex right now. He comes straight from the park—whoever he was there with—and asks for a towel, so he can shower here. We try to get him to play guitar for a little over an hour, learn chords and the names of the strings, and then we order food. Nick turns on another one of his reality TV cooking shows he likes so much, while we eat. He's a sucker for reality TV. He knows all couples of 30 Day Fiancé and feverishly watches Married at First Sight. Cooking shows are just the cherry on top for him.

When we're done eating, he's determined about what he's going to have for dessert. I was pretty clear last time when I said I wasn't going to have sex with him anymore. And I meant it. And why would I? I always enjoyed it, but the fact that I never came to experience my peak made it frustrating, especially when considering the fact that I'm not even his girlfriend. But my will isn't as strong today, and when Nick slowly takes off my pants, after gently kissing my neck, I think I might have just lost control a bit.

I'm laying on the couch facing him. He's right above me and takes my head into both of his hands, like he knows exactly what it takes. And when we kiss, we melt with each other. It's so perfect. Like there was never, and will never be, another puzzle piece that fits me better. I forget everything around me for a second, and then he moves down towards my thong. He starts kissing the soft skin on the inside of my thighs and then takes the small piece of fabric off, now kneeling between my legs. "Let's go to the bedroom," is all I get out and Nick gets up, scoops me up and carries me to my room, where he throws me onto the bed and finishes what he started on the sofa.

"I missed you, Kathrin." He slides his arm under my back and with one quick movement moves me up towards the head of the bed. I love it when he does this. I wrap my legs and my arms around him tightly and don't remember what part of myself convinced me that this wasn't something I needed.

He decides to stay over and we curl up into our spoon positions, and before I know it, our conversation turns into gibberish. "It's competitive," he mumbles. "People should get the best awards show, you know. The Grammy's. And on top of that, he likes to run."

"Who?" I ask.

"This guy named, uh, Montero. I think he's Jamaican or something..." He starts snoring for a bit and when I nudge him, he has a sassy tone. "Swiper, no swiping, girl." He says this with a slight valley girl accent.

"What? Swiper, no swiping?"

"Yeah, it's a Dora the explorer thing."

"What?" I'm so confused.

"Yeah, you never watched that expedition on YouTube?"

Now I know there's no coming back for him tonight anymore. I just laugh and say goodnight and we fall asleep booty to belly, with my head on his outstretched arm.

Then

I've had about four major fights with my family already. I know it's not their fault that I have to be here. And it's not even that I don't like being here. It's just the fact that I don't have a choice. Every night I sneak into my room to talk to Eddie. But they know, when I disappear with my iPad for more than an hour, and it's not even bedtime yet. They know that I'm talking to him. But we don't talk about it. The big elephant in the room.

I started working at a flocking company almost two hours away from home. The company belongs to friends of my aunt and uncle, and they give me a ride every morning. But that means I have to get up at 4am some mornings, others at 6am. I wear a mask almost all day because all we do is spray car parts with glue and tiny little black hairs that stick to it and make it feel like carpet. I never questioned how my glove compartment became so fuzzy. But now I know.

I stand up all day, and work like I'm a machine, from 6am to 3pm. It's the same thing every day. Sometimes they move me to a different car part and I get a bit of variety in what I do. But at the end of the day, I'm pooped, my feet hurt, my eyes and nose are full of black stuff, and when I get home I shower, eat—my mom is the best cook—and fall into bed. I don't know how these people do this every day of their lives. I start to appreciate my teaching job a lot more these days and I promised the Universe that I won't be ungrateful anymore, once I'm back, and get to return to my California life again.

Part of me does wish I could just relax while I'm home and sit it out while I'm waiting. But I do need the money for the visa—I still have to pay off my credit card—and to go back to LA. I'll need a new place to live. The money I'm making here won't even go far, but it's something. And I'm showing my parents, and the Universe, that I'm serious. I'll do whatever it takes.

I'm also occasionally doing some extra work for some TV shows, which are being filmed in Munich. On those days, my dad drops me off, since it's close to his office. Last week I played a slutty coworker who was a married man's side piece, and next week I get to be a nurse on a classic Bavarian telenovela. Both times I actually got lines. I wish I could do those jobs every day. Way less exhausting and a lot more fun. I also played a female cop quite a few times now, but all I do is run around in the background of a scene, and for the most part, I just sit around waiting all day until they need me.

I asked Eddie if he'd come visit. Or if he'd meet me somewhere. The visa application was filed, but it's November already and I still haven't heard back. I even offered to pay for his trip, with the money I'm earning, but he declines every time I ask. I miss him so much, it hurts. I hate being apart for this long. And while he says he misses me, it seems like he's just fine by himself. Hopefully, I'll be back before Christmas, so we can finally be together again.

It's my birthday in a week. Eddie was on a trip the last few days and, even though we were texting, I wasn't really able to call him, because of his side business thing, and him not being alone. I've been very understanding since he told me the truth, but I am impatient regardless. He told me he'd be back Monday morning and since it's midnight in Germany, it's 3pm in LA already. So, I call. I know he must be on his way to Silvio's studio right now, but he's not answering. I call again. Again, no answer. OK, I'll try one last time. On the eighth ring, he picks up. "Bunny, what is wrong with you? You can't be calling me like that." He's seemingly annoyed, if not angry with me. I've called him more times than three before.

"Why? What's wrong? You said you'd be back by Monday, and I haven't talked to you in days, so I wanted to reach you before your rehearsal with Silvio."

"I still had a client in the car, and you're blowing up my phone like that. You can't be doing that. If I don't answer once, why do you keep calling?" He really *is* angry.

"Because sometimes you don't hear your phone right away. And because you told me you'd be back and done with your trip by now. I'm sorry. I didn't know you had someone in the car, obviously. Why did you pick up then?" I feel the anxiety rising. Once I messed up, in his eyes, there's no talking myself out of it.

"Well, we just stopped at a gas station because you didn't stop calling. The trip ended up being longer, and I had to cancel rehearsal for today. Why are you so insecure? I would have called you when I had time."

"I'm sorry, babe. I didn't know. I had a really rough day. I miss you, and I still haven't heard about the visa. And it's my birthday next week, and you won't be here, and my family still doesn't get it, and work is hard."

"You know what? What you did really wasn't OK. I think you should think about what you did. I'll give you some alone time. I'm getting really tired of this whole situation. If you don't have that visa by the end of the month, we can just be friends."

"What? Babe! No! Don't you think I'm tired of this situation, too? I've been trying to see you. I even offered to pay for plane tickets. I'm doing everything I can. Don't do this!" It's almost 12am, but there is little chance now of me falling asleep after this call.

"You're handling this all really badly, and I'm tired of it. Like I said, you can call me when you get that visa, and we can talk. Until then, I won't be answering the phone anymore. Goodnight, Kathrin."

"No, please. Wait. You can't do that."

"I can. Good night."

And before I can say anything else, he hangs up. Tears are falling down my face, and there's no one I can go to because everyone already told me what they think of him.

Now

I've been worried again. Every time I move on from Nick, I feel that freedom and strength. And then I miss him. And when I start talking to him again it feels refreshing, and it also feels like I have it all under control, and that I can keep it casual and not expect anything from him. We made a deal. He won't lie to me anymore when I ask him something. But how do I know that's true? It wouldn't even bother me so much if he was just upfront about what he's doing outside of seeing me, that way at least I'd know what to expect. This way, it always feels like he's in love with me, and that we both can't escape the chemistry between us. But I also feel stupid when he tells me things just to avoid conflict, extremely stupid. Like he can just do that with me.

Last weekend I freaked out, first internally and then out loud via text. He told me he went on a weekend getaway with colleagues, but when he sent me a picture of the pool, there was a second pair of legs in it, right next to his. And it wasn't a man. He assured me that I'm overreacting and, despite me not knowing what to believe anymore, I told myself that I should stay calm, for my own sake, and recognize my need to control things that I can't control.

This was something we talked about a lot in therapy, and apart from being patient, I know it's one of my biggest life lessons. I look up the note on my phone that I wrote about a year ago, when I started talking to Nick again, after our three-month hiatus. I was going through the very same motions then, and somehow I was able to calm myself, with affirmations that I partly found on the internet, and partly wrote myself.

☆ Don't put anyone on a pedestal.

☆ All we have in life are experiences.

☆ Nothing is ever really safe.

☆ I don't have to lose myself because I met someone.

☆ Hold on to the future you saw before meeting him.

☆ Remember YOUR dreams.

☆ Remember that you want meaningful connections.

☆ Goodbyes are a part of life and can make you feel alive.

☆ Hurting means you've lived.

☆ Don't buy into your horror imagination!

☆ Let go of *What if*'s (good and bad ones).

☆ Trust what life gives you.

☆ Be patient.

☆ Let the answers present themselves.

☆ We have control over nothing in life, so just accept things how they are.

☆ Be OK with not knowing!!!

☆ Don't hurt yourself with creating problems in your head! It doesn't help you with being in control.

☆ It's OK to be confused.

☆ You have a powerful soul.

☆ Nobody can give you wiser advice than yourself.

☆ Listen to the calm voice, not the crazy, erratic one.

☆ There are multiple versions of reality. You choose the one you want to see.

☆ Don't try to impress, or be liked.

☆ You call the shots.

☆ Sit back and observe.

☆ Feel your feelings.

☆ You can be independent *and* in love. It's not an oxymoron.

☆ All the answers are either inside of you, or in the future.

☆ He is just one of many beautiful experiences.

~

I'm meeting Andrea tonight. And I'm looking forward to that. Besides longing for a romantic relationship, I've been wanting to find a real girlfriend for a while now. Someone who's close enough to actually be able to hang out more than every other month. Someone I can fart in front of, and discuss dirty details with, or gross things our bodies do. Somebody I can confide in and do things with.

Like going out to eat or going to the beach. I haven't seen Alana all year so far, and with her being married now and working at Disneyland, I never get to see her or talk to her much. We still love each other like sisters, but we did grow in different directions.

Andrea is from Germany as well. And she's vegan. She lives five minutes away, and one of the best things is that she makes handmade vegan chocolate that she sells at local farmers markets. My taste buds have definitely profited from our friendship. But the funniest thing is that she used to live with my best friend from music college when they lived in Germany, and I already lived in LA. But I didn't know that, until I accidentally met her in a Facebook group. Especially with me being stuck here right now, I'm so grateful to have her. We even speak the same dialect, and it feels like I found a little piece of home far away from home.

I'm walking Trooper in the park this evening. My phone vibrates, and I'm surprised to see Nick's name pop up with a text notification. He rarely texts me first these days. He just got back from his fourth of July weekend trip with his "friend only" Carey and her family. It would be an understatement to say I felt slightly jealous and left out. But I remember my resolution to let things evolve naturally, and not get upset about things I can't change.

> Hey. How's your day going?

> Hey. Pretty good. About to walk Trooper.
> You back home? How was it?

KATHRIN JAKOB

It was fun! Beautiful weather and cool people, and the time on the lake was a lot of fun.

I am. Not. Jealous. Or envious. Or anything like that.

What you got going on tonight?

I can imagine. Lake time sounds amazing.

Just digesting all the food I ate. You?

That's funny. I'm just thinking about what I could eat.

Also thinking about all the sexual things I wanna do to you.

You already know you're gonna end up at Chipotle. Stop thinking.

All he's been eating lately is Chipotle. At least every time I saw him.

And then addressing his sex comment.

Oh yeah? What's that?

Basically, me inside you. Of course, me trying to make you come by going down on you. I enjoy doing that.

The text gets dirtier as it goes on. But immediately after, he switches gears.

388

*Also, I think I'm gonna get some pizza from
Papa John's. :P*

Way to ruin the mood. But really, I don't know him,
talking like that. He must really not have had sex this
weekend.

Papa John's? I'm disappointed in you.

*Blaze is too far. What do you want me to
do?*

Oh, I have a lot of answers to that one.

*Spend more time with me, be nice to me,
spoon me, give me a massage, kiss me, tell
me I'm your favorite person in the whole
world...*

*Adopt a dog, stop eating eggs, stop making
up fake stories, buy me food all the time.
The list goes on...*

Taking notes...

Oh, really?

Yes.

Enjoy the pizza.

Thank you!

Do you have a date tonight?

A date? I did, with Trooper. And now with my couch. Why are you asking?

I was just curious.

I have been telling him about my recently very frustrating dates, not too long ago. About the small guy—I usually only date taller guys—who got to the restaurant minutes before me, then ordered and paid for his food before I even got there, and then wanted to invite me to a beach cabana stay with him on the first date. About the guy who only called me when he was super drunk, and who, on our first FaceTime call, took me to the bathroom with him, and just started peeing, unapologetically. I don't mind it when Nick does this, but I already know him, so it's different. Then there was the guy who knew every vegan restaurant in town, and on the planet apparently, and was so promising, but in person looked 40lbs heavier than his profile picture, and during our hour-long walk asked me maybe two questions. And the nice guy, who paid for everything on our Downtown date and shared my birthday, but who I had no chemistry with.

I vented and told him everything. On top of all that, my PMS hasn't gone lightly on me.

I might hurt someone if I go on another bad date with the mood that I've been in this

> *week. I wish you could bring me strawberry lemonade from Veggie Grill!* 😔😣🍪🍪🍪

> *Oh, man. Why don't you bring dat ass over here?*

> *Because you're not allowed to have visitors. Because I'm still in a food coma. Because you also don't have strawberry lemonade. Because it's my first day at work in person tomorrow. Because you can come here if you want to see me last-minute. And I'm hanging out with Andrea tonight.*

> *It's all good.*

The next day, Mila messages me on Instagram, with a screenshot of me liking one of her posts. That must have been from weeks ago because apparently she restricted me from her account and I can't see anything when I try to go to her profile.

Hey. I'm not sure what the point in this is but can you please just leave me be. You won! So I don't get it. You got your way. You got him, and he left me completely and utterly broken; what more is there. Just please. Thank you.

I forward it all to Nick. Maybe he knows what's going on. But when he texts back, I find out that he doesn't. By the time I send Mila a voice message saying I'm sorry that she feels that way, she has already blocked me.

I call Nick and when he picks up it seems like he's in a mood. That doesn't happen often. "What's wrong?" I ask.

"Nothing. Why?"

"You just sound different," I remark. He's not his bouncy, fun-making self.

"No. I'm OK," he assures me.

"OK. I need you to sing me a goodnight song." Time to pick up our old tradition.

"Kathrin, I don't really feel like singing right now."

"I knew you were weird. Something's off with you."

"Nothing's wrong. I'm just a bit tired."

We talk about other things, Mila, and how work is going for both of us, and that he will be going on his seven-week training to the East Coast soon, since he made it into the team. I'm so excited for him. It's his big dream. But I'm terrified for myself. I can cope for seven weeks. But this makes his moving date pretty final. And it won't be too long after he returns from this training that he'll have to pack everything and leave for good.

I'm rambling on about Baloo's routine in waking me up every morning when he interrupts me. "Kathrin, be quiet." What is wrong now?

"Why?"

"Just be quiet." And then he clears his throat and starts singing. "When you watched Cinderella, you wished that it was you. And then you asked your Mama: Do fairy tales come true?"

My cheeks lift towards my eyes as high as they can, and my lips spread into a big smile while I'm listening to my impromptu goodnight song. How many times has he sung this song for me when I asked for the "Cinderella song," time and time again. It never got old, and he sang this for me as a goodnight song over the phone, or sometimes when we hung out. I still have a hard time remembering the actual title of the song.

"Aw, thank you," I say when he's done.

"You're welcome, Kathrin. I'm gonna get off the phone now. Have a good night."

"Good night, Nick." That was sweet.

I make myself ready for bed and when I return to my phone I have a text from him.

> I know it may not seem like it at times, but you are special to me, Kathrin. Not many people could have gotten me to sing when I was in my "leave me alone" mood. 🧑‍🦰😳

> :) I knew you was weird. Thank you for doing it anyway. 😊

> Have a goodnight.

~

Two weeks later, Nick invited me to eat Chipotle at Point Fermin Park by the water with him. I'm having a stressed out week. My PMS is through the roof and I still haven't heard back from Immigration, about my visa, and my 'what if' thoughts are killing me. If I had to leave the country now, coming back would pretty much be impossible until this whole pandemic is over, and who knows when that might be. My type of visa is in the category that wouldn't allow me to come back into the country right now. And even if they changed that, everything seems to be taking three times as long right now. We're still not quite far enough in the Green Card process for me to be able to stay here like that, so I need this visa approval. What would I do with my job? What would I do with my apartment? Do I have to sell everything? Just thinking about it stresses me out and robs me of all my joy. I'm glad I'll get to see Nick today.

He already picked up our food and laid out a big blanket on the grass. He brought his wireless speaker, and we lightly chat, while we eat our food and listen to his collection of romantic songs.

"So they finally gave us the dates for the training. It looks like it's finally happening. I'll be leaving in two weeks," he announces.

"Oh wow!" I finish my bite. "I guess they had to do it eventually. Doesn't look like this pandemic will be over so soon."

"Yeah. And then, if I make the team, it'll be four more months before I move."

"OK. So, like early next year." I try to stay calm and composed.

"Yeah, something like that. But I have to make the team first anyway. We'll see what happens."

"I believe in you. And this is what you always wanted, right? I remember you telling me about this on our first date."

THE ONE I LOVE MOST

"Really?"

"Yeah, I have a good memory." I grin.

"Was that when we were at that pie place in Downtown, and you had that fluffy black off the shoulder shirt on?"

"Oh wow. Yes, it was."

"I remember. Are you done with this?" He points to my bowl. "Yeah, I think I'm gonna take the rest home. I can't fit any more."

"I told you. You can't hang with a real G."

"Yeah, yeah, OK." He has been saying this lately, whenever I can't finish my food, after I told him that I used to challenge my exes with eating competitions. Those times are over.

We put the trash and my leftovers away, and then I crawl into the space between his legs and hug him. I turn over, he puts his arms around me from behind me, and we just sit there. I don't know why, but his physical touch all of a sudden summons all my emotions, and when a slow song comes on his Spotify, tears start running down my cheeks. I don't even know the song, but all of a sudden, the heaviness of my fears hits me. I've been carrying this visa burden with me for years, and I still feel like somebody could pull the rug out right from under me, at any moment. And now there's the reality of Nick leaving, first for almost two months, and then forever. It scares me. I can't ignore this whole belonging feeling, not in the long run. What if we miss out on something great? My nose starts to run. I sniffle, and wipe my eyes. Nick notices.

"Are you crying, Kathrin?"

"Yes. I don't know what's going on right now. It's just all coming over me. And you, hugging me, feels so good. I know I'm always crying."

"It's OK. Just let it out. That's good, right?"

"Yeah."

"And you know what Shrek says..." I laugh, but with that, even more tears are being squeezed out of my eyes.

"Come here." He motions me to turn around, into a normal hug, and as I rest my head on his shoulder, my tears fall onto his sweater. And with that, I start to sob. I can't stop it.

"I'm so scared. Everything's just too much right now. And knowing that you're leaving doesn't make it easier."

He holds me tighter. He doesn't try to make me feel better or talk me down from where I am, or tell me everything's not so bad. He's just there. And he lets me cry all the tear stains on his sweater that it takes.

"Come on, stand up."

I willingly follow his lead, and before I know it, we're slow-dancing in the park, on a blanket, while I'm crying into his chest. I don't care who watches, or who sees, or what people might think. All that matters is that I'm here with him.

We go over to the railing to watch the last few minutes of the sunset, and for the first time in one and a half years I ask him to take our picture, and he takes one. I look OK, he looks cute, as always with his dog smile, and there's a tear stain on the very front of his sweater. This will be a good memory.

As we look out into the water, he says, "Oh man. It's so beautiful. I can never get over it. I won't want to leave." This is the first time I've heard him say something like that, but I know it won't change anything.

We drive home to his place, and that night I can't stop crying. Every sad song provokes waterfalls coming out of my eyes. A slightly touchy-feely commercial has me wipe my eyes, and when we have sex I sob without him noticing it. Then I cry myself to sleep, and the next morning I put on my sad song playlist while I'm driving home. I cry all the way home. I know this is PMS, but nonetheless, the emotions are real.

Then

It's my birthday, my first birthday at home, in Germany, since I left to go to the States four years ago. My family baked cakes, wrapped presents, sang for me, gathered with me, gave me all these surprises, and all I can think about is that Eddie hasn't even sent me a text, let alone called me. He was serious about making me pay for my mistake, but I was hoping that he'd make an exception for my birthday, at least. I'm putting on my happy face. I wish I could feel it, too.

I am genuinely grateful for everything my family did, for how much they love me. And yet, that one little missing phone call taints the whole day blue for me. I just can't believe that to him, his pride is more important than my birthday. Him not being here or giving me a present is one thing. But not calling? It hurts. My mom knows. As much as I want to avoid telling her. Another thing that makes them right, and me stubborn and naive.

"Eddie hasn't contacted you today?" She asks because she knows I'm hurt. And I know how angry she is at him, and she's not letting any of that show today because it's my birthday. I want to run upstairs to my room and cry. It's one thing to feel bad, it's another thing to feel horrible when you have so many reasons to be joyful and feel good. It makes me feel even worse.

My extended family is still here, my aunt and cousins, and my grandma. And at least there is a ton of vegan food today, that I can eat my sorrows away with. Today is one of those days. It shouldn't be. But eating until I can't feel anything, except for my full stomach, and relieving myself right after sounds like the perfect thing to do right now. But I know it's wrong. And I'm done with that phase.

It was Eddie, actually, who pushed me over the last edge, in a good way. I had defeated my bulimia for the most part, but I still had days, once in a while, when I accidentally ate too much and relapsed because it was the easy way out. The day he noticed, he took on the parenting role and told me that I had to be done with it. That it was for kids, and the woman he'd be with can't be doing such things. So, I stopped, just like that.

He isn't only bad for me, he's taught me so much. But he also has all the power over me. My mood is in his hands, and all I'm trying to do lately is constantly fix what we have, be with him, try to make him see... when in the beginning I didn't even want him. I had a whole different picture of the person I wanted to be with. But he pursued me. And now? How did the tables turn like that?

~

I start a Google search. My birthday is long over, and I still haven't heard from Eddie. I need to get myself under control. Why can't I trust him? Why can't I just relax? And why am I always so paranoid about things with him? Or, maybe, I'm just paranoid about things in general?

I type '*how to know you're paranoid vs him cheating on you*'. A bunch of therapy ads pop up, but then in fifth place I see a Quora listing. '*Ten signs your partner is a narcissistic sociopath*'.

I would usually scroll past that, but the highlighted text gets me. *He won your heart like Prince Charming and now calls you paranoid?*

That does sound oddly familiar. How did things change this much? He worshiped me in the beginning. And now he's calling me crazy, annoying, and incapable. I click on the headline and start reading.

He won you over, things progressed quickly, and then things turned around all of a sudden? There are many narcissists and sociopaths out there. About one in every 100 people is, what experts call, a narcissistic sociopath and 1 in 5 women have dated one. So, the chances aren't slim. Here are 10 signs your partner might be a sociopath.

My heart starts beating faster, and I notice my palms getting sweaty. This wasn't the type of article I was trying to find, but I have to keep reading. I just need to rule everything out. When my mom called him a sociopath half a year ago, I thought that it's just a curse word, something bad to call someone. But this article suggests otherwise.

THE ONE I LOVE MOST

1: *Things between you progressed quickly in the beginning, and they worshiped the ground you walked on. But once they reeled you in, things changed.*

Things did happen pretty fast between us. He told me I'm the love of his life super early on. We shared secrets, and we hung out almost every day. He made sure I was committed to him, but once we came back from our holiday trip to Germany, nothing was the same anymore, and everything he valued me for were my looks.

2: *They always have an excuse for everything, and they are really convincing.*

I always took comfort in the fact that Eddie was able to explain everything, no matter what my question was. But looking back, a lot of these explanations were so random. I wanted to believe what he said. But what if they were just that? Excuses...

3: *They always talk about what others do wrong, but somehow nothing is ever their fault. That includes your relationship with them.*

I remember how many times he talked bad about his exes. How it was his ex-wife's fault that things didn't work out between them, how his ex-girlfriend's culture was just wrong, and how Ines just couldn't get her life together enough for him. And then, of course, I was always blamed when something went wrong in our daily life. The time he locked us out of my car, he made me call and pay for the locksmith. The day I locked the door, and he unlocked it. The time I found out about Carina's car, and he ended up blaming me for supposedly not believing him, when he did tell me the truth initially. Everything was so backwards. How did I never question this?

4: *They accuse you of being paranoid, insecure, a drama queen, or all of the above.*

More than anything, I've been calling *myself* paranoid. But what if I'm not? What if my gut was trying to tell me something all along? Eddie does call me insecure all the time. "Grow up," he likes to say.

5: *You can't stay mad at them long, or at all. They have a way of charming you right back into their lure.*

That is true. For Eddie, that is true.

6: *They're spending your money.*

7: *They just don't get why you're upset or down, and might even get angry at you for it.*

All those times Eddie told me to 'go home 'when I was on my period, and to 'deal with it.' Calling me a cry baby when I was emotional, instead of hugging me. He never seemed to understand when I wasn't doing great. But then again, he also built me up, when I didn't get my visa, and when I felt alone.

THE ONE I LOVE MOST

8: *They have extreme charisma. They seem to win everyone over instantly.*

Eddie always makes everyone laugh, even when they're not in a good mood. He talks to people, and everybody that I know he knows, has extreme confidence in him. Even my dad was so quick to give him the OK. I thought all of that was a good sign. How is someone a bad person for this?

9: *They guilt-trip you.*

He made me feel guilty every time I so much as uttered a doubt I had about him, or Carina, or his whereabouts. He'd make me buy him dinner with my parent's credit card for the emotional turmoil, and the waste of time I caused him. He made sure I regretted it, and more and more often he threatened to break up with me. How did I just accept that?

10: *They're verbally or physically abusive.*

He never laid a hand on me. But he did, with his ex-wife. He told me how it all went down and how he became "Don't be so sensitive."

So angry, but the fact is that he 'wanted to kill her 'and his mom stopped him. He hit her in the face, but they made up. But he sure talked to me in ways, which, according to this website, would fall under verbal and emotional abuse.

— "You're just being paranoid."

— "You're overanalyzing everything."

— "You're overthinking."

— "You need me. You wouldn't survive without me."

— "Stop being so dramatic."

— "You're lucky to have me."

— "I could be with anyone else, if I wanted to. Someone more together, someone better."

— "You owe me."

— "I don't have time for this."

And then I start writing down the things he has said to me over time, just to have it black on white.

"There you go crying again. Go ahead, but don't think I'm like those other dudes who come over and give you a hug to comfort you."

"See, I'm not like those other guys. I know how to treat a woman."

"I can get anything I want. I know how to talk to women. I could find somebody that's a better fit like that. *finger snap* I'm that confident."

"Don't ask me if I want water. That's fake. You know, I only like cold water. So why would you ask me that?" (I offered him room temperature water.)

"You're too soft."

"You shouldn't even have to ask me to never cheat on you. You're just lacking confidence."

"I'm not breaking up with you right now. I'm just keeping it 100. We will see how long this will go. I'm just warning you."

"I'm not gonna do that. Why would I look into your eyes that long? That's stupid. See, that's because you're still searching and trying to figure your life out. I already have it all figured out. My life has come full circle."

I'm shaking. Somehow, I feel like I'm having a big revelation. A revelation I'm not ready for just yet. What if there really is something wrong with him? What if none of what I did was actually wrong, stupid, or insecure, but just straight up my gut, telling me that something is wrong?

For the next two days, I watch countless YouTube videos and read articles. I find a blog called 'Dating a Sociopath, ' and I read everyone else's story. And while everyone's experience with 'their sociopath 'is slightly different, they all sound the same.

All of a sudden, I'm able to shift my point of view, and I'm looking back at last week, the last few months, the last two years, realizing that I've kept myself small for him. When he wasn't even what I wanted, not even close. He gave me all the attention I wanted, but he used that against me, once he had me.

I am so angry. All the lies he told me, and all the gaslighting he did every time I asked him questions and gave him the benefit of the doubt. I also check Carina's Facebook page, where, according to my previous research (aka light internet stalking), not much is happening usually. But she changed her profile picture. It's an Avengers Halloween outfit. Eddie loves Avengers and everything Marvel. And then I see the watermark and the backdrop she is posing in front of. It was the same club Eddie was working security for that night. I already know that he will have a very convincing explanation for this, but I am not interested in hearing it anymore. I can't take it anymore.

I send him a text. This time I'm not the pleading, small girlfriend. I am the woman who's starting to realize that she's been worth so much more all along.

> *You know what? You don't have to break up with me because I'm breaking up with you.*

It doesn't feel quite right just yet, but it does feel good!!

Now

I got my visa! One day before Nick left for his training on the East Coast. After all the worrying, I was so relieved, and I told him right away. He was also the one who had to listen to all my crying and all my doubts about it, after all. He came over that day, and we said goodbye, for the next two months.

I am so relieved. I mean, this same visa will expire in just two and a half months, but the threat of me having to leave the country all of a sudden is gone. And if everything goes well with this green card application, then I'll just be good to stay here until all of that is through. I feel like I have my life back, my soul, my joy. I'm still learning to lean into that momentary feeling of security. I'm one step closer.

Before Nick left, I made a deal with myself, to finish my book before he gets back, and use this time. That way I have something to look forward to. And to get this big task done, I think I really need to have a temporary goal, to at least finish the draft.

Nick should be back mid-September. And so far, I've really been on it. I've been reading more often, and have written a chapter almost every day. He's been gone for two weeks now. I took several trips to the beach with Anne, who's now my neighbor, and have been hanging out with Andrea, my German girl-friend, a lot more. And I am content. I am thinking about Nick, but I don't need him to be here. I love my cozy nights with Baloo, watching a Netflix show after a long day of being busy. I'm also finally planning to release my new single, "Big Space In My Heart" soon, and on top of that, a new yodeling cover for YouTube.

I'm finally back in my flow, and I know that I can have whatever it is I want, if I just manage to believe in it. I've been checking in with Nick frequently. He hurt his knee the first week already, and he said the training is really hard. This week, he said he wasn't 'feeling it 'as much as he thought he would. They have long days and it's probably best not to bother him much. Also, I want to focus on my own projects, and not distract myself too much. I am preparing for the next extension of my visa already, which I'll need, in order to 'maintain lawful status,' while I'm waiting for my green card application to be approved.

I am so close now. All this time, all this anxiety, the planning, the money. My parents helped me out big time, and so did Fred. I can't believe how lucky I am to have these people in my life. I can't imagine what it would be like to try to come here from another country, one that is less liked by the administration. It's hard for *me* already. How do people with a different background, and less money, do it? And the fact is, I have a safe place to return to if, for whatever reason, I need to.

I catch myself getting caught up in my thoughts and return to my computer. My follicular phase will only last so long, and I need to take advantage of it. Once my luteal slow self is back, I'll probably have to dial it back a bit anyway. I've been learning a lot more about my menstrual cycle and how it affects me at different times of the month. It's definitely been helpful to know when to take advantage of my energy and when not to get mad at myself for feeling slower.

~

It's Friday. I will call or text Nick this weekend. I mean, I'm sure he's alive, but I haven't heard from him since Sunday. It's his third week there, and I just want to check in and make sure he's OK. I do wish he'd miss me a bit more, enough to call me, but I can't be mad at him, if all he has time for is eating and sleeping, next to the torturous training they put him through.

My workdays at the school are slowly getting longer again, and I'm back at work in person, at least two days per week out of the three that I'm teaching. Back when the pandemic hit, we taught all lessons online, from home. How bad I wanted to push the right piano keys for my students when they messed up over and over, and I tried navigating their hands to the right spot. And how frustrating it's been trying to accompany my singing students with a time lag and the occasional freeze. More and more students are coming back to the school in person now, and while at least half of them still prefer Zoom because it's safer, at least I'm not glued to the screen all day long anymore.

I'm sitting in the foyer when my phone starts to ring, immediately before my next student walks in. NICK WATTS calling. What? How does he have time to call me right now? It's 1pm. That's 4pm EST and would mean he's still occupied, unless they finished early? Or, unless he got sent home?

I hit decline and send a text.

> *Sorry, at work. Can I call you later?*

> *I just wanted to see if you're free tonight.*

> *You're back? Since when? And yes, I'm free after work. Come over if you want?*

> *Since yesterday. And I'll explain later.*

He's back! What does that mean? And he just got back and wants to see me first thing? I mean, almost first thing.

I rush home from work once I get out, to meet him at my place. He let me know he can't do any physical stuff and that he just wants to stuff his face with ice cream and pizza tonight, and then take me to breakfast in the morning. I agree to all of the above and while we're in the car he explains. "I just wasn't feeling it."

"So you broke it off?" I ask.

"Yeah, I left."

"Wow," I say, "I know how much you wanted this. So, it just really wasn't what you thought it was, and you realized it wasn't for you? That's good."

410

"Yeah."

"Wow." I don't know what else to say. I thought Nick would be too stubborn to give up on anything. But I guess he meant it when he told me a few weeks ago that, if at any point he wasn't happy anymore, with his job or the city he lived in, he would find something else. Maybe I don't know him as well as I thought I did.

Then

It's November 29th and my phone rings. It's an 818 number. I'll definitely be answering it this time. Last time I was in Germany I got two calls from the Ellen Show and I thought it was just more spam calls. So, I didn't answer. And when I called them back, they said they wanted me to be yodeling for an audience segment the following day. I was never so upset that I was in Germany, and that I couldn't cross the Atlantic fast enough.

"Yes?" I answer, ready to hear one of Ellen's producer's names.

"Hi, Kathrin. This is Emily," a girl with a British accent says. "From Kenna and Associates."

Oh my God. I'm starting to feel a small panic attack starting. Emily is the paralegal that has been assigned my visa case at the lawyers' office Eddie sent me to. I've been so stressed about my visa application, and the possible outcome, that I've been emailing her almost every week. I've been so anxious to get back to the States. Her calling must mean that there's a decision, and after two denials, it just seems logical that would happen again.

"Oh. Hi, Emily," I say, trying to keep my voice from shaking.

412

"Good news," she announces. "Your P-3 petition was approved."

"Oh my God, really?" Did she really just say that?

"Yes. We just got the approval notice, and we'll send it out to the address on file tomorrow."

"Oh my god. I'm so relieved right now. Thank you! I almost can't believe it."

"See? I told you it was going to be fine." I can hear that she's happy for me. I feel a thousand bricks falling off my shoulders and realize that this means that all the struggle wasn't for nothing. It means, if you really want something and fight for it, you *can* make it happen. "Congrats!" She adds.

"Thank you, Emily! Thank you so much for everything."

"You're very welcome. I'm glad it all worked out."

"Oh, one more thing," I remember. "Could you send the approval notice to my friend? He's going to send it to me via express shipping. I want to get back as soon as possible."

" Sure. We can do that."

"Thank you, Emily!"

I run outside. My mom is sitting on our patio and I hug her, more excited than I was the whole last four months I was home. "My visa was approved. My visa was approved," I shout with tears in my eyes.

"It was?" She asks, taken aback by my sudden appearance.

"Yes, they just called me."

"Congratulations, Mausi! It all worked out after all. Is that still what you want, though? Now that you and Eddie aren't together anymore?"

I told her this while we were in the car together just yesterday, and to say that she was visibly relieved would be an understatement.

"Yeah. I thought about that, too. My life was pretty much all about him. But I do want to be in LA. I still want that. It just feels right."

"OK, Mausi. Then I'm happy for you!" She smiles and hugs me. "I'll miss having you here."

Now

Dear Kathrin,

This is just a formality, but I saw that you missed a question on one of the forms we have to submit. Do you have any criminal record or history of arrests?

Kindly,

Emily

Shit shit shit. Why didn't they ask me that sooner? If they need that, why have they not asked for this at the beginning of the process? And why did I not just mention it? I was always worried this would get in my way, but I thought I went through the thick of it already and that now was only a matter of adjusting my status, and I'm good, forever. My 'priority date 'finally became current, and that means I can officially adjust my status to 'permanent resident 'here, that is, if the last form thing goes through.

Hi Emily,

Could you give me another quick call? There might be a problem.

Best,

Kathrin

My phone rings. My heart beats in my throat. All the ease I've felt these past two months is leaving my body in mere seconds. My palms are sweaty, and I'm right back in the horror world of fearing for my legal status here.

"Hi Emily. Thank you for calling. Um. I got your email. Um. So, the thing is. I got arrested once for domestic battery and there weren't any charges and I thought it wasn't a big deal, but now I'm scared."

"OK. This shouldn't be a problem, but of course, I cannot guarantee that."

Shit, shit, shit. "OK, so what should we do?"

"I think you should schedule a phone call with Kenna, so she can advise you on how to deal with this."

"OK, I'll call the office then. Thank you, Emily."

Five minutes later I get an email.

Dear Kathrin,

As discussed on the phone, please schedule a phone consultation with Kenna at your next convenience to talk about the next steps. Please hold off on getting your pictures taken, and the medical exam done.

Kindly,
Emily

I totally screwed this up. I messed up. All this time. All the money. All the effort. Everything my parents gave me, all that Fred did for me. My dreams. It's my fault if it goes down the drain now. I text Nick. I need him to tell me he can fix this. If nothing else, I need him to calm me down.

> *Please call me. I'm not doing good.*
> *Something happened.*

When he doesn't respond immediately, I try calling him, but he's still at work. He doesn't answer. I'm scared out of my mind, and all of my mindful practices and wisdom can't pull me out of this right now. I was just at Nick's place yesterday. I wanted him to come over, but he was tired, and if I wouldn't have gone there, I wouldn't have seen him at all. I bought new underwear, just for him, because he always makes such a big deal of my underwear. I was finishing up my music video and stayed up until 2:30am, lying on his stomach, while he was already asleep on the couch.

For a second, we thought we were going to record another video clip of the both of us, to add to the video. But we ended up kissing more than acting, and had Mila seen it, I probably would have had an anonymous death threat by this morning. But the good news is that I have a video of Nick and me, making out, on my phone now.

I'm texting Andrea about what's going on, when yet another friend sends me a screenshot of a message from my very newest hater. Or not so new, actually.

PSA, if you fucked Kathrin Jakob, go get yourself tested. She slept with my man behind my back, and now I'm dealing with this mess. Just trying to help others out.

I thought it was just a random troll when I got a *"Ur ugly, bitch"* message three weeks ago. But then it kept going. *"I know about you and George."* George? My friends-with-benefits-George? How? *"Stop stealing other people's men."*

I texted George, and he promised me that he never told anyone about us. After all, I see him maybe three times a year. This could only be one person, and it has nothing to do with George. Mila. I sent her a link with a fake lure, to track the IP address of the account, and it turned out to be in Albany, Georgia. It had to be her. Nick also thought it's her, so he decided to block her on every single social media platform. Let's just say that didn't make the problem go away. *"Kathrin Jakob, you ruined my life,"* was one of the nicest things she's said.

This didn't really bother me all that much, to begin with. After all, none of my followers who she sent this to, believed her, an account with zero posts and zero followers. They all sent me the screenshot, warning me that someone out there is trying to hurt me. But now? With all of this going on, my visa situation proving itself to be yet another big hurdle, I can't deal with this anymore. Nick already offered to talk to her and bring her to her senses, and he still hasn't done so.

Tears start rolling down my face, sparsely and slowly, as if I didn't have enough left to really cry all the fear and frustration away. The anxiety returned in full force, and nobody can save me.

But then George somehow messaged me at the right time, and now we're on the phone talking. Or more like,

I'm crying, and he's talking some calm into me. I told him about Nick, and Nick now knows about him, thanks to Mila. Then, finally, my phone rings, and it's Nick. Two hours after I tried calling him.

"Hey George, he's calling. Can I call you back in a second?"

"Yeah, sure."

I hang up our Instagram call, and answer Nick. "Hey."

"Hey Kathrin. What's going on?"

"It's my visa. I'm worried about that arrest on my record."

"But that shouldn't be a problem, right?"

"Well... I don't know. They weren't super clear on that, and now they want me to talk to the main lawyer of the company. I had to schedule a phone appointment with her, and I have to wait the whole freaking weekend for her to be available. I'm so scared."

"You know, worrying doesn't help right now. Just try to stay present and positive. It sounds like you can't really do anything but wait right now."

"Yeah, I know that. But it's just really hard right now. It's hard to turn it off. I wish you could just fix it, or at least be here."

"Well, you know. Feel free to use my name. And unfortunately, I don't think I'll be able to tonight."

"Use your name, tss. Like they're gonna know you and be like, 'Oh yeah, Nick Watts? She gets her green card, no questions asked.'"

"Why don't you and Mila just get married, and you can get your green card, and you guys can stalk people together."

"What? Not funny. Actually, *really* not funny."

"I'm just trying to make you laugh a bit and lighten the mood."

"Yeah, I got that. But with that? By the way, have you called her yet?"

"No, but I will, soon."

"Please!? I just got another message, and it's getting a bit extreme. I'm just worried that she will send this to my students." I only have one or two students following me on Instagram. But after my colleague pulled me aside to carefully tell me that there's someone out there spreading lies, I realized this could very well land in my students' inbox as well. And I don't want to take that risk.

When we hang up, I call George back. "Did he make it all alright?" George asks nonchalantly.

"Not really, no. I'm sorry to whine to you so much." I look at my half of the screen, at my puffy face. Thank God there wasn't any mascara involved today.

"Hey, it's OK. You're human."

"I wish you were here, and we could watch a movie." I know I'm being selfish in even saying this. And I know he won't want to come over at the last minute, especially since I'm crying, partially because of another guy, again.

"You know what? That actually sounds pretty great right now. I think I could."

"Really, Georgie?"

"Yeah, I'm leaving in ten minutes. See you soon." And he hangs up.

We end up watching *A Knight's Tale*, one of my favorite movies, which I used to know by heart as a teenager, in German at least. I loudly envy the love scenes and start crying when Will meets his father again after 12 years of being away. I also find myself in the movie, when Will decides not to run, even though he's done something wrong, and he ends up being the knight he always wanted to be. He changed his stars.

I'm lying on George's chest, wet from my tears, while he caresses my head and plays with my hair. He puts gentle kisses on my forehead and then on my lips. I don't remember him being this sweet. Every time we met, we had sex, and we usually didn't have time for more than that.

As the credits roll, things heat up between us and my desperation turns into something else all together. He carries me into the bedroom at my request, and I tell myself that I don't have to feel guilty for anything. Nick could have had me all to himself, if he wanted to.

~

A week later, I wake up to see that Nick texted me at 4am. That's unusual.

> *Are you up?*

That was four hours ago.

Since when are you up so late? Are you ok?

Another unusual thing happens, and he responds immediately.

Yeah, I'm ok. Just couldn't sleep.

Are you still sleeping with George?

What?

I don't think I want to anymore. Why?

This is not a lie. As much as I appreciate George, most of the time we don't really get along. And sex with him isn't the same as with Nick, or someone I have real feelings for, and can see myself with long term.

I looked at his Instagram last night.

What? Why?

Cause I did 🫣 And Kathrin, that guy is wack. He looks like a typical wannabe LA star. He's an "actor"?

Are you being jealous right now?

Maybe I am.

THE ONE I LOVE MOST

> *I'm not in love with him, but he's a good guy, and I'm in the industry too, so I guess that also makes me a typical wannabe star.*

> *But why do you want to be jealous right now? I don't get it.*

> *You don't give off that wannabe LA star vibe. But maybe I'm a little biased.*

He keeps rambling on about what he thinks is wrong with George, very much unlike his kind and usually composed self.

> *And yeah, you don't have to defend him. Just telling you the truth about why I texted you at 4am.*

Every time I think I couldn't be any more confused, he says something that puzzles me even more, about what's going on inside his head, or heart.

Then

Eddie has been acting like I never sent that text about breaking up with him. We still bicker on the phone, about the same things we always do. I asked him to send my visa papers to me with overnight express mail, as soon as he gets them. Part of me still wants to spend Christmas with him.

We're on FaceTime right now, and he makes fun of me again for pointing out that there's long brown hair in his apartment. He goes to the rug that was in the apartment already before he moved in, and that is now laying under yet another new deluxe air mattress model, and starts pulling on the fibers. "See, Bunny? Hair everywhere. I told you it's from this rug. Somebody with long hair must have lived here before."

"Yeah, whatever," I say. "I don't really care anymore." It's mostly true. But as he's making fun of me on the floor, I see something else. He gets back up to walk back to his kitchen counter. "Wait, was that a lube bottle?" He doesn't react and just keeps rambling on about the hair. "Babe, was that a lube bottle?" I say louder this time.

"What? Where?" He asks.

"Over by the bed, on the floor."

"Ooh, that," he says nonchalantly, and picks it up from the ground. "I bought it for us. For when you're back. Something new to try."

"Uh, OK. The other bottle wasn't even empty yet, before I left. And why is it open already, then?" If he thinks my detective skills are any less sharp via FaceTime, then he's wrong.

"It's new."

I don't feel like doing this debate again.

~

The next time we talk, he shows me the lube bottle up close, to show me that it's still sealed. I didn't ask for that. I know he went to the store and bought a new one. Because I know the other one didn't have the packaging on anymore. I might still be back and forth about having feelings for him and finally being done, but I know good and well that he will always try to be right, no matter what. Even if it takes bending the truth until it's the complete opposite. I know what I saw, so I just agree with him, to let it go.

"Have you received the package with my visa papers yet?" I ask again. I've asked him every day over the past two weeks.

"Not yet, Bunny. I'm sure it's gonna get here soon. And I'll let you know. You know, aaall this holiday mail, they must be busy. It might just take longer than usual."

"I'll check back in with Emily."

Emily emails me back right away with the tracking number and said it was sent with priority mail the day after our phone call, and that it should be there already. As I click 'track package,' the delivery date says it was delivered two weeks ago.

"Eddie, it was delivered two weeks ago already. What the fuck?"

"OK, let me go check. I didn't see it. I'll call you back."

Five minutes later, he sends me a text with a picture of his apartment complex mail area and then a picture of my visa approval notice.

"It was there all this time? Did you even check?"

"Of course I did. It was buried beneath all these other packages."

Somehow I don't believe him. And I barely have a doubt that he just wanted to keep his 'peace' for a few weeks longer. Especially during Christmastime. If I didn't check the tracking, he might not have found it for another three weeks. As a matter of fact, it might have been laying on his kitchen island all this time. Maybe he wanted to play God in my life one last time.

"OK, please send it right away tomorrow."

"Alright babe, but you know express shipping isn't cheap."

"I don't care. I want to come back soon. And I can't have this take two weeks to get here. Also, you do know you still owe me all that money, right? At least $1500."

"What? It's not that much."

"It is, and I have to pay off that credit card! They've been calling."

"Just don't pay it. After a few years, it just goes away. That's how things work here. You're already late for paying it, so now it doesn't really make a difference, if you pay them back, or not. Why would you give them that money?"

"Well, I want to pay it back, so please."

"OK, I can give it to you little by little."

Two days later, I get the package in my parents' mailbox and make an appointment at the consulate in Munich.

Now

"I've had enough of this. I'm calling her brother now. She freaking threatened me with my address. So, I went online and I found hers. Along with the phone numbers of all her family members. And guess what? Her brother's name is Michael Michaelson. Who does that? Name their child like that? It's like my parents named me "Jakob Jakob" if I had been born a boy. Should I call him?" I'm determined and unsure at the same time.

"Yes," Anne agrees. "I can be here for moral support if you want."

"Yes, please. OK, I'm just gonna call."

While it's ringing, Anne says, "If he doesn't answer, just say you need to talk to him about his sister." I'm redirected to his voicemail and I do just that. I guess I had to expect that someone wouldn't just pick up the phone, when an unknown number from across the country is calling.

Anne heads back home when we haven't heard back after half an hour. And that's when I get a text from a 229 number. It must have been the one I called.

Who is this? Do I know you?

THE ONE I LOVE MOST

I record a voice message. Too much to explain for a text. He has an iPhone, so I might as well explain.

One of her last messages to me after I offered her, or rather her Instagram alias, to meet up close to the 568 freeway, which anyone, living in LA, knows doesn't exist, was:

Nah, baby girl, we don't get to do that now. I tried meeting with you and you blocked me. The woman that claims to be all about women empowerment couldn't even help a woman in distress. You instead ran to George and had him fuck me up. Just pretended I don't exist, so harshly. Had your friends DM me to call me names and tell me I'm crazy. No, thanks, I'm good. Now that you know I'm going to expose how EVIL and MALICIOUS and PATHETIC of a human you are to your friends, family, men, business partners; you wanna meet up, so you can have peace. Nah. I'm good. Where is my peace? And my health? You took that away from me Kathrin, and now you can see how it feels having your world/life torn apart. And I know where you live, dummy. Apartment building, red brick and white pillars. Second floor, I think. I followed George there at the beginning of the year. You have a blue Yodlemobile. It was in front of his house. His neighbor told me. How I found out about you. So no, thanks 🖐 But good luck to you tho!

I know the pictures she must have seen that made her think I live in a red brick building, but if she was actually here, she'd know there's only the tiniest bit of exposed brick on the house. And this so clearly isn't about George. It can't be. And her IP address tracked to Albany, GA. There

429

is only one person I ever talked to who lives there, and even knows about me and George. I wish I hadn't told her so much about me. But oh, how much one can bond over a broken heart, with somebody who shares their pain.

My phone rings. At 11pm. It's the Georgia number. When I answer with a slightly shaky, but as much as I can muster it, strong voice, I already know whose voice I'd be hearing, before she speaks. "Hi Kathrin," she says, sweetly, but also a bit snappy. But I've learned earlier this year that that's what she sounds like. I can't believe she just called. It's 2am in Georgia.

"Hey Mila. Thanks for calling."

"Yeah. I was a little surprised when my brother just drove me out in the middle of the night. He told me what you told him."

"Yes, OK. And I do want to say there's no evil intent in saying that I think this is you. I just don't know who else it could possibly be, you know? There's nobody else I know who knows these things about me, who would do that to me. And I tracked the IP address of the account, and it turned out to be in Albany."

"I understand, and I'm really sorry this is happening to you. But I would never do something that malicious. It's not me."

"And again, I apologize if this really isn't you, but I hope you know why both Nick and I believe that. I saw that you blocked me on Instagram a while back, and I didn't really do anything then, and then *this* happened."

"I blocked you because it felt like you were rubbing it in my face, that you met up with him, and he fixed your ceiling fan or whatever. And honestly, I'm done with him. And since he's not moving to DC anymore, or coming back to Georgia, since he'll be staying in LA, there's really no more reason for me to hold on to this. So no, it's not me. And honestly, I was wondering why some people randomly messaged my Instagram account and said weird things. But now that makes sense."

I take in the rest of what she is saying, but I got stuck in a very particular part of this rant.

"He's staying in LA? What do you mean?"

"He hasn't told you?"

"No, I mean..."

She cuts me off. "No, I won't even say any more. I'm gonna stop. I won't say anything else. Just that this isn't me, and I find it a bit extreme that you call my brother."

We go back and forth a little more. She makes me feel like she's genuine, but when we hang up, it all makes even more sense now.

Kathrin Jakob, you ruined my life. She thinks he's staying here because of *me?!* And here I am, silly me, who doesn't even know that he's planning to stay. You'd think a 'friend 'would be informed of such a big decision, but maybe I was wrong. Or maybe I'm not even a friend after all. This was the main reason why things would not work out between us. The distance and, of course, his fear of commitment, which he can only admit to, every once in a while.

I'm shaken. I know she's behind all of this. I'm also shocked by how close this all is to what I intended the ending of the book to be. I had that thought a lot recently, after he didn't finish that training, and gave up on his long-term goal. Is he actually staying? But clearly I'm not the reason, or I would know about it already. He probably doesn't even want me to know because he knows how much I'd be on his case. And that realization really hurts right now.

I feel angry, left out, and stupid. I decide to tell him I took matters into my own hands and type.

> *I just talked to Mila. Let me know if you want an update.*

After my walk with Trooper the next morning, Nick calls. If I thought I was nervous and anxious last night, that was nothing compared to how I'm feeling now. What is he going to tell me? Am I going to confront him about the big news that I don't really know yet?

"Hey Kathrin. How are you?"

"Um, I'm alright. I've probably been better. You? You have work this weekend, I thought?"

"Yeah, I did yesterday. And I'm still going to Utah tomorrow, for the debate."

"Ah, I see." What I don't say is '*It's convenient to just say you have work on the weekend, that way there's no risk of me wanting to see you on Sunday.*'

"So you talked to Mila?" He proceeds. "How?"

"Well, I called her brother," I state.

"You did what? Kathrin!"

"Yeah, don't sound so surprised. You didn't really do anything about it, and she more or less threatened me with my address, so I went and found hers and her family's numbers. I didn't know what else to do, so don't make me sound like I'm the crazy one now."

"No, it's OK. So, what happened?"

I tell him about my talk with her brother and then her. "She kind of made it very believable, she was nice to me, you know. But I think I know now why she would think that I ruined her life."

"Kathrin, what? I can't believe you believed her. You know it's her. We both know it's her. I can't believe you let her talk you out of that again."

"I didn't. I said for a second I almost believed her, but it makes even more sense now, that it would be her."

"And why is that?"

"Apparently you told her you're staying in LA?" I phrase this as a question. And he doesn't immediately say anything. So, I continue. "So of course she'd then think I ruined her life because she thinks you're staying because of me."

Silence.

"I would have gone about this a whole different way. You were way too nice to her again." He sounds angry. Why is he angry?

"So is it true? You're staying here? Why didn't you tell me?"

"What? No. *I* don't even know what I want yet. I love California, yes. And I've been thinking about staying, but I don't like how much I have to travel for this position here. And I do want to be home with my family."

He's talking about his family like he's already built one. He's not talking about his actual family because as far as I know, his friends in Georgia are more like family to him than his actual family. He's talking about a wife and kids. And he has it in his mind so surely that it gives me a sting.

"Of course Georgia would be nice, too. It's home and my friends are there. But I just don't know yet. I have to make up my mind."

"OK." I don't know what else to say. He might not have made his mind up yet, but he did know that he's not moving to DC. He was able to come over first thing after giving up on his plan to join that team, but he doesn't even discuss things like that with me?

"You know, when I talk to her, I'm gonna make it clear that I won't believe her, if she tries to talk herself out of it. I'm gonna tell her that, if she doesn't stop the nonsense, I can find out who's behind the account. We had an IP program as part of our training, and hopefully if nothing else, that will stop her."

"Hold on a second. You can actually do that?"

"Yeah, but obviously, I'm not supposed to. That would be an abuse of resources, but she doesn't have to know that."

All of a sudden, the Mila thing is only secondary in what bothers me. How is he such a smart and kind human being and then doesn't know how to express himself, or talk about his feelings, or treat me like an actual friend when he says I am so important to him? I can already sense him wanting to get off the phone again.

"You know what bothers me about you? It's that you're always just quiet when I'm trying to talk about something real. Yes, we got a bit better at arguing, but it's always about superficial stuff. You don't really let me see you. If it's anything more than a small annoyance at the grocery store, you keep it to yourself. And I know I can pour my heart out to you, and you won't judge me, but you also don't respond. You're just quiet. I know I've told you all of that before, but it just really bothers me. I can't deal with that. People who can't open up, or at least try." I stop for a second and, as expected, there's silence on the other end of the line.

"See? You're doing it again right now. This is exactly what I mean. You get overwhelmed by feelings, or my feelings, and you just shut down. It's super frustrating. I need people around me who can express themselves, who can have honest conversations."

"I still need to finish making this breakfast and the dishes. So I'll have to go soon, but I know we will pick up this conversation the next time we watch *Insecure* or something."

"And then you try to get off the phone. All the time. I don't know why I even bother. I tell you all the time what annoys me, or what bothers me, but you never do that, you just keep it to yourself."

"Ok, since you want me to tell you something that bothers me. I knew that you had called someone over last weekend, even before you admitted it."

"I knew you could tell. That was part of the reason I told you."

"OK, well. Who did you call?"

"George." I say quietly.

"Did you suck his dick?"

"What? Nick! First of all, no, I'm not lying when I say that's something I don't do a lot, and that I give you way too many privileges, and, second of all, why do you even bother?"

"I don't know. I just don't like the idea."

"Why are you even jealous? And why are you bringing this up right now?"

"I don't know, Kathrin. I thought you said you didn't want to have sex with him anymore."

"I said, I don't think I want to."

"Oh, OK. You didn't *think* you wanted to. Got it," he mutters sarcastically.

"I needed someone here. I was not doing well, and you didn't even text me back. It's not like I didn't try. You know

THE ONE I LOVE MOST

that I wouldn't be seeing *anyone* else if you asked me not to, right?"

"Yeah, but that wouldn't be fair."

"Because you also have sex with other people," I bluntly state.

"Kathrin, I think you think that every day that I'm not with you, and that I'm not working, I'm sleeping with someone else."

"No, I don't think that."

"I haven't had sex with anyone since we had sex."

For a second, hope flares up in me, only to realize that what he means is since 'the last time we had sex'.

"You mean, since the last time we had sex??"

"Yeah, like one and a half weeks ago."

"Oh, Bravo!!!!"

"I haven't had sex in a while before that either, actually." Is he trying to win a medal?

"Oh yeah, and how long's that? When was the last time?"

"It must have been one and a half months ago."

"A very long time indeed," I mock. "Good job. It must be hard to keep it in your pants for that long."

"Stop it."

So, what's her name? Since you know everything about me, I guess I can ask that, too, now."

"It's Marcy."

"Marcy... Was it protected?"

"Of course, Kathrin! Why do you even ask that? You know you're the only one I trust like that. I haven't done that with anyone else. It's because I feel like I can trust you."

"I feel honored."

I can't believe where this conversation is going right now, and for all the little things he seemingly pats himself on the shoulder for. The thought of him being with other women, while we are seeing each other, makes me sick. I just want to curl up. I wish I had more than those few tears left that are dampening my eyes right now. I don't know how to get rid of this anxiety. And isn't it me, after all, who puts myself in this very same position over and over and over again? Insanity, they say, is when you do the same thing over and over again, expecting different results. Who can I really be mad at but myself? It's so much easier to be angry with him, but he won't do anything about it.

"I don't like her anyway. Matter of fact, we just talked on the phone yesterday and I told her it's not going anywhere."

So, he wasn't working all day, and he could have easily texted me back. Everything he says to soothe my mind only drives the screw deeper into my heart. It's only getting worse. "You know, I think I know why you're jealous. But you don't want to see it. I think I'm almost at the point of no return with you. It's always come to this. Every single relationship or guy I've dated. I tried to tell them for so long, what it is I needed or wanted, and they didn't get it. I tried SO hard. And eventually, I was finally over it. And somehow that's always the moment the guy gets it, and he tries, and does all the things I ever wanted from him, but it's too late."

"And you're at that point with me?"

"I don't know. I think I'm close. And I'm not saying this as a threat, but just because that's how it is and how it's gonna be."

"And that would be OK, too," he says calmly. He is such an asshole right now, and he doesn't even know it.

"Yeah, I'll let you get back to your breakfast now."

"Ok. Let's hope Mila will stop, now that you talked to her. And if nothing else, if George's career *does* go bad because of this, it wouldn't be so bad either."

"What? Are you serious, Nick? I can't believe you seriously said this."

"It's just a joke, but yeah, I wouldn't mind."

This is so unlike him. "It's not funny right now, or at all. He got pulled into this whole thing, and has nothing to do with this. You might not know him, or like him, but he still doesn't deserve any of this."

"Ok. I'm sorry your friend got pulled into this," he says, but he doesn't mean it. What happened to him? Is this the *real* him? Is he finally showing me who he is? Is that nice persona just that, a nice persona?

"I deserve someone who really loves me and wants to be with me," I finally say.

"You do."

I have the hardest time letting go of this conversation because we haven't arrived anywhere, but are deeper into

Shithausen than we've already been. But knowing that's the only direction it's going, and he's about to exhaust his talking capacity, I say "Let me know if you hear from her. Bye."

Why did I ever think he really cared about me, or actually was in love with me? What fairy tale compartment in my head was spinning that tale, and made me believe it?

~

I set up a co-writing session with Kim this week. We met at one of the songwriting events I went to last year. I don't feel ready to be creative, so I look through some of my more recent ideas. Once we get on Zoom, she asks me, "Do you have any ideas right off the bat, or is there anything you want to write about?" Immediately, I'm thinking I have a whole lot to write about.

"Hmm. I wrote down this line not too long ago. 'You might not love me, but I do.'"

"I love that. I think we got our title," Kim grins.

Then

It's March. It's been almost two months since I came back to California. It was a bit rough at first, without a place or a car. Eddie told me he'd take care of my little Scion, but he didn't do anything other than drive her, and at this point, fixing her wasn't even worth it anymore. I sold her to a junk dealer, for not even $500.

I stayed in a sublease situation for six weeks, and just moved into a permanent place with my new roommate Anne, who's lived here for a while, and also has a cat. Eddie helped me find and buy a car these last few weeks, and I was truly grateful for his help, even though he sent me walking straight through Skid Row when we were meeting up one day. But I am the proud new owner of a blue Prius now. And I'm finally reunited with Baloo. I thought he was going to be mad at me, or worse, that he might not even recognize me, but we're inseparable.

Eddie and I had many 'back and forths' the past few weeks, and he somewhat felt like a rock because he was the most familiar thing I had here. But after several of his sociopathic stunts, including tearful tries to get me back, calling me names, and heavily arguing with him, I was finally able to let it go, once and for all. It's been two weeks since I responded to any of his texts, and I just signed up for all the dating apps.

I'm back, and I'm not here for Eddie. I'm here for me. I am so excited for what's to come, and I'm grateful for everything I've learned.

Also: The Universe *did* have my back. If it wasn't for the five months I had to spend in Germany, I might have never realized how unhealthy and bad for me my relationship really was. It was a blessing in disguise, and I can finally say "Thank you, God."

Now

It's been three weeks and I haven't heard from Nick. No update about if he reached Mila. Who knows, he might have not even tried anymore after our talk. No checking in how I'm feeling about my visa situation, or if Mila is still harassing me. Just nothing. I want to say I'm not bothered by it, but I am angry, more than anything.

I cried that day, when we hung up the phone, out of frustration, and the feeling that I was left alone, again, by someone who I thought actually really cared about me. But I haven't had any tears left since. I've been through this so much with him, and I have almost gotten used to it.

When I tell my friends, I say, "I'm just so angry that he is taking this away from me. I finally found the person who fits, that one person you just feel is right for you, and he's too fucking proud to work on his issues. And because of that, whether he wants it or not, he's hurting others. He doesn't even see that he's in love with me. Why else is he so jealous of George?" And then I think I sound like Mila, who's convinced of those very same things, just with herself in first-person perspective, and it would be *her* ending up with him because he's *her* person.

443

And then I remember all the times he's lied to me. The times he didn't have time for me, or want to make time for me. And how seeing me once every two weeks was more than enough for him, while he simultaneously met up with other girls. I remind myself that he missed my birthday, most likely on purpose. That he never gave me that housewarming gift he insisted on getting for me, and how I only got that Christmas card from him because I told him I want him to write one.

I remember the tiny red flags from the beginning, that now seem pretty obvious. I just didn't want to see it. I thought that, just because he treats me really well and like a valuable human person most of the time we're together, it doesn't mean I'm a priority or mean that much to him overall. It's just who he is. He's like that with everyone because he wants to be a nice guy.

Andrea sent me a voice message. She's still going through her own heartbreak. Sometimes things are really hard for the heart, even though our mind already knows what's best and what we need to do. But something pulls us back so strongly to the Comfortable, the Known, even if we know it's not good for us, and that it most likely won't make us happy in the long run. On my way home from work, I send her a voice message.

"I get that. And I'm really sorry you're feeling so shitty. You know, sometimes things are hard to do, even if we know it's the right thing to do. I think I'm at a point where I've accepted that I might just have to go through this Nick cycle over and over again, until I really get it, until I'm

444

really fed up. And honestly, I think I'm close. I'm so used to this whole process, me getting hurt, him not caring, that it's not even that bad anymore, most of the time. But I do think I'm close to just having had enough. You'll get there, too. It's OK if it has to suck for a while. It's part of the process." Maybe I really should take my own advice more often.

I park my car in Old Town and run out to grab the food I ordered. I've had a long teaching day and the last thing I want to do is cook.

Baloo is yelling at me, as usual, when I finally walk in through the back door. I drop my bags and phone and lie down on the floor with him to give him his much-wanted attention. "Just let Mama change real quick, OK, baby?" I go to the bathroom, he follows me, screaming. More screaming when I go to the bedroom to finally get out of that bra and into some sweatpants and my oversized Rams shirt that I scored at a movie premiere three years ago. With my yelling pet in tow, I return to my phone and I have three more texts from Andrea. And one from Nick, as well as a missed call.

Call me back when you get a chance.

OK. My appetite just left without thinking twice, and my pulse doubled. Just 15 minutes ago, I told Andrea how I think I'm out of hard emotions for this thing, and then I get a simple text and my body is going to 'Alarm level 500?' What is wrong with me? Is this excitement? Anxiety? Why am I so nervous? I can't be happy about this. I don't even know what this is about. Most likely it will just be a "*Hey, how have you been? Let's hang out"* thing. I call him back, my pulse now tripling. I hate myself for how much control this man has over my body, without even being present. He picks up.

"Hey Kathrin."

"Hey," I answer. I notice that I am indeed still mad at him and while I'm not letting it 'hang out, 'I also don't have a problem hiding it with short answers.

"Let me preface this by saying I want to talk to you. I didn't mean to ignore you. I know I haven't been in touch. And there are some things I want to apologize about. I just don't have time right now. Work has been crazy. I've been crazy busy. And I know other people are busy too, but they sent me on all these trips lately. I just got back from Israel, and then Florida."

"Israel?" I exclaim loudly. That's a first.

"Yeah, and I got back at 10pm last Wednesday, and they sent me to Florida at 7am the next morning."

"Oh wow. OK. But if you don't have time to talk right now, then why are you calling?" I say coolly.

"I do want to talk, but again, it's just been crazy busy with these elections coming up. And I'm calling because Mila finally called me back today."

"Oh, so you talked to her?"

"No, not yet, that's why I'm calling. I wanted to check in with you to see if she's still bothering you, or how it's been since we talked. Is she still sending those messages?"

I think. "Not in the last week, but before that, yes, I still got a few screenshots from some friends. So no, it hasn't stopped completely."

"OK, I just wanted to get a sense. I will call her now."

"OK, cool." I don't know what else to say anymore. I tried so hard to get him to call her, to talk to me, to make an effort, that I'm burnt out now. I haven't been doing great anyway with the days getting shorter, Covid still being a thing and not working out much at all. All I want to do is sleep, eat, and repeat.

"And Kathrin, I do want to talk to you. We will. And you might not believe me, but I do miss you."

"OK," I say again. "What are you doing now?" He asks.

"I just got home and was about to eat."

"OK, enjoy your food then."

"I will."

"Bye."

"Bye."

I would usually say so much more. 'Tell me about those trips. Where are you going next? When can I see you? Tell me how the talk with Mila went. How much do you miss me? 'But I simply don't have the energy. I send a voice message to Andrea to tell her, and when I send it, I see I have another message from Nick.

It was nice to hear your voice!

He used an exclamation mark. But I don't know what to say. I can't be happy about him missing me this time because it doesn't change anything. It's too easy for him to come back like that, and after seeing me one time, everything reverts to the usual: me feeling like I have to beg for attention.

So, I don't say anything back.

Then

January 5th, two years later, I get a text from Eddie. The first one in over a year. I have to click the little ">" to open up a separate page that scrolls down a very long way.

Hello little lady! Good morning! I hope this message finds you well and in good spirits! As I reflect over this last decade... There are so many things I could say but the main thing that's been weighing heavy on my heart these last 2 days, as I sent out my warm holiday wishes, was that I needed to reach out to you! Not to ask for anything, or any favors, but I write this in the spirit of gratitude for all that I actually learned from you. And I've been feeling like I just need to give you a sincere apology for the way I was during our time together. Let me start with apologizing for how long this text might be and how long overdue this message is.

Kathrin ...no matter what I may have thought about you, or thought about what I was doing, or what was a priority, through it all you were always so sweet and innocent and so good to me! I was so stuck in my mind with making progress and making money, that I didn't really see all the good and the treasure that was right there in front of me! You had a lot of answers to my thoughts and concerns, but because you were so young, inexperienced and foreign I gave little credit to your thoughts and input! Because I was so caught up in my own crap, and trying to hide from you and everyone else how I was making money on the side, without getting in trouble, I became rigid, hard, impatient and coldhearted! Not at all who I really am! Especially knowing that deep inside I wanted to be in a meaningful relationship that would lead to a lifetime partnership! So I just want to apologize to you and your family for all that I put you through! All your stresses that I caused. All your concerns that I pushed to the side. The times I wouldn't listen. The times that I made you feel less than! For not supporting you when you go through your thoughts and anxiety! For not giving you my vote of confidence and not encouraging you enough and boosting your self-esteem. Honestly, every single time I looked at you, I truly felt like I had the most chill, sweet, kind-hearted, silly, fun-loving soul I'd ever had in my life.

On top of that, you were drop-dead-gorgeous, and you wore little to no makeup at all! You were so incredibly beautiful from the first time I laid eyes on you, and I feel ashamed, and sorry, for the times I didn't reassure you, when I knew you struggled your whole life with thoughts of being less than pretty and overweight. I'm really sorry for that! For the fights and the unnecessary blow ups and tantrums I had because you wouldn't do something "my way!" For sending you to jail, which I regretted as soon as I saw you in cuffs! I honestly tried to stop it all right then, but they wouldn't allow it. I should have just hugged you before they came and told you the truth of what I was doing, and probably just should have stopped all of that at that time! I'm sorry I let you down, Kathrin!

THE ONE I LOVE MOST

Let me say that I've learned so much from you, it's not even funny! I won't go into too much detail in order to keep this as brief as possible, but... So much from health, so much more about food and so much more indirect stuff about simply betting on myself rather than a job! Kathrin, I sincerely apologize for all of these things and if there were any that I didn't mention, please charge it to my head and not my heart! I hope that the hurt, pain, and damage I caused you, you've been able to heal, move past and move on from! This city, as great as it is, is all about perception and full of schemes, scams, and imposters! I hate to admit my part in that and how I hurt you and let you down, all with the intent to simply have a good life here in LA. I hope that the Creator has given you the strength to forgive me for all my offenses toward you! In retrospect, I should've been a much better partner for you, and I'm sorry that I wasn't! If I had a chance to take it all back and do it all over again, I totally would and it would be so much more free, easier, so much more open, and so much more like a real team effort, and a flow in the same direction for the same purposes and goals! This isn't an attempt to get you back (and not that I'm opposed to it) but it is an attempt to make a connection and agree with you that I was wrong and should have been a better man for you!.... I'm sorry and ashamed of being so stuck on myself and my own goals and intentions to the point of letting a good thing go bad! I don't really expect you to respond if you don't want to, and I don't mind if you do. But please, if you don't mind leaving an emoji of any kind, so I know you received this, that would be cool!

451

So with this huge Spirit of Gratitude for everything I've done and been through this past decade, I apologize one last time and I say thank you for all you've done and for who you are! You're quite the inspiration to me and to all the others I've seen you touch! As we enter into this year, may the Creator continue to bless you, your life, your career, your family and everything you touch! Happy New Year, sweet and beautiful Kathrin S. Jakob.

When I'm done reading, my cheeks are wet with tears. I had forgotten what it felt like to be in this emotionally abusive chaos. And I'm glad I forgot it. I am also grateful it happened.

I reply with a thumbs up emoji and put my phone to the side. If there's one thing I learned, it's to listen to my intuition. And it's telling me that Eddie James won't be a completely different person in this lifetime.

Now

It's my birthday month. Half way done already. And so far, it's been off to a great start. Trump finally got voted out and while 'we,' or shall I say 'the Americans,' have another pretty old president again, things, in that regard, can only go uphill. I'm a bit hopeful, at least.

I also got a haircut, the first one in over a year, and the first one that wasn't a buzz cut in over two years. And what can I say? I'm blonde again. I did want to abstain from using bleach and go the 'all natural 'way, but seeing other blondes started an itch in me. My roots are still my natural brown, but now I am the wearer of an ombre blonde long bob, and I love it.

I started fostering this adorable bunny that looks just like Baloo, color wise, but lighter. I might adopt her when she's old enough. For now, I named her Billie. I am also super excited to shoot that game show I was booked for, that I will be yodeling on. Those are the gigs that I love the most, and I'm so happy the Universe is bringing those opportunities my way after this crazy year.

And Nick... I feel so much better not trying to make a meeting happen, or trying to make him see something. I just feel relaxed in that aspect. While I do miss the great connection we had, and the way I feel when I'm with him, when he kisses me, I prefer the peace I feel over not stressing it, or waiting for his call or text. Or waiting for him, period. This way, at least I have *me*.

And I still have Andrea. We already planned a trip for my birthday in 10 days, Thanksgiving week. I'll be off all week. I've been looking forward to this all summer. We've been planning to take a special 'trip 'for a while now. Finally, we've made 'nails with heads' (as we say in Germany) and booked an Airbnb close to Joshua Tree. I'm really looking forward to getting out of LA for a few days, and not teaching for a whole week. To take a deep dive into the magical workings of my mind and the Universe and find some powerful truth that I haven't been able to see before.

My green card process is still stressing me out, but all I can do right now is wait. And since I don't have a solid reason to worry, I keep reminding myself not to do that.

My phone rings. It's a Saturday. I'm surprised to see Nick's name light up. He waited another three weeks to call me again. I wasn't trying to count, I guess I just do it automatically now. Even though I am not stressing over this anymore, it's an automatic response my body developed over the last 2 years: Mentally chart all interactions with Nick Watts and don't ever forget a word, or a date.

"Hey, Nick," I casually say when I pick up. I don't even feel the anger anymore that I used to feel. Most of it is gone. My body still reacts in the habitual way of sweating and getting nervous, but even that is mild compared to before. I think I'm simply, finally, getting to a place where it doesn't phase me anymore. If only I could have found that peace sooner. Or kept it, those few times when I did find it.

"Hey Kathrin. How are you?"

"I'm actually pretty good. It's birthday month. I can't complain," I say with an upbeat voice.

"Oh, right," he says, dragging out the 'raaaaaiight' pretending he didn't already know.

"How are you? Are things a bit calmer, now that the elections are over?"

"Much calmer. I actually got to organize quite a bit of stuff at the house. And I even cooked three times this week."

"Woah," I say, mockingly. "Did you also have time to sleep longer than 5am?"

"Believe it or not, I did sleep in a few times. You'd be proud of me."

"I'm happy for you. I'm sure it must feel good to finally get some downtime."

"It does. But hey, I wanted to see if you're free tomorrow, by any chance?" And before I can say anything he adds "And I know, it's another last-minute request. If tomorrow doesn't work, then next week works too for me. If you're up for it, that is, of course."

"Um, look, Nick, I don't think I'm interested in what we had anymore. So..."

"No, Kathrin. I told you I wanted to clear the air about some things and talk to you, remember? Let me take you out, if you know of a place that offers outside dining, maybe? Or I can come over, I don't have to stay the night, if you don't want me to. Or we can go for a walk."

"Now you finally wanna walk with me?" I laugh. "OK, I'm free in the afternoon, we could go on a hike?"

"OK, hike it is. Let me know when and where, and I'll meet you there."

"So flexible. Wow. I like it."

"Haha, girl, you thought I couldn't surprise you anymore, did you?"

"Hush now. I'll see you tomorrow."

"See you tomorrow."

I'm not getting excited anymore. We're simply going on that friend date he offered me over a year ago when he told me that we can also just be friends, if the benefits are making things too complicated. I never really went for that offer because, no matter what we do, I was convinced I'd always want more, or at least *feel* more.

Now I figure it's a good way to take advantage of birthday month, get a good hike in and let him apologize, so he can feel better. I don't want to be mad anymore. I also don't want this to be what it was anymore, just like I told him. And I think I can hold my ground on this now.

~

I park sideways into a spot by Del Cerro park in Palos Verdes. I came all the way down here to his neck of the woods, not because I want to save him the drive, but because I simply love this place. And one day I will have that land and build a house on it, close to the ocean, but close to the city, too. And I'll have space to save so many animals. 'If you can dream it, you can do it. 'Cheesy but true.

I see Nick pull in two spots behind me and then quickly walk towards my car, opening the door for me. He's wearing one of his brightly colored pair of Nike shoes, and classic for him, a Patagonia shirt. We hug, and for a moment his laundry-scented clothes take me on a trip down memory lane. I will never understand how this particular laundry detergent has such a strong power over my state of being, and the feelings it evokes. "You smell good," I say.

"Still as always?" He asks, smirking.

"Yup. But don't get too cocky about it."

"I'm not. And you look really cute, by the way. Your hair got so long, and blonde. You look great." I'm wearing my new matching workout gear, bra top and long pants. It's warm enough today.

We start walking down the trail and my gaze drifts towards the ocean. "It's so beautiful. I can never get over it." And then I playfully add, "Too bad you won't be able to enjoy this for too much longer."

"Actually, Kathrin, this is part of what I wanted to talk to you about. I'm not going anywhere. I'm staying here. I still need to figure out what position exactly I will be taking in the long run, but I'm staying in California. I do have to get out of that house, though. So, you might be right. I might not get to see this every day."

"You are?" Something inside me is twisting, and I don't know whether I want to jump, or throw up. "That's great. I mean, you figured out what you wanted. Good for you."

Immediately, my mind goes to all the places. Him finding his 'the One 'and starting a family here, and I have to live with that fact, knowing he's here, but that he didn't pick me. Him probably wanting to stay friends, and I'd have to see it because I can't say no. I thought I was getting over this once and for all, but this new piece of information is quite shocking to say the least.

He's quiet for a bit, just like when there's something he doesn't say, and when he knows he disappointed me but can't put it into words. His lips are shut tight, and he looks like he's about to hurt me. Not physically, but worse, where it hurts the most. And I thought he didn't have that power anymore.

"Is there something else you want to say?" I nudge.

He's giving me the puppy look, and I almost want to turn around right there. We aren't that far into the hike yet, and I'm starting to regret coming here. My anxiety is as high as ever.

"I think this wasn't a good idea, actually," I say. "I've been doing really well, and you know I care about you and enjoy time with you, but your silence is making me so anxious. I hate feeling like this. I think I'm gonna go home." I start turning around. I don't feel too bad because his drive here can't have been more than 15 minutes. For a moment, I think he's just letting me walk away without even saying anything, not so much as a goodbye, but then I hear his footsteps behind me, and he grabs my wrist.

"Kathrin, don't go."

"I can't keep doing this, Nick. I told you so many times how it makes me feel when you don't talk. When I'm left guessing what it is that's going on in your head. Now you're telling me you're staying here? What am I supposed to do with that? It doesn't change anything for me. If anything, it makes it harder." He holds my face and starts kissing me. I push him back.

"You can't just kiss me to shut me up. It doesn't work like that anymore." I walk away again.

"Kathrin." He takes a deep breath. "I'm sorry, I'm just having a bit of a hard time saying what I wanted to say. You know I'm not a talker. And usually, I'm the one running away." He looks at me, then takes another deep breath. "I signed up for therapy. I'm starting next week."

This is something I never expected to hear coming out of his mouth.

"You are?" I say non-believing. "Wow. I don't know what to say. I'm so happy for you. This will be good for you. And this is a big step. I'm proud of you."

"Thank you." He seems unsure.

We're still in the middle of the trail, and about 10 people have already passed us on both sides.

"Look, I know I did all the wrong things. What I did wasn't fair. And I thought I was fine, just by telling you I can't commit. But it still wasn't OK. I hate how I made you feel, again and again."

"Oh, it's spilled milk now." I'm referencing him. That's something he used to say all the time, and half of the time I didn't agree that something was already 'spilled.' I don't even believe myself as I'm saying this right now. I just don't want him to keep talking because I know how this goes. He apologizes, says how much I mean to him, and that he doesn't want to lose me. He'll try really hard to be extra nice and sweet, and then we end up in bed together again, and we're back to being friends with benefits while he's on dating sites looking for 'the One.'

"I know it might be too late now to say this, but Kathrin, you were right. You were right all this time."

"With what? That you indeed are an asshole?" I mock.

"Kathrin, I was in love with you."

"Oh."

"I *am* in love with you. And every time we get close, I get so scared that I resort to doing something stupid. And you kept trying and trying, and I just kept being stupid."

I did not expect this. I am walking over to the next rock of a decent size, and I sit down. "Why are you telling me this? You, realizing what I knew all along doesn't change anything now, does it? I'm tired of trying to convince you to be with me."

"I know. It's my turn to convince *you* to be with *me*. And I understand if you're over this. I really do. But I want to be with you, Kathrin. I want to make this work. And it might not be easy for me. But I promise I won't ever lie to you again, or not make you a priority, as long as you can stand being by my side and helping me get through my fucked up brain. I've waited too long to deal with this. And if you'd rather be with someone who has their shit together, I get it. I won't blame you. I will leave you alone if you say that's what you want. But I had to tell you this. I had to try."

He never said this much at once to me, I think. Especially not when it was about feelings. I stare at him, not knowing what to say, if I can believe what I just heard. Nick Watts wants to be with *me?*

And I know I should already be over this, and be with someone who knew how to value me from the get go. I shouldn't cave in at the first admitting of feelings, the first attempt to right things, but I notice right then that I would never get over the way I felt with him. I could never forget how we fit like two puzzle pieces, how no one else could lift me up and hold me the way he does, even if they were ten times stronger.

"I hate you," I say. "You are such a fool. And I love you. And I wish I wasn't so easy to have."

"Is that a 'Yes, I'll be with you?'" he starts smiling.

"Let's see how long you'll actually last with me around," I joke. "But yes, princess Kathrin Simone shall give you a chance to unspill the milk."

"Almond milk?"

"Of course, Almond milk."

"There's something else, though."

"Oh God. What is it?"

"I have to be out of the house by the end of the year. So, assuming you can still stand me by then, would you have me at your place? For a bit? Until I find something new? Or maybe until *we* find something?" He carefully asks.

"Woah! Watts. Where did you find the gas pedal all of a sudden? You haven't even proven to be able to spend two full days with me yet. What makes you think you can live with me? Also, I don't even know if I'll get my green card. Who knows, *I* might be the one moving."

"Let that be my worries. And no, you won't be. If all else fails, we'll go to Vegas and do what crazy couples in Vegas do." I laugh at this. Did he just use the word 'couple?' "But on yet another note. I would love to take you on a real couples thing vacation. Catalina Island for your birthday?"

"I already made plans with Andrea, sorry."

He frowns, and I add, "But I'm free that weekend. Let's do it."

Somebody will have to pinch me tomorrow morning, and I'll have to fact-check everything that just happened. This might be another one of my weird dreams, the good kind this time. But for now, let me hope it's real and let me enjoy the heck out of it.

Nick lifts me up, grabs my thighs and cups my butt with his hands. I hug him as tightly as I ever hugged him and kiss him, knowing I can have these lips anytime I want them. Someone is posing next to us, taking pictures with the view behind. I have an idea. "Excuse me, sorry? Sorry for interrupting your hike. But would you mind taking a few shots of us and maybe airdropping them to me? We're just having a really special moment."

"You got it," the girl says, snapping away already. "You guys are so cute together."

"That was so very LA of you," Nick says when she's gone, and we're looking at our cheesy 'kissing with an ocean backdrop' pictures. "But I think I'll have to frame that one."

"You?" I laugh.

Maybe crazy dreams do come true. Maybe there's always a bit of hope left that can turn your fantasy into reality and can make reality feel like a dream.

Who knows what the future brings, but the potential is unlimited, and I'm in love with that. And I'm in love with him. This time officially.

Don't keep reading if you loved that ending! But if you do keep reading, you might find out that there can be more than one happy ending.

Epilogue

That was my dream ending. That's why I wrote this book. Actually, that's not true. It's what motivated me to write this book at a time when nothing else did. Love has always been my biggest motivator.

And no, it didn't happen. Not that way. At least not yet.

I officially adopted Billie the bunny, I dyed my hair blonde and I really got booked for a game show that aired a few months ago. But apart from those things, the last chapter was the story I dreamed of, the future I wanted to manifest, and that didn't happen.

But something even better happened. I found out that the One I love most isn't Eddie, or Nick, or anyone else for that matter. It's Baloo. Just kidding.

It's me. And this sounds like some cheesy self-finding stuff. I knew this all along, that I am my person, that I am the one, who needs to love me, that I am the one human I can always depend on. But until now, I guess I never really truly felt like that.

I do now. I don't always love myself, not every single day, but I wholeheartedly know now, that only I have all the answers for me. Not a therapist, not a psychic, not a coach. They all helped me, but in the end the answers were already inside of me. Looking back, and looking at myself now, I must say I'm pretty awesome. I already am what I want from life, I just have to claim it.

Eddie and Nick showed me how much I didn't value myself. And yet, I had so many good times with both of them, and I learned so much, not only through their less-than-perfect behavior towards me, but they did teach me things. Eddie taught me how to be a fun music teacher. He taught me about the American way, even if that wasn't always the correct way. He taught me about Seattle and the Pacific Northwest and, most importantly, that everyone calls each other 'babe' in the US.

Nick taught me how to throw a Frisbee, he taught me a variety of Urban Dictionary slang and showed me so many great songs I didn't know yet. And most of all, he helped me experience the feeling of being in love again, which I am now ready to find again in a healthy relationship, with somebody who truly values me, and isn't afraid to put a label on it.

Both of them taught me to trust my gut instinct, even though they didn't know that's what they were doing, of course.

They both made me laugh SO many times, and they cared for me, each in their own way.

I am grateful I knew them, but I am even more grateful that time allowed me to fall out of love with both of them. Being in love is wonderful, but it can also become a prison, when the other person doesn't know how to love you back.

Of course, this won't be the end of my love stories, but I know that I can't rush the Universe.

Meanwhile, I finished writing my story, and my green card was finally approved. I don't have it yet, but fingers crossed, I hope I will soon.

I don't know where Eddie is, and what he does, but I do hope he picked a better path for himself, and that he'll treat whoever he chooses to pursue next with as much love as he possibly can.

As for Nick, he's still in California, but he's leaving at about the same time as this book comes out. That will close this chapter once and for all. I still have love for him, but there are no more butterflies when I think of him, which feels so liberating. Now I know that he won't be the one to '*show me, that love can be true,* 'even though I loved being serenaded with that song. I hope that he'll find the person who will make the emotional work he has to do worth it.

And as for me, I am finally confident that I can have whatever I want from this life, and that I don't have to hide my self perceived 'otherness 'any longer. In the end, aren't we all a bit 'special?'

Much love,
Kathrin, the one I love most.

Extras

To get to the extras of this book, such as Spotify playlists and a list of my favorite vegan spots and favorite places in LA, please visit the following link or scan the QR Code:

www.kathrinjakob.com/book-extras

Acknowledgments

I want to express my gratitude to everyone who helped bring this book to life.

Thank you...

... to my parents, without whom I wouldn't be where I am today. You always believed in me and supported my crazy, unconventional dreams. I can never thank you enough.

... Cynthia Byrd, for volunteering to go through my many pages and being my editor. You were such a tremendous help.

... to my test readers, who were the first to ever lay eyes on my story and encouraged me to bring it into the world.

... to my dear therapist, who I hope to meet again someday. You always made me feel understood and encouraged me to be me.

... to Sarah, an incredibly sweet and helpful life coach, who helped me set realistic goals, and without whom I might still be procrastinating on the first edit.

... to singer/songwriter Katie Buxton, who agreed to let me use her song lyrics to "You flew" in one of my chapters.

... to my co-writer Kim Krenik and producer Ananada Dhar-James for creating a self-love anthem with me.

... to my lawyer team and my boss, who helped make my dream of becoming a permanent resident of the United States a reality, and who went through this excruciating process with me.

... to my friends, who love me, support me, and are there for me. I love you!

... to Baloo. Not that he can read it, but he's my little family here at my home away from home, together with Billie.

And, of course, thank you to all of my readers, however few or many of you there are. I feel honored that you read my story, my debut (and possibly) only novel/memoir.

Last but not least, thank you, Eddie and Nick, for without you there wouldn't have been so much to tell and so much to learn. I hope life treats you well.

About The Author

Originally from Bavaria, Germany, Kathrin currently resides in Los Angeles with her cat, Baloo and bunny, Billie. She's a singer, music teacher, and yodeler living life unabashedly honest and happy. When she's not writing, she can be found reading, hiking, and discovering people's stories through engaging conversations. She loves healthy vegan food, is an animal lover through and through and she wishes to rescue more animals throughout her life. Through her writing, she hopes to inspire her readers to be themselves, love themselves, and believe in themselves, because there's only one of you, dear reader, and you are amazing!

If you are interested to find out more about Kathrin you can follow her Instagram accounts @kathrinjakob or @yodelstar, or visit her website www.kathrinjakob.com

Made in the USA
Monee, IL
17 September 2021